GRAMBLE STREET

GRAMBLE STREET

L. S. BLACKWELL

ThreeLinePublishing

Published in the United States by Three Line Publishing
threelinepublishing@gmail.com

Cover Design
German Creative
and Amelia C. Blackwell

ISBN: 9780578676685
Library of Congress Control Number: 2020910200

Printed in the United States of America
First Edition

Blessed are they who hunger and thirst after righteousness:
for they shall be filled.

Matthew 5:6

PROLOGUE

Georgia Homewood had been lying facedown in her front yard for three hours before anyone noticed and called it in. When the Los Angeles County coroner declared the death as a myocardial infarction, the authorities closed her file, along with any suspicions they had, and Georgia became a guest of the county morgue, awaiting instructions from the next of kin; however, a week later she was still there. The only living relatives found were two minor children—her grandkids. No one was coming for Georgia. After thirty days, without ceremony, her unclaimed body was cremated.

"A real shame," the county clerk said while processing the records. She knew the procedure. Without a will, Georgia's grandchildren, nine-year-old Kiandra Spence and her little brother, Jackie, who was only five, became wards of the state; but by the time the clerk was leaving for the day, the kids' plight, along with all the other unfortunate cases she had handled, were forgotten. Her main concern at five-thirty that evening was meeting her friends for margarita night at Don Felipe's, so she was beyond thrilled when her coworker, once again, offered to finish the last of her entries.

"You are spoiling me! Don't work too late," she said, and waved backwards to the dark figure as the clicking of her high heels faded down the hall. Left alone with access to the clerk's computer again, the accommodating coworker settled in for a long night.

CHAPTER 1

"I killed them!"

The agonizing cry pierced the sterile quiet until a door slammed, barely missing the young nurse outside Room 1610. With the patient's medications in her hands, she spun around, wide-eyed, searching for her supervisor. "Did you hear that?" The question, amplified by her adrenaline, landed on every set of ears in the hallway, including the head nurse, Katy Beecham's.

Katy lifted a stern finger to her lips, and her eyes traveled to the closed door.

"What do we do?" The nurse's volume control still wasn't working.

Muffled high and low pitches of despair were seeping through the walls and Katy took an unnoticeable step closer. Then another. If the young nurse would be quiet, she might decipher some of the conversation. Working her good ear, her right one, closest to the room, Katy extended her own silence, but it was useless. All she caught was the young woman's rattled breath and the fax machine coming to life in their workstation. Then, like a magnetic force pulling the other employees into a perfect huddle around Katy, three more closed in.

They were on the sixth floor of the UCLA Medical Center in Los Angeles, and the flickering fluorescent bulb overhead animated the concerned expressions of her staff as they looked to each other, then to Katy, waiting for her response. She gave them a definitive nod. "We get back to work, is what we do. You guys check on the other patients to make sure they weren't disturbed, and I'll handle 1610."

The new male nurse from South Carolina pointed toward the room. "And you're going to report that, right?"

Whatever was going on behind those closed doors had to be handled delicately. On the job eleven years, Katy prided herself on the discretion and privacy her floor provided for the rich and famous, so, leading by example, she broke away from the pack and walked several feet ahead to the nurse's station while addressing him. "Of course. It will be recorded in the patient's file." She lifted her sweater off her chair, slid her arms into it, and grabbed up a small stack of folders. She glanced at the clock. Only one hour before the 11:00 p.m. shift change, with two hours of work left to do.

"No ... um, I mean ..." The same young man stammered. "Aren't we required by law to call that in to the authorities?"

Like an anvil, the question slammed Katy, along with her judgment, and she jerked her head to face him, offering a smile that didn't reach her weary eyes. "Do you know anything about the patient in that room?" Without waiting for an answer, she barreled through. "They've had a head injury, and until we get the test results, we are treating it as severe. You're aware of the mental confusion that sometimes accompanies a concussion, right?"

"I wouldn't classify killing someone as mental confusion," the employee said in his slow southern drawl that had once charmed his supervisor, but as he pressed her in front of the others, he might as well be dragging jagged iron across the floor. The effect was the same.

Exhausted from the day's shift, Katy took a quick breath that helped straighten her shoulders before countering with a hearty, condescending chuckle. "Evidently, you're unfamiliar with HIPAA laws. I'm not sure how you missed that in school, but I am expecting you to study them after your shift tonight." Then she swept a look across the other nurses, ready for any other challenges, but they nodded in agreement with her. One even rolled her eyes at the bold coworker. Satisfied, Katy continued, "Until the patient's testing is conclusive, what the law requires is to protect the patient's privacy. Now, again, let's check on the others."

The male nurse stood alone as the crew got back to work, then he followed as well. Despite her own words, however, Katy stole a quick glance at Room 1610, absently chewing on her cheek.

* * *

"Tom! What happened to the children? I hit them, didn't I?!" The brown, watery pools of Ginny Vinsant's eyes left no room for the fear or misery filling them, and the overflow left a growing wet imprint on the fresh hospital linens. She reached for her husband, tugging desperately on the sleeve of his jacket. "How many were hurt? OH ... what have I done?" She laid her head against his arm.

"Ginny, I told you, there were no kids at the scene of your accident. Stop this. You weren't even conscious when the EMTs arrived." He looked down at the grip she had on him and slowly edged backward, away from the bed, which passively forced her to release him. He straightened his sport coat. Free from his wife, but still a prisoner of the room, he loosened his tie. "You're disoriented, but that's expected with a concussion. The doctor wants to keep you overnight as a precaution ... so just lie back and get some sleep."

The sound of keys jingling was like an alarm going off for Ginny. One of his many tics of impatience, and she knew he would be gone within minutes. "Disoriented? Tom, listen to me, I saw people! Kids! They were in my path! In the middle of the off-ramp!" She leaned in, clutching the sheets. "I was going too fast to stop, so I swerved." Her voice broke, trying to stifle the sob in her chest, but there was no way to hold back the tears. "And it could—could be criminal, because I—I had a glass of wine before I left your fundraiser!" Her head rocked from side to side. "The car was spinning ... I just don't remember anything after that!"

Tom Vinsant, the United States senator from California, made his way back to the bed. He loomed over his wife so closely, she smelled the coffee on his breath and blinked with every word he spat. "You. Aren't. Listening. Are you intentionally trying to sabotage my re-elect—" he stopped. The veins in his flushed neck were bulging, throbbing. He took a deep breath, then stood upright and released it slowly, never taking his eyes off her. Once. Twice. *Get control.*

"I needed you at the fundraiser. What—" Tom took another deep breath. "Whatever possessed you to sneak off to that wretched community center? You put it before your own husband and look where it landed us." His voice was calm, but the white knuckles of his clenched fists said otherwise. "We will discuss this further at home, but for now, you lost control of your car and hit the light post. End of story." With a hard stare he drove his message home to his wife, who stared back, unmoving, except for the involuntary spasms from crying; then, breaking away, Tom was at the door in three long strides.

A quick jerk of the handle exposed the cool hallway air which enveloped him, promising delivery from the growing confinement of the room; however, instead of leaving, the square shoulders of his tailored jacket froze. It was as if he'd forgotten something.

He left the door open and retraced his steps back to Ginny's bedside as she pulled the covers tight, close to her chin, and watched him transition into the caring lover who'd captured her heart so many years ago. Gently, leaning over her, Tom brushed a lock of blonde hair from her brow and placed a kiss there before drawing away to engage her big brown eyes. "Ginny, sweetheart, you can't imagine what I felt when I heard you'd been in an accident. Please, no more crazy talk. Rest."

The swagger Senator Vinsant had perfected over his career, accompanied him to the door once again and directly past him, in the hallway, was a small cluster of nurses with a clear view to Ginny's bed. Only one of them pretended they weren't looking.

Tom pulled the handle softly behind him and joined the attentive staff with nothing more than an exhale and a concerned smile. Senator Vinsant was an attractive forty-four-year-old, and, at five-eleven, he still had an athletic build due to his occasional jog and active lifestyle, but it was his arrogance, masked as capability, that captivated. It gave those around him a sense of well-being, as though he could make everything right. It lured audiences, who hung on his every word; but that night, outside his wife's room, he played vulnerable to this small group, and even Katy Beecham was not immune. She motioned for the other nurses to disburse, to give him privacy, but when turning to leave as well, her feet wouldn't cooperate and she tripped, falling into his shoulder.

"Excuse me, Senator." Regaining her balance, Katy re-straightened her cardigan, shifting her eyes from her shoes, to her watch, then to the files she was carrying, before locking on his. A beat or two passed. Her eyes fluttered. Breaking contact, she asked, "Is there anything else I can do to make you ... uh, I mean your wife, more comfortable? I was just coming to check on her."

"Actually, yes," Tom said. He read her name tag. The crow's feet at his eyes deepened and he gave her a nod. "Thank you, Ms. Beecham. She's very agitated ... unusually so, and confused. Ask the doctor if she can be given a sedative."

In a quick glance, Katy shot a silent message to her male nurse, then with full attention back to Tom, she met his nod with an affirmation of efficiency and said, "Absolutely. I will ask him, Senator."

"Also, refuse visitors. She needs rest." Tom made his way to the elevator. The senator hummed as he rode down to the lobby. He loved his position. Not only the Senate seat, but the committees, sub-committees, and the unlimited connections he had, which wielded great power. He relished it all. Even simple situations like watching the head nurse doing the backstroke for him. Ginny had no other close relatives; therefore, under Nurse Beecham's watch, he was assured Ginny's ramblings would not be witnessed by anyone else. When he reached the ground floor, he was in motion. *Time to see what damage she's done and take control of the media outburst before it even starts.*

CHAPTER 2

"Listen up," the caller said in a hushed tone, muffled, as if someone's hand was over the receiver. "That senator you've been after? His wife was in an auto accident last night. Off the Harbor Freeway, but it ... like, won't be in the news ..." There was a brief pause, then the caller continued, "... even though she was overheard claiming to have killed someone. No DUI test. No investigation. And her car? Totaled." The caller's dialect changed with the word "claiming." It popped through the phony Valley accent with a southern twang.

"I'm sorry, *LA Diggs* is no longer on the air. We've stopped taking viewer tips," said KDLA TV's former news anchor, Nicole Portman. "Who is this?"

"A friend." There it was again, a slight drawl, but the caller disconnected. The ID on her phone said *UCLA Medical Center*. Nicole had been accustomed to unsolicited news tips coming in, since KDLA had encouraged them from the viewing audience through her weekly investigative program; however, by the time she received them, they had always been thoroughly filtered.

The caller referred to the senator I've been after. He's talking about my last segment! The one that got my show canceled! If this is real, she could be at the Medical Center now! Without the luxury of a staff to validate it, or the time to do it herself, Nicole had to make a quick decision. It was around five in the evening. By six, she was at the hospital.

* * *

The woman at the information desk tapped away at the keyboard with unusually loud clicking, and, after waiting her turn, Nicole found the source: a set of extended acrylic nails with a dark burgundy finish. They loomed from the woman's fingertips, typing rapid-fire. "I'm sorry," she said, without looking away from her screen, "we don't have a listing for a Virginia *or* a Ginny Vinsant here. Check with emergency. Maybe she's still there and hasn't been admitted."

Approaching the emergency room doors, Nicole was assaulted by the smell of antiseptic, and she stalled. It immediately triggered the memory of that same marbled hall where a shocked twelve-year-old girl was led away after the doctor on duty pronounced her parents dead. Now, at age thirty, her personal horror from that night was ignited by the odor. Her chest rose and fell jaggedly. She needed oxygen, but instead the familiarity of death covered her nostrils.

Visitors and employees crisscrossed around the tall, motionless brunette, then Nicole gave a quick shake of her head. *What am I doing here?* She pushed her hands deep into her jacket pockets as if she were chilled and turned. There was an exit door about twelve steps away. *But ... what if? The caller was confident about his "tip" ... and obviously knows I've been after the hidden truth concerning Senator Tom Vinsant.*

She turned again, mentally confronting the double doors. *What if the senator did arrange for his wife to skirt a DUI charge or even a possible manslaughter? Could those doors be my portal to redemption? I'd rather nail him on his illegal activities at the waterfront, but ... maybe ...*

Back at the information desk, Nicole enlisted the clicking employee's help. Within minutes she was facing the looming doors once more, but this time was equipped with a borrowed cotton face-mask. The mask would help hide her identity as long as she didn't look squarely at anyone, since her crystal-grey eyes were a signature of the celebrity anchor. But it wasn't only her identity she was hiding. It was the haunting odor. The mask would protect her from it and allow her to maneuver through the emergency room.

With the mask firmly in place, Nicole was ready and bolted through the doors with purpose. Judge Judy's voice met her first, thundering from a mounted television, as she lectured the distressed crowd waiting on urgent care, but the judge was no match for the screaming toddler across the room. The child had a halo of tangled red hair and each scream came with an arched back that threatened to bust out of her exhausted mother's arms. From the tears in the young woman's own eyes, it was difficult to tell which one was in need of care.

Blended conversations rose to match the decibel level, and between the choruses, a man moaned, writhing in his chair for any moment of comfort. It was medical mayhem, and no one noticed as Nicole popped open the second set of doors to the restricted area as if she belonged there. Working quickly to stay ahead of her own recollections, she scanned from bed to bed, but there was no sign of Ginny Vinsant.

The next stop was the gift shop. A get-well bouquet would be her ticket to the patient rooms. Floors three and five were pediatrics and cardiology, so skipping those, she maneuvered through the second and fourth floors, using her prop to ward off personal contact. However, soon she was back in the elevator with nothing to support the caller's allegation. *Even if it's true, Ginny could've been released by now. The caller didn't mention the extent of her injury*, she thought, but still, she punched the button for the next floor. Before the elevator doors could close, a group boarded.

"... Then the clip is placed around the base of the aneurysm, sealing it off from the flow of blood and pressure, thus, neutralizing its threat." The physician loudly articulated the process while five others hovered around him, and the car was shrinking. Nicole lifted the flowers slightly and looked through the arrangement for a brief second, her brows tensing when she saw the control panel. No other floor was selected. They were getting off on six with her. "... We believe this could redefine the way we ..."

She took a silent step backward. Then another. When the car stopped, she didn't move. Oblivious to Nicole or to the commotion they caused in the otherwise quiet hall, her fellow passengers exited in a sudden gust, leaving the elevator and Nicole in their wake, and Nicole's brows finally eased. Choosing the opposite wing to start her search, and moving quickly, she read the names on each patient door. Nothing. The nurses' station was coming up on her left. Raising the bouquet again in the crook of her left arm for coverage, she kept going.

Toward the end of the hall, outside Room 1610, Nicole slowed. The pattern changed. There was a lone "W" on the room tag. No patient name, not even a physician's. She stared at the tag for a moment longer than safe, then, jarring herself back into action, Nicole kept moving. But just as suddenly, she skidded to a stop. Her eyes widened. *That's not a W! It's two V's!*

Her heartbeat rose in her throat and pounded in her ears. She dropped back to 1610 and slowly, gently, eased the door open. "May I help you?" A voice sprung from behind her. Nicole jumped, spinning around.

"Oh! You startled me!" Her free hand joined her other around the vase of flowers, stabilizing them; her breath, quick and shallow behind the mask. "Actually, yes, I'm looking for my friend, Ginny. Virginia Vinsant. This is her room, but it's empty."

"And you are?"

"Nicole."

"Family?" The nurse was a couple of inches shorter than Nicole, and she tilted her head back, eyeing Nicole down the length of her nose, as if she were looking through bifocals that weren't there.

With a soft smile, Nicole kept her voice low and tender, while keeping the flowers in slight motion. Movement, so the nurse couldn't detect they were shaking. "As good as."

"Hmmm." The nurse maintained her evaluating glare. The badge clipped to the white jacket pocket, read 'Beecham, Supervising RN'.

Dramatically, the eyebrows above Nicole's mask lifted, and her right hand left the vase, landing in a thud over her heart. "Wait! She's all right, isn't she?"

"I'll phone her husband." Nurse Beecham kicked the stopper down on the door to prop it open and started toward the nurses' station.

"NO!" The word spun the nurse around, but not quick enough to catch the alarm in Nicole's eyes. She softened, "I—I mean, please don't bother him. I know Tom is busy."

"We all are, and he made it clear no one is to disturb her. Especially reporters. I'll walk you to the elevator." The nurse waited for Nicole to join her in the hall.

"Ginny will be disappointed when she hears I wasn't allowed to see her!" Nicole tried, but only got a hard stare. She matched it for a few beats, thinking, then pushed the flowers into the arms of Nurse Beecham. "At least give her these. They're her favorites."

Before the other woman could respond, Nicole turned and retraced her steps to the elevator, glancing back only once. The nurse, holding the bouquet, was steadily eyeing Nicole, who slapped the call button and tapped her foot, urging the car's arrival. The seconds stretched out to a minute. When the digital number six lit up and the sound announced the car's arrival, Nicole looked over her shoulder. The nurse was retreating down the hallway and turned toward the west wing, out of view. Nicole hurried to follow.

Passing the nurses' desk, she kept her chin high, forging ahead until she heard the masculine voice, "He claims there wasn't any ..." Something was familiar. She'd heard that voice before. She jerked a backward glance as she was rounding the corner and didn't see the lanky security guard who had jumped to attention to block her. She plowed directly into him.

Nicole shrieked. The impact was solid and together they teetered, fumbling. The guard grabbed Nicole's arm. Instinctively responding, she pushed him away and regained her balance, but the guard wasn't so lucky. Before the show ended, and backup was called to escort Nicole out of the hospital, she had noticed the closed doors behind the fuming officer. They had a key swipe for authorized personnel only. High security.

* * *

"I can find my own way, thank you," Nicole said. With her identity exposed and no risk of passing the emergency room area again, she had ditched the mask, and walked ahead of the two security officers.

"I'm sorry, Ms. Portman, but the head nurse said she'd already asked you to leave. Just doin' our job."

From the sixth floor down, the elevator stopped at three other levels, adding more visitors and personnel. Surely it had a reputation for being slow, because no one decided the car was too full. They pressed in. The occupants squeezed closer, shifting toward the sides and the rear, and Nicole took advantage, staying against the control panel, offering space between herself and her escorts. At ground level, with the door only open two feet, she bolted. Her long legs weaved through the clusters of people that hovered in the hall, and she didn't look back, even when she heard the growing commotion from behind. When she reached the exit she burst through, allowing the cool Los Angeles air to catch her.

It was the last week in May and the evening breeze was perfect. Nicole took a deep breath, then another, before resuming her pace and sprinting to her car.

CHAPTER 3

There was a loud drumbeat coming from Nicole's purse, and on any other day, it would likely cause her to smile. It was the special ringtone she'd chosen for Blind Dog Mike, the deejay who hosted the morning drive show—*Your Mornin' Jamm*—on KDLA radio. Mike was popular with Angeleno commuters, knowing what they needed each day to get moving, and they were as dependent on Blind Dog Mike in the a.m. as they were their caffeine. The success of his show eventually gave way to national recognition, and Your Mornin' Jamm was picked up for syndication from coast to coast, in over one hundred radio markets. Blind Dog's fame had erupted. But to Nicole, he was still her closest friend, Mike Hutchens.

Whether Mike was in his Blind Dog mode or not, he had a rhythm all his own, earning him the unique drumming sound from her mobile phone; however, this time she ignored it. She had just pulled out of the hospital parking lot and was too distracted to chat. Even to Mike. Lost in thought behind the wheel of her black Range Rover, she let it ring. *What did I just discover? And what do I do with it?*

* * *

Until four long weeks ago, Nicole had worked for the same broadcasting company as Mike and was at the top of her career as KDLA TV's evening news anchor. News was her life. That is, until Sidney Drummond, the founder and president of Drummond Media, sent her packing on an indefinite leave. She had been with them for eight years. Eight years of sweat. Eight years of forgoing a social life to get where she had. Eight years of proving she was promoted because of her abilities and not her looks or her last name which she shared with a famous actress. And Mike was there through it all. When he congratulated her on the anchor position, she had casually said, "I was at the right place at the right time." But Mike knew. He had witnessed her relentless work ethic.

And as if suspending her as their anchor wasn't enough, Drummond also canceled her original, self-produced program, *LA Diggs*. *LA Diggs* was a weekly show about her audience's problems, and it had been a hit. The program encouraged its viewers to contact the station with issues or suspicions that Nicole and her team could investigate on their behalf. Nicole and her staff worked, or *dug,* as the show suggested, to fight their battle or solve their mystery, all with a camera crew in tow. Each show had the right ingredients for success, but even more, *LA Diggs* was personal to the viewers. It told their stories.

One of the most heartwarming was the episode where *LA Diggs* helped one viewer find her two siblings. Formally wards of the state, the three children were separated at an early age, and the viewer was adopted at four years old. Fast forward: now in her twenties, she wanted to find her brother and sister but didn't know where to begin. With the unique team Nicole had put together, they helped the viewer find them. It aired as a special edition just before last year's Thanksgiving holiday.

Another segment that received wide recognition was about a convicted killer who sat on death row in the state of Texas. His family had contacted Nicole, pleading his innocence. With her team on board, and after finding new evidence, Nicole encouraged an attorney to reopen his case and file an appeal. The new evidence ended up being a digital highway-toll. It had captured the prisoner's car twenty-six miles north of Highland Park, the place the shooting occurred, at the time of the incident and had never been paid. He was acquitted.

The show was a hit. Tips became more and more interesting, and when Nicole received the call about "rumored security breaches" at the Port of Los Angeles, she was intrigued. Intrigued enough to get her in motion, but the fact that she ran into a brick wall is what got her hooked. Scheduled interviews canceled on her, and the ones that didn't cancel, were a no-show. Contacts not only became uncooperative, but openly hostile. All her resources waned, and even her boss, Sidney Drummond, joined in and ordered her to drop it, but she couldn't. *Something's there. It's not like I've run into a dead end ... this is more like an intentional roadblock. People aren't just changing their minds; they're frightened to talk to me. Why?*

Nicole was determined to find out.

On off hours, stealing into her personal time, it took almost four months, but she finally made connections with insiders that validated her suspicions. They personally witnessed ships entering and leaving the docks without inspection through customs and also knew of invoices for labor and inventory that were nonexistent. However, the only reason Nicole was able to pull this information was because of the employees' anger with human resources. They claimed the administrative positions that oversaw these departments were not being promoted from the inside. Instead, they were being appointed by contacts of Senator Tom Vinsant. They described a solid smokescreen at the Port of Los Angeles and the senator's name kept surfacing; however, she had nothing tangible to support these claims and her contacts refused to go on record. She needed something big. Something bold.

Arriving with her crew in tow at the Human Resource Department of the state docks, she asked for the department head. "I'm sorry, Ms. Portman, you'll have to come back another time. Mr. Johannsen had to leave unexpectedly."

Nicole gave a nod to her camera man to start filming. "Is it true that Senator Tom Vinsant has been involved in the appointment of key management positions here at the Port of Los Angeles? And why would a US senator be making these appointments?"

"I'm not at liberty to answer that question." The woman gave Nicole a polite smile and waved her hand toward the door as she tried to escort the news crew out.

"Is it true some of these positions are in the customs division and have the authority over the inspection process of the ships that enter and exit our port?"

"I wouldn't have that information, and I must ask you to leave. Please turn those cameras off." She had emphasized her request with her hand held toward the lens. The cameraman backed away, but kept filming, and when security arrived, the commotion he captured wasn't award-winning, but it was all Nicole had.

After seeing it, Sidney said, "It's speculation! All of it. What are you trying to do, Nicole, damage the station? I've told you before, drop it!" He left her office without another word, but Nicole couldn't drop it. With Senator Tom Vinsant's reelection campaign in full swing, she had felt it her duty. Perhaps she could merely prick the minds of her viewers with a "what if" segment.

The "what if" piece on the waterfront was cleverly constructed to protect the station, but still, on the day of the report, Nicole was nervous. While she drew large ratings for the network, she knew the segment would put her on thin ice. Still, she didn't care. She was willing to face the consequences. Nicole checked her mic and took a deep breath.

"According to an anonymous source, we've had reason to investigate ..."

The response was lightning fast and, whether favorably or not, it was record-breaking for the station. When Sidney called Nicole, she prepared for his praises. "Hello, Sidney. I promise not to gloat."

But the smile quickly dropped. She had glazed over, vaguely remembering colleagues giving her the thumbs up through her open door. Sidney left her with, "Let things cool down, Nicole. Take time off. *LA Diggs* will be replaced by a cooking show or something, and maybe in a few weeks this scandal will blow over and you can ease back into your evening news slot." Sidney had chosen Senator Vinsant over her. Eight years. And in a day's time, it was ripped out from under her.

* * *

Now, gripping the steering wheel of her black Range Rover, she raced to put distance between her and the hospital, and her thoughts were spinning just as fast. *The mysterious caller has seen LA Diggs ... but how did he get my cell number? This could be a setup.* Nicole shook her head. *No, that Nurse Beecham more or less validated Ginny Vinsant's presence when she threatened to call the senator. Something is going on there. Something they don't want public!*

As she drove, the loud drumming from her purse persisted. Again and again. She still needed time to think, and if it were anyone other than Mike, she would not have answered. "What?"

"Well, I must've called at the right time," Mike said. Her silence gave him his answer. "I'm at Samm's and have us a table out back. The sun will be doin' its thing soon—I'll hold it for you if you hurry," he chuckled.

"I've had an odd day, Mike, and I want to wallow in it."

Mike heard the road noise from her tires. "All the more reason to join me. You're probably passin' by now on your way home. I'll order a cold glass of chardonnay to be delivered the minute you sit down." Then he disconnected before she could say no.

Samm's Restaurant rested along the California coast in Marina Del Rey and was centrally located in the radius of Mike and Nicole's worlds, partway between the Los Angeles airport and Nicole's home in Malibu. Then, equally distant to the west was Beverly Hills, where Mike lived, and West Hollywood, where he worked at Drummond's Studios. It had become their go-to place, where the outdoor setting delivered the entertainment—breathtaking sunsets behind a forest of sailing masts, all resting in the harbor.

When Nicole arrived, the host recognized her and guided her to the back patio, where Mike was waiting. He stood and kissed her cheek. "Hey, baby. Your wine will be here shortly. Talk to me."

As usual, the light show was brilliant on the horizon, and, through the lenses of her dark-framed Versace's, Nicole simply looked out to sea. The server left the chilled glass, and Nicole watched a cluster of birds chase after a small fishing boat, squawking for the two fishermen to throw their discards. Conversations in the light breeze were subdued by the sound of waves pushing into the bulkhead and by the clanking of hardware from the sailing masts. A light tune from the piano bar mingled onto the patio and joined the refrain. It was nurturing to the senses. Nicole took a savoring sip from her glass before she left the serenity for conversation. "I've been to the hospital."

"As a visitor? Or ... is there something I should know?" Mike's brows drew together. His body shifted forward. Closer. Tilting his shades down, he watched her response. To him, you didn't simply listen to Nicole, you watched. From the first time he saw her, he couldn't imagine an artist doing a better job at chiseling out that strong jaw line and long, straight nose that flared its nostrils when she debated anything she was passionate about. There was one vein that popped out on her left temple when she cried, and he didn't think anyone else knew that but him. Her eyebrows lifted often, and she'd switch from left to right, depending on her emotion. Then there were her hands, always adding animation to the conversation, so you didn't merely listen to Nicole talk. You watched. And he could watch her talk for hours. But that evening, there was no animation. She absently twirled the stem of her glass. It had Mike's attention.

"Actually, it was work."

"Baby, that's great! You got your job back! So ... why the heavy vibe?"

Nicole smiled solemnly at her friend. He was the one person who knew how difficult her suspension had been and still supported her as she continued to secretly research the waterfront, the senator, and anything else she felt the citizens of California needed to know. She was pursued by publishers to write a personal tell-all about her life at Drummond Media, but there was only one tell-all she was interested in, the unreported rumor-mill surrounding the senator and the city officials whose names were attached to him. It was how she filled her unemployed days, that is, until the anonymous caller.

Nicole sighed. "No, Mike. Drummond hasn't called ... not yet, but he will." Conviction sparked her eyes. "And I'll get vindication!"

Mike tilted his beer in her direction. "So, what was at the hospital?"

A platter of freshly fried seafood waved past them. The aroma stirred growling sounds from Nicole, reminding her that she hadn't eaten since morning, and she inhaled deeply, enjoying the sensation, but evidently she wasn't the only one. A crash jolted her, and she spun around. The unusually large wingspan of a lone seagull was wiping out every vertical object on the neighboring table as the shocked couple scrambled backwards. Before the staff could get to him, the bird grabbed a clump of calamari from the platter and fled to the safety of the beach. Behind her shades, Nicole's eyes smiled at the sneaky bandit, then turned back to Mike. "I was following something that could be newsworthy. The subject is in UCLA Med Center and I went to investigate."

"You didn't," Mike said, then raised his index finger in the air for the server.

"Didn't what?"

"Try to see Ginny Vinsant."

Nicole removed her shades, her grey eyes piercing Mike. People tended to talk freely with Mike, and he had more dirt on the rich and famous than he cared to, but he was also a vault. Nicole respected him for it and usually refrained from squeezing gossip from him, unless she deemed it necessary, and to her, Senator Tom Vinsant and his wife qualified.

Mike shook his head. "Baby, that's no way to get to her husband. Word is, she had a pretty bad head injury."

"Excuse me?" The response was louder than Nicole intended. Looking around, she saw everyone was still lively over the seagull incident. She lowered her voice. "Time to open the vault."

The server was back and set a frosted glass of beer in front of Mike. Tiny streams of dark bubbles chased each other around, then right up the middle of the glass, waiting to be tasted by the man holding it, and he obliged before answering her.

Nicole pressed. "I know the Vinsants gave a huge donation to The Rock, since it's Hollywood's 'charity of the year,' but please don't tell me he's on the board or something repulsive like that! You would have said something, Mike ... right?"

The Rock was a faith-based community center for urban boys and girls, a non-profit; therefore, it depended highly on donations and volunteers who mentored the kids, and Blind Dog Mike became involved early on. His firsthand knowledge of a dysfunctional childhood with no father figure inspired him to be a positive influence in the children's lives. With his bigger-than-life persona, he was a huge draw for the center, not only for the kids but also for attracting other celebrities. Currently, it was trending as *the* "photo-op" spot for the rich and famous, who promoted themselves on every social media platform; so when the Vinsants hopped on, Nicole wasn't surprised.

For all the patience Nicole didn't have, Mike had a double dose and took another swallow before calmly placing his glass on the small, square napkin. "No, baby. He's not on the board, and yes, I would've told you." He leaned back in his chair. "Mrs. Vinsant still donates musical instruments. That's her thing. She's helping to build up the music department. Word is, she wrecked on her way there."

Nicole's left eyebrow rode high.

"What?" he asked.

The steel of her eyes bore through him. "It never crossed your mind to tell me she was still around?"

"That's not around." Actually, he had only seen her a couple of times, but those times made an impression. With her dreamy, childlike brown eyes that belied her forty-two years, the kids were fascinated by Ginny and her choppy yellow hair. The younger girls had gathered around her when Ginny sat to show the proper form of holding a violin, and a few bolder ones touched her hair, eventually braiding it. And she let them. Mike hadn't known too many women—no matter what ethnicity or social level—who would let a room full of children mess with their hair like she did. He added, "She drops off instruments, baby. That's it."

"And I was doing a segment on her husband!" Nicole grabbed her purse and threw the strap over her shoulder.

Mike tilted his head back slightly, sighing. "Now what could you gain by knowing she drops off donations? Other than learning she has a penchant for music, like you and me. Or that she has a givin' spirit. The only insight into her husband would be the obvious ... bad choice in men twenty years ago."

They had a rhythm. Nicole didn't respond, but Mike knew she wouldn't leave. Not without pumping him for information about the accident, and he didn't have to wait long. Nicole flipped her chin toward Mike, as to go ahead, and said, "Back to her head injury. What do you know?"

He took another slow drink of his beer, obviously not as eager about the conversation as Nicole. When he returned the glass to the table, Mike's fingers brushed the outer condensation mindlessly as he said, "Only that she was stopping by the center to pick up some instruments for repair but was a no-show." He tapped the napkin, drying his finger-tips, then looked squarely at Nicole. "Later, the director heard she'd been in an accident coming down the exit ramp off the Harbor Freeway."

"You said head injury. How bad? Was she drinking?"

Mike shook his head and crossed his right foot over his left knee. "That's all I have. The Rock's director tried to visit her, but they wouldn't let him. You?"

Looking down at the concrete of the patio, Nicole spoke softly, but Mike didn't catch it. He uncrossed his leg and leaned closer. "Try me again?"

Their heads were inches away when Nicole shared her experience, leaving out the sickening smell and memories she fought. She ended with her run-in with security and the escort out. Mike's signature smile flashed. Then he gave a light chuckle. But when he caught the slight twitch of a grin from Nicole's face, he let go with a roaring laugh, slapping his knee. When a tear escaped from under his glasses and he wiped his face with the back of his hand.

"As if I wasn't humiliated enough. I thought I could get a little sympathy from my best friend." Her words contradicted her expression, which was softer than it had been all day, and Mike squeezed her hand, but as quickly as he'd turned on the laughter, his smile faded and his eyes narrowed.

"An escort isn't cool, baby. So whatcha gonna do?"

Nicole pulled her chair closer. "I've got to go back."

Mike was shaking his head.

"Yes. Listen to me! The reason I ran into the guard? I was distracted. I recognized a voice, and I know who it is now!" Nicole looked around the patio before continuing, keeping her voice low. "My anonymous caller? He's a nurse on the sixth floor of that hospital and I need to talk to him!"

CHAPTER 4

Mike and Nicole had met at the beginning of their junior year at the University of Southern California, when Nicole came to him looking for a job. The young Marvin Gaye look-alike examined her résumé while she picked the invisible lint at the hem of her jacket.

Nicole's Great Aunt Naomi, who had raised her from the age of twelve, had passed away, and Nicole was relocating from her aunt's house to the campus dorms. She needed a paid internship. According to her career advisor, the only opening that qualified for credit in her major of communication and journalism was with the small radio station at the university. The decision was up to Mike. Nicole fidgeted until he finally said, "This is beautiful, baby, but all I'm reading here is journalism. You're a writer. What are you doin' *here*?"

"I'm interviewing for the position you have."

"Um huh. And you wanna share the air with me? With Blind Dog? Look at you. You're wound so tight, I ain't got room for that."

"I thought it was administrative ... or, um ... editorial ... I could write copy for you. I'm a fast learner," she threw in. Even though he shook his head, she persisted. "I need this job, and from what I've been told it's the only one I DO qualify for. Give me two weeks. I'll prove myself."

"I'm sorry, baby, but I need talent. I got a station to run." He turned, tossing her résumé on the file cabinet behind his desk, then began shuffling through a stack of new applications.

Nicole raised herself slowly out of the chair, but she simply stood, unmoving, watching Blind Dog Mike's back.

"A school filled with talent and this is what they send me ... Miss 'Stuck-up-tight-ass-white-sorority-I-want-a-journalism-degree-girl,'" he muttered, and when he turned back, he jumped. She was still there. "Did you forget somethin'?" Blind Dog's cool exterior was ruffled, knowing she'd heard him. Nicole just stared. Unblinking. Mike tried again, "I got work to do, so if you don't mind ..."

Still, she didn't leave. Her fight might have abandoned her, but her tenacity hadn't. It ground her to the spot where she was standing, and she stared, holding him captive with those crystal-grey eyes. Eyes that had seen their share of tragedy and were not accepting his answer. The piercing glaze had him repeatedly clearing his throat.

"Naaww, baby," he said, shaking his head. "Stop lookin' at me like that."

She started the next day. Mike's compassion, along with his patience, was rewarded, because Nicole had a natural ear for music. Especially discernment on what aired well. Their tastes were so similar, it wasn't long before Mike actually asked her to join him on-air and pinned her with the pseudonym "Nikki Slate." Slate, because of her grey eyes. Intriguing eyes that had persuaded him to give her a chance. And they became a team. The faceless audience of radio gave Nicole freedom, but Mike still had to remind her from time to time, to keep it loose. "This ain't the news ... it's entertainment, baby. Chill. Out."

She was the straight man. Strong willed, but still naïve, and her persona collided ingeniously into Mike's inflated ego and unconventional groove. Man to woman, black to white, they had a unique banter that ignited the radio waves, and their popularity drove record donations into the college station. Blind Dog Mike and his sidekick Nikki Slate became a commodity that even grabbed the attention of Sidney Drummond, media mogul and owner of KDLA Broadcasting. Before their graduation, Drummond offered them an afternoon show with his local radio station, and that's where their careers took off.

Work was Nicole's favorite pastime, so when she wasn't prepping or taping a show, or at a promotional event, she honed her writing talents at home, staying in touch with the journalism world. She dated from time to time, but always found reasons to break it off, so dry stretches were more common. The only relationship she was committed to was her professional one with Mike. He had gambled on her, and, because of him, she belonged somewhere.

Mike's lifestyle was much different. Sometimes his weekends ran into Monday mornings, and he'd be dropped off at the station by his latest long-legged fan, just in time for work; but his loyalty, too, was always to Nicole. He still saw her as his protégé, even though they were the same age, and wanted to protect her. And she let him. He had become family. The constant in her life.

In just two years at KDLA FM, Mike and Nicole celebrated another huge achievement of driving their time slot to number one. They were reveling in their success when a prime job became available in the newsroom. Mike saw the look on Nicole's face when she got word. He knew the news would always be her passion, and, although he didn't want change, he also didn't want to hold her back.

"Hey, baby, it's time you stop depending on me to prop you up," he had said one afternoon. He kept his shades on and did everything he could to keep from looking into her eyes. He dug through file drawers, pushed items around on the counter, then fired up his computer. "I've talked with Drummond about becoming a solo act. You know ... um ... if we wanna grow we gotta get out of this comfort thing we got goin'." He stopped, but looked like he wasn't finished. His mouth opened, then closed. Nicole waited. "... Anyway, Drummond said he might be able to find you somethin' else. I believe the newsroom is hirin'."

Nicole walked up behind Mike's chair. There were no files open on the computer screen. He was blankly staring at it.

"Um hmmm ... and how long have you been thinking about this?"

Mike shrugged.

"Since the position in news came open? It's okay, Mike. I'd rather be here. Us." Then she tried to mimic Mike and said, "We're the boss!"

He playfully shook his head from side to side, grinning. "Baby, you are too stiff to be tryin' to talk like me. It just don't work."

Mike never turned around; he was still facing the monitor, and Nicole put her arms around his neck, leaning her head against his. "I don't want to go without you."

"You'll always have me ... but go before someone else grabs it."

The position was hers. Nicole shed her alias and plunged herself into the news, initially writing wire copy for the reporters of Drummond Media, working herself up through the trenches.

It had now been eight years since college, and they were both at the height of their careers, or at least Mike was.

* * *

They were in Nicole's black Range Rover, headed to UCLA Medical Center, with Mike riding shotgun. He held the grip over the door as she made the corner onto Sepulveda without braking. "Whoa!"

"We need plenty of cushion before the nurse's shift is over." Nicole was an aggressive driver on a normal day, so with her rushing, Mike's chill was challenged.

"And what am I supposed to say to this dude?"

"I'll write a note and you can hand it to him. Simple." Nicole described where to find the nurse and what he looked like, then pulled in front of the hospital, waving off the valet attendant. She scribbled something quick and passed it off to Mike. "I'll keep making the block until I see you."

It was close to ten at night and the area around the hospital was still congested. Nicole uncharacteristically stayed in the slower lane behind a city bus, and by the time she made her second pass, Mike was already waiting. "His shift is over at eleven and he'll see us at Cap't Jack's at eleven fifteen."

"He talked with you?" She studied him.

"Yeah, name's Johnathan. He read the note before I left the floor and said no way," Mike said casually.

"And?"

"I assured him Cap't Jack's was a dive, and no one would see us there. Also," Mike said smiling, "I promised he can sit with me." He didn't tell her Johnathan actually was a huge Blind Dog Mike fan.

Nicole rolled her eyes and pulled onto Westwood heading toward Cap't Jack's to wait.

Mike wasn't wrong about Cap't Jack's being a dive. It was. Located in a small, overlooked strip mall between the hospital and the 405 freeway.

The area wasn't seedy, just a bad development located on a one-way street with very limited parking and even that was hard to get to. You had to round the corner of the cross street to enter the lot. Any business that depended on walk-in traffic was doomed from the start, but for some reason people kept trying. Before becoming Cap't Jack's, the space had originally been home to a convenience store. After it closed, someone opened a dry cleaner, and next, a check-cashing business. It didn't look like Cap't Jack's was going to be long-term either, but in the meantime Nicole took advantage of it for the obvious privacy.

"Dude's punctual," Mike said, and nodded to the sandy-haired man coming through the door. Mike and Nicole had taken a booth against the far wall, and Mike sat facing the entrance with Nicole well-hidden on the opposite side. Their guest looked military, except for the slight goatee. He walked with efficiency, as if his every move had purpose, and in a day where people were becoming less likely to wear a watch, his black wrist-band shouted discipline.

"Thanks for coming," Nicole said to Johnathan as he slid in the booth beside her.

"I didn't realize it was an option." He looked from his watch to the bartender. "Your note threatened to oust me as a snitch." Mike shot Nicole a quick eye, brows high, and she met him with a leveled gaze. The tension broke momentarily when the bartender walked to their booth. He was pulling double duty, but with only two other patrons it wasn't an issue.

"What can I get you?" he asked. Subtle details told this man's story—the slight Latino accent, the grey in his beard, the simple wedding band hanging from a chain around his neck, were all overshadowed by the gold embroidery on his Vietnam War veteran's cap, and Mike gave him a respectful nod.

The newcomer fidgeted with his keys and Nicole looked away, faking patience. She twisted the stem of her glass and heard the bartender clearing his throat, prompting Johnathan. "I'll have a Black Jack, on the rocks, with a water back."

Boz Scaggs was serenading them over the surprisingly clear surround speakers with a song from a different time, most likely the same era as the blue paisley carpet. Without the chatter of a full bar, every noise was heightened. Ice cubes clinked in a glass; the air conditioner kicked on. The other two patrons were talking and laughing over a competitive dart game, and the activity surrounding them helped balance the awkward group of three in the back. "This has to be quick. I have somewhere to be," said the nervous, sandy-haired man.

"Fine," Nicole said. "Is what you told me on the phone true? Is the accident more than we know?"

"Are you recording this?" His eyes darted about the booth.

"No." Brushing her hair behind her ear, Nicole took a slight sip of her wine. Casual moves, overplayed to appear calm. She turned in the booth, facing him, her back against the wall.

"Listen, I shouldn't have called, I just got caught up in the moment." Without hiding under the pretend "Valley" dialect, there was no mistaking his southern heritage. His forearms rested on the table, and he turned his keys over using both hands. His right leg bounced.

"But you did. And I understand." She sat her glass down. "I've been through this so many times with the viewers on the show. Once we had the ball rolling on an issue, they regretted getting involved and didn't want their names attached. Didn't want trouble ..." She stopped and watched his face. "I get it. Don't worry. If you answer my questions, we'll go our separate ways and you'll never be mentioned."

Johnathan turned to her and for the first time kept eye contact, but he couldn't hold it long and looked back at his hands.

"Is she still there?" Nicole pressed.

His nod was so slight, had Nicole not been staring intently, she could have missed it. The black pendant lamp that hung over the booth accentuated Johnathan's pallor. He looked ill, and Nicole kept an eye on him, even as she lifted her feet, right, then left, trying to unstick the soles of her shoes from whatever had been spilled under their table. Johnathan's drink came, offered with pride on an impressive Cap't Jack coaster, and after a tip of his head to the bartender, the Jack Daniels became his focus. He sipped, then set it back on the coaster.

Mike gave it a try. "How serious are her injuries?"

They waited. Then muffled popping sounds "poof ... poof, poof," echoed around the room and Johnathan jerked toward the bar. Nicole didn't bother; she smelled the fresh aroma of popcorn. The bartender was optimistic.

Bringing his attention back to their group, the nurse took another quick sip of his drink and played with the edges of the coaster. He looked at Mike. "Concussion. Should've been just a twenty-four-hour observation." He shook his head. "I called because the tests showed she was fine." Again, the bobbing knee, rapidly up and down. "And I figured, if she wasn't hallucinating like we were told, then they were covering up something. But I was wrong. Seriously. So y'all need to forget I called."

"Covering what? What hallucination?" Nicole asked.

"Didn't you hear me? I was wrong. You need to drop it!" His color reddened.

"I didn't get where I am today by 'dropping it.'" As an afterthought, Nicole forced a smile. She didn't need to run him away, but she also wasn't letting go.

His drink was empty. Mike got the bartender's attention, pointing at Johnathan's glass, but the young man shook his head. "I gotta go."

He stood and Nicole scooted toward him, across the booth seat. "Wait! Did you or did you not overhear her claiming responsibility for someone's death?" If someone could be mentally pushed by a look, Nicole's intense expression would have done it. "I don't want to hurt you," she said, "but I *will* expose you if you leave me hanging."

The jazzy tune from Michael Bublé steadied the friction at the table, and after a long pause Johnathan sat back down—barely. He sat on the edge of the bench and kept his eyes on the floor. "We all heard the same cry—that she had killed someone. I over-reacted." His jaw clinched. "I'd seen it before. Folks getting away with stuff because they have power or money. Like they're above the law." His keys were back in hand, turning, and he was covered in regret. "Like I said, I was wrong. I wish I could take it back. Her husband spoke with the doctor and they decided to move her to a more secured area."

"Secured?"

"Well, for our floor it is. The real mental facility is at another location."

* * *

It was after midnight and Nicole had driven back to Marina Del Rey to drop Mike off at his car. Before he stepped out of the Range Rover, she asked, "Mike, is anyone at the youth center close to Ginny Vinsant? Enough to verify what he said?"

He shrugged.

"I know what the center means to you and I hate to ask, but this is a game-changer. Please. Can you find out if what he said is true?"

He touched her arm. "Baby, get some sleep. We'll talk on the flip side."

She didn't push.

The adrenaline yo-yo she had been on was on a downslope and Mike was right. They had tomorrow. By the time Nicole made it to her small Malibu cottage, she was spent. Setting her alarm to awaken early was habit, even though she no longer had an office to go to. As soon as it was set, she was fast asleep.

CHAPTER 5
THE CHILDREN

"Where are we, Kiandra?" The small voice asked. Jackie Spence was looking to his big sister for answers.

There was a guard at the door. He never seemed to be watching them, but he was. He wore black athletic pants and a black T-shirt that looked two sizes too small, as the short sleeves stretched over large biceps. There was a stool beside him, and he rotated between sitting and standing, but he never looked bored or anxious. He also never revealed their location or what was planned for them. With no information, the four frightened foster children couldn't know if the past forty-eight hours or the next would be their worst. "I wanna go home. To Grammy's home," Jackie cried.

Kiandra Spence was only nine, but she did her best to comfort her little brother. Two days ago, their lives had taken another drastic turn when they ran away from their foster home, their second one since becoming orphaned after their grandmother, Georgia Homewood, died months earlier. This last one was heinous, and though the children wouldn't have known to question why a house located in a gang war zone, or the drug-dependent woman inside, had ever qualified in the foster system, they did know she frightened them. Their caseworker, a Mrs. Smith, handed them a business card with one instruction, "Call *only* if it's an extreme emergency," then left them with the woman and two junior-high boys, Jorge and Angel, also fostered.

Before the door closed behind Mrs. Smith, the foster mom hurled warnings at them. "I agreed to give you a place to sleep, but you keep your greedy self outta my kitchen! You be gettin' 'nough food from school." The kids stared wide-eyed at the woman with the white, smacking substance that collected at the corners of her mouth. She pointed a shaky finger at them, and Jackie jumped backward. "I'm paid to watch you, so don't be tryin' to run away, neither. You do ... an' my brother's gang will hunt ... you ... down." Her eyes were all pupil but they narrowed to angry slits under her sparse brows.

And the children had done as told. All four slept in the front room together with tattered furniture blankets as their beds, and they lived in constant fear. Not only of the neighborhood but of the foster mom and her boyfriends.

School was their sanctuary with schedules, fairly clean bathrooms, and most importantly, there was food. Breakfast and lunch were a sure thing during the weekdays. While most children delighted in the sound of the Friday afternoon school bell, the thrill was lost on the four foster children. To them it meant a long stretch without a warm meal. The hunger scars from their first weekend at this new home forced them to become resourceful. They began collecting scraps daily from the leftovers at school, saving what they could for Saturday and Sunday. Whole untouched apples or bananas could usually be found and pieces of peanut butter sandwiches. "Collect all the pizza bones, Kiandra," Jackie had told her. That's what he called the leftover crusts, and he loved them, which was good for her—they saved well enough. They wrapped their findings in napkins and hid them in their pockets until they got home. Jorge had located a couple of plastic bags from the junior-high kitchen, and they all contributed to the bags each night. He sealed them tight to bind in the odors so they wouldn't get caught and to protect their treasured rations from the pests that scurried inside the rotting house.

Then, two days ago, after Kiandra had put her homework away, she located the frayed business card from Mrs. Smith. It was her pastime, fantasizing about calling her and being rescued. With card in hand, Kiandra laid down, and it wasn't long before she fell asleep, dreaming of her grandmother and their home together. Grammy was at the kitchen table whipping up some of her funny stories right along with her yummy mashed potatoes, and Kiandra was giggling, but her laughter quickly turned to choking and suddenly she couldn't breathe. She was smothering ... fighting ... for air. Jolted awake, she found that her fight was with the foster's boyfriend. He was on top of her. One of his hands covered her mouth and her nostrils flared and constricted fiercely for breath. His other hand worked at the knotted drawstring of her pants.

Squirming and writhing with all her might, Kiandra found a primal, survival kind of strength and clamped her teeth into the hand that was mashing her face. For a brief moment she was free, and she screamed, but his backhand slammed across her jaw, silencing her, and the attacker became more aggressive, ripping the drawstring, popping it apart. Then everything stopped.

The boyfriend went completely still. The full weight of his body was crushing. Kiandra's eyes were squeezed tight and tears dripped down the side of her face onto the floor as she laid there, shivering. "Get up!" Jorge, one of the older foster kids, rolled the boyfriend off her.

When Kiandra's eyes opened, she saw the boyfriend lying next to her. Blood was dribbling down the side of his head, and Jorge was holding a handgun. "Where'd you get that?" she whispered, wide-eyed.

"That don't matter," said Angel, the other child, standing behind Jorge. "He only clipped him with the butt. Our problem's the foster. We gotta think fast 'fore she calls her brotha!"

Using the boyfriend's cell phone, Kiandra had used her lifeline—the business card with Mrs. Smith's name and number. They were told to meet her at the Bullard Street Airport at eight o'clock. It was several miles away and they would have to stay under the radar as they cut through yards and between buildings, keeping ever mindful of the gang tagging from hood to hood. Jorge and Angel would have been challenged by the restless streets if they were alone, but traveling with the little kids, they had a chance of making it to the airport in time.

With only two miles left, Jackie stopped. "I can't." His words were barely audible, but the silent tears making a path down his soiled brown cheeks were deafening to his sister. She heard the fear and pain that stamped her baby brother's face.

"You my superhero ... lil' ... man. You ... you ... doin' good," Kiandra sputtered between her own gasps for breath. "Jump on my back. I'll carry you." She knelt next to him, but a cramp seized her side and she doubled over, clutching it with a trembling arm.

"I got him," said a voice standing behind her. It was Angel or Jorge, she wasn't sure and couldn't think clearly past the pain. She needed rest too, but they couldn't be late. The voice sounded again over the sirens and sounds of the night. "Ready?"

Kiandra gave a slight nod and pushed herself up. Her body pulled to the right, favoring her side as the enemy within her wrestled to take her down again.

"Stay close," Jorge said, moving ahead with Jackie on his back, "We gotta hurry." And the four children had disappeared into the night.

CHAPTER 6

Nicole's Malibu house was California contemporary, with lots of white painted concrete and glass, and since the earth sloped downward from the road to the water, you could only get a full view of it from the beach. Mostly what was seen from the highway was the paved driveway leading to a two-car garage on the left, and a solid privacy wall with an electronic entry gate covering the right. It wasn't until you were inside that you would realize the size. The rooms were huge; however, it was only a one-bedroom, originally built to be an elaborate vacation rental or for Drummond Media's visiting business associates. The kitchen, dining area, and living room were all one large living space, divided only by a long island counter that was lined on the beach side by five zinc barstools with grey leather seats. The oversized master suite ran parallel to the living area and both rooms had full views of the beach. With the French doors open, the house extended onto a full deck, where cozy gatherings of chairs under the blue skies invited the ocean in, or, if you'd rather go to where the water lives, one flight of stairs would take you down to the beach level, and Nicole used them every morning.

Before work each day, Nicole descended the back stairs and ran the same brisk run. Two miles up Malibu, then back, taking slightly over thirty minutes to complete the four miles, then she'd start the coffeemaker while she showered. It had been a good routine, but since leaving her job at Drummond Media, and with no office to go to, it had become harder to get out of bed. And the run was taking longer. On that morning after Cap't Jack's, for the first time in four weeks, Nicole had awakened before the alarm. Her eyes popped open wide, and she jumped out of bed, slipping into her grey sweatpants and the Hawaiian Tropic T-shirt she'd cropped in college with its ragged hem that barely covered her navel. With running shoes laced, she walked onto the back deck of her house and stretched. As dawn broke, she descended the stairs with purpose.

No therapy matched that wide-open sweep of sand. The marine fog was like a filter hovering over the early hours. It greeted the Pacific shoreline most every evening, wanted or not, staying until the sunshine and warmth from the next day drove it away again, and Nicole was one of the few who welcomed it. Routines, and inanimate things like this, were part of her nucleus, something she depended on. She disappeared into the cloud-like landscape without headphones, opting to listen to the rhythms of life, and her own feet pounding beside the crashing waves. When the seagulls were at play, they added the perfect accompaniment.

The beach house was Sidney Drummond's. He rented it to her for a nominal amount, considering the area—a perk that came with her position at Drummond Media, but that could change at any moment if her relationship with him didn't. The last time they spoke she got the same response, "Our attorneys have advised us to put a little more time between the incident and your resurfacing. Soon, dear. Be patient." Then he would disconnect.

Sidney! Sidney siding with Tom Vinsant. And now the wife should be making headlines too ... but isn't. "There is no doubt he is corrupt ... and I'll prove it, Sidney!!" She said aloud, then picked up her pace.

The run was invigorating, and Nicole started the coffee before going into the bath and turning on all three showerheads to bask in the warmth and the steam they created. It was her guilty pleasure, since there was a water shortage in Southern California and the reason it would be brief.

Returning to the kitchen wearing linen shorts and a white tank top, she finger-combed her hair and left it to dry. Holding her steaming coffee mug, she booted up her laptop at the island counter. "Let's see what the internet says about you today," Nicole said as she typed in "Virginia Vinsant."

"Surely someone is following you ... other than me," she muttered as she reconfigured the site to check for newest results, instead of the most popular or trending.

Nothing caught her eye. A charity event here, another there, even a few about her style. Then, a day-old link appeared with the headline with the words "Auto accident" and "Campaign."

"Bingo!" Clicking on it, Nicole tapped the counter, waiting for the website to deliver. It kept searching. She brought her mug up to her lips with both hands and took a sip, waiting. Her little cursor turned and turned, stuck in a cycle. Nicole sighed heavily, then moved the pointer to the X in the top corner to close out the window, and just before she clicked it, the page came to life. It was CMbz's website, a Hollywood gossip-type magazine, and she wasn't surprised they had the story, since their street resources reached far and deep; however, the page said the content had been removed.

"What!? A Ginny Vinsant story removed after only one day?" Nicole said aloud, then closed out of the link and tried again. Same message. Her left eyebrow lifted. "Did you strong-arm them too, Senator?" Then she shook her head. "No. Not seeing it. Not with that group." Nicole knew of the editor, Rusty Willmore, and more than once she'd given him an on-air plug for breaking news. "Hopefully, he'll remember and extend a little professional courtesy to me today." She quickly logged their Hollywood address from the contact information and made a quick change into jeans and threw on a black jersey blazer. The three-inch heels were intentional, elevating her to six feet, and with her recorder and camera in her tote, she was on the move.

CMbz took up the entire second floor of a dated two-story office complex off Vine Street, and Nicole was stunned by the extravagant design of the entrance when she walked in. The foyer was the full height of both floors, with an elegant crystal-looking chandelier that hung fifteen feet from the ceiling, and in a loft style, a section of CMbz's office was on display through an upper glass wall. Contemporary leather furniture in a deep pumpkin color was nestled in settings of lush potted trees, and the décor emitted an energetic luxury that extended to the sleek, stainless steel desk, where a female in a security uniform waited to help. After alerting the news group to Nicole's arrival, she pointed to a narrow passage behind her desk with the promise of an elevator. And the grandeur ended.

Transported back to the seventies, like the outside of the building, Nicole walked the tunnel-like hallway with low-hanging ceilings and fake paneling, past hollow wood doors, each labeled with a small stamped plate. One, an accounting office; another, a PI firm; and so on. Other than a slight murmur of conversation, the first floor was eerily quiet, so the resounding ping that announced the return of the elevator definitely could have been dialed back.

The second floor was the total opposite, with an open, breezy feeling, and abuzz with life. *What a strange building,* Nicole thought as she stepped off the elevator. A hipster-looking intern popped up from his desk to assist Nicole, and recognition turned to curiosity as he escorted her through the maze of desks to his editor. All eyes were on Nicole. It was like a mental gauntlet, and, with her smile locked in place, she nodded to a few, sashaying past them in the heels that gave her a four inch advantage over her escort.

Rusty Willmore's face lit up when he saw her. "Nicole Portman. Whatta ya doin'... slummin' today?"

Nicole had never met Rusty in person, who looked like an aging surfer. His hair, which was once copper, covered his ears with a permanent windblown effect and was laced with silver. Looking to be late fifties and wearing a wrinkled linen jacket and a pair of Nike sport shoes, everything about the man stated unconventional, like the news he produced. Freely and *usually* without malice, CMbz reported gossip electronically and also partnered their exclusives with an entertainment television program. With millions searching the web for gossip each day, CMbz had become huge.

"I heard you were hiring," she countered, cheekily, with a broad grin.

"Yeah. Intern position. Bathroom duty included. You interested?"

"Let me see the bathrooms first," she said, and Rusty started laughing.

"Coffee?"

"Sure. Black." When Rusty turned toward the coffee maker on the counter across the room, it gave Nicole a moment to gauge her surroundings. It didn't look like an office nor would it be considered a conference room. It felt more like a common area. The chairs looked exceedingly comfortable and faced each other. Intimate. Rusty's outstretched hand offered her a white mug with a large crimson "A." His had a navy and gold "ND." The coffee was perfect.

"Is this your office?" Nicole asked.

"No, but it's where I spend most of my time. My office is too confining."

Nicole knew enough about the company's history with Rusty at the helm and therefore wasn't surprised. He started CMbz, which was short for Celebrity Media Business, giving his readers what they wanted. Gossip. News that entertained them. When it started blooming, one of the larger entertainment groups saw the potential and tried to purchase CMbz for millions, but Rusty wouldn't accept the offer, and here he was, still in the same building he started in. He was a multi-million-dollar gig and growing, with a low-budget attitude, living on his own terms.

"So, do you need foreplay, or are we going to get right to it?" he asked, startling Nicole from her thoughts.

She gave him a full one-hundred-and-fifty-watt smile. "I can get right to it if you can. What happened to the story on Virginia Vinsant?"

"Can you be more specific?" Rusty sat in one of the cozy chairs. Too cozy. Nicole leaned against the counter.

"You ran a story only a day ago about Senator Tom Vinsant's wife in a car accident. I clicked on the link, but it said the story was removed from your website."

"Not familiar with it." He watched her over the top of his mug as he casually sipped.

It was difficult to read him. He could have been entertained by her position—the prime-time news celebrity who was stripped from her glorified position at his rag looking for information. Or he could've merely been suspicious, like most reporters were. She sipped and stared right back. "Can you ask?"

He crossed his leg, comfortably, like he wasn't going anywhere soon. "What's this story to you? Better yet, why is it so important that I would bother my employees to find out?"

"You don't find it odd that your group published a story and within hours it was pulled? If you're not familiar with it, and you didn't have it removed ... who did?"

"Again, why would that be important to you?"

Leaning against the counter, Nicole tilted her head. The long layers of her brown hair tumbled to the side, her steel eyes sparkled, flirtatious. She looked as cool as he did, as long as you couldn't see the flutter of her shirt, moving with the intensity of her elevated heartbeat. Making the decision to come here aroused her professionally; however, she'd been humiliated in the news circles by having her show pulled from her, and this man knew it. This pulse was different. Like she was caged. "Maybe I just like puzzles and have a little time on my hands."

Through narrowed eyes, Rusty watched her and sipped again. Slowly, he returned her smile and lifted a phone next to him. After several minutes, two of his staff members joined them. "I checked the post you're referring to," said the young man in the camo blazer. His black jeans were rolled up past the high-tops of his Converse sneakers, exposing the muted colors of his tie-dyed socks. It was a combination that alleged to have been thrown together in the dark, but actually took a lot of style to achieve the visual appeal and earned him a nod from Nicole. He continued, "It was published yesterday, but today it's not there. It's not even in the saved file."

"What about a printed copy?"

The young man shook his head, then threw his thumb toward the woman with him. "We looked before coming in here. It was written kinda tongue-in-cheek about Senator Vinsant's wife totaling a car coming off an exit ramp. Like, 'What sober person leaves the danger zone of the freeway unscathed, but crashes on the sidelines?' Something like that. An undercurrent suggesting alcohol, so we figured you pulled it." The woman nodded in agreement, her brows tight in worry, like she was about to be on the outs with her boss.

"I didn't pull it. See if you can find anything else," Rusty said, dismissing them. Nicole had his attention, in more ways than she wanted. "You're on to something, sunshine. You gonna share? Over dinner tonight?"

Dodging dates was simple. Nicole had years of experience there, but evading his questions about Virginia Vinsant was another thing. She couldn't make light of it, because if there was nothing to it, then why *was* she there? "I have the same information as you ... a wreck on the off-ramp ... however, I caught wind of another person's involvement, and I'm not exactly in the position to check out the police records." There. She planted the seed. His group *could* follow it through. Promising to stay in touch, Nicole left him at the elevator and in the privacy of her own car, took a deep breath, then blew out, "You're right about one thing, Rusty. If you were hacked ... then I AM onto something."

Leaving Hollywood, she turned the Range Rover west onto Sunset Boulevard instead of getting on the freeway. She passed close to Drummond Media and thought of Mike. He would still be in the studio, but

Nicole no longer had her pass and wouldn't easily get through the gate, so she'd have to wait until later to see what he'd found out at the center. Staying on Sunset, she opted for the scenic route to get to the Pacific Coast Highway, taking the long way home.

CHAPTER 7

"Where were you yesterday?" Nicole asked Mike. It was Friday morning and the day was perfect for a California tourism ad, so taking full advantage, Mike had removed the Targa top from his Porsche 911 and Nicole was buckling her seatbelt as he pulled out from her bungalow in Malibu.

"I thought you would call with something, *anything*, on Ginny Vinsant." Both brows lifted above her shades. "If she's not a story, Mike, I need to know. I've been digging scraps off the internet while waiting, and meantime," her hands waved, palms up, "your group at the center has all this access to her!" Mike was wearing his favorite Persol sunglasses, the Steve McQueen edition, and they weren't dark enough to cover the grin in his eyes.

"So, how's your book coming?" he asked.

"You're changing the subject."

Laughing, he said, "I really want to know."

"Fine."

"Fine? That's it? Fine is all you got?"

"I don't like surprises, Mike, so I can't be charming and chatter about my book when I have no idea where we're going." Nicole held her chin high, over-exaggerating her interest in the landscape as she continued.

"AND, by the way ... you said to dress for a 'casual business lunch.' You know how I hate those cutesy invitations that say 'dressy-casual.' So, what is it? Are we having lunch with someone? Is it casual? Or is it business?" Then, as if something brilliant occurred to her, she spun to him. "Are you sneaking me into the hospit—?" Then caught herself. They were heading further into Malibu, the opposite direction. "Scratch that." She crossed her arms.

A passionate, gypsy-jazz tune by Roman Street was seeping from the speakers and had been competing with Nicole's rant. It was a tune they both loved, and Mike's head started moving to the beat even before he turned it up. He was driving them north along the Pacific Coast Highway, and said, "Enjoy the ride, Nicole."

He didn't use her given name often, but when he did there was something peaceful about it. The sun was high and Nicole breathed in the cool ocean air from the opened top and, for the time being, she resigned herself to that peace, reminded of why they put up with the endless hours of traffic and waiting in lines to get ahead in LA. It was for this. The Pacific Coast. Water, sand, rocks, mountains, rich vegetation, and a steady breeze all come together along an endless shoreline, and there's no jockeying required when you're near the water. There's plenty for all.

She closed her eyes and when they opened again, Mike was calling her name. "Nicole. Wake up. Time to stretch our legs."

A black sport-coat opened her car door and, with an extended hand, helped her out. There was a fountain to her right, and the display around the motor court would impress even the most elite car enthusiast. She recognized the Lamborghini and the Bentley, but the other two metal beauties went above her limited knowledge of exotic automobiles.

"Where are we?" Nicole whispered to Mike.

"Right outside of Santa Barbara at the Ritz-Carlton Bacara. Pure luxury, baby."

"I thought it looked familiar, but the Bacara is well over an hour away from my house! I slept that entire drive?" Confused, Nicole postured toward Mike. "I'm limited on time, Mike! Why here?"

"Why do you always need the facts up front?"

"I'm a journalist, remember? Or I was, at least."

"You always will be. *That's* why we're here."

She eyed him suspiciously, then followed the black sport-coat through the sweeping arched entry of the main lobby. Its polished tile floors held several groupings of furniture for intimate circles around two massive fireplaces. Everyone, whether host or guest, seemed to have an agenda, but the light melody from the Steinway on the far side of the room added a graceful tranquility to their movements. It was a five-star resort, and it would be easy to shed their concerns and float across the marble with the others, but they kept walking to the back terrace, where a golf cart awaited them.

Through a winding concrete pathway with meticulously trimmed edges, the golf cart transported them to another world of secret gardens filled with fragrant flowers and lush greenery. The majestic palms danced slightly, gesturing to them as they passed, and a young child would have certainly waved back. Grounds as flawless as a putting green were an impressive accessory to the architecture of the buildings, which were a blend of Italian and Spanish influence, and planted perfectly throughout. Brilliant pink bougainvillea clung to the walls of the smooth white stucco, and brown clay tiles lay in waves, floating across the rooftops. Everything about this paradise was romantic, and Mike's enthusiasm was evident. Instinctively, Nicole's eyebrow shot up, and Mike chuckled, "No, baby."

They exited the cart, following the driver through a corridor of the spa, and, keeping his voice low, Mike said, "You asked me to check around at The Rock, remember? Well, I did. You've got your meeting." Her brow shot up again.

A bronze number eleven was on the mahogany-stained door that Mike knocked on, and it swung wide for them to enter, welcoming them with the heady scent of lilac, salt air, and freshly brewed coffee. Across the room, a set of French doors were opened allowing the Pacific Ocean in, and to the left was a table set with white linens, china, and a large, stainless carafe. On either side of the table, silver cloches covered two trays, and the smell of baked goods seeped through. Centered, and tastefully arranged, was a crystal vase overflowing with lavender roses and lilac.

"Mike, thank you for coming." Nicole heard a woman's voice and turned in time to see Mike embracing a figure with medium-length, choppy blonde hair. There was a familiarity to her, and Nicole was smiling as she anticipated Mike's friend, but when she turned around, Nicole was anything but smiling.

"Hello Nicole, I'm Ginny Vinsant."

CHAPTER 8
THE CHILDREN

"My feet hurt," little Jackie said when Jorge sat him down, but Jorge needed a break. He'd been carrying Jackie for two miles. He leaned against the fence just outside the Bullard Street Airport, gasping, trying to get his breath, and Angel and Kiandra joined him. The four foster children had finally arrived after running and walking several dangerous miles from the home they'd escaped, and it was a minute or two before anyone noticed Jackie's feet.

Blood was seeping through the threadbare heel of his sock.

"No wonder you was cryin'," Jorge said. "You straight-up tough, lil' dude." Despite their lack of nutrition, the children's feet had steadily grown inside their only pairs of shoes. Little toes and heels had pushed against the restraint, and each day the pain had increased, but they had also not run or walked this far before. Jackie's feet were more than bloody. They were swollen. Jorge was gentle with Jackie when he removed the shoes. He and Angel had experienced this before and had customized theirs. Jorge had pushed in the heel of his shoes to lay flat, so the back was open, and Angel had simply cut the toes out of his and called them sandals. Jorge pushed Jackie's heels inward, like his own, then slid them carefully back on. "We'll take care-a those feet when we get settled. Maybe they'll have somethin' on the plane." Then he knelt again. "Okay, jump back on."

Wiping his hand across his cheek, Jackie nodded and climbed on the offered back. The four of them continued along the rear of the property, until they found a small opening at the bottom of the fence where the earth dipped. It was shallow, but the four thin frames had no problem sliding under. They kept to the brush for cover, hiding in the darkness it provided, and steadily moved through the property toward the front, until they could see a couple of airplane hangars and the parking lot. There was no one moving. No vehicles where the children were told to be, and no planes were prepping for a flight.

All four tried to be quiet, but they were winded and breathing heavy. "Did we miss 'em?" Kiandra whispered too loudly, her eyes stretched wide to see in the darkness.

Having no way to know the time, still, Jorge said, "Nah, we jus' early. It's all good."

The adrenaline from their fear, plus the excitement of a new future, had been their fuel, and the only reason they were still standing; but, with this simple assurance, they bent their weak little knees and dropped to the ground. All but Jorge. He was as tired as the others were, his chest rising and falling rapidly, and his pant legs trembled from his strained muscles, but he wouldn't sit. He kept vigil. Kiandra watched him. *Maybe he thinks we won't hear the car over all this heavy breathin'*, she thought, and her eyes closed a moment to deal with the pounding in her chest. When she opened them again, Jorge was squinting, looking back and forth across the airport property. Even in the darkness of the thicket, she saw the worry on his face.

Somethin's wrong.

CHAPTER 9

Nicole stared at Ginny Vincent for a beat or two, then turned to Mike and narrowed her eyes. She took a moment to adjust before facing Ginny again. When she finally accepted the extended hand, her broadcast persona was turned on and fully charged.

"I'm surprised to see you looking so well. Actually I'm surprised to see you at all. It was my understanding you have been, um ... ill." Nicole said. Mike flinched.

"Would you like coffee? Or perhaps tea?" Ginny asked. Mike was the first to turn toward the spread of pastries. Whether anyone wanted any, it was a welcomed distraction, and they all went through the motions before moving to the sitting area. Addressing Nicole, Ginny said, "I understand you tried to visit me in the hospital. I doubt it was solely to check on my well-being, but, still, thank you."

Nicole looked down at her coffee, watching the reflection of the light ripple over the top, then looked intently at Ginny. "You know I'm a reporter, right?"

"Yes, I'm well aware."

"Then you know I was looking for a story about your accident to use against your husband," Nicole said, then looked from Ginny to Mike.

She remained professional and even smiled, "So ... why don't you two explain what's going on here?"

Mike followed suit, glancing from Nicole to Ginny, then back to Nicole. "Mrs. Vinsant is close with one of The Rock's employees. Yesterday he overheard me askin' about her ... and, well, it seems Mrs. Vinsant is in need of help."

"Please, Mike, Nicole, call me Ginny."

"Okay, *Ginny*," Nicole responded. She was cool. She set her coffee down. "What is it you think I can help you with? You already have the rest of the media on your payroll, you surely don't need me." Although she behaved professionally, this was personal. Nicole stood. The air between them was thick. "Unless this is a Vinsant family effort to quiet the only one standing?"

Ginny's phone started ringing. The sound was low but with the stark silence that hung, it was demanding. Expectant. Enhancing the tension. Ginny pushed a button and the interruption was removed, but its impact lingered.

Looking overly attentive to the phone she just suppressed, Ginny kept her eyes diverted, then smoothed the hair that framed her face, tugging at it. "This is not about my husband," she finally said with a shake of her head, then took a deep breath and looked up at Nicole. "Me. I need your help."

The seconds that followed were long and Nicole regarded Ginny cautiously. A heavy breeze came through the open French doors, stirring the heaviness in the room. When Nicole finally spoke, her steady, steel eyes challenged Ginny. "I was at the hospital because your accident had the makings of another cover-up by the senator. It never made the news, you know." She paused, not breaking eye contact with Ginny. "I can't imagine how I can help you, but before we go any further, I need a question answered."

Ginny met the challenge and nodded once.

"Was anyone else injured in your accident?"

The hands placed on Ginny's lap squeezed together, then her left hand went to her hair, tugging once more at the fringe, pushing it behind her ear. Her mouth opened; at first nothing came. Finally, she breathed, "I don't know. That's why I need your help."

The waves that steadily crashed against the rocks could be heard in the quiet that fell over the room. Although faint, the soothing sound cushioned the absence of conversation. Mike leaned back in his chair. His hands were spread facing each other, and, with thumbs together, his fingertips tapped. It was unlike Mike to display a tic, and just as quickly as he started it, he stopped, and left his chair to refresh his coffee. The clang from the silver dome was extraordinarily loud when he placed it back over the scones. It served to jar the standstill, and Nicole prodded, "I'm listening."

"You see, I thought there were others at the scene, but Tom says I'm dreaming because I was brought into the hospital unconscious." Ginny looked to Mike like she needed assurance that she could trust Nicole, but his back was toward them. She took a ragged breath. "He thinks I'm trying to sabotage his campaign, so he had the doctor move me to a secured area. I'm here *only* because they couldn't prove I was mentally incompetent." Mike turned around with lifted brows to swap glances with Nicole, then pushed the rest of his pastry into his mouth. Nicole sat back into her chair. With minimal coercing, Ginny began her story, telling them everything she could remember from her accident. Time moved forward, but Nicole and Mike were suspended in the moment, listening.

"So, you believe you hit at least one child, if not more, who was crossing the off-ramp?" Nicole asked. She had uncrossed her legs and was leaning forward, her body language encouraging Ginny.

"I hope not, but I don't see how I could've missed them. I was moving fast, and they were the reason I swerved and lost control of my car." Ginny lowered her head.

"But no one else saw them?"

Ginny shook her blonde waves. "No."

"Had you been drinking?"

"One glass of wine over a two-hour period. As I told you, we were at a dinner. A fundraising thing," she said.

"But you can't recall anything after crashing into the street lamp?"

Ginny continued smoothing the fringe of hair. "No. I awoke in the hospital. When I asked Tom about it, he told me there were no pedestrians involved."

"Why don't you believe him?" Nicole asked. Mike choked on his coffee. He sat his cup down, coughing. Nicole cut her eyes at him.

Ginny watched Mike with concern, then continued. "Because, when I tried to discuss it in the hospital, anger overcame him—but before the anger ... before he could hide it, there was a flash of fear in his eyes. I know he's worried about his reelection, but ..." She let her thought hang. "Anyway, when I didn't drop it, I was moved to the high security area. After one day in, Tom came to my room and said he was fighting the hospital to get me released, but first I had to promise to put the accident behind me and come here. He doesn't know I saw the records. They had no valid reason to hold me ... the doctor had already released me." Before anyone could respond, she added, "My car was declared totaled and was crushed at a metal recycling yard the very next morning."

Nicole's pulse accelerated, but she delivered her next words as flatly as possible, "This is an interesting story, Ginny, but I'm not following your purpose here. I assume you don't want this in print, so why aren't you dropping it like your husband asked? Why tell me?"

Ginny lowered her head again. The sporadic breeze from the terrace had entered again and danced with her blonde hair. "This is hard." Her voice was subdued and her audience of two strained to catch every word. "Do you have children, Nicole?"

Nicole shook her head once. "No."

"Me either. I guess that's why The Rock pulls at me. It was only supposed to be a one-time publicity thing for my husband's campaign. However ... " Ginny looked at Nicole and with a shy smile said, "I fell in love with it," then she stole a glance at Mike, too, and took a sip of her coffee. She swallowed hard. "Tom hates me going there, and I believe it's the only thing I've really stood my ground on." Then her face darkened. "However, he still controls me when I'm there."

"How's that?"

Ginny stood and walked toward the serving table but with no real purpose. She stopped, then started again, ambling about. "I'm sure neither of you know this, but my degree is in music, which I've never used. When I found the need at The Rock for instruments, I felt it was a calling ... at least I could gift music to others. But Tom had a different purpose. He knew charity events for The Rock were trending and only wanted publicity from the one donation. He'd moved on." She walked to the middle of the room. "Well ... to summarize, I found my own way to get involved without him knowing. I started locating good, second-hand instruments and having them delivered. On occasion, I went just to show the children how to use them ... you know, technique and proper

69

position first, then a couple of chords. It was all I'd have time for ... but ..." she shot a glance at Mike, then turned to Nicole. "A couple of times, I saw marks on their little arms. Marks that should've been reported ..." She stopped, then turned her head away.

They waited. Nicole had done enough interviews to know the consequences if she interrupted now. Most wouldn't finish, or, at the very least, they veered off course.

As Nicole hoped, Ginny continued, "But I didn't. I never reported it because Tom would find out I was there. So, I stayed silent." She stopped at the French doors, looking beyond the balcony, and threw her words over her shoulder as she watched the seagulls dance in the air. "The custodian, Gabriel Simon ... he's such a dear ... he knew something was wrong with me...." Emotion rose in her voice. "I promised him to secrecy, then burdened him with my finding ... just to clear my own conscience!"

She spun around and they saw tears balancing, threatening to fall. Her arms crossed, hugging herself. "Those children I suspected of being abused? They haven't been seen at the center lately ... and I still haven't followed up on them to make sure they are all right." Ginny looked directly at Mike. "I'm so sorry, Mike."

Looking down at the floor, Mike took a moment. When his head rose, he met her pleading expression. "I figure we're all creatures of conditioning, and it sounds like your conditioning took over. It was stronger than your own conscious. But ... what you just did—owning up to it— well, that's cool. A right step in breaking free."

The words were kind, and she gave a slight bow of her head, but the pain on her face didn't recede. Ginny walked back to her chair, sat, and addressed them both.

"You're right. I have been trained. Since we married, I've been reminded that every move I make is for the sake of Tom's career. Unless approved by him first, I stay quiet. You asked my reason for this confession, Nicole? There's a place I've buried all of Tom's secrets ... and ... well ... that place is finally filled up ... I can't do it anymore." Ginny couldn't keep seated. She popped up again. Her mouth was dry. She poured ice water and took a few sips before returning to her company. "I don't know where this will go, but I have to know the truth. And if my husband finds out we've talked, he'll have me put away until after the election ... but why? Is the truth that bad?" Ginny looked to Mike, then back to Nicole. "I need to know where those children went. Where is their family? Why haven't there been reports of missing children from Tuesday night?"

"What do the police reports say?" Finally, Nicole was going to know about the police reports without having to go through Rusty at the gossip rag.

"Nothing. No children in the accident. No missing children at all. I have so many questions." Ginny lightly shook her head, causing her hair to spill around her head. "I'm sure you don't think much of me, Nicole, but it's not about me. This is about them, and ..." Loud conversation carried from the cart path, but the three in the room didn't show they were aware. They waited on Ginny's next words, which appeared to be thoroughly considered. "If I pursue this, I'll pay you well for your help! You are the only person who can help me."

Nicole, naturally guarded, took a mental step back. "How's that?"

Ginny's early anxiety seemed to have worn on her and she lowered herself into the chair facing Nicole. "Because I don't believe you would settle for some false explanation but will dig for the truth ... just like the segments on your show. Also, you are the only person with investigative abilities that I believe isn't in Tom's pocket. And lastly ..." she exhaled. Her shoulders dropped, her large brown eyes baring themselves to Nicole. "You also have reason to keep this discreet, so I can trust you. I *have* to trust you."

* * *

The ride home from Santa Barbara was much livelier than the ride up. "You did this! You scored, Mike!" Nicole's face was lit up and she gave his hand a loving squeeze. "Although I should be angry ... why did you wait until we were knocking on her door before giving me a heads-up?"

"It was a gift. You don't tell ahead of time what the present is."

Nicole gifted him back with a soft smile. Mike had his own way, and she knew he meant it for good.

* * *

Over the years, Mike had been told many times that he looked like a young Marvin Gaye, including his height, his coloring, and all his cool ... and it was true. Add these traits to a set of light hazel eyes that he insisted came from his great-grandmother, and you had the combination for a real babe magnet. Mike's approach to life was so laid back, a casual observer would assume everything came easily to him. Nicole had. It took years for her to find out differently.

He didn't talk about the childhood he never had due to his drug-addicted mother. She was a single parent whose twisted idea of safeguarding her child was to lock him in a closet while she got high to ensure his whereabouts. When he was five, he almost died of dehydration after being forgotten in the closet for three days. Upon his release from the hospital, Child Services interviewed his mother, but they still allowed Mike to go back home with her. She never put him in the closet again. No. Instead she sent him off to the neighbors. One day when he was thirteen, she sent him away, and he never returned.

Living on his own since, and overcoming his past was a marvel in itself; however, he went beyond that. Mike put himself through college and found his niche—the celebrity deejay that he was. Once, over a bottle of wine, Nicole asked about his deejay name, "Blind Dog Mike," and she couldn't have been prepared for such an honest response. "There's a lot of evil out there, baby, so while I was pullin' myself out of it, I became Blind Dog. I chose to stay blind to the bad and forget the things I'd seen. I choose to look for the good in everything."

And he did. Mike shared a perpetual optimism with the inner-city kids at The Rock, which had become a passion. It gave him purpose.

Nicole was amazed at him, since she still harbored anger over the car accident that claimed her parent's lives when she was only twelve. "Objective cynicism" was the name she gave her own outlook and credited it for giving her a successful career; however, she had learned to rely on Mike for balance. Other than their emotional differences and their skin color, Nicole and Mike were remarkably similar. Neither had family. Both were driven in their fields. Both had worked for Drummond Media since college. And both were still single at the age of thirty. Physically, they were both tall and athletic, and both had unique eyes that drew others closer, and that's when their differences became apparent again. He welcomed close. He loved interaction and wanted folks around him. And the obvious fact that she didn't, initially drove him to become her friend. Her compadre. He had recognized her fear.

* * *

The top was still open for their ride home from Santa Barbara. "Who'd a thought you and Ginny would be looking for the same thing?" Mike asked, over the whistle of the wind. "So ... you gonna do this?"

Nicole's resentment over being ousted by Drummond Media and her mission to expose the senator had been her driving force. It was the energy behind her book deal with the publisher and she *would* finish it ... however, she couldn't walk away from this chance to redeem herself and her job through the senator's own wife. They could go hand in hand.

"You mean accept Ginny Vinsant, the subject of my investigation, as a paying client?" Nicole let out a laugh, and the afternoon sun coming in through the roof spotlighted her enthusiasm.

Moving her hands to accentuate her thoughts, Nicole shared them with Mike. "When we met with Johnathan, the nurse, his story took a one-eighty from that first 'anonymous' call ... however ... this confession from Ginny supports his original 'tip,' and I have no doubt Tom is behind it—just like her car being crushed for scrap metal. How convenient! And he's still holding the threat of hospitalization over her."

The traffic became more congested along the stretch near Carpinteria, so Mike paid close attention to the road and missed the gradual tightening of Nicole's eyebrows. Nicole was quiet for a spell and chewed on her lip. "Unless ... what if this *is* her imagination? She admitted to being mentally evaluated in the hospital." Nicole raked her fingers through the top of her hair and down the back. She spun back to Mike. "Or worse! ... What if she's setting me up, Mike?!"

"I don't see it, baby. Ginny Vinsant looks like she's tormented, if you ask me."

"It could *all* be an act!" She paused, but Mike didn't bite. "Think about it—she said she heard I had been at the hospital. How?"

Mike let her run.

Nicole was shaking her head. "Tom could've found out. He could be using Ginny to sabotage me ... again ... somehow!"

Mike started nodding. A soft smile appeared at the corners of his mouth.

"What? You agree?"

"NO, baby. I'm nodding, because I'm happy."

"Happy? Care to explain?"

"You're back! Your wheels are all turning in the right direction. Just keep 'em goin' and you'll figure this out!" Mike kicked the accelerator to pass the car ahead of them, and Nicole had to hold onto her hair as the Porsche disappeared down the highway toward Malibu.

CHAPTER 10

There was a light knock on the door of Senator Tom Vinsant's California office, and Rita Morgan, his assistant, stuck her head in. "I'm sorry to disturb you, Senator, but you have a call from George Lupe on line two."

"Remind me, Rita, who George Lupe is with."

"He's one of the executive producers from *The Morning Report.* He's calling to schedule your appearance on their show. Do you want me to take his number, or have him call you back this afternoon?"

Tom paused, his brows pulled together in concentration, drawing out the scene with his secretary. Across the desk from him sat a prospective financial backer, a billionaire from the Bay Area, with two of his colleagues, and Tom had orchestrated the producer's call to come in while this meeting was taking place. Folks loved that morning program, especially women, and his appearance on it could raise his lead in the polls by a percentage or two. Tom wanted these new partners to see he was a solid investment, because if he was going to become independent of his current blood-sucking associates, he needed their funding.

"Get whatever information we need to finalize a date, Rita, and I'll call him back." He then gave full attention to his guests. "I'm sorry, gentlemen, now where were we?"

"I think we've covered everything, Tom." The billionaire stood, cueing everyone present that the meeting was finished. "I'll have my attorney draw up the necessary papers. We should be able to finalize our arrangement by next Thursday if you're available."

"Thursday works. I fly to Washington in the morning for a few social engagements, but I'll be back by then," Tom said, giving them his campaign smile, and stepped around his desk to shake everyone's hand.

As they made their way to the office door, one of them turned back. "By the way, rumor has it your wife was in an auto accident, but nothing was in the news. Is this true? Is she all right?"

"A minor thing. Nothing that would've made the news. We still tried to get her to take a day, but you know Ginny, nothing slows her down." Tom patted him on the shoulder.

"A lovely woman, Tom. Please send her my best."

They made their way to the elevator, and, as Tom turned back to his office, his grin faded. Ginny was becoming a cause of concern, because like these men, his constituents all loved her. As did the press. Tom had used Ginny and her charitable efforts anytime he needed a boost in his image, or to deflect attention, like when the Nicole Portman attack came. Tom's publicist had arranged an event for Ginny at an elementary school, and as she emerged from the building, news cameras were waiting with set questions about a recent shooting at a midwestern elementary school and her opinion on gun control. Ginny's wide-eyed response and the timing of the broadcast brought such positive press into the Vinsant camp, they milked it for days. With Sidney Drummond's help and his wife's interviews, the Portman story was soon buried.

But recently, Ginny was becoming too unpredictable to have that much leverage over his campaign. He brooded. *Even with Ivan watching her, she skated out of the fundraiser and totaled her car. At least he caught it in time to do damage control, but if the press catches wind of this latest story about running over little children, the damage would be irreversible!* He slammed his fist on the desk, then caught himself and looked around. His door was closed. He was alone. Tom exhaled. With the election only a few months away and him traveling with the campaign, it would be impossible to control her new obsession: the accident.

"Time to amp up her security," Tom said quietly to himself. Dialing a contact in his phone, he skipped the pleasantries when the other party answered. "I need you to do something."

CHAPTER 11
THE CHILDREN

Kiandra, Jackie, and Angel rested, but Jorge couldn't. As exhausted as he was from the journey, plus the strain of carrying Jackie on his back for two miles, he still couldn't sit. *This ain't right*, he repeated to himself, scanning their surroundings. *They wouldn't a left and we can't be early.* They were in the brush behind the airport, hiding. Waiting.

Night sounds of the commercial area were all around. Horns, pulsating beats from rap tunes, and the loud humming of tires were the backdrop to the occasional shouts and the revving engines. Then one engine separated from the rest, and was coming closer. Heavy tires rolled over gravel, then onto the asphalt of the lot.

Jorge, being vigilant saw it. There was movement under a security light near a back hanger. "They're really comin'!" He wiped his arm across his wet eyes, took a huge breath, and in a spasm, he released it. The other three stood.

Headlights of a white utility van flashed. "You think it's her?" Angel whispered, coming alongside Jorge.

Little Jackie didn't miss the concern in Angel's voice, and he stretched his eyes in the dark to read Angel's face, then he turned to Kiandra. She put one arm around him and a finger to her lips.

The van stopped. A burly white man got out and gruffly called, "Kids!" They all stared, unmoving. Kiandra held her breath. He tried again, but this time said, "Ki-AN-dra?"

She looked at Jorge, the whites of her eyes growing larger, and he shrugged his shoulders. The man called again, and Jorge nodded, then nudged his head toward the voice. She nodded in response, then called out, "Where's Mrs. Smith?"

"I'll take you to her." The voice was moving closer. "Come get in the van."

No Mrs. Smith? The kids looked to each other, wide-eyed and confused, and Angel's head shook back and forth. Kiandra's slight voice carried into the night, "I thought we was flyin' out o' here. Why we meeting at the airport if we ain't flyin'?" The man didn't answer. She looked at Jorge. The hope that was there only seconds before were gone and he started shaking his head too. He motioned backwards with his thumb, and she nodded. Backing up with the others, Kiandra said, "We don't go with strangers. We'll wait for Mrs. Smith."

A van door slammed. A second voice shouted, "We don't have time for this, kid. GET IN THE VAN!" Then heavy footfalls. Someone was running in the kids' direction, into the thicket. Kiandra screamed, and they all took off.

Branches slapped at their faces, but it didn't slow them as they raced frantically through the brush toward the back fence where they had entered. "Go, go, go," Kiandra chanted, pushing Jackie under the small opening. It looked even smaller than the first time, as all four scurried to get under. Angel and Jorge were quick to shimmy through, but Kiandra got caught. A prong grabbed her clothing and wouldn't let loose. For the second time that Tuesday she had struggled violently to get free. She tossed their backpack of meager belongings to her little brother as a second man, creepy and bald, was coming for her. He reached out to grab her. "NO! NO!" Kiandra thrashed to get loose. His hand was closing in as the barb miraculously released her, and she sprang up on the other side of the fence, grabbing the backpack from her brother, and they ran after the others.

Down into a ditch and darting up on the outer bank, a cacophony of skidding tires and car horns sounded when the four silhouettes bolted across the busy road leading to the intersection of the off-ramp for I-110. Disoriented by the commotion, they froze in the headlights of a silver BMW speeding off the interstate. It was barreling into their path, and the eight eyes stared wildly when the BMW swerved in front of them and started spinning. A surreal slow motion took over. Before the BMW stopped, the children were sucked away from the destruction.

That was Tuesday night. A lifetime ago to them. It was now Friday, and they were still trying to remember how they had gotten to the place they were being held. Jackie's small voice asked his sister, "Why won't they tell us where we are, Kiandra?" He leaned his head into her as she tightened her arm around him, but it was Jorge who answered.

"Hey, lil' man," he said, "you lucky to be here. You was inches from that Beamer, dude! This place gotta be better than the hospital. Right?"

Jackie looked at him from under thick, black lashes, and Jorge added, "Remember. Me an' Angel gonna take care-a you two."

Jorge hadn't let him down yet, so although Jackie's eyes were still sad, they weren't saturated with fear. At least for the moment.

CHAPTER 12

"Hello?" Nicole's voice was hoarse in the phone as she scanned her surroundings trying to remember where she was.

"Good morning, beautiful, have you had your coffee yet?" Mike asked.

Arriving home from her Santa Barbara outing with Mike the evening before, she'd had numerous emails and messages from her publisher. They began with reminders of her deadline, and ended with "Where are you?" With work to do before she could return their calls, she wrote all night and had fallen asleep on her sofa. Nicole checked the time, then cleared her voice before speaking again. "Are you at work?"

"It's Saturday, baby. Good thing I called! This writer gig can't be healthy. Come by The Rock and see me."

"I appreciate your concern, but I can't afford the time—" She broke off. She needed coffee. She made her way into the kitchen.

"Word is, Ginny Vinsant is coming by today, around eleven. Gabriel said she's slippin' in from Santa Barbara to bring a saxophone she found."

"Gabriel. He's the one who helped arrange our meeting ... so how is it he knows Ginny Vinsant?"

"That would be a Ginny question." Sounds of cheering and balls bouncing resonated in the background. Mike raised his volume. "Later, we can break outta here and have a margarita at Samm's."

Mike could hear the smile in Nicole's voice when she answered, "I have a few errands to run anyway, so ... sure, I'll be there around eleven."

"See you then. Call when you're close and I'll meet you in the parking lot," he said before disconnecting.

Nicole didn't bother with her morning run on the beach and was on the road by nine, checking off errands from her to-do list. By ten o'clock she swung by Two Sisters Bakery to get a pastry. Although her favorite bakery did a huge volume for an independent business, it still maintained a quaint, homey atmosphere, including the tiny bell on the door that announced Nicole's arrival.

"Let me guess, one chocolate croissant," the older woman behind the counter said. She grabbed a small bag to put Nicole's pastry in.

"Yes, thanks." Then she held up her index finger. "Ummm ... If I needed around a hundred pastries, how would you ring it up? Like, do you have a price break per dozen ... I hope?"

Nicole let Mike know she'd be early and was glad to see him in the parking lot. The kids center was in an area of poverty, broken homes, and drugs, which sometimes produced gang activity, so she knew to be alert. Mike greeted her enthusiastically and gave her one of his trademark hugs, wholesome and solid, and she felt loved all the way to the bone. At the back of her SUV she opened the hatch door and presented him with five extra-large boxes from Two Sisters for the kids.

"What's this? You buyin' your way into their hearts?" Mike teased.

"No, and don't make an issue of it. I don't want anyone to know I'm here." There was a smile playing at her lips, no matter how curt her words were.

"I'll take them to the kitchen," Mike said. "Why don't you go upstairs to my office? I'll be right behind you."

The design of the center was paramount to its success, with different rooms for different interests, and for the children's safety each of these rooms had a large picture window on the inside wall, facing the hallway. They even had glass doors so their activity, whether homework, crafts, or music, was fully exposed. Strolling along, Nicole was reminded of nursery windows at a hospital as she observed each room filled with kids of every size and adults overseeing them. There were plants, books, textured rugs, and brilliant paintings to give the rooms life.

As she approached the gym, kids were lining up for a new game of basketball. A couple of teens stood to the side, reluctant to join in, and one of the volunteers dribbled a basketball over to them. He spun the ball on his forefinger, and their faces changed from bored to awestruck. Nicole gave a nod of appreciation. She recognized the Clippers player about the same time they did. "S'cuse me." The running of feet accompanied the warning and Nicole moved aside as two boys hurried past to join the game starting up.

Back when the center had its ribbon-cutting ceremony, Nicole was there representing KDLA news to help with its publicity as a favor to Mike. The ministry behind it was using it as a prototype for future outreach programs in major cities. Other than a handful of employees the board hired to run it, it relied heavily on these volunteers, and it was rewarding to see the success. The center was getting a lot of attention, and she could see why as she wandered the building. The positive energy was so thick, it was buoyant. It was Mike.

Over all the voices and laughter, Nicole heard the moans of a double bass beckoning her. It was faint, but there was no mistaking the particular tone of that magnificent instrument, one of her favorites. The sound lured her around corners and past workshops, until the volume was full and the music room was in clear sight through the glass wall.

The door was open.

Easing toward the entry, she nestled outside, spellbound, leaning against a nook near the doorjamb.

Layered braids and a ripped hoodie hung over the shoulder of the large wood bass, the artist's body enclosing it. They were one. His left hand manipulated the strings, while his right guided the bow, extracting the deep, soulful sound. Nicole, being familiar with this complex piece, was mesmerized by his light, graceful touch that created an extraordinary precision. Despite his young age, he masterfully interpreted the composer's intended anguish to the hearts of the privileged audience, and Nicole momentarily forgot to breathe as the bassist swept her into his emotionally draining finale.

"Beautiful, isn't it?" whispered the deep, masculine voice from behind Nicole's left ear. She felt the breath from the voice linger heavily in her hair. The warmth of it, mixed with cool spearmint, sent a shiver down her spine. Slowly turning, she was drawn into a pair of sensual dark eyes with thick, black lashes that boldly searched her own.

Still transfixed from the music, Nicole's senses were pushed into an emotional overload, causing an unexpected tear to spill out and land on her cheek. The stranger's hand slowly lifted to her face and brushed it lightly, transferring the lone droplet to his finger. Nicole just watched, mesmerized by him. By his intimacy. Her neck flushed, and the seconds of time kept stretching. Breaking contact, she forced one foot in front of the other and made it to the end of the hallway, distancing herself from this stranger as he called after her.

CHAPTER 13

"Hey, your pastries were a big hit! That was cool, baby," Mike said to Nicole as she entered his office. He had gotten there before her and was waiting. "Around here, all these kids get is the value-priced, packaged stuff. That, or leftovers from the afternoon cooking class."

Mike's office was a reflection of his personality. Social. Friendly. So it felt more like a café, with a grouping of low-profile cushioned chairs positioned around wood and metal coffee tables. The desk in the back was strictly for computer or paperwork when he was alone. Nicole lowered herself on the first available chair.

"Since you've been roaming around, you must've seen Ginny," Mike said, walking back to his desk with keys in hand.

"No. I, uh. No. Didn't see *her*," she said, and took a quick glance toward the hallway.

"She should be in one of the music rooms," said Mike. "We have several, but she'd be around the band room or the classical. Those are the instruments she's been bringing." Mike walked to his desk and locked it. "Shall we go look?"

Ginny? Virginia Vinsant? Responsible for what I've just witnessed? And the mysterious stranger ... when did he slip into my personal space?

Although, oddly enough, I knew he was there. Smelled him. Expected his words, like a movie I've watched before, Nicole thought. She was staring down at the floor, and Mike was saying something. She simply muttered, "Uh huh." The stranger's smell lingered with her now. Crisp but warm. Masculine and clean. Spice and soap all wrapped up in new leather. Difficult to describe, but impossible to forget. Her stomach fluttered.

"Stop!" The whispered command wasn't supposed to slip out.

"Stop? I thought we were going to find Ginny. What's goin' on with you?"

"What?" A quick beat passed, and Nicole forced her puzzled expression into a firm smile. "Yes, of course we are!" Popping up and flinging her purse strap over her shoulder, she moved ahead of Mike, but after only three step she froze, and Mike, coming up behind her, grabbed her arms and skidded to a halt just before butting into her. The stranger she had forced out of her head had made his way back. He was standing at the door.

"Whoa," Mike recovered from the near collision and followed Nicole's stare to the door. "Great timing, my man." Mike stepped around Nicole and shook the stranger's hand. "Come in and meet my gal, Nicole." Mike turned toward her. "Nicole, this is our new director and counselor of The Rock, Pastor Rand Coleman."

With the same intimacy as before, Rand's eyes locked unapologetically with hers, and he took a few steps to close the space between them, extending his right hand. "Nice to meet you, Nicole."

But the distance between them grew again when Nicole sidestepped Rand with nothing more than a polite nod. "Would you two excuse me?

I'm sure you have things to discuss," she said, and left the room. Just outside the door, Nicole leaned against the wall.

"Your girl, huh? Isn't that Nicole Portman, from the nightly news?" asked Rand.

"Same one. But she's on a short leave right now."

"Yes, I heard." Rand looked toward the door.

Nicole was trained to eavesdrop, to gather information, but listening to her name coming from the mystery man was unsettling. She walked lightly down the hall. Once she was sitting in the driver's seat of her Range Rover, Nicole sent Mike a text.

* * *

Mike and Rand both remained standing in Mike's office, indicating neither planned a long visit. Mike noticed Rand still watching the door. He grinned. "Nicole might help me with a project here, if that's cool with you."

"Sure. Sure." Rand turned back to Mike. "But for security reasons we'll need to do a background check if she wants her own access to the building. Have her come in Monday, and I'll take care of it myself. Just no stories about our kids."

"That's cool, I'll tell her," Mike said. "So, what's up?"

Rand slipped his hands in his pockets. "A volunteer coach mentioned that one of the neighborhood kids, Philip, has a missing friend."

"Runaway?" Mike asked.

"Not sure. The information is vague, so I'm following up to get the kid's story and need a witness."

"Sure. I just need to check on Nicole," Mike said.

"Great. See you in the Dolphin Lounge in fifteen."

After Rand left, Mike grabbed up his cell phone and saw a text message from Nicole. *I got to peek in Ginny's music class. Not feeling well. I'll take a rain check on lunch. Apologies to the director if I was rude. BTW, did you say "pastor"?*

CHAPTER 14

The Dolphin Lounge was a perfect meeting room for the kids. As the name implied, it had a marine-life theme with lots of aqua accents, but what made the room special was the mural. Instead of hiring artists to create it, the center had allowed the kids to paint it themselves. Some of the children were filled with unbridled talent, and others were not, but each one of them was encouraged to draw freely. The outcome of the combination of talents resulted in a composition greater than a professional could have achieved. It was brilliant. Childlike. And when Mike arrived, Rand was there, waiting for Philip.

Mike knew Philip to be an after-school regular who loved basketball. After homework, which was a center rule, he could always be found on the court. Other than stopping for snacks, he'd play until they closed at night. He was an aggressive player. Confident and agile. But from the looks of the kid who joined them, those personality traits stayed on the court.

Standing in the doorway of the Dolphin Lounge, Philip lifted his eyes, then dropped them. He rolled up on his toes, hands folded in front of him, one over the other, and with the fingers of the top hand grabbed an elastic band from the opposite wrist and popped it repeatedly. Mike flashed his signature grin at the boy. "Chill, man, you're not in trouble. Come in. Relax." He patted the small sofa, where he made himself at home. Philip's lips pulled almost into a smile at his radio idol, and he took a timid step inside the room but remained standing.

Sympathetic to the boy's anxiety, Rand cut straight to it. "Philip, one of our volunteers here at The Rock mentioned you were concerned about a friend."

Philips eyes darted from Rand to Mike, then he looked at his feet.

"We only brought you here because if you're concerned, then we are, too."

Philip shrugged. "Nah, I'm good."

"If someone's in trouble, you know we want to help, right? That's the purpose of The Rock." Rand had a notepad in his lap, but laid it on the table, then sat back in his chair. Mike didn't miss a step, especially in noticing Rand's body language. "Let's say he is in trouble. Is it with the law?"

Again, the shoulders shrugged. "Nah. I don't think so."

"Trouble on the street?" Rand brought one leg up and crossed the ankle over his opposite knee, resting his hand on the crossed leg. It was a relaxed position, calming. He looked almost as laid back as Blind Dog. Almost.

Philip popped the band and the adults waited patiently, allowing Philip time. "Like I said. I don't know."

That wasn't working. "Tell you what." Rand uncrossed his legs and leaned forward. "Just let your friend know, if he needs help, to come to the center. Blind Dog or I will make ourselves available anytime to talk with him." Rand stood.

Philip kept his head down, then his eyes shot up at Rand, then to Mike, then back down at his feet. "That it?"

"Yep." Rand said. "No pressures. However, just so we'll know who to watch for, I need his name."

Snap. Snap. The rubber band popped. Philip struggled. He shifted his weight from one foot to another. *Snap. Snap.* "I don't mean no disrespect, but it don't matter ... his name. He won't come by." Rand slid his hand into his side pockets, casually. He said nothing, but he turned on the dark stare. Philip kept his lids lowered to keep from looking at Rand and said, "He just ain't around."

They all heard the announcement over the main paging system. A new game was gearing up. Mike stood and stepped closer to Philip. "So, if his absence was somethin' chill ... like he moved or on vacation, we wouldn't be havin' this convo. Somethin' ain't good, and we have a couple a minutes before the game. Talk to me, man."

They didn't learn much, only that Philip's friend hadn't been around for three or four days. Word on the street was the friend and another junior-high student were seen running down the road with two smaller children, and no one had seen them since.

They were silent for a moment. Laughter, muffled conversations, even a guitar being strummed, could be heard. Mike's head bobbed and he asked Philip, "So, my man, why would the word be out on that? Like, why was it newsworthy, who he was running with?"

Philip turned slightly as if they'd lost him and he was about to leave, then he looked toward Mike. "You from the hood?' He asked him.

"Yep," was all Mike said.

Philip's eyes instantly turned hard, removing all traces of the previous timid child. "You see a couple of guys runnin', you look to make sure you're not in the line of fire. You know." The eyes shot a look at Rand, then back to Mike. Eyes that had seen more than they should. Eyes too old for this young man. Mike nodded. He understood. Philip continued, "But you never see 'em runnin' with little kids. This made news 'cause they was running with the two little temp kids that live with 'em. One's even a girl. Middle school don't hang with little kids unless they blood and teaching 'em the street. An' from what I hear, no one was even chasin' 'em."

"Wait. Temp?"

"Yeah. Foster."

"You got names?" Rand asked.

Philip looked at Rand. His eyes were jumpy, and his feet followed suit. From right to left, he bounced. He'd said too much, and Rand wasn't asking casually, this time. "Angel. Jorge's the other dude. That's all I know. Can I go?"

Mike walked out with Philip, leaving Rand behind to make notes, and from the overhead speakers Mike heard his name being paged to the gym. The kids loved having Blind Dog Mike call the game when he was available, so with Nicole's lunch canceled, Mike and Philip headed to the courts together, and Blind Dog jumped on the microphone, giving the players and spectators a real show.

An hour passed, and Mike caught a glimpse of Rand rushing down the hall. "You two take over for me," he said to the two boys sitting nearby, who high fived each other and ran to Mike's table. The tall, skinny one grabbed the microphone.

"Hey, Coleman." Mike was still smiling from the kids when he caught up with Rand. "How'd Philip's story check out? Anything?"

Rand slowed. "The local police station has nothing that fits. No Jorge or Angel missing, but we'll follow through on Monday. Listen man, I gotta run." He bumped knuckles with Mike and headed out to his truck.

CHAPTER 15
THE CHILDREN

As always, the "Keeper" was at the door. That was the name Kiandra had given the rotating guards. It was easy to watch over the children, since all of their living quarters for the past few days was in one large room, sectioned off. There was a recreation area, a dining table, and along the back of the room were four soft, extra-long twin beds. The bedding had down comforters, and for the first time since her Grammy had died, Kiandra looked forward to crawling into bed. She didn't remember a bed feeling so good. Even her pillow was made from down.

Although the Keepers were ever-present, they gave the kids their space, and each time they traded shifts, the new arrival said the same thing: "Everything's going to be fine." The woman guarding them last night added, "You can leave here in a couple of days. We're making sure you're safe first." And that was as specific as anyone had gotten. The kids weren't allowed outside or near a phone or to watch live television; instead, they were redirected to the video games or encouraged to watch movies. Every children's movie imaginable was at their disposal.

Breakfast was delivered and broke the anxiety of the room, and whether the kids trusted these current strangers or not, the Belgian waffles with happy faces drawn on them using whip cream and chocolate morsels broke down any barrier ... or at least the kids' willpower. They tasted heavenly. The night before, they actually had a steak with creamy mashed potatoes. Kiandra didn't think the potatoes were as good as Grammy's. Grammy would whip them up with the electric mixer, and when she finished adding her milk and butter, they were better than any icing. "Me and Jackie fought over who'd get to lick the beaters or the bowl," she said, smiling. Then it slipped away. Mashed potatoes also reminded her of the nightmare that brought them here.

Kiandra Spence pulled the folded card from her pocket and looked at it again. "If we could get to a phone, I'd call Mrs. Smith."

"You can't call her!" Angel blurted. "Mrs. Smith set us up. I recognized that bald dude. He's the one that took Hector away."

"Who's Hector?" Kiandra asked.

"One of the kids at that Gramble Street house when we got there. Weren't there but a day when bald dude took 'em away."

"They gonna take us away too, Kiandra?" Little Jackie's eyes were wide. "They feedin' us good! Maybe they fattenin' us up like Grammy's poppa did their pigs."

"They not gonna kill us, Jackie!" said Kiandra. She took his hands in hers, reassuringly.

"You right," said Angel, "They not gonna kill us like the pigs, they gonna sell us."

"Angel! Stop!" Jorge quietly hissed at him. "Not cool, man, trying to scare lil' kids."

Pure reaction overcame Angel. He jerked his entire body toward Jorge with balled fists, ready to take him on, but then, unexpectedly, a helplessness peeked through his anger. He spun around, retreating to the other side of the room before anyone could see his tears and began pacing.

Kiandra's, breath quickened, looking from one to the other. "What?"

Jorge shook his head. He set Jackie up on an electronic game in front of a huge television monitor then walked back to Kiandra. In a hushed tone, Jorge said, "We saw Hector and some other kids loaded in a van and that bald dude from tonight gave the foster mom cash. We didn't think nothin' of it until a few days ago. Me an Angel heard her talkin' to the boyfriend. She said, *'Just one mo' month for their records to get lost, 'for they can sell 'em.'* The foster was so high she didn't know we was listenin', or she just didn't care."

Kiandra's mouth hung open in confusion. "What do you mean sell? Like for rich people to adopt?"

But Angel had walked back. He didn't wait for Jorge to explain, "No. Like to work in sweat shops or as sex slaves. We ain't gonna be someone's kid. We gonna be their slave."

Jorge stood and grabbed Angel's shirt by the collar, "I said stop talkin' to 'em like that."

"I'm sayin' the truth, man!"

Kiandra's eyes were wide and the guard started over to them. "Everything okay over here?"

"Yeah," Jorge told him, "we just messin' wit' each other. It's all good." He let go of Angel and raised his hands, showing his palms to the man. Satisfied, the guard retreated to his position by the door, but faced the kids and crossed his arms, with his bulky biceps straining against his chest. The kids waited a while before continuing in a whisper.

"What'd I get us into?" Kiandra's meager voice was filled with grief.

"Hey, we didn't know Mrs. Smith was in wit' the bald dude. We was excited as you to get away," Jorge consoled.

A subdued Angel leaned against the wall near Jorge, then slid down it to sit. He used his shirttail to wipe his eyes and cheeks, then started talking to no one in particular. "The foster can't keep no drugs 'round long enough to sell 'em. An' she too nasty to be a ho'. I guess only thing left is sell kids." He hung his head, shaking it from side to side. "It ain't your fault. Our month was almost up; it was gonna happen any day."

They heard a low moaning sound from somewhere outside the building. "What's that?" Kiandra asked. She stiffened, then looked around for Jackie. He was still watching his movie.

"Sounds like a ship horn," Jorge replied.

"Ship?" She stiffened. "I've never been in no ship. I'm scared, Jorge. We can't sit here and do nothin'!"

Angel lifted his head. "Whatcha gonna do, half-pint? Take down the muscle at the door?" he asked flippantly.

The horn sounded again. The sad wailing in the distance matched the growing fear in their hearts. Kiandra looked around the room, then stood tall and called Jackie over. Taking his small hand in hers, she extended her other one to Jorge, then directed Angel to join them. They formed a circle, an endless chain of four, and it was empowering. "I'll do what my Grammy taught me. It's all that's kept us safe since she left."

And she began to pray.

The guard broke protocol and entered a number in his cell phone. Keeping his hands in front of the mouthpiece to divert the sound of his voice, the four children didn't hear his quiet conversation coming from the door. "Hey man, these kids haven't settled down. If anything, they're getting worse. We need to move them soon."

"What are they doing now?" asked the man on the other end.

"Praying."

The guard listened for another minute to the man on the other end. "Yes, sir, Dominic." He closed the phone and was in action.

CHAPTER 16

Living in Los Angeles, you grow familiar with haze. The seamlessly cloudless days might be described as sunny, but you will seldom hear them referred to as crisp. The locals have grown accustomed to the skies looking like a big smudge across their lens, so they don't notice it. That is, until a rare light rain happens, or the Santa Ana winds charge in from the east and overpower the ocean breezes, sending the questionable air out to sea. It changes everything. Then, the sky becomes flawless. The heavens appear to be endless again, and the vivid blue elevates everyone's mood, and after an unexpected shower had just cleared that's exactly how it was that Saturday afternoon.

It was late May, and the beach was reaping the benefits of the day, especially the stretch behind Nicole's place. It was on a curve of the ocean-front and one of the best locations to catch a wave. Nicole was back from her visit to The Rock and was sitting on the back deck with her laptop and a cup of tea. Two young surfers dressed out in their black wetsuits walked past her place with their boards. "Dude, I don't trust air that I can't see!" They were both still laughing as they headed into the water.

Everyone's mood is affected! Perhaps that explains the encounter with that director? Rand. A quick shudder rolled down her spine. Loud conversations, laughter, and music were magnified, and the quote pinned at the top of her screen danced. It was a quote from her estranged employer, Sidney Drummond. *"You'll find as life goes on, the greatest stories were in the slightest corners of the world."* She had saved it. He was her mentor and his advice usually paid off. Usually. It reminded her to look where no one else was.

The surfers were lined up and Nicole watched them until they became only a backdrop to her thoughts. She was muttering under her breath, "If Ginny Vinsant *did* have anything to do with that bassist's performance, then maybe she really isn't as shallow as her husband. And why would she bother going there today when no one expected her? She wasn't getting accolades for it. She was actually sneaking in."

She called Mike, and he answered on the first ring, his voice concerned. "Hey! How ya feelin'?"

"What?" she asked, momentarily forgetting that she'd run out on him at The Rock. "Oh. Better. Listen, did you see Ginny after I left?"

"No, baby. There was no need since you were gone. What's up?"

"She didn't try to contact you? She really only dropped in to bring something to the kids?"

Mike released a slight chuckle, "Maybe she likes coming here because, like the kids, she needs a refuge from her home, too."

Too concentrated to acknowledge his attempted joke, Nicole said, "Mike, Ginny said she checked with the local police, and there were no missing persons reports filed that night. No missing children. So, IF they were involved, but no one is missing them, then they'd be accounted for ... like hospitalized. Parents notified. Tom could squelch Ginny's accident, but not the injured parties ... or could he...?" Her voice trailed off. Nicole stood and went inside to get her notepad. Mike waited. They'd been here many times together when Nicole started on the trail of a lead and needed to talk it out. It helped her.

"I'm listenin'."

"Well, what if Tom *was* able to keep the injuries out of the news? We've seen what he's capable of." Nicole sat at her counter and wrote "Tom Vinsant" at the top of her page. As she talked, she underlined it. And underlined it again. "I threw the idea of others involved to Rusty Willmore at CMbz. He has enough connections to find out, but that was two days ago, and nothing." Under "Tom Vinsant," she wrote "injured children." "Let's say there was an injured pedestrian. Where would they have been taken? They wouldn't have been brought to the UCLA Med Center like Ginny. It's in Westwood, eighteen miles away from the accident. She or Tom arranged that."

Nicole opened her laptop on the counter, but before she could begin a search for hospitals around the site of the accident, Mike said, "It'd have to be Memorial South LA. It's right by that exit. You need me to ride shotgun—or deliver threatenin' notes to the staff? I'm finished here."

This time his humor wasn't lost on her. There was slight laughter in her voice. "Sorry to disappoint you, but I actually have a contact there who could at least let me know if anyone was admitted Tuesday night under similar circumstances. But thank you for the kind offer."

"Anytime, baby. Stay loose."

"Wait! Mike!"

"I'm here."

Renewed energy bounced her from her seat and she paced to the window, looking out over the ocean. "What about the center? That area has its own grapevine like any small community. There would be word on the street, so there would have to be at least one kid who knows something! Like if someone hasn't been at school or if they were in an auto accident!"

Mike didn't answer.

"I'm not trying to infringe on your center again, Mike, but I don't see me getting access to the school records. I have to go through the kids! That, or wait for the authorities to inquire at the school, and I don't see that happening, from what Ginny said."

Mike still didn't answer.

"Mike? What?" She could hear the road noise in his car. Mike was on the move and she was now on speaker.

"Rand said you can't write about our kids."

"I'm not going to write about them, but if Ginny's right, then you know The Rock is our most logical place to start! I won't expect you to ask around … I'll do it! Just get me in. When does it open again?"

"Slow down," Mike said.

"What? Do you know something?" Nicole heard loud sirens blaring through the phone. If Mike did answer, she wouldn't have heard him. She waited for the noise to drop. "Mike? Were you talking to me or to another driver?"

"I'll call you back."

* * *

The CHP's siren was perfectly timed. Mike disconnected from Nicole, and the music from KDLA radio graduated louder to fill the void. Mike stared ahead, his eyes narrowed behind his dark shades, and it was several miles before he left the interstate and was nearing his home. He pulled into Via Alloro Italian Sports Bar near Beverly Drive. The neighborhood eatery was his local favorite, and he usually opted for the patio, especially on a day like that Saturday. The skies were brilliant, but everyone else thought so too, and the patio was packed. Mike asked for the lounge instead.

Sitting off by himself, Mike made a call.

"Rand here."

"Hey man, got a minute?" The server nodded to Mike and he nodded back. Code for Mike's dark draft beer.

"Sure. What's up?"

"I've been running over conversations and, well, I know what the kids share with us is confidential, but—Philip's wasn't personal, so ..." It was rare for Mike to be at a loss of words.

"What did you hear?"

"Nothin', really. It's just, well ... if we're goin' to check this out for Philip, we got to ask around, right? I just didn't want to do it without checkin' with you first."

"And that's it?"

Mike gave a light nod of thanks when the server sat an ice-cold glass in front of him. "Yeah, man. That's it."

"Okay. Just don't use Philip's name."

"Cool. Thanks, man." He disconnected. Instead of driving home after he ate, he headed to Malibu.

* * *

The sun was slowly setting, and the body count on Malibu beach had thinned tremendously. The churned-up sand told the story of a successful day. Sitting out on the sundeck, Nicole was startled by the sudden tone from her doorbell, and it chimed a second time before she reached the intercom. "Yes?"

Mike's voice was alive and warm through the speaker, "Hey baby, would you like some company?"

"I'm out back." She punched the button for the gate to open, and Mike followed the narrow concrete patio along the right side of the house. It was like an alley leading to the back deck and was lined with potted plants and the brilliantly colored leaves of bougainvillea that clung to the stucco wall.

"You didn't think to call me before now to let me know you're okay?" asked Nicole as soon as he was in sight.

"Everything's fine." Mike gave her a quick hug, then walked toward the railing, looking out toward the Pacific. "Beautiful. Every time. Sea mist or not."

Nicole followed his gaze and joined him in the serenity but quickly jerked herself out of it and confronted him, arms crossed. "Fine? I see you're fine, but you left me hanging. Sirens in the background, you mysteriously hang up, and now you're here. What's going on, Mike?"

"Might be something ... might not. But I had to run it by Rand first."

The name caused Nicole's eyes to flinch ever so slightly, she turned away from Mike. "Let's go in. Can I get you something to drink?"

"How about tea? You have any green jasmine?"

Mike sat at the counter and Nicole moved efficiently around the kitchen getting the kettle on and the tea out. She pulled a stool around and sat opposite him. "Time to open the vault—and don't worry about the merit of your 'gossip.'" Nicole playfully did finger quotations over the word she knew he avoided, then smiled. "Remember ... that's what I do, Mike. I filter through information, and you're right, it's usually worthless ... so spill!"

Drumming his fingers on the bar, Mike said, "Well, there's a kid at the center who mentioned a group running through the 'hood near his home. Running fast. But nobody was chasing them." Nicole pushed his cup over, and Mike worked the tea bag through the steam as he continued. "It was a couple of junior-high kids with a couple of elementary taggin' along. Four of them."

"And?" Nicole blew the liquid in her own cup before taking a sip.

"That's it."

"That's it? That's why you drove over here?"

"Well, except it seems they haven't been seen since."

Nicole held the cup in front of her, the steam rising, and she watched Mike through it. "When was this?"

"Tuesday night."

"So you're thinking ... close enough to Ginny's accident. Same night."

Mike shrugged.

"But how likely would it be...?" She left the thought, and from the open doors the sound of waves breaking rolled inside. She moved on. "So the kid who confided this—how does he know them?"

"They hung at school."

"Hmmm. I don't know, Mike ..." Dusk began casting shadows, and Nicole moved around, turning on a few lights, then punched the control for the music system. It was last on a café playlist and she left it, walking to the French doors to close them, performing mindless tasks as her mind wondered. "However ..." She turned back to Mike. "Wouldn't someone be missing those kids as well? If those kids from the center haven't been seen, someone in their family would have contacted the authorities! And even if they had to wait twenty-four hours, their report should've shown up when Ginny checked two days later for her kids."

"You got it, baby."

"So once again, this isn't adding up ... but why? Because of the kid's families? Or is it the police?" She snatched up her notepad. "Do you have names? Have they been to the center? Could they be on file?" Nicole's eyes were bright.

"I have two first names," Mike said. "Monday, we're gettin' someone in administration to do a search in our system, but they won't find anything. I would have known them."

"What are the names?"

"Angel and Jorge."

"What else, Mike?" Nicole didn't sit, she stood, her foot tapping to the slight beat of the music. "Replay your conversation with this kid at the center."

Mike thought a moment, then carefully picked his memory, and Nicole jotted down keywords. Her head jerked up, "He said foster kids?" She pointed her pen at Mike. "That's it! That could be why no report was filed immediately with the police. Maybe they called Family Services instead ... and it's a process." The remark caused her to lose all steam as it left her mouth. It was a reasonable thought, removing all mystery.

"Did you talk with your contact at the hospital? Were any children taken in Tuesday night under the same circumstances?" Mike asked.

"Yeah, I talked with her. Nothing that fit our situation."

Mike took a sip of his tea. "Time to change the music, baby. We need something more upbeat or I'm switching to tequila!"

A slight smile played at her lips, and she used the remote to change the music. After jumping around playlists, she handed the control to

Mike then, disappeared inside her pantry to look for tequila. "Mike!" Her abrupt change caused him to jump, but when she came running out, he was his cool self. "Mike, what if those kids were abused! And that's why they ran. And that's why the foster parents didn't report it!"

Mike nodded. "Wouldn't surprise me."

Back and forth across the kitchen area, Nicole paced. "I'll contact Family Services on Monday! Somehow, I'll find out if they were notified about these two missing foster kids. If the foster parents didn't call it in, then I've got something to work with."

She was getting traction.

Nicole sat back at the counter across from Mike and began writing, then stopped and looked at him with a question covering her face. "What *are* we listening to?"

"Bluegrass, baby."

She lifted both brows. "Since when do you listen to bluegrass?"

"It's my new thing and you should listen to it. This is a Celtic-bluegrass band. Locally grown right here in LA and they've got soul. Just a little livelier than Marvin."

"Because Marvin wasn't Celtic."

"You don't know that!"

"Yes, I do!" Nicole argued through light laughter. "You are full of yourself today!"

Mike danced around, kicking up a foot here and there, but he'd lost Nicole to her thoughts. She was writing vigorously. "I'm outta here." He kissed her on the cheek. "Good to see you on track, baby, and if you need a hub closer in, use my office at the center while you're lookin' into this. I've mentioned it to Rand, and he's cool. Just go by Monday to sign the release for a background check."

Nicole lifted her hand in a slight wave goodbye and was still standing against the gate long after Mike's Porsche was out of site. *Rand.* Nicole raked her hand through her hair, shaking it loose, and headed inside to her computer. There was still nothing about Ginny or the wreck on CMbz's news feed. Next, she searched keywords to check out Mike's information but got nothing relevant to the time and situation she was looking for. Monday morning couldn't come quick enough.

CHAPTER 17

Tom Vinsant closed his eyes for a brief moment. The heady aroma of expensive perfumes insulated the clinking sound of champagne flutes. Chatter and snippets of laughter danced around to the slight melody from a trio of violinists. The black-tie event in Washington, DC was abuzz with energy as the celebrity guests and a core group of politicians waited for the secretary of state to announce his daughter's engagement to a dot-com visionary, and Tom happened to snag an invitation. The young couple were trending; therefore, to ensure Tom's own share of tomorrow's headlines, along with the invite, his campaign manager had also arranged for him to interview with two different reporters during the evening, and he was drinking it in.

"Senator! Good to see you." The boisterous voice of Congressman Duke Stanton attacked a half-beat before his right hand did, gripping Tom's, while his left hand buried into Tom's right shoulder. "Where's that enchanting wife of yours?"

Tom's professional smile was so practiced, only Ginny would've noticed the flecks of anger that darkened his eyes. "Duke." The soft tune from the violins were lost on this exchange. "Ginny couldn't make it—a charity thing, but I'll tell her you asked about her." He moved, twisting just enough to free himself from Stanton's controlling clutch. "We'll have to catch up later, I have someone to see," said Tom jovially, moving away, but Stanton gripped his shoulder again to hold Tom back. A famous model, escorted by her country-music-star boyfriend, walked by, and the seasoned politicians kept smiling. Tom started counting under his breath, and Stanton was turning his head left, then right, as though he were looking for something, then with a sweep of his right arm he addressed a young woman approaching them. "Senator, I believe you know Ashley Martin, my goddaughter. She's been hard at work on your campaign in the Bay Area."

"Hi, Senator!" Ashley's fingers twinkled at Tom, just above the natural-looking size 34DDs she was leaning toward him.

Dismissing the congressman, Tom reached with both hands to take her offered one and held it affectionately. "Ashley. Good to see you, dear. What brings you to DC?"

Ashley Martin was one campaign worker he remembered very well. Attractive enough, but to Tom her greatest asset was brushing up against his arm.

"Uncle Duke flew me in for my birthday. Aunt Marcy couldn't come, so I'm his guest for the evening."

"Well, by all means, let's celebrate." Tom raised his glass in a toast.

"Ashley, dear, I hate to leave you two, but the senator from North Carolina is waving me over and I must see what he needs," Stanton said, patting Tom again, then left, making his way through the crowd.

Ashley leaned in closer and her long blonde hair perfectly framed her deep cleavage, demanding Tom's attention. "I hope you don't mind me hanging with you. I really don't know anyone and it's all so intimidating. I mean, I LOVE politics, and working on your campaign has been so exciting ... but this," with palm up, she pointed her hand across the room at the various celebrities, then brought it back across her chest, "I'm outta my league here."

"Believe me, sweetheart, you're in a league all your own." Tom grabbed them both another flute of champagne, and he listened as her nervous chatter turned into a free discourse about his campaign, the volunteers, and different issues he was running on. Her arms were in constant motion when she spoke, and Tom's eyes were, too—from her, to the clusters of influencers and their dates around the room, to make sure he wasn't being watched before he brushed, bumped, or leaned into those breasts that were screaming at him to touch. He was enjoying the game, hiding in the center of the room.

Encouraged that Ashley didn't object to his contact, he eventually offered, "If we're going to work closely together, I need to know something. Are you my number one volunteer? Can I count on your help?"

"Of course, Senator!" she said, her smile wide, and as she drew closer to hear, Tom felt every rise and fall of her breath, excited at the prospect of helping him.

"That's what I was hoping to hear, Ashley. As I look around this room, I see a lot of glitter. Outrageous gowns. Fake breasts. Fake eyelashes, hair and nails. Then I watch you. You're fresh. Radiant. Wholesome." Tom looked around once more before leaning his head toward her and in a soft, confidential manner said, "A true beauty. I'm pretty sure nothing about you is fake, but you could be fooling me, too. That dress you've chosen accentuates every detail ... so it could be the design of it that has me so mesmerized. Or is it you, Ashley?" Tom stopped. He backed away, momentarily taking her in with a long, appraising look, and when they came together again, his question was delivered seductively against her ear. "If everything were totally stripped away, would you still take my breath away?"

Tom was always confident in his gift of persuasion, and tonight he was riding high. The gorgeous, young Ashley had stayed as he directed and mingled for another twenty minutes, before leaving with Tom's spare hotel room key. Tom worked the room, shaking hands, laughing, being seen. Alone.

He located the reporters his campaign manager had arranged and delivered his prepared statements. His words were brief but powerful, and when he left, he was walking even taller, sure that he would receive his share of publicity in tomorrow's news. The night was his, and power radiated from Tom as he entered his hotel lobby. "I trust you had a good evening, Senator, is there anything we can get for you?" The night manager was following him to the elevator, groveling over him as Tom expected.

"Actually, yes. I might be up for a while. Working. Please send a bottle of champagne. With two glasses."

"Very well, Senator."

Tom rang for the elevator and was on the ninth floor putting his key in the door when he felt the vibration of his cell phone in his jacket. He opened the door to find the young Ashley Martin lounging on the chaise sofa in the large suite and forgot all about the phone.

She rose slowly. The long, blonde hair was pinned up away from her body. Loose pieces that had fallen, softly framed her face and were her only accessory. "Well, Senator, have I helped?" Tom had already noticed her dress lying across the back of the sofa, her shoes and accessories placed neatly together.

Tom didn't answer; he just stared. She was a little thicker than you'd expect around her waistline, and he loved it, but Ashley couldn't read him and started shifting, transferring her weight from foot to foot, then rolling up on the balls of her feet. Finally, she tried again. "Was it the dress?" she asked.

Without breaking eye contact, Tom removed his coat and tie, deliberately allowing her question to hang in the air. The knock at the door startled Ashley, and she moved to cover up, but Tom shook his head and waited another moment to assure she would stay before going to the door. When he returned into the main room with the hotel cart from room service, Ashley was still standing tall, uncovered, with her arms down by her side; however, her fingers were tightening, curling into fists, then straightening, then curling again, releasing her anxiety. She stared in the direction of the drawn curtains. Expertly uncorking the chilled bottle of champagne, Tom took his time pouring two glasses. Anyone who didn't know Tom would assume he was unaware of the discomfort he was causing Ashley. One corner of his mouth twitched, suppressing a grin.

"Look at me," he said, and she did as commanded. "You listen well, Ashley. Another great asset." He took a sip from one of the glasses, drawing out the scene. "Put your shoes on, they won't distract from the canvas, and we'll mingle just as we did earlier tonight to see if it was the dress, or not. Just let me look at you."

Ashley did as instructed. She had relatively thin ankles and good, strong calves that led to a pair of fleshy thighs, and Tom's eyes took it all in. As she started across the room, Tom commanded, "Slowly." Her neck was flushed by the time she accepted the flute Tom offered. Their fingers touched and she quivered. He had total control over her. She stood there, exposed, because he said to. Power was intoxicating to Tom. His breathing became heavy, rapid. He took her glass back, grabbed her by the hand and led her into the bedroom.

By the time Tom reappeared to the living area for their drinks, he heard a slight humming, and remembered the earlier vibration from his cell phone. Retrieving the phone from his jacket, he looked at the caller ID and answered abruptly, "Yeah?"

"I've been trying to call. Mrs. V left the Bacara today. You said she'd be staying there for a few days, at least until you got back, but she's not, so I wanted to let you know."

"WHAT?" Tom asked, his grip tightened on the phone. "Where'd she go?"

"To that youth center. The Rock, where she was heading the night of her crash. She met some tall black dude in the parking lot, and he walked in with her." The caller waited for Tom's response. Nothing. "Hello?"

"Finish telling me! Don't make me ask you for details!"

"Uh, right! She stayed for a couple hours, then I followed her back to your house in Beverly Hills. She hasn't left."

"Let me know immediately if she moves! I don't care what time it is!" He disconnected.

Tom grabbed up his and Ashley's glasses and walked back just in time to see her emerging from the bathroom, and he strode over to Ashley, expressionless. His eyes held hers, and he handed her a glass. "To you, my beauty," he toasted. "It definitely was NOT the dress." They both drank.

Promising to call, Tom got Ashley's cell phone number and encouraged the night to end, insisting she take money for a cab. She had just left when the telephone in the hotel suite began ringing. Tom turned toward it. The unusual sound of a land line at such a late hour stirred his curiosity. "Hello?"

"Tom ... Duke here. I hate to bother you, but is my goddaughter, Ashley, there with you?"

"Duke, now why would you be calling me about your goddaughter?"

"Well, I left her in your company and don't remember seeing her after that."

Tom let out a small chuckle. "I was busy working the room like you, Duke. Sorry."

"Well, I'm sure she can find her way back to the hotel, but I'm responsible for her. I've got to see she makes her big birthday celebration tomorrow night."

"Yes. That's right, she mentioned this was a birthday gift from you. Well, I bet she's moved on to party with some young people she met there."

"I doubt that. She's not old enough to get into any of the clubs."

Tom let the receiver slip and quickly recovered it before it hit the lamp. He sat down. "How's that?"

"She's just a baby, Tom. She's not even eighteen yet, well, not for a couple of weeks, but we're celebrating it tomorrow night, like I said." He left a void in the conversation, intentionally allowing the information to resonate in the silence, then threw out, "By the way, I've got some ideas for my district and I'd like your help. Maybe we can meet before I leave. I'll call Monday night and see how your schedule is for Tuesday."

Tom pressed the disconnect button on the phone. The receiver slipped from his hand, and in a quick, fluid move he jerked it up and banged it twice on the table before slamming it into its cradle. He paced a few moments, cursing through clenched teeth. "What are you up to,

Duke?" The armoire held a bottle of Chivas Regal 25, and Tom was on it, breaking the seal and pouring a small amount of the dark amber liquid, and before he lowered himself into the deep cushion of the wing-back chair he had already taken a liberal drink, letting it roll around his tongue. He sat, thinking, with scotch in hand, and took another drink; then suddenly his eyes grew wide. He jerked around, looking about the bedroom. Slamming the glass down, Tom shot over to the closet and opened it, then the curtains, then any other logical place to hide a camera. Nothing. He let out a deep, grateful sigh.

Tom knew all about Congressman Stanton. Stanton had come into public service for his district as a moderately successful man; however, after serving eight years, Duke was now very wealthy. There were still honest men and women on Capitol Hill who supported bills solely on behalf of their constituents, but for the rest, there was an art to passing bills that benefited them directly or indirectly. "He's learned well, but he's still small time, and I'll crush him," Tom said aloud, reassuring himself.

He looked at the time. Two o'clock. It was already Sunday morning. *If I reschedule my Monday meeting for today, I can leave on the first flight tomorrow, before Duke's even awake.* Tom relaxed and sipped on his reliable liquid friend. "Duke, ole buddy, we need a little space until I find out what you're up to. Then I'll quickly put this to bed." He toasted his own pun.

CHAPTER 18

"If you started your Monday off as jazzed as you are on Friday night, just think how great your week would be!" The voice of Blind Dog Mike came through Nicole's bedroom speakers as she listened to his show, *Your Mornin' Jamm.*

It was a great diversion while she dressed for the day, and he was wound tighter than usual. "What you need is a little funk rhythm! We're going back in time to a tune your parents ... maybe even your grandparents ... danced to if they were as cool as you." Mike's energy was high, but his delivery was still silky smooth. "... a beat that should never be archived. The year was 1976, and this movie soundtrack is sure to make you move parts of your body that normally won't budge until around Wednesday afta-noon ... I'm gonna crank it up and get your groove goin' at the 'Car Wash' first thing this morning with *Rose Royce*!"

The clapping intro of the song could be heard before Mike was finished, and Nicole began moving as promised. After changing outfits twice, she gave herself a final inspection in the mirror and decided on the black slim-leg jeans with a loose, white, jersey blouse intentionally half-tucked to give it a carefree look. She slipped into a pair of black mid-heel pumps. Not too tall for a daytime professional appearance, but not too low, so her legs looked even longer than they were. Her jewelry was simple, with a silver cuff bangle and silver hoop earrings.

Although she hardly ever wore rings, today she placed her Great Aunt Naomi's platinum engagement ring on the index finger of her right hand. The low-profile setting, with its flat, rectangular cut diamond, fit perfectly on the long, slender finger, and she loved the feel of it there, sometimes turning it with her thumb. A stroke had taken her Great Aunt Naomi suddenly, ten years ago, and Nicole still missed her terribly. Wearing Naomi's ring was comforting. "I need you today," she muttered softly, looking at the brilliant stone. When she looked back at her reflection, she tilted her head and asked, "But why? With all the powerful people I've interviewed ... why would I be uneasy about meeting with The Rock's director?" Her movements slowed, her purpose drifting, until Blind Dog's voice started booming through her speakers. The song was over. Nicole shook her head, as if clearing it, and snapped. "I'm following a story. Bottom line."

Storming around the room, taking control, she made a call to Family Services and left a message, then, after one more look in the mirror, Nicole placed her notebook and laptop in her tote and was on the move. When she finally made it to The Rock Community Center, her phone started ringing. She didn't recognize the number. "Nicole Portman."

"This is Kim Argnaut from the Los Angeles County Department of Children and Family Services. I'm returning your call."

Nicole found a parking spot and left the car idling while she talked. "Yes. Thank you for calling me back so quickly. I'm doing a segment on the foster system in the Los Angeles area and need someone with your knowledge to advise me. Like a technical advisor of sorts. Is there a time you could meet this morning?"

"This is a busy week for me. Hold, while I look at my calendar." The static crackled louder than the music and mercifully, Kim Argnaut didn't leave her on hold too long. "Ms. Portman? I'll be free from three to four today. That's all I've got."

"I'll make it work. Thank you." As Nicole logged the address in her phone, she felt a shadow pass and an intense tremor swept through her. Quickly twisting, she looked over her left shoulder and down the side of her car, but it was clear. A small, uneasy laugh escaped her, and she absently stroked the ring with her thumb.

Nicole unfastened her seatbelt and reached for the ignition as a sudden burst blew the passenger door wide open, and before she could register what was happening, wild, bulging eyes were in her face. Threatening her. Matted dreadlocks and incoherent screeching filled the front of her car. Then a glint, and Nicole grasped what was in his hand.

A gun. Aimed at her.

Bile rose in Nicole's throat from a surge of fear, and when it met with his foul odor, she gagged. Urgent and explosive sounds too erratic to understand were hurled at Nicole, and the gun jammed into her side. The only word she understood through the scrambled shouting was "DRIVE!"

Other than the quivering of her limbs, Nicole didn't move while the crazed invader steadily screamed, poking the gun into her side. He removed it briefly and pointed toward the gear shift, and again, only one clear word surfaced from the piercing rants. "DRIVE!" Then he shoved the gun back into her ribs. His hand shook so violently, the trigger could have easily been pulled by accident, so Nicole worked the gearshift to do as he said, but it wouldn't budge, and his panting increased. He pushed the gun against her temple, then jabbed it, knocking her head against the door frame.

Nicole gasped but didn't cry out, and before he could jab again she fumbled at the controls. Her foot wasn't on the brake, and it wouldn't go into gear. Deliberately remembering to lift her leg and place her foot on the brake, Nicole tried again. That time it gave, and closing her eyes to shut out his hysterics, she slowly eased the Range Rover into reverse then lifted her foot from the brake. The car began to roll.

In Nicole's earlier career, she had done her share of chasing police reports and even resorted to scanners in order to get something "newsworthy." This story was familiar and she knew the odds if she left the parking lot with this man. She needed to think. Fast.

Inch by inch the SUV moved. Running into another car would bring attention, but when she opened her eyes, all she saw were empty, parked vehicles. If she hit them, no one would notice but her angry kidnapper. Jumping out was going to be her only option. The screaming continued, but if she focused on a plan of action, she could work through it. Nicole carefully slid her left hand to the bottom of the steering wheel, closer to the door handle. As her right hand tightly gripped the wheel, she turned it slowly while her left went unnoticed. Her fingers were reaching below the armrest. Any moment she would be touching the handle. There were plenty of cars around to duck behind, but her timing would have to be perfect. She took a deep breath. Almost there … her fingertip felt the metal, then suddenly the passenger door burst open wide, and as if by a huge vacuum, the crazed body in her front seat was sucked right out of her car.

The door slammed shut. "Lock your doors!" she heard over the commotion.

Nicole punched the automatic button, and then grabbed for the phone to call for help. Her car rocked as someone hit the side of it, jarring her, and she dropped the phone on the floorboard. Nicole dove for the phone and made her call over the rising clamor outside her car. The phone was ringing. One powerful thud hit her car again, then everything went quiet. Trying to control her shaking hand, she put the phone against her head and sat up slowly to see what was happening.

"9-1-1, how can I help you?" came the voice through the lifeline in her hand.

Nicole jumped when Rand rapped on her driver-side window. "All clear. May I escort you inside?"

"Hello? This is 9-1-1. How can I help you?" she heard again.

Her hand still trembled holding the phone. "I've called 9-1-1," she said to the image on the other side of her window.

"That won't be necessary. It's over. Thank them and let's go in." He tipped his head toward the building.

"Ummm, thank you, but I guess we don't need you after all." She disconnected, still watching Rand.

"Nicole, you can unlock the doors now."

Once inside the building, Rand left her resting in a chair near the receptionist's desk. "Bethany, would you watch Ms. Portman for a moment while I step out?"

"Sure, Pastor Coleman," said the ever-helpful Bethany. She asked Nicole, "Can I get you anything?"

"No. Thank you." All of Nicole's responses were on autopilot, until Rand walked back in with the crazed person, and she flinched. His hands were bound in front of him with what appeared to be a necktie, and he looked worse than before, since he had a new cut above his eye, and his nose was bleeding. His clothes were torn from the scuffle, especially the knee of his pants, and it was bleeding as well. Rand had a firm hold on his arm.

"It's okay," Rand said, reaching out to Nicole with nothing more than a look that amplified his calm assurance, as though he knew it had the power to sedate. And it worked. "Says his name is Timbo and he was being chased and was trying to get away ... at any cost, it seems."

"Da gun is empty. I hav' no bullets," Timbo said in a heavy accent, and tears were coming down his face. He dropped his head. "Please. I cannot go back."

"Back where?" Rand asked him.

With hands tied together, Timbo fretfully picked at a scrape on his left arm, creating a larger wound.

Rand repeated the question and still nothing. Security rounded the corner and came over, standing on the other side of Timbo. Rand tried another tactic. "When was the last time you've eaten?"

Timbo shook his hanging head.

"Bethany?"

"I'm on it, Pastor!" She took off toward the kitchen.

Nicole was watching them all. The filthy face with bulging eyes raised up. He did look frightened of something, but it was most likely from a hallucination. He was heavily wired. Rand's eyes found hers again. They locked. "I'm sure you'd like to press charges," he said to her. She nodded.

Rand pulled Timbo's gun from his own waistband where he'd tucked it, and Timbo flinched, ducking his head and bringing his hands together to block his face. "No one's going to hit you." Rand checked out the gun. He didn't have to drop the magazine; there wasn't one. It was missing. He looked in the chamber. Empty as well. He raised one brow and looked back to Nicole. "Empty. Like he said." Rand turned to security. "Take him to your office and stay with him. Have Bethany take his food there. No need for the kids to see him."

"Excuse me, I'll be right back," Rand said to Nicole, who was still pinned against her chair. She watched him walk away as chaos evolved into peaceful order again. With great composure, everyone at the community center had played their part to move the situation forward, unruffled by the incident.

Nicole's rapid, shallow breaths gradually slowed, and the bulging vein over her left temple calmed too. Rand wasn't long returning with a freshly washed face and his shirt properly tucked. She accepted his offered hand to stand but started slightly when a third person appeared. Nicole's eyes darted right to left of the stranger, searching for hiding areas that could justify his sudden presence, but there was nothing. Not a wall or even a column he could've been leaning behind. *Odd.*

"Hey, Gabriel," Rand said to the man. "Could you hang out with security until his charge has finished eating, just to make sure there are no more surprises from the young man? They should be in his office. Oh, and I bet he'd like to get cleaned up. Perhaps some new clothes."

"I'll see to it. You have a good morning now, and take care of Ms. Portman," he said, heading in the direction Rand told him.

Nicole turned back to watch Gabriel walk away from them, her eyes narrowed. He was of average height and medium brown hair. Attractive, but no unique features, but still, he was familiar. "Do I know him?"

"That's our custodian here at The Rock. Gabriel Simon."

"Hmmm," was all she said as she watched him turn the corner and out of sight. *Ginny's friend. Did she show us a picture of him? I'm sure I know him from somewhere* . She was distracted, and Rand was talking. "I'm sorry, what?"

"Let's go to my office. We can call the authorities from there. But before we do ..."

They continued walking side by side. Their long strides were in perfect unison. Nicole looked down or straight ahead, whatever to avoid his eyes. "... Our center does have a program for kids like him. Since his gun wasn't loaded, and he's obviously messed up, the center might be the only answer for rehabilitation if he's to stand a chance. Because at seventeen he'll be tried as an adult." He stopped and turned to her, and as before, those dark eyes seized hers. The hold intense. "Of course, you're the one who's owed justice. I'll do whatever you say." The rapid breath, the rising pulse, they were returning. She looked away.

When she didn't answer, he moved on. "Mike told me you were coming. I was watching for you."

Her head nodded. "I'm thankful you were."

"I understand you were coming for a temporary pass?"

Rand strode casually beside her. Not a bruise on him, with perhaps one scuff mark on his shoe. She simply said, "Yes."

"And you still want one?" Rand asked lightly, smiling, as though they shared a secret. And they did.

They stopped in front of a door that promised to be Rand's office, with his name and title in block letters. It was a solid wood door, one of the few, so she couldn't see the room until she entered and couldn't have been more amazed by the life inside. Nicole's eyes didn't know where to start. The walls were filled with pictures. Homemade drawings by the center children on one wall; on another, photographs. Pictures taken of the kids in action. Playing, eating, laughing. Some with the volunteers, and many with Rand, the director. She momentarily seemed to forget the parking lot, and used the photographs to study him.

"Nicole?" Rand called softly.

She was absorbed. The children captured in each image looked comfortable in Rand's company and he was quite photogenic, with his olive complexion and thick, dark hair. It was longer than most men wore it at his age, which looked to be mid-thirties, and it was tousled, adding a soft contrast to the scar above his left brow and his firm, square jaw. In some of the pictures he sported a slight stubble, and the added ruggedness caused Nicole's stomach to flutter. At six feet, he towered over the younger children, and they hung on him with love and affection.

The pictures were intentionally placed for occasions like this. They were a kind of therapy for the kids when they were sent to Rand's office, to divert energy, and he leaned against the bookcase and watched. "Nicole?" He called again.

"I'm sorry, did you say something?" She turned to face the living replica.

"Are you all right?" Rand asked.

"Of course." She looked around again, avoiding the connection. "Why wouldn't I be?" Eventually facing him, she was captured. "I'm used to crazy people with guns jumping into my car, holding a barrel to my temple, attempting to kidnap me, and super ninja moves from an amazing, but unlikely source. Did I cover everything?"

"So, you think I'm amazing?" Rand gave her a crooked smile.

"Seriously? That's all you got from that spiel?" asked Nicole.

They looked at each other for a beat or two, then burst out laughing. The laughter was good, releasing the pent-up nerves, the adrenaline, the anxiety, and then Nicole stopped, and her eyes flooded, as a lone tear sat on her lashes threatening to fall out. Her lip quivered. She reigned it in. But she couldn't control the shivering that followed.

The compassion in Rand's eyes held her close, even before he walked to her and took her in his arms. And she let him.

Rand's face was a mixture of emotions as he held her, sharing his warmth to calm her tremors, and as they subsided, Nicole quickly pushed away, struggling with embarrassment. "I met you just two days ago through a very limited introduction, and in those two days we were alone twice. And both times I've cried. If you knew how often I cried you'd understand how odd this is."

Rand took his time to answer, waiting for her to look at him, but she wouldn't. "I believe you," he said. "But the only part I find to be odd is we only met two days ago."

Her head jerked up, the crystal eyes wide. "You too?" Nicole said softly, but was interrupted by hard rapping on the door.

Mike stormed in. "Nicole! BABY! Are you okay? Bethany told me."

"Hey," Nicole greeted him half-heartily until she saw his concern. "Yes, I'm good, thank you, Mike. I can't imagine what would've happened if Rand hadn't been there ..." She looked around Mike to acknowledge Rand, but he was gone.

"Where'd he go?" she asked Mike, and stepped out in the hall. Rand was already engaged in a conversation with someone.

Back in the office, Nicole answered Mike's questions, then told him about the empty gun and the decision she still had not made. She started pacing. "If you'd have asked me while he was still in my car, there's no doubt what my answer would've been! No one that deranged should be on the streets. But now ..." She let the words hang and shook her head. She stopped and looked at the pictures on the walls. All of the lives touched. "You guys are conditioned to helping these kids. I'm not. To me, a bad egg is a bad egg. I don't get to see the results of your program. What if it doesn't work for him?" She turned back to Mike. "Is there a way he can be monitored? Because if it doesn't work, then the authorities need to know."

"You'll have your own ID for entry, you can stay on it yourself ... make sure."

They left Rand's office, and she turned in the necessary paperwork needed for her ID.

* * *

Unnoticed, Rand had quickly slid from his office, leaving Mike and Nicole. He had taken Nicole there to make sure she was okay and give her a moment to recover, not to be moving in on Mike's woman.

He had watched as she became lost in the display of art and photo collages along the walls, and he had used her distraction to openly observe her. She was remarkably composed after what she'd just experienced. She had the physical appearance of an athlete; specifically, the build of a runner, with long legs and narrow hips, and he had watched her move. When her hand reached out to touch a photograph, he also noticed the vintage platinum and diamond ring quietly displayed on her forefinger. Its value wasn't lost by its subtly. It was remarkable, like its possessor. As she moved her head, her hair fell behind her ear, exposing the long, graceful neck and the dark, full lashes that once held the single tear he'd captured just two days ago. *What if I hadn't seen her pull up in the parking lot?*

Rand's attempt at a quick exit was blocked by the volunteer coach from the local middle school. He stopped Rand in the hallway to discuss the fundraiser game coming up, but Rand had difficulty focusing on the coach. In his peripheral vision, he saw Nicole step out and look in their direction, then go back into his office. With Mike. Rand had to go. He patted the coach on the back. "Thank you for all you do, and if you want to discuss this later, I'll be back in about an hour."

Rand jumped into his black Ford F-150 Raptor, and his phone vibrated in his pocket. "Yeah?"

"I got an address," said the voice on the other end. There were no preliminaries. The two men knew each other well and got right to the point.

"Leave it in the email account. Save it as a draft, like before, and I'll get it."

"Copy. Where are you now?"

"Driving," was all he offered before disconnecting. Rand had set up the joint email account with his friend for times like these. Once he opened the saved draft, he could delete it after reading, and, because it was never sent, there wouldn't be a footprint of it.

His windows were tinted in the truck, but he looked around anyway before reaching around to the small of his back and pulling out the gun he had taken from Timbo, placing it in the console, then driving to his favorite coffee shop, *Everyday Joe*. As he waited for his espresso, he checked the email account. The address he was looking for was there. 5161 Gramble Street.

CHAPTER 19

Nicole arrived early for her three o'clock appointment with Family Services, even after swinging through Richie's Auto Wash to erase evidence of the madman in her car. Images of him sent a shiver up her spine, and she rubbed the arms of her jacket. Timbo had breached her private world that morning, and she was repulsed by the event; however, by awakening her survival instincts, it also reminded her how much her job had changed. She hadn't felt that adrenaline of danger since her first years of combing for news stories. Even with her waterfront segment. It was like most of her journalism. It had the marks of good investigating. Painstakingly diligent work, filled with a lot of confrontation, and it was bold; Nicole loved bold reporting. *But was it really a risk? Although I lost my show, I never imagined my job was really in jeopardy.*

The incident from that morning left her reflective more than anything.

Outside Kim Argnaut's office was a cramped holding area with only one empty chair, and the mood of the room was oppressive, like a twenty-pound weight was laid onto the shoulders of all who entered. The only ray of optimism came from the empty chair, as the tan foam wrestled for its freedom through the cracked, green vinyl, and was winning. Nicole looked around again for any other sitting option and caught the glare of the woman across the small alcove, as though she took Nicole's reaction to the room personally. Nicole nodded politely, then set her things on the chair, opting to stand. She leaned against the wall and used her extra time to look over the questions she'd be asking Ms. Argnaut to keep the interview on track.

"Ms. Portman?"

A heavy-set woman in her fifties with grey streaks through her lifeless, pinned-up hair was peering over the top of her reading glasses that hung on the end of her nose. She looked like Nicole's second grade school-teacher, and she called again. "Ms. Portman?"

Nicole quickly pushed the notes into her tote and walked over to the lady. "I'm Nicole Portman."

"Well of course you are," the woman said, neither pleasant nor rude, just matter of fact, then introduced herself. "Kim Argnaut." Nicole stuck her hand out in greeting, but Kim turned. "Follow me."

Kim Argnaut barely hit five feet and moved impressively for someone who was carrying an extra eighty pounds on such a small frame. And she was all business. Most often, getting information from a source was simply building a relationship. Nicole had her work cut out for her.

"So, what can I do for you, Ms. Portman?"

"Please, call me Nicole." Nicole captured the room in one quick glance. It wasn't as depressing as the waiting area, and Kim's desk, although it was at least forty years old and held stacks of paperwork, was clean and well organized. The chairs were newer, purchased in the last decade, and there was a fresh scent that almost masked the dust coming from the air vents.

Like an actor, Nicole had perfected her expressions for the camera, and she used her polite smile, not overdone, then began. "I'm doing a news segment on the county's foster system ..." The pitch was well-planned, with a few hooks to lure the woman in front of her, and after her uninterrupted spiel of a sympathetic piece on those who carry the burden of the system—the caseworker—she got no response.

Nicole paused and took a long, deep breath, shook her head, and began to zip her black tote. "I don't know, it sounded good to start with. I was going to do a complete television special focusing on you guys. The understaffed. The underpaid. Too many cases pinned on one worker. But now ... now, I come here and look around, and ... I feel a bit foolish." She added a slight laugh. "Everything looks so organized ... so together. Perhaps the county IS taking care of you guys and I'm just chasing an urban myth."

The readers that had been resting below the bridge of Kim's nose were removed and placed on the desk. Her chair creaked as she leaned back, waving for Nicole to go on.

Nicole was in. She moved quickly.

"I just know in the newsroom we were always understaffed but still expected to cover every bit of the news, even before it happens." She flashed her smile at Kim Argnaut in conspiracy, continuing, "AND do it better than the other networks and news sources." Then Nicole pulled her brows together in concern. "But at least we weren't dealing with thousands of children and making decisions for them that will affect their entire lives. I just wanted the viewing audience to get a feel of what you're up against each day. Actually, I was looking for you to be, like, my technical advisor."

"Nicole, can I get you coffee or a water?" asked Kim.

"Coffee would be lovely," Nicole replied, successfully keeping the excitement from her voice.

Two hours later they shook hands, and Nicole promised to call Kim the following week for lunch. Once she was inside her Range Rover, she looked for Ginny's number, but since her earlier encounter, she didn't idle while waiting for Ginny to answer. She started driving. It took several rings before connecting, and Nicole heard a faint "Hello".

"It's Nicole. Can you talk?"

Ginny's voice came alive. "Nicole! Yes. Mike said you'd be calling!"

"I've just come from a meeting at Family Services with some information and got an address that might be significant. I can check it out on my own but if you want to join me, we could meet, and I'll fill you in."

"When are you going?"

"Soon. I'm going to let traffic thin out, first." Nicole turned her signal on and pulled into the parking area of Everyday Joe's.

"I'd love to ... but ..." She paused. "Tom's on his way home from Washington and could be here any moment. He wasn't scheduled to return until Wednesday, so I'm not sure what's up." Before Nicole could respond, she threw in, "Are you free in the morning? I want to meet and hear what you've found. I can break away then."

There was a small silence while Nicole thought about it. "Sure. Around eleven would work, I guess. Where?"

"How about the Beverly Center? There's a day spa, Plush Salon, on the second floor. The owner is a dear friend of mine and she'll find us a comfortable room to meet."

"Great. I'll see you then."

"Oh, and Nicole? Thanks for asking me along."

* * *

Ginny disconnected her call with Nicole and heard her garage door rising. Looking through her phone, she pushed the "recents" button that listed all her conversations for the past week. She deleted the last two calls. "Whatever you're up to, Tom, I'm ready," she whispered and started toward the door.

CHAPTER 20

"Stop that knockin'!!" the voice snapped. It came from the other side of the hollow front door with the fist-sized hole on the outside panel. The exterior of the small house was once white, but the paint had been flaking off for years, and the exposed wood was rotting. Martha Vaughn moved to the side of the door, then knocked again. She wasn't taking any chances at being on the receiving end of a fist or even a gunshot when someone finally answered.

The sound of rusted hinges creaked a warning while a slight opening revealed the grotesquely sunken eyes of Theresa Chastang. "What!" she spewed toward Martha. It wasn't even a question.

"I'm Mrs. Smith from the foster service. Remember me?" She flashed one of her cards with her alias on it. "I need to see your children."

"My kids ain't home, and you don't have no appointment."

"I don't need an appointment, if you'll remember. I understand your children have run away and we need to find them."

"Who told you that? Liars! You just tryin' to cut my money!"

"I'm not trying to cheat you, Ms. Chastang, but we had a schedule for your children and now that's been disturbed. If you'll tell me everything you know, I'll make sure you get replacement kids, so your funds won't be cut." That worked. The door opened further to allow her entry.

When Martha Vaughn, the woman Theresa Chastang only knew as "Mrs. Smith," finally exited the house on Gramble Street, she climbed into the van that was waiting at the curb. Fuzz was behind the wheel, "Jeez! What were you doing? Having tea?" Fuzz got both his nickname and his demeanor from fifteen years with the LAPD before being discharged. His real name was Charles Keel, but his snitches dubbed him Fuzz, thinking themselves clever. With a shaved head, the street slang for police described the total opposite of the bald, sarcastic man. Before she could answer, he added, "Or perhaps you were exchanging recipes? Any new variations of meth you'd like to share?"

"Don't get wise with me." She jerked around to face him. "If you hadn't lost the kids in the first place, I wouldn't have to step foot in that living hell. Or have you forgotten?"

Fuzz ran his hand over his bald head, "For the last time, we did exactly as told! We were at that little airport when they arrived, ready to transport them! You said they were on the run, but you forgot to mention they'd run from us too!"

"Normally after placing them in one of these houses, they'll do anything we want. I guess these kids were more shaken than we realized. But you two *idiots*," she held her hands up at him, "chasing them around!"

Harp Grisholm popped forward from the backseat, challenging Martha. "You were the contact! That little girl wasn't expecting two men. You didn't tell her, and you didn't tell us, so the way I see it, YOU messed up."

Fuzz looked in the rearview mirror at his partner. With a full head of sandy-brown hair, Harp Grisholm reminded Fuzz of the lion in the Wizard of Oz. Not only because of his mane, but at six foot four and looking as menacing as any man, Fuzz saw him as soft, like the weepy lion. Today, however, Grisholm was really out of character and was still going at Martha. "You mishandled this one, Martha." Grisholm was leaning in between the front seats. "Those kids can ID all three of us now, and they've been gone for six days! I hope you got something inside."

Martha held Grisholm's stare for a long beat. He was right, and she had no comeback. "The only firsthand information she had was something about a boyfriend." Her mouth was in a snarl. Then she turned to Fuzz. "I didn't exactly understand her, but when I promised to get her some more kids, she became a little coherent and shared some 'hood gossip I think we can use."

"What about missing persons? Did she call them in?" Fuzz asked.

"NO. And she won't. I made sure no one will be hearing from her again. Fuzz, tell me again exactly what happened after the children took off running."

"I already told you." Fuzz looked around, cutting his eyes left and right. He was uneasy. They'd sat too long in front of the house. He put the van in gear. "We couldn't catch 'em on foot, so we got back in the van. The last we saw, they ran across the exit ramp from I-110. That's when the accident happened, but by then, a large travel van had blocked our view. We couldn't see." He looked over at Martha. "I told ya. I jumped out, ran toward the scene, and when I made it around the big van, they were gone. Nothing but smoke and the smell of burning rubber. Emergency vehicles sounded in the distance, so we got outta there." Fuzz looked back in the side mirrors again, then over his left shoulder; uneasy, he pulled away from the curb.

"Was the obstructing vehicle black?" she asked. She was grinning now, but the tight pull of her thin lips looked the same as her snarl.

Fuzz hit the brakes and his head spun around.

"She knew that?" came from the back. Grisholm leaned forward again, his hand on the back of Fuzz's seat. "Stop jerkin' us around—what'd she say?" Both men were scowling.

Martha ignored them and crossed her arms. "That was her news from the 'hood. Drive, I'll tell you what I got."

Fuzz quickly checked behind him again, then continued on.

As they passed through the intersection, Martha looked in the side mirror of the van and saw a striking brunette sitting behind the wheel of a black Range Rover. Although the car and the woman were out of place, she might not have thought any more about it, except this woman lifted a camera in front of her face and held it in their direction.

* * *

Nicole left a message for Mike while waiting for the evening rush of traffic to thin. "Hey, I got an address of a foster child named Angel. It's on Gramble Street, just a few miles from the center. I'm headed to check it out. Don't need back up," she said jokingly, "just FYI. I'll phone you when I'm headed home."

The drive didn't take long. It was still light enough to figure out the numbers on a house—for the few that had numbers—but the one her navigation system marked had a rental van idling in front of it, and a driver behind the wheel. Nicole didn't stop. Instead, she drove to the next stop sign, then took a left and crept along for a few blocks, then took another left, repeating this pattern until she could see Gramble

Street again. She stayed back at the curb, two stop signs away from the house, and reached behind her seat for her camera bag. The new telephoto lens attached to her Nikon worked as good as binoculars, and when the front door opened and a lady emerged walking toward the van, Nicole's professional impulse took over and she started clicking the camera, capturing the woman's image, along with the van's. When they pulled away from the curb, they turned in her direction, and she was able to get a few frames of the driver as well before they came toward the intersection. Lowering the camera, Nicole pretended to be on the phone, but as soon as they passed she got in two more shots, getting their license plate from the rear as they went down the road.

With the white utility van out of sight, Nicole drove to the house and fished out her small can of mace. It had a hook at the top, and she attached it to her key chain, then, retrieving the magnetic KDLA television signs from the cargo area, placed them on the doors hoping they would ward off vandalism. Pressing the key fob for her SUV to lock, she cringed at the beep it made and quickly made her way to the door.

"What?" The voice on the other side croaked out after Nicole knocked for the second time.

"I'm looking for Angel," said Nicole calmly, but when the door gradually creaked opened, Nicole worked hard to stay expressionless. She checked the address again on the house, but there was only one number there and it looked like it was once a six. The house next door had "5163" spray-painted on the curb. It had to be the right address, but there was no way this was a foster home, or the woman before her a foster parent. The frail frame, along with the sores on the face of this vacant-eyed woman, tagged her as a drug abuser and addict. "I'm sorry to bother you," Nicole said, watching the small figure struggle to stay standing.

"I done told you everythin'. You said you'd get me more children. Don't you go changin' our agreement." The woman pointed a brittle, boney finger at Nicole with one hand and held onto the door, for support, with the other. "I need the money. It's not my fault they run off!"

That confirmed it. It WAS the right house. Nicole had to be quick before she lost this woman's cooperation or her consciousness. "Angel was supposed to meet me. I have money for him, and I need to know how to find him."

The fragile woman's eyes became slightly more alert at the mention of money. "Give it to me. I'll see he get it."

"Well, there's a problem with that," Nicole said. "He had information he was going to sell me."

"I done told you, I don't know where they gone to. Little Two saw the van. Big and black, like in the movies. He said it had a Mercedes emblem on the front of it."

"Little Two? Is that someone's name? Did the kids get in the van?" Nicole was leaning in, trying to watch her mouth to read her lips as she talked, but the woman kept moving her head around.

"He know my brother. In his gang." Then she turned away from Nicole and staggered a few steps. She didn't answer the last question.

"Can I take a look where the kids slept? Maybe he left me a note. If you let me do that, I'll give you the money," Nicole said, following her in.

The foul stench of the house was soaked into the small room the children had shared. It was dark and looked like an abandoned cabin in an old black and white movie. There was no furniture, so the dirt and rat droppings had nowhere to hide, but gathered mostly around the baseboards of the room, along with piles of trash. There were a few worn, moving blankets strewn on the filthy, barren floor that seemed to be their sleeping arrangements. She lifted each one, hoping to uncover anything personal of the kids', but other than stirring up the soiled odors trapped within, she didn't find anything more than an old napkin wrapped around something that used to be edible and a family of cockroaches that scattered. She was already anxious, so when they took off and two of them ran across her foot, she dropped the blanket and squealed. Nicole quickly recovered, then froze, listening for the woman, in case she had heard Nicole. Nothing.

Back in the living room she was alone, so she crossed over to the kitchen. The swinging door made a slight noise, and she found the source of the underlying stench of the house. It wasn't fresh, but it was the distinct cat-urine odor of meth. Putting her arm up to her face and using her shirtsleeve as a filter, she walked around the room, scanning as quickly as she could. She was in the same black and white movie and was about to leave when she noticed something bright sticking out from under the refrigerator. Getting closer, she slid it out with the tip of a pencil and brushed it off. *Mrs. Smith—Smiling Tribes Foster Care.* No address, just a phone number. She slipped the business card into her pants pocket.

Nicole backed out of the kitchen and realized she never got the woman's name. She called out, "Hello? I'm ready to leave. Here's the money I promised you." No response. The house was tiny; surely the woman heard her. She looked down the hall, and this time the stench was so overwhelming, she gagged. *That's twice today*, she thought. The feet were the first thing Nicole saw, hanging out of the doorway as the scrawny body of the woman lay crumpled just inside her bedroom. She grabbed her phone and dialed 9-1-1, also for a second time that day.

* * *

Nicole had found out her name. The shriveled woman in the house. She was Theresa Chastang. Unfortunately, they weren't going to be talking any more. Theresa was pronounced dead at the scene by the paramedics, although it wouldn't be official until the medical examiner arrived. It was an assumed overdose, but for the record would have to wait for the autopsy. Nicole was their only known witness, so she was detained for questioning. "Please," she asked the detective who just arrived, "can we go back outside to talk? I can't stay in here another minute." The EMTs confirmed the latest stench to be Theresa's loose bowels at the time of her death.

She walked out with the detective and sat on the rear bumper of the first vehicle she came to. She was seriously nauseated, but even more, she was trying to buy a little time to figure out what she was going to tell him. Why was she there would be his first question.

"So, Ms. Portman, I don't peg you for a druggie and I can't see where this woman was front-page news, so care to tell me why a celebrity news reporter like yourself was here this evening?" came the first of many questions from Detective Ernest Graves of the South Street police station. She leaned forward, bending at the waist, and rested her forearms on her knees, her head down, looking at her feet.

"Do I need to send a medic over?" he asked.

"No. Thank you. I just need a moment. Between the shock and the smell ... Just a little more fresh air and I should be fine."

"Take your time, I'm not goin' anywhere."

She closed her eyes. *I must be faint. I smell him. That marvelously warm, clean, leather smell of Rand Coleman.* Peeking through the curtain of hair that cascaded over her shoulder and covered half of her face, she saw shoes that looked like his within four feet of her, and when she heard Rand's voice, she raised her head. He was shaking hands with the detective, then approached and lifted her by her arm in one smooth movement, guiding her away from the emergency vehicles, the people, and the excitement, as well as the sadness, and they walked straight to her SUV.

"Your keys?" He asked. He helped her into the passenger seat and, after pulling the magnetic signs from her SUV's doors, he got behind the wheel and they drove away.

CHAPTER 21

Heading west, Rand drove with no particular destination in mind to get Nicole away from the chaos. "Where are we going?" she asked.

"Just driving—getting distance from that scene. Do you want me to drive you home? I can get someone to pick me up." Rand glanced at Nicole. She was staring off into the distant landscape, which was filled with lights now. Streetlights. Headlights. Brake lights. Thousands of cars all in a hurry to escape their own scenes—or to get to them.

"No. Not home. Not yet. Can we drive to the ocean?"

They had missed seeing the sunset, but the reflection of the harbor lights in Marina del Rey still made it magical. The sailboats clustered along the marinas were peaceful. Each harbored in their own slip, swaying with the movement from the water. Samm's Beachside was one of the few restaurants in the area customers were not required to valet, so, driving to their lot, he parked.

Nicole stepped out once the car stopped. Her grey eyes sparkled beneath the lights from the boardwalk but it didn't hide the sadness in them, and Rand didn't rush her to speak or encourage her toward the building. He simply waited.

"I guess you were destined to keep rescuing me today," she eventually said. "Thank you." She looked to Rand, who stood close. Protective. "A pastor?" Her lips spoke the words slowly. Her head tilted, and Rand's eyes darkened as he watched her. Her sadness was replaced with a momentary appreciation. Momentary, because a slap to her senses switched her brain into gear, and she stiffened. "Wait! Why *were* you there? Did Mike send you?"

The abrupt change and mention of Mike caused Rand to retreat. In a slow move, he turned his back to Nicole and looked out at the vast display of yachts dancing lightly with the breeze. He breathed in the salt air, and when he faced her again, asked, "Do you realize that house is only about eight blocks from The Rock? Emergency vehicles, blaring so loud … I feel it's my job to keep watch …" his dark eyes narrowed. "And what do I see surrounded by flashing lights? A black Range Rover with news station magnetics attached …" He let his words hang.

Nicole swallowed hard, then moved, taking a step, pausing, then another. He fell in beside her. His dark, wavy hair was tousled by the light wind and to avoid watching him, she took in their surroundings. The water. The marina. Samm's. Then her feet stopped. Her arm spread wide toward the restaurant, and her steel eyes were suddenly challenging him. Again. "And how did you know to drive me here?"

"Whoa," he laughed and spread his arms wide like hers, toward the same scenery. "You wanted the ocean."

"But here? This particular place? How do you know this is my hangout—mine and Mike's?"

"Excuse me? You think you're the only one to use this mirage in the middle of the 405 traffic? I personally don't enjoy Venice Beach, and Santa Monica is so crowded, the only place to park is one of their big garages." He dropped his arms but was still smiling. "And they all look alike. If you've ever forgotten which one you're parked in, it kinda ruins the experience. No, this fits me. But after hearing it's your hangout, too, I can't believe we haven't run into each other before."

He was right. Nicole's claim over the marina was irrational. The day was taking its toll on her. "Perhaps we have," she said, with one brow still raised.

"Impossible. That wouldn't be something I'd forget." He motioned toward the building. "Would you like to go inside?"

There was the promise of a smile, but Nicole suppressed it. "I can't sit right now."

"A walk?"

Strolling side by side along the wide path leading to the water, their rhythm was intentionally slow. They were on the boardwalk before anyone spoke. "How are you?" Rand asked gently, breaking the silence. Then added, "I'm a good listener."

She turned her head to look at him. He wore testosterone effortlessly and seemed to possess an equal amount of empathy. The lights from the dock danced around him, illuminating him. Her smile finally surfaced.

"What?"

"You only asked a simple 'How are you,' but it felt like true concern," Nicole said.

He slowed and turned toward her; they stopped. "It was. Why didn't you take someone with you this evening?"

Nicole shrugged her shoulders. "It should've been a simple stop. Just following a lead to a possible story." She shook her head and said, "Dead end." Suddenly her eyes widened. "I didn't mean it to come out like that!"

Under any other circumstances, it might've been comical, but there was no trace of humor in Rand's voice. It was calming. "You've been through a lot today." He guided her on, resuming their walk. "Was she dead when you arrived?"

It was a reasonable question, but she didn't rush to answer. He waited. And they walked. Her voice was faint against the night, "No. She let me in. We talked and ... I knew something was wrong ... she could hardly stand ... and ..." She stopped abruptly, then faced him. "I should've called 9-1-1 earlier ... maybe she wouldn't have died."

"Don't." He placed his hands lightly on her arms, reassuringly.

She backed away, shaking her head, "I don't want your understanding!" Nicole hadn't been physically harmed in either encounter of the day, but the heavy frown and dark shadows under her eyes were revealing a deeper affect. "Didn't you hear me?" Not waiting for an answer, she pushed on, "I knew something was wrong ... but what did I do? I asked to search her house! I thought, 'Oh good, she's so stoned she won't notice me digging around'! What kind of person...?" Suddenly she stopped and turned away, toward the wind and the dark, moving waters. Had he not taken a step closer, he could have missed her words, "You wouldn't have done that."

Rand started to reach for her again, and instead shoved his hands in his pockets. Standing behind her, his deep voice was gentle. "I can't tell you what I would have done, Nicole, but the woman was obviously a drug addict. Now ... tell me ... how were you ... a total stranger to her, supposed to recognize if this 'high' today was any different than yesterday's?" He let the comment sit before adding, "Don't do this."

Gradually, they began walking again. Minutes passed in silence, and Nicole was more herself when she asked, "So, 'Pastor' –is that a casual term? Or are you the real thing?"

With a shrug of his shoulders, he said, "I guess you can say I'm the real thing; however, I consider my job more like mission work."

"Mission work? ... Like you're on a mission? Undercover?" she asked playfully.

A broad smile lit up his face, but that was his only response.

Returning his smile, the white of Nicole's teeth radiated in the night but after waiting an awkward beat too long for him to answer, it dimmed. "Just joking. Go on ... tell me about your mission work." It was a more serious note, but at least her heart was lighter than before, and she added, "I could surely stand to hear something good."

Rand shrugged, his response thoughtful. "The term usually conjures images of a Third World country, but you know, you've covered enough news to see the needs here in our own city." He glanced at Nicole as they strolled beside one another and caught her quick nod. "The poor and the homeless are right under us, within blocks, as we drive home on the overpasses. It's glamorous to have a photo shoot helping impoverished children in a foreign land, and I commend anyone who does because it brings awareness, but there are children in our own backyard who are going hungry tonight. They deserve the same awareness. As does The Rock." He looked off toward a sailboat coming into the harbor and Nicole took the opportunity to study his face.

As he talked about the kids at the community center, Rand exuded an intriguing mixture of immense strength with compassion, he was obviously invested in his work, but there was something else. Something he was hiding, like he was guarded. *Why would a pastor be guarded? I'm*

147

sure that's what I see. It's a trait Nicole would recognize because she saw it in the mirror daily. So as he continued, she watched.

"Some of these kids are still innocent, some not so much, because they've had to grow up too quickly. Many are victims of abuse, living in a nightmare that they never wake up from, so they take to the street, dishing out what they've learned. Abuse." Rand's brows pulled together, and there wasn't the slightest trace of the smile he wore earlier. His concern was contagious. "If The Rock and its volunteers can make the slightest difference in their world, then as Emily Dickinson said, 'I shall not live in vain.'" His smile returned, and he said, "It begins with one."

"Like Timbo." The crystal-grey eyes softened, "And The Rock, it becoming the new 'glamour photo-op' ... you did that." Nicole watched in fascination, until he turned to face her with the dark eyes that didn't seem to know their boundary. Or maybe the issue was her. Nicole looked away and steered back to the conversation, something she had more control over. "What did you tell the detective to get me away so quickly tonight?"

Rand took a few steps before answering. "He'd gotten your basic statement. He really didn't need anything more for now."

"Does he know you?"

"Everybody in that area knows The Rock," he delivered to Nicole with a mischievous grin, and everything in her body responded, beginning with weak knees. She became off-balanced, and he took her hand to steady her.

Holding hands. A common act for many, but to Nicole it was so intimate that she flinched at his touch, until his eyes met hers again, and she relaxed, leaving her hand with him. The sea was alluring them with its bevy of activity, and they stopped again to watch. Boats coming and going. The clanging of the ropes against the masts of the docked yachts was like soothing wind chimes in the night, and Nicole locked in on a double-mast sailboat in the distance, watching the magnificent sails arch against the wind as it left the protection of the harbor. She breathed in. It smelled like freedom.

"I don't like feeling vulnerable," she said, "much less admitting to it. I was caught off-guard ... twice today." Nicole paused. "If not for you ... the ending might ..." She stopped. The unfinished sentence hung heavy between them.

Rand watched her stare out to sea and couldn't help trying to rescue her once again, to move her past this verbal struggle. Also, to downplay his own heroics. He tilted his head and through a puffed chest and a crooked grin said, "Yeah, I get that a lot."

As charming as he was, it landed flat and Nicole casually slid her hand from his grip. His mouth opened, then shut, thinking of a recovery, but something past Nicole caught his eye. On the far side of Samm's, a white panel van was idling in their direct view. Instead, he said, "The temperature's dropping. Do you have a jacket in your car?"

Nicole hadn't noticed the chill until now.

They made their way back to her Range Rover, and, in a measured turn, Rand studied the area around them, then folded his arms and leaned against the car door. "We have to be in Detective Grave's office tomorrow morning."

"Unfortunately." Nicole's voice was soft.

The salt in the air mingled with aromas from nearby restaurants. Snippets of music and laughter from Samm's could be heard and although it had been an enjoyable escape, as they stood in the parking lot,

Rand addressed the unavoidable topic. "The woman tonight–did she say anything significant to you before she died?"

Nicole's eyebrows lifted. "Not exactly a 'how's the weather' question, is it?" She rubbed her arms, reminded of the chill.

"I already know the answer to that one." He flashed a smile and opened the door of her SUV to remove her jacket. Rand draped it over her shoulders, then he resettled against the car, scanning the road behind Samm's once more.

With a slight tilt of her head, she let out a playful, "Hmmm." Exaggerating her evaluation of him. "Considering you've rescued me all day, *and* I'm in your custody, I guess I'd be asking, too."

He waited.

"Her name is Theresa Chastang. She didn't say much—actually, she thought I was someone else ..." She narrowed her eyes and said, "A social worker!" Nicole was always guarded with information, but the outrageous notion that someone listed that house as a foster home wasn't anything to stay quiet about. "Did you go into that house?"

He shook his head.

"The living conditions were horrid!" Nicole used both hands to drive her point across. "It's listed as a foster home! Theresa Chastang, a foster parent! An apparent drug addict!" Shaking her head from side to side, she continued, "There is *no way* she should've been given a child! Something isn't right!"

"Were you looking for a child?"

Nicole froze. Her flared nostrils calmed, and she crossed her arms, reeling it in. "I'm working privately for a client and don't have the privilege to discuss it, but," she challenged Rand with a look, "... I will say there are holes in what I'm investigating, and until I know where the problem lies, I don't trust the detective from that station. I don't trust anyone."

"Not even me?" Rand asked. Leaving his position against the car, he took a step closer to her.

Nicole opened her mouth to speak, then closed it again, watching him closely. "It's late. We should go." She slid her arms into the jacket draped over her shoulders, then gave exaggerated attention to the simple act of buttoning it.

Rand let it go. "I'm going to assume you don't care to revisit Gramble Street tonight to pick up my car."

Nicole shook her head.

"Why don't I drive you home, then pick you up in the morning since I have to go to the precinct with you?" He was standing upwind to Nicole, and the night breeze was collaborating with Rand, the way it delivered his warm scent to her.

The offer was bold, coming from someone she'd met only two days ago, and later she could blame the wind on her decision, but tonight it seemed logical. "That works," she said, and climbed into her own passenger seat as he held the door for her.

* * *

The questionable white van Rand had seen loitering at Samm's had left. He didn't see it again, and it was probably nothing, but he still watched for a tail on the drive to Malibu. Sitting in front of Nicole's home, the silence between Rand and Nicole was comfortable, like a conversation in its own right. Words were unnecessary. When Rand finally spoke, his voice was gravelly.

"We've shared an eventful day."

Nicole smiled softly and nodded.

"Will you be all right? I'm reluctant to leave you here alone."

Nodding again, she said, "I'll be fine."

"You'll set your security alarm?" he asked.

"Always." Nicole opened the console where she kept the garage re-mote and with it in hand, she gathered her tote. Rand started to open his door. "That's not necessary, I can see myself in."

"I'll be here at seven, if that's not too early for you."

"Seven's fine." And she closed the passenger door with a thud. The light from the rising garage door silhouetted Nicole's long limbs as she walked away, but before she entered, she stopped and turned back to-ward Rand. He lowered the window. Words, gently spoken, navigated the dark to find him, "Thank you, again. I can't imagine today without you." They landed on his chest.

While watching her safely inside, Nicole still enveloped the interior of the car, moving through the air vents. The fragrance was alluring and classic, just like the owner. He sat a moment longer after the door was completely shut, then turned abruptly, doing a quick inventory of her car. He found what he was looking for on the back floorboard. There, forgotten after all the evening's events, was the camera case.

Making his way home, Rand phoned Jocko Green, and Jocko an-swered with a question. "How'd the showing go?"

"Different," Rand said. "It seems a visitor brought snacks and the homeowner ended with a bad case of food poisoning. Not good. Did you get anything on the license?"

"Yeah. I'm coming your way. I'll be there shortly," said Jocko.

Approaching his condo, Rand released a long sigh. He still had work to do, but he let himself relax for the first time in hours. Nicole was safe.

* * *

Earlier in the day, Rand had been edgy. It was impatience creeping in, as he waited on a call from his friend, Special Agent Jocko Green. Jocko had given him an address to check out, but had forgotten a crucial part. Rand needed a reading on the power meter from Jocko's contact at Southern California Edison. Checking the meter activity was essential; it would give an idea of the activity inside the building.

His phone vibrated, and Jocko gave him the news he'd waited for. "The meter is barely moving. Probably the refrigerator. We watched it for a few minutes with no change, so I'm going to assume you're clear."

Wearing a faded black ball-cap, Rand sat low in the driver's seat of an old blue Nissan Altima. The car was a loaner from a friend, the legendary stunt coordinator and director Conrad Palmisano. Conrad had a collection of these unsuspecting vehicles that he rented to the studios and production companies. The dings in the doors and fenders made it perfect for what Rand needed, and just as planned, no one had looked his way as he sat one block down from Theresa Chastang's. After disconnecting from Jocko, he stepped out of the vehicle, but a white panel utility van pulled directly in front of the house he was watching. He slid back into the Nissan and gently pulled the door shut.

The passenger side of the van opened and a woman in her mid- to late forties emerged. Her dark hair was pulled back in a clasp, and she was dressed professionally, in slacks and a blazer. Approaching the house, she knocked with purpose. A second round of knocking proved even more aggressive, and Rand watched her move a couple of steps to the left of the door. He lifted a pair of binoculars and caught her mouth moving. Unless she had an earpiece, she was talking to someone on the inside. The door opened. It was too dark inside for Rand to make out the image of the occupant, but within seconds it opened further, allowing the woman entry.

Without taking his eyes off the house, he called Jocko back. "Yo?" answered Jocko.

"Our listing? Activity just picked up. Looks like they're showing. I need a tag run. California D3691."

"Got it."

Rand was the first to click off, and he replaced his cell phone with a Glock, checking the magazine clip and the chamber. It was good to go. He slid it in his belt at the small of his back under his sport jacket. Movement to the left of him caught his attention, and he pulled the cap down further before glancing over. Almost forgetting his position, he jerked upright when a black, late model Range Rover crept past, but just as quickly ducked back down. "What! What is she—" He watched as the SUV slowly disappeared around the next corner. It wasn't long before it approached the same street again, staying back at the stop sign. Nicole hadn't seen Rand. It was evident she was preoccupied with something else when she leveled a camera with a powerful lens at the same house he had been watching.

The door of the house opened again, and all eyes were back on the female from the van as she emerged and went straight to the vehicle waiting on her. It sat for another three long minutes before pulling onto the road. When the van made the corner, the angle gave Rand a clear view from the front and exposed a third person who was leaning forward talking to the woman with the dark hair. Once the van party was out of sight, Nicole had driven to the same house, placed magnetic KDLA signs on her car, then approached the same front door.

From the dented Nissan, Rand had observed it all, his head barely above the window line.

* * *

The night had taken a much different turn than Rand had expected, and he arrived to his own home in Nicole's Range Rover. The flickering gaslights mounted outside his garage welcomed him and, punching a code in his phone, the doors lifted. His two-car garage wasn't really meant for two large vehicles—most in Los Angeles weren't—but with great precision Rand landed her SUV in beside his truck, and, before exiting, he reached behind the seat and grabbed the camera case. He might still be able to salvage something from Gramble Street.

CHAPTER 22

Special Agent Jocko Green wasn't far behind Rand, arriving at Rand's condo with his tweed flat-cap twisted backward and an olive army jacket on his slim frame. His slight goatee had flecks of grey that belied his youthful style and carefree banter, but they did match the intensity in his speckled amber eyes. He dropped his backpack on the counter, and, making himself at home, grabbed a water bottle from the refrigerator, unloaded his laptop, and set up to work. "I ran the ID on the license plate you gave me, registered to a 2011 Toyota pickup. Obviously stolen."

Rand nodded as he walked back to his own laptop, where he had downloaded the pictures taken from Nicole's camera. "There were three people in the van. I have pictures of two of them for you to start a face recognition." He airdropped them to Jocko.

"Cool. I'll take it from here." Jocko sat on the tall swivel stool in front of his laptop, ready to work. His foot jiggled back and forth.

While Jocko worked, Rand briefed him on the evening, and ended with, "... and Nicole has to be at the police station in the morning."

"So, she mentioned the children?"

"Yeah, then caught herself. Said she's on an assignment, and since she doesn't have anything solid yet, she's not talking, especially to the detective. She doesn't trust him, or his station."

Jocko stopped and looked at Rand over the top of his round silver readers. "All they have is a presumed overdose. I don't see them being aggressive with this. She's used to this dance with the heat, she'll be fine," said Jocko.

Rand nodded again. "True." He handed Jocko a printout. "Here's the report you gave me last Thursday." It looked older than a few days. The edges were curled, and it was marked up with Rand's handwritten comments. "You're right. It's been doctored. I went back two years, and the numbers under the different categories of missing children haven't changed much; however, new names are added weekly. Now, you know very few of these kids are being found ... so if the totals aren't changing ..."

"Then someone's deleting data," said Jocko.

"Exactly. Read my notes. You're going to need more manpower on this; get your cyber buddies involved."

With the files transferred, Jocko logged off his computer and shook his head, "Leak in that department, I only have a couple that I trust right now."

"You sound like Nicole. Do what you have to. We've got to know who's hacking the data. Surely they've left signs of footprinting. Somewhere. The county's files, yours, wherever. They had to leave something."

Jocko thoughtfully stroked his goatee. "Anything else?"

"Actually, yes, I need your help moving some vehicles around."

They followed one another to The Rock, where they left Rand's truck, then rode together to get the Altima and returned it to Conrad.

On the drive back to Rand's, Jocko gave Rand a side glance and asked, "So, what's Nicole Portman like? When she was doing live newscasts, she came across no-nonsense, but ... still ... very hot. Like the sultry librarian thing." He waited only a beat and asked, "How about in person?"

Rand chuckled, "Fair description," was all he said, and they rode in comfortable silence down the highway. After a mile or so, Rand said, "Substance."

"What?" Jocko did a double take at Rand.

"If I had to sum her up with one word that would be it. Substance. She's solid. Driven." He raised one hand. "And guarded! Like she's hiding something." Rand stopped, shrugging one shoulder. "Although it might only be vulnerability." He turned toward the passenger-side window and gazed out. "It's in her eyes."

"Her eyes?"

Rand didn't answer, but even over the loud noise of the off-road tires, Jocko could hear what his friend didn't say. He smiled and drove ahead, then suddenly, with a puzzled look, he startled Rand from his reflection, "WAIT! How did Nicole get that address on Gramble? I got it to you as quickly as I could—and barely beat an unemployed news reporter? What was her source?"

Unexpected laughter bellowed out in the small cab of Jocko's truck and the sound was so consuming, Jocko grinned along. Shifting his attention from the road to his overly amused passenger, he waited for insight into the joke, but the longer Rand went without explaining, amusement turned to irritation and Jocko's lips tightened, along with his driving. Like a New York cab ride in the heavy traffic, he accelerated urgently, then hit the brake, catching Rand's attention. Rand wiped his eyes and with a piece of smile still hanging on, he said, "There I was, in the beat-up Nissan on surveillance with information secretly passed along from my special-agent friend, when around the corner comes her shiny Range Rover, and she parks directly in front of the house, station call-letters and all." As quickly as the humor had entered, it left. Rand turned to Jocko, and his face hardened. "Thing is, Jocko, she has her bite into this. She's not going to let it go."

CHAPTER 23

Tom Vinsant pushed away from the dinner table. "I'll leave you with it, my dear, since I still have work to do," explaining as if he would have actually helped Ginny clear the dishes. He was back early from his Washington trip and retired to his study to work. There were several pressing emails to answer, and Congressman Duke Stanton had said he would be phoning, so when the call came through, Tom was ready for him. "Duke, ole buddy, what can I do for you? Missing any more family members? Or perhaps it's your dog this time."

"Good one." The congressman forced a laugh. "Actually, Tom, I was thinking you and I could get together early tomorrow. I have some things to discuss—ways to benefit our fine state."

"That won't be possible, Duke, not unless you'll be in Los Angeles. I flew back. Unexpected business." Tom crossed his legs, took a sip of his scotch, and savored both–the flavor of the fine liquid and the awkward pause coming from Stanton. Tom allowed it to stretch out before adding, "When you get home, give me a call. I'm open to listening, *if* it will benefit our constituents."

The pause continued.

"Hello? Do we still have a connection?"

"Well, Tom ... from what I understand ... you do." Stanton waited another beat before adding, "So like I said, we need to talk in person."

"I don't have time for riddles, Duke. If you have something to say, say it."

"You know, it's been months since I've been in Los Angeles and visited your thriving port activity. You know how competitive I am."

Tom set his glass in motion, swirling the remaining scotch. Watching it. His mood darkened.

"This one-sided conversation isn't working for me, Senator. Maybe instead I should just visit my old friend, Sidney Drummond. He loves to listen. Hell, I could even bring my goddaughter with me. Such a delightful girl." Stanton waited.

Tom allowed his ice to jingle against glass. "Like I said, Duke, I don't have time for riddles. Say hello to Sidney for me." He pushed "end."

Sidney Drummond was powerful. He owned people, and his influence could crush anyone's career, even Tom's. Tom took another sip and swished the flavor around his mouth, thinking. *If Sidney hears about the girl, he'll hold it over me, and I'll never break free ... however, Sidney hates Duke Stanton more than I do. He won't meet with him.* "So, I keep moving on things I actually have control of," Tom said aloud, and set his glass on the desk before pulling up a contact in his phone. "What have you got?" Tom asked the man when he answered.

"Hey boss, nothing new to report, other than I found out who the black dude was that Mrs. V met at that youth center. He's a radio personality. Name's Blind Dog Mike. Great Show! Funny, but real hip, he's on in the mornings ..."

"Cut to the details!" said Tom curtly.

"Yes, sir. Anyway, that's it. Like I said before, after a couple of hours she went home and didn't go back out."

"What about Sunday and today?"

"Nothing except the fitness center. After her workout, she went straight home. Your housekeeper went for groceries."

"Good. Stay close for the rest of the week. She'll be getting a new BMW on Wednesday to replace her wrecked one, so watch for the change from the loaner car to her new one. It will be white."

"Yes, sir. No problem."

Tom found Ginny in the living room, reading. "Here you are. So, tell me about your weekend. I thought you were going to stay at the Bacara to get some rest."

"Oh, Tom. I know you wanted me there, but with you gone," she shook her head, "I needed to be here. At home. I knew you'd understand." She put her book aside. "I read your interview. It was really good, Tom! Touching but determined ... just the combination I'm sure you were after!"

"Thank you, and even though you are biased, I agree, it did turn out well." He walked over to her chair and kissed the top of her head before sitting in the chair beside her. "But tell me about you. You didn't really answer; what have you been up to?"

"What's there to tell? Same things. So, other than the interviews, were you able to get any business done?"

"No, no business. And you know how boring that was for me, so I took the first plane out." Tom watched his wife closely, a glint of appreciation in his eye. *She's learned well, dodging unwanted questions.* "Next week will be more productive. I'll probably stay the whole week, but then I'll need to get back to my campaign." He crossed his legs and took a small sip of the scotch in hand, then said, "I have an idea! Why don't you get my campaign schedule from Rita and go with me? At least to a couple of junkets. Our constituents love you, and who knows, we just might find a little 'us' time."

Ginny smiled at him. "That would be nice, Tom. I'll call her tomorrow. I'm getting a little tired. I think I'll get ready for bed."

"You do that sweetheart, and I'm right behind you."

From the outside of the closed bathroom door, Tom heard the hum of Ginny's electric toothbrush, so he picked up her charging phone and quickly checked her recent calls. The insurance broker, his phone, Rita, and the housekeeper. He nodded as though confirming what he had hoped. Perhaps her visit with the deejay was nothing to be concerned with. He placed it back just where she had it, and began his routine as well.

CHAPTER 24

It was late Monday night and Nicole was safely at home. Alone. Security alarm set. But she could not settle in. "To call this an eventful day is a major understatement, so why is it I'm more disturbed by the fact I have no transportation?" She poured a glass of wine and checked the voice mail on her phone.

"Hey baby, don't leave me a vague message that you're ridin' around in the 'hood, alone in that shiny wagon, then let me hang to guess what happened. Call me." Mike's words were as playful as ever, but his tone wasn't. After finding Theresa, Nicole had forgotten simple things, like her promise to call him. She punched call.

"Well, you must've found something. Was the address good? Did you find our Angel?"

"Mike, it has to be the same one!" She sat at the counter. "It was a foster home and the kids that lived there are gone ... missing. For days." She felt her pants pocket, then pulled out the business card she'd found under Theresa Chastang's refrigerator, turning it over, inspecting it, while talking. "So, I have Angel's name, his address, and my connection at the county office. It's something to work with." They talked for a while longer, and she shared with Mike the living conditions of the house and the room she assumed was the children's, but the fatigue was settling in. With their goodbyes said and the coffee pot ready for morning, Nicole turned out the lights and slid deep into her bed.

* * *

The kids. It's the same as Debbie.

The monster was jabbing at her mind. The stories from Family Services and the vile images of Gramble Street had danced too loudly in the darkness and had awakened it.

Your best friend. Remember?

It badgered. She tried to stifle it, but like a sneeze or a hiccup, it wasn't something she could hold back.

You didn't help her. You can't help them.

Nicole slapped the light back on and looked around the room. The voice hid. It always hid from the light. Getting up, she found the remote for her sound systems and turned it on. It would override the unwelcomed voice if it came back. She searched for the Jack Johnson playlist, since Mike always called it her "flip-flop" music: happy. And Nicole needed "happy."

With Jack serenading her, there was no room for the nasty voice, and she tried again, leaving a soft nightlight on and pulled the comforter close around her. It worked, and she finally drifted off to sleep. Until the hammering started. At first it was far away, then grew louder and louder. *Who could be hammering so late?* Fighting the mental fog, she stretched in bed, looking around the room to get her bearings and to get the spiderwebs out of her head. Then the hammering started again. She looked at her clock. The blue digital number read 7:17 a.m.

"Seven?!" She sat up. The hammering was rattling her front door. "Rand!!"

Nicole bolted to the bathroom, gargled, then shook her hands through her hair. She grabbed a hooded jacket that had fallen from its hanger to throw over her little lace camisole and shorts as she ran through the house.

Jerking the door open, Rand's fist froze in mid-air, and Nicole's chest rose and fell with her rapid breath, as she simply stood, watching his face transform through a whirlwind of emotions. Concern—to anger—to re-lief. By the time he spoke, his voice was calmer than he appeared. "I was to pick you up twenty minutes ago. You didn't answer your door. You didn't answer your cell phone. I was concerned."

"Good morning to you, too," she said, finally breaking from her stu-por, and she pulled the door wider, inviting him in. Rand turned to the small ledge behind him, and when he faced her again, he was holding up two coffees.

"I hope it's still warm." He handed her one.

"Thank you." Nicole took a sip and gave Rand a guilty grin, then walked to the coffee maker and pushed the "on" button. "Excuse me a moment."

Nicole's phone was charging in the bedroom. Seven missed calls. The setting was on "do not disturb" from when she took the meeting with Kim Argnaut yesterday, and with all the craziness afterward, she'd for-gotten to switch it back. No wonder she didn't hear her alarm or her calls. Six of them were from Rand, between seven and seven-fifteen, and one was from Ginny. She listened to Ginny's message, "Checking to make sure we're still on for today. You don't have to call back—see you at eleven." Nicole deleted the message.

"Nicole? Listen, if you need time, I can come back." She turned from the bedside table, and he was leaning into her bedroom, his arm raised, braced against the doorjamb. Nicole had been told many times that she had a good poker face, and she hoped it was working now. He was relaxed, confident, with a quiet authority, staring openly at Nicole.

"Ummm ... I was checking my phone," and she held it up as if she needed to support her statement. "It was still on DND from a meeting I had yesterday, which explains no alarm. My entire yesterday was filled with firsts," Nicole said a little clumsily, nervous at his ease in her home.

A high-pitched beep came from the kitchen. "The coffee is done. Would you like a hot cup?" she asked playfully. He shifted, barely, to allow her passage, and she felt his warmth radiating the small cove as she slid past. Her full, tangled, "bed-head" look with no makeup complemented the shorts that exposed her long, strong, runner's legs and had she turned seconds sooner to hand him the steaming mug, she would've caught his appreciative glance.

"I don't want to mess up your schedule." Nicole embraced her cup with both hands and blew into it before taking a sip. "It won't take me long to get ready, but if you need to leave, I understand. Just take my car, and I'll get a ride in later."

Rand moved to the French doors to look out toward the beach. The morning waves broke softly against the shore, barely seeking attention through the cottony air floating above them; still, they chased away the family of seagulls walking the wet sand. When he turned back to Nicole, he locked eyes, and before he spoke, she nodded, knowing what he was going to say. "I'll wait."

CHAPTER 25

"What time is Detective Graves expecting us?" Nicole didn't care about the detective or whether they were on time. She was simply making conversation as she drove along the Pacific Coast Highway because Rand Coleman was riding shotgun, half-turned in his seat, watching her.

"Whenever we get there. I called him while you were in the shower, so we're good."

He called while I was in the shower. It was a simple comment but so personal. Nicole adjusted the collar of her shirt.

"Penny for your thoughts," he said, and Nicole whirled around at him, accidently jerking the wheel and hitting the shoulder of the highway. They bounced along a few more feet before she completely righted the car.

"You've been through a lot in the past twenty-four hours, Nicole, how about I drive?"

The past twenty-four hours had done far more than he would know ever know. They had honed her. Nicole's edge was sharpening. The only problem she was having this morning was the scrutiny of his deep, penetrating gaze. She thought, *If he drives, he can't watch me so closely.* So, without answering, she pulled into the parking lot of Zeke's Restaurant and pivoted the car around to face the entrance before stopping. And that's when they saw it. The white utility van from yesterday. It passed Zeke's, then slowed and pulled over, stopping on the side of the road. It didn't have the magnetic signs, but it did have the same thick scratch on the right back panel.

The driver got out to check the left rear tire. With a medium-brown ball cap covering his head, he positioned himself to watch oncoming cars from under the brim, and as Rand and Nicole pulled onto the road, the driver was suddenly satisfied with his tire. As soon as the Range Rover passed, he maneuvered his vehicle back onto the highway.

Nicole played cool as she unfastened her seatbelt and twisted behind her, reaching to the floorboard for her camera bag. She hurriedly scanned through the pictures from yesterday. Stopping on one and enlarging the image, she then switched to camera mode and turned to face the rear of the car. The zoom lens on her camera gave her a clear look. The passenger was a large man with shaggy, sandy-brown hair, but there was no mistaking the driver. It was the same man who was in her pictures from Gramble Street. Rand heard the shutter click.

Why would they be here? How did they find me? Pulling her shades up to hold her hair back, she looked closer at the pictures from yesterday, enlarging each one. Her answer was in one of the last shots, the one of the van from the rear. Reflected in the mirror on the passenger side was the woman's image, staring directly into the camera. Directly at Nicole.

"Everything okay?" Rand asked, puling Nicole from her thoughts.

"Just remembered something." She offered a phony grin. Drawing from years of conditioning, Nicole kept cool and engaged Rand while monitoring the van behind them. Thinking. "So, tell me about you ... Rand. Is that short for Randall?"

Rand's eyes moved from Nicole, to the road ahead, to behind, and to the cars passing alongside. His awareness had amped up, and traffic was heavier, but he was still working the crooked smile when he said, "Randolph."

"Ahhh ... Well ... Rand was a good choice." Nicole let out a light laugh. She glanced in the mirror again, then around to the sea of cars they were swimming in, but the van wasn't in clear sight. Absently she said, "I'm assuming you spell it with 'ph' and not an 'f' since you don't look German ... more like Black Irish."

"I'm impressed." He tilted his head, nodding once toward her. Cool. Appreciative.

"Eh, too much study time left me with a lot of unnecessary data roaming around in my head. I have to use it sometime." She saw his head kick back with a small laugh, and she was grinning too when she checked the side mirror. Still no van. Looking back at the photos in the camera, Nicole quickly picked all the ones from the day before and transferred them from the digital camera over to her cell phone. When she finished, she flipped around in her seat to put the camera back and used the moment to scan the entire field of cars. With miles of big rigs, large delivery trucks, and six lanes, it was easy for a simple van to hide. She had lost them. For now.

They rode in compatible silence, and with her occasional glance over her shoulder to see if the van was still around, she couldn't help but steal a look at the driver. The way his bicep pushed against the fabric of his sport coat while he casually draped his left hand over the steering wheel. He wasn't overly muscular, just fit, and he wore it like an accessory. *And his physical appearance isn't even his best feature ... it's that calmness ... like he silently knows he's in control ... even a little mysterious ... alluring.*

"Tell me more about you," Nicole said. "I mean your work. At The Rock. Like, do the celebrities that profit from the photoshoots, do they really volunteer there? Like Mike?" She brushed her hand through her hair.

He smiled, but didn't answer right away, so she nudged him. "Yes, some of the celebrities actually come back. We've been fortunate with the talent that've donated their time; faces that the kids actually recognize ... and respect. Actors, comedians, recording artists. We have a few regulars that come every other week, some come once a month, then others at random, just whenever they can. During the week after school, however, you can usually find a member of the Clippers basketball team on the court. It's cool."

Nicole waited for more. "Please. Go on."

"Actually ... we're here," Rand said, exiting the 105 freeway, jolting Nicole back into their current situation. She checked behind them, but the white van didn't come off the ramp or go by on the overpass. Somewhere along the route, they had actually lost them. At least she had their tag number.

* * *

After Martha Vaughn had screamed at Fuzz the day before about the pretty brunette in the Range Rover taking their picture, he had written down her license number from the front tag and swore to check it out. He still had access in the department and within hours had a name and an address in Malibu. Unfortunately, the brunette was the famed news celebrity from KDLA, so they had no choice but to pay her a visit, stay on her, and find out what she knew. The following morning, Fuzz and his partner, the burley Harp Grisholm, were waiting outside her home when the black Ranger Rover left her drive and pulled onto the Pacific Coast Highway. Following her down the road, once again Nicole was aiming her camera toward them. "Well, there's our answer!" Grisholm was nodding toward Nicole. "She's started with the camera again... she's on to us, Fuzz!"

Fuzz hit the brakes and backed into the congestion of cars for coverage, his face tense. He was stingy with his reaction, but said, "Well, now we know." They drove for a quarter of a mile before Fuzz spoke again. "We gotta take care of her ... and get that camera."

"But how?" Grisholm looked from Fuzz to the traffic in front of them.

Fuzz flipped the brown bill of his cap backward. "I need to think."

The heavy traffic was great for hiding; however, that worked both ways. Soon after merging onto the 405, they lost the black SUV, and Fuzz was beating the steering wheel, furious at himself and every other driver around them for his circumstances. Grisholm waited until his partner was calmer, before offering, "Should we cruise by the police station that covers Chastang's neighborhood? Make sure that's not where they're goin'?"

Fuzz took off the cap and rubbed his bald head. *Why didn't I think of that?* Speechless at his partner, he looked at Grisholm and merely asked, "Are you growing a beard?"

When they passed the South Street Station, they saw the black Range Rover squeezed into the small, crammed lot. "Lucky, call H-Man." Fuzz used the nickname he had for Harp Grisholm, relief in his voice, but within seconds it flipped. "You realize she could be handing them our picture right now! Someone in there is liable to identify me ... I can't just sit here and do nothing!"

The chartreuse coat coming down the street was so loud, it announced Good Oscar's approach well before he arrived, and Fuzz's face altered into an evil grin. "And opportunity has arrived."

"What? Why? Who's that?" Grisholm asked.

"Good Oscar. Use to hang near the Seventy-Seventh. Always talking to himself, telling himself to be good—like correcting a child. The hapless and homeless could be our ticket today!" He popped open the console and removed a Taurus 9mm. It was one of many handguns he had taken from a drug bust years ago, the serial number ground off and impossible to trace back to him. With a gloved hand he cleaned off the prints, then drove the van onto Buckman Lane, put it in park, and ran to the corner in time to catch Good Oscar, walking in step with him. "Hey, I've been looking for you."

"Really? Me?" Oscar said, showing a smile of fairly white teeth, considering the years of living on the street. The fanned-out bristle heads of a couple of old toothbrushes were peeking from the top of his soiled shirt pocket. His own peculiar obsession.

"Yeah, and you've been taking really good care of your teeth, I see."

"Yes, yes." His head bobbed. "Brush after every meal and don't forget to floss. After every meal and don't forget to floss. Four out of five dentists ..."

"Wonderful," Fuzz cut him off. "Oscar, your smile deserves to be in a movie!"

With Oscar on board and in motion, Fuzz ran back to the van.

CHAPTER 26

All the seats in the reception area of the South Street police station were taken, as well as any of the cool air that might have escaped from the rattling air vents overhead. Everyone was on their cell phone trying to talk above each other, and the officer at the front desk was straining loudly to explain the booking process to a couple of angry women who wanted to see their relative. When Nicole and Rand walked in, the officer recognized her from the news and motioned Nicole to the side door, where he buzzed them back.

"Celebrity definitely has its advantages," said Rand, and placed his hand in the small of her back, accompanying her into a long corridor. Nicole had never been to this particular station but was familiar enough with the basic layout after years of interaction with the LAPD, so she led the way past offices and departments, until arriving at the busy workstations, where Detective Graves was on the phone at his desk. They took a seat in two of the few empty chairs against the front wall and waited.

"Ms. Portman," Detective Graves said as he approached them, then nodded to Rand. "Pastor. Let's get started," he said, making his way back to his desk. Graves looked more like a retired linebacker than a police officer, with his short, cropped hair and black mustache. It was hard to tell how old he was. His skin was dark brown and silky smooth, except for the few pockmarks along his cheeks. It reminded Nicole of the Agent Orange effect on Vietnam veterans, but he didn't look old enough for that. Nicole noticed a protein bar wrapper on his desk and another in the wire trash-basket, which meant that's probably all that was sustaining him; a clear warning not to antagonize him.

There were no preliminaries. "I'm figuring a basic overdose here with the Chastang case, since it's obvious she was a heavy user, but what I'm not getting is why her place was a revolving door yesterday. Word is, she had a visitor before you. Then you show. I'm still trying to figure that one out. You want to enlighten me, Ms. Portman?" he asked.

Nicole kept her purse strap on her shoulder. She wasn't planning on staying long. "The address was a lead. A witness to an accident, and I didn't realize until I was already inside that it had to be bogus information."

"So you're saying she invited you in, not knowing who you were or why you were there since she wasn't your source after all. Then, she walked into another room and collapsed? You want to talk about bogus information, Ms. Portman? You're giving me a line of it, so I'll ask again. Why were you there?"

"I know it sounds weak, but that's all I have." Nicole didn't flinch at the detective's scowl.

"There was evidence Theresa Chastang had once used her house to cook up meth. People in meth houses are paranoid, Ms. Portman. She wouldn't have welcomed you."

"Well," Nicole said, leaning in, "it was obvious something was wrong with her, I just didn't know how bad." She broke eye contact with the detective and looked down at the printout in front of him. He flipped it over, not taking his eyes from her. When she looked back, neither acknowledged the dance. She kept talking. "She was frail, detective, but even so ..." Nicole's head moved slowly side to side. "Something else was going on. When she stepped out of the room, I wanted to leave ... to just get out while I could, but I had to check on her ... and ... that's when I found her."

Graves stared at her for several beats, then he started typing into his computer. "And how about you, Reverend? What were you doing there? Were you going to see Theresa Chastang, too?" Graves stopped typing and, with his voice growing louder, said, "I want to know why I was the only sucker in town that didn't know how popular Theresa Chastang was!"

Rand smiled at the detective. "The Rock is near that neighborhood. I heard the emergency sirens and followed them out of concern. When I recognized Nicole's SUV, I stopped."

"Everybody's got an answer. So," he said, addressing Nicole again. "What do you know about the children?"

"Excuse me?" Nicole didn't have to act shocked; it was genuine.

"Some of the neighbors said she had children, but we didn't find any signs of them."

"I didn't see any, either. I can't imagine a child living in that filth."

Detective Roma Ortega walked over to Graves's desk, addressing only her partner. "We have a neighbor's statement. Chastang's brother is the leader of the local gang, SOTIS." She and Graves shared a look, and his lips puckered out as he ground his teeth. She handed him a copy of the statement, then kept moving toward the coffee machine. "Want one?" she asked him, as she poured a cup of caffeine to sustain her another hour. Her straight, black hair was pulled tight in a long ponytail, and although her name suggested a Hispanic heritage, she had the striking features of a Native American.

"Nah, I'm coffee-ed out," he answered, then addressed the two sitting in front of his desk. "But how rude of me; would you two care for a cup of coffee?" Still sarcastic, as though everything wrong with his day was their fault.

"No, thank you," came from Rand, but Nicole only shook her head while trying to discreetly type "SOTIS" into her phone. Graves was glaring at her when she looked up, and she barreled past it.

"Why is her connection to SOTIS of significance?"

Graves didn't respond. After a few beats he stood. "Thank you for coming in. Remember, Ms. Portman, you're the last person to see Theresa Chastang alive, so until we have confirmation on cause of death, don't leave town." Suddenly eager to be rid of the newswoman, he turned to Rand. "Reverend, good luck with the work you do. Maybe your place can make a difference, keep 'em from ending up here."

"I appreciate it, Detective. Stop in sometime and let me introduce you around so they can see the positive side of law enforcement." He shook Graves's hand and was releasing his grip just as they heard the gunshot. Rand pivoted toward Nicole, who was already headed to the floor behind Graves's desk. Graves pulled his Glock from his holster and, crouching, disappeared around the wall, then down the hall toward the front of the building, where the shots were coming from. Shouts, scuffling, and furniture scraping across the floor filled their ears, then a stark quiet. Then murmuring.

Nicole popped up and, with her cell phone in hand, flipped over the paper Ortega had dropped on Graves's desk and took three rapid photos before flipping it back and straightening her jacket.

A low voice behind her pressed close. "Intriguing." The same minty voice from The Rock. She didn't turn around. And she didn't answer.

Detectives Graves and Ortega came back into view with a wild-haired man wearing a bright green jacket. His hands were zip-tied in front of him, and he was smiling. "I'm gonna be in the movies!" he kept repeating, looking around. Ortega escorted him toward the back for processing, while Graves and another cop came toward the desks, steamed.

"... said it was a UPS guy because he had a brown ball cap—told him we were filming a movie, and his part was to shoot at the ceiling with the 'fake' gun he gave him!"

The other officer went straight to his desk, wearing his anger in his walk. "I'll take this one, Graves! Oscar's deranged, but he's never been a threat, and now we gotta lock him up!" He grabbed up keys and his jacket and pushed his chair in. "Somebody had to see something! I'll find the smart-ass who did it!"

They had mentally dismissed Rand and Nicole, who slipped out unnoticed. The ride to The Rock was a quiet, but intense, few miles. When they arrived, Rand drove her Range Rover straight to the front of the building and parked in a handicap spot closest to the door. "Seriously?" Nicole asked. Motioning to the sign, "You can't leave my car here."

"Hmmm," was all Rand said. He exited the driver's side.

"I'm leaving, anyway. I have an eleven o'clock appointment in Beverly Hills." Nicole stepped out to get her keys and to switch places with Rand, but he locked the doors with the key fob, then, with his hand on her back, walked her toward the building.

"I have to make a quick call, then I'll go with you." He was moving quickly and glanced back, scanning the parking lot while opening the door for her.

"That's not necessary. We've already made our appearance at the station, so I'm good to go ... unless you need a ride to get your car," Nicole argued. "I've already taken up too much of your time."

"Good morning, Pastor Coleman," said Bethany as they entered the building.

"Good morning to you, Bethany. You look exceptionally lovely today," Rand said, which was surprising, because they passed the woman at lightning speed, and Rand didn't look her way. Nicole looked back. Bethany *did* look different. Like she had a makeover.

"Is there anything to eat? Ms. Portman hasn't had breakfast yet."

"Absolutely. I'll bring it to your office!" And Bethany hurried away.

Nicole moved alongside Rand and, although he revealed little, there was no question he was driven; in control, as always, without discarding his charm or calm manner. He unlocked his office and stepped inside, alone, checking the room before bringing Nicole in. "Make yourself at home. Bethany will be here shortly with coffee and something to sustain us. I have just a few things to take care of."

"I'll wait for the coffee, but after that, I'm out of here." He was already on the landline phone on his desk, retrieving messages and making notes, so he placed a finger in the air, as if asking her to wait one moment. When he finished, he walked around his desk to where Nicole was standing and closed the gap between them. He lifted a piece of hair that had fallen across her forehead, and her breath caught.

"Pastor Coleman, I have coffee," Bethany said, after rapping on the door.

Rand didn't move immediately, as he allowed his gaze to move past the mystical grey eyes and follow the contour of her face. He brushed it slightly with the back of his fingers that still held the single strand of hair. His eyes longed to talk, and not just about the story she was working on and the apparent danger involved.

"Pastor?" Bethany called out again.

Still engaged by the intensity between them, Rand spoke only for Nicole to hear, "We have things to discuss." He let another beat pass, then he stepped away, breaking contact, and opened the door for Bethany to enter with the tray. "Please, eat something, and I'll be ready to leave in ten minutes." He fixed a coffee and left the room.

Nicole paced in front of the photos on his wall. In one picture Rand was surrounded by six or seven kids, and they were all laughing. It was infectious. Her breathing picked up, and she shook her head.

It would be so easy to let him come with me today, but Rand doesn't simply join; he saturates. And one day he'll be gone too, and then what? That kind of void breaks people.

Nicole hurriedly wrapped a couple of pastries in a napkin, shoved them into her purse, and grabbed her keys off his desk. Then, with a fresh cup of coffee in hand, she was gone.

CHAPTER 27

"Have a blessed day, Ms. Portman." Nicole's step faltered. She had made sure no one was in the hall, but there he was. The custodian.

"Gabriel, right?"

He nodded with a smile.

Regarding him with the same recognition as before, Nicole's curiosity slowed her step. "You're so familiar. Have I interviewed you before? Possibly a witness from one of my reports?" They both turned at the sound of the car alarm. She knew it was hers. She recognized it from the few times she'd set it off, and the incident at the police station raised the probability.

Forgetting about Gabriel or the consequences, Nicole darted out the door, scanning the parking lot as she ran, and, ducking to look under cars, saw nothing out of the ordinary. She let the alarm keep sounding as she cautiously approached her SUV. The busted back window was obvious, so before circling her car, she knelt and checked underneath for leaks or any other tampering, including her tires. There was no other damage or activity, so Nicole pushed the button to silence the alarm, but quickly jumped into the driver's seat and locked the doors, since the possibility of the van people being nearby was high. Within seconds, Nicole had the Range Rover leaving the community center, getting distance from everything there.

All the way to Beverly Hills she watched for a tail. Utility vans are a common work vehicle during business hours and now that she was looking for them, they were everywhere.

It was ten thirty when Nicole got to the Beverly Center. She rode through the parking structure, circling each level until she was confident she was alone, then decided to park on the top floor, backing into an end space against the concrete wall so her broken back window wouldn't be seen. Sitting in the car too long would leave her vulnerable, so she hurriedly checked her phone for the downloaded pictures of the van, found one with the license plate visible, then wrote down the number.

There weren't many things to remove from the car, but Nicole started with the garage-door opener and car registration, stuffing them into her large tote. The console held a couple of CDs, an extra phone charger, and, when she saw the small automatic digital camera, her entire being changed with a sickening realization. "My camera!" Nicole jerked around to the back floor, looking for the bag that held her professional camera with three lenses, including the new zoom she had gotten only last month. "GONE! All of it gone!" She froze in place, swallowing down bile that was threatening to rise, then slammed the door closed.

No one was parked nearby ... only a few other spaces taken, but she still scanned the area, seething. "Stupid thugs. You always mess up when you start trying to cover up ... that's usually how you're caught ... and whatever you're guilty of, you *will* be caught!" The tapping of her heels echoed a lone sound of determination across the concrete. "I'm sure they have no clue that digital cameras are wireless, so they'll feel safe for now."

Nicole had a new sense of empowerment, but still jumped with a start when she heard the engine of a vehicle approaching. She pressed the call button at the elevator as the front end of a utility van crested the ramp. The ping of the call button was loud and welcoming, but Nicole waited to see if it was *THEM.* The van stopped. The sun caused a glare across the windshield, and she couldn't see who was driving. It turned. She was pumped and angry, but she wasn't stupid. She got inside the lift. The concrete and steel construction overexaggerated the tug and squeak of her ride to the third level of the mall.

"Welcome to Plush," the beautiful young blonde said to Nicole, guiding her inside. Eucalyptus greeted her, reminding her of a childhood vacation in Palm Desert with her parents. A happy time. Her racing pulse dropped a couple digits, and the young voice asked, "May I help you?"

"I'm meeting Ginny Vinsant."

"Of course. Follow me." They made their way through the makeshift paradise to a small lounge, where candles added a soothing illumination to the soft lighting. The soundscape music pinged and hummed. "Please make yourself comfortable while you wait, and let me know if I can get you anything."

Left alone, Nicole said to no one, "A massage," and rubbed the back of her neck.

"That could be arranged."

She spun around to find Ginny standing beside a curtained alcove. "I'm sorry! I hope I didn't startle you," Ginny said, smiling as she took a few steps into the room. "I've been in Sue's office waiting and saw you from her monitor. Thank you for coming to meet me."

"I understand you can't be seen with me in public, but," Nicole waved her hands to address their meeting place, "isn't this a little over the top?"

The room was furnished with carpet that tempted Nicole to remove her shoes, not just from courtesy, but because she wanted to feel that cushy, thick pile under her bare feet. Two ivory club chairs faced each other with a sleek, stainless table between them. A crystal pitcher, filled with iced water and cucumbers, was on the table with two chilled goblets and a platter of freshly cut kiwi and pineapple. Every detail was intentional. All for Ginny's meeting. She sat in one of the chairs, offering the other to Nicole. "I don't mean to act mysterious," Ginny said, "but Tom has me followed, and since it's escalated recently, I'm not sure yet if he shadows me into buildings."

Nicole didn't sit right away. "Why do you think Tom has you followed?"

"I don't think. I know. Has been for several months. A tan Ford Explorer. At first, I thought Explorers were becoming popular again, and it was normal to see them everywhere, but ... because of the way I drive, he couldn't help being exposed." Ginny gave Nicole an impish grin, as she said from the corner of her mouth, "I'm not the best navigator. I rush out of our drive without planning ahead and eventually pull over somewhere to look at my GPS. Keeping up with me without being noticed would be close to impossible."

"If that's so, it could be anybody. They could be watching Tom, too." Nicole leaned against the chair, still opting not to sit.

Ginny shook her head, "No. If they were investigating my husband, they would be more professional, discreet. Maybe more people assigned, so I wouldn't have noticed so easily." She looked at Nicole, but didn't hold eye contact; instead, she looked at the floor, her hands, and the door as she explained her theory. "And it's not paparazzi. They would've gotten their pictures by now and moved on to the next flavor of the month.

No, it has to be a private investigator, which makes sense." She looked sideways at Nicole. Her certainty lowered, watching for Nicole's reaction. "Tom's very controlling, you see. And the elections are coming up. It's just ... it's become more noticeable, you know, since last week. Since my accident. So, it has to be Tom."

Nicole's expression didn't change, and with an opportunity to peek into the intimate world of Tom Vinsant, she jumped on it. "And you accept that from your spouse? Has he always been like this?"

Ginny mindlessly groomed a lock of hair framing her face. Pulling on it, then slicking it behind her ear. Her nervous tic. Nicole recognized it from the Bacara a couple days ago and from TV interviews she had seen her on. It was either insecurity, or she was simply stalling, so she waited. Nicole poured herself a glass of water from the crystal pitcher, and sat across from Ginny, who finally answered, "Well, when we met, my very first year at Berkeley, things were different. He was a junior—an 'upperclassman'—and everyone on campus knew him, so I was beyond flattered he even noticed me.

"Tom was always so sure of himself, just as he is now ... I guess it was much more attractive on a young college student." Ginny's head tilted with a slight twitch of a smile. "Anyway, when he graduated, he came to Venice Beach and shared a condo with an acquaintance a couple years his senior. Said this guy would be a 'great connection,' and he started his career while I stayed at Berkeley to finish my degree."

Ginny paused and sat erect, looking to Nicole. "Actually, it was Sidney Drummond, your boss." It was good Nicole had swallowed the water she'd been sipping before she heard this, or it would've certainly sprayed all over Ginny's freshly applied makeup. She looked down to where her bag was and diverted her eyes until she recovered.

If Ginny noticed Nicole's reaction, she didn't show it. "My parents expected me to get my master's degree, but I couldn't stand being away from Tom. I moved down here as soon as I graduated college and the next month found out I was pregnant," Ginny said. Her brows pulled together, then she spoke without looking at Nicole. "Tom's family were such strict Catholics, he whisked me off to Las Vegas, and we were married before we told them about the baby. It wasn't a very romantic proposal, but at the time I was so crazy about him I didn't care." Sorrow filled her big, brown eyes. "But losing the baby changed everything."

Soft music that was barely audible before suddenly seemed inappropriately loud when Ginny stopped. She swallowed hard. Took a sip of water. "Miscarrying in the fourth month, I was so depressed, I don't really remember the details of that first year. Tom was still Tom, of course ... driven," she said with a gentle smile. "His family owned a lot of land in the northwest part of Los Angeles County, and he got into land development. He was brilliant, and every deal he closed was intoxicating for him, so I simply let Tom and his ego soar while I lived in his shadow, which was easy to do, since I was cowering around feeling sorry for myself. I tried to conceive another child, to give our lives more purpose, but I guess it was never meant for me."

Ginny accepted the tissue Nicole handed her and touched it to her wet cheek. "I've never accomplished anything, Nicole, so to sum it up, yes, I guess Tom has always controlled me. And I let him. It was my own fault. I let my degree waste away to become someone's shadow."

Getting way more than expected, and not wanting to hear the Vinsants humanized, Nicole moved the conversation forward. "Forgive me for changing the subject, but we need to talk about the accident."

"Of course. I'm so sorry." Ginny composed herself quickly.

"No worries, let's go back to that evening. Close your eyes if you need to. Try to remember everything. Even what was playing on the radio. Sometimes that helps."

Their surroundings were peaceful. The music still seemed a little loud, but Ginny did as Nicole asked. "It was Tuesday evening and it had just turned dark, so ... I guess after eight. I had been to a fundraising dinner. I left early to swing by the center and pick up a flute for repair. I took the exit off the 110 and was coming down the ramp pretty fast. I was rushing so I could get home before Tom, and he wouldn't know. Out of nowhere, children appeared." The private meeting room at Plush was perfect for meditation. Play by play, Ginny delivered the events. "I knew I was going to hit them." Her head went from side to side. "I slammed my foot on the brake and jerked the wheel of the car. I spun, and I couldn't tell what was happening. It was dark. The landscape swirled past my view. Tires squealing. Crashing sounds. Horns." Her eyes opened. The two women faced each other in the matching chairs. Ginny said softly, "I was told I finally stopped when I went side-long into the light post, and some of the sounds were from the cars behind me."

Nicole nodded in acknowledgement. "When your car finally stopped moving, do you remember anything? Were you awake then? Or had you been knocked out already? Think. It's very important."

Ginny closed her eyes again, and Nicole waited, patiently, letting Ginny revisit every detail she could. Ginny's mouth worked silently, the space between her brows crinkled. "I'm sorry. I'm trying. I'm picturing a dark van. Like those tall ones Mercedes makes. The travel kind. It appears in my mind from nowhere, just like the kids did, but I must have been seeing things by then." Ginny let out a nervous laugh.

"Why?"

Ginny shook her head.

"What?"

"You won't believe me."

"We've come this far, Ginny. Tell me," Nicole pushed.

"That's when I saw Batman."

CHAPTER 28

"Ginny, do you take prescription drugs? Like for headaches or depression?"

"You mean, do I hallucinate!" Her yellow hair tossed around her head as she shook it. "I knew this would happen! I shouldn't have told you."

Nicole had wrapped up the meeting at Plush Spa shortly after Ginny's reference to Batman, but when she told Ginny she had another lead to check on, Ginny followed Nicole to the garage. "I know, drive my car! Well—it's not actually mine, it's a loaner until I get my new one, so that's even better. You won't feel bad if we mess it up in a car chase or something." Ginny was on Nicole's heels, grinning with excitement over the prospect of that happening.

Nicole picked up her pace, but when she approached her Range Rover, she stopped and took in the reality of her back window. It was gone. What Ginny was proposing *would* be convenient. She swallowed her stubbornness, and they dropped Nicole's SUV off at the dealership.

Nicole was driving east on I-10 with Ginny riding shotgun and the business card she'd found at Theresa Chastang's house on the dash. It was her next move; actually, her only one, since the registration check on the white utility van had led nowhere, and the photos she had of the van driver and the brunette passenger couldn't help her identify them. They would be useless until she was ready to turn them over to the authorities, but she couldn't until she had more to go on. So, with Ginny in tow, she was on her way to Smiling Tribes Foster Care and Martha Smith.

The loaner car was a red BMW, and Nicole was behind the wheel, enjoying the response of the sports car; however, the pleasure didn't outweigh the close confinement with her passenger. Nicole didn't hide her annoyance. "I thought you had someone following you. Won't they see me driving your car and tell Tom?" She jabbed.

"Again, you don't believe me."

"It's who I am," Nicole said flatly. "I question." She always wore shades while driving. She had on her Ray Bans today, and they didn't cover up much of her face, but they didn't have to. She showed no emotion behind them, still processing Ginny's comments from Plush Salon.

Ginny looked out the window. The sun's reflection hit her from somewhere along the infinite stream of metal that overcrowded the freeway, and she pushed her own sunglasses snugly against the bridge of her nose. "You wouldn't be the first to question my mental stability, especially since Tom has planted that seed with the doctors in the hospital. It's his insurance in case I do anything to endanger his reelection." With a bite, she said, "So, it's not just my marriage I'm risking here."

Nicole cut her eyes at Ginny, then back to the road. "Exactly my point. So why chance coming with me now? What changed?"

"Didn't you hear my purging at Plush? I haven't voiced those things out loud before. It was so humiliating ... but ... also cathartic! I've been cowering on the sidelines of life! *Tom's life.* Hiding!" Ginny's hand went to her bangs to tug at them, but she stopped and instead, she shook her hair out and said, "At this very moment, I actually feel free. Really free." She reached to open the sunroof. "You mind?"

Nicole shook her head, which Ginny interpreted to mean Nicole didn't mind, so she opened the sunroof. The next few miles they were left to their own thoughts with limited interruptions from the navigation system, then it announced: "In four hundred yards you have reached your destination on the right." They had arrived. Ginny turned it off.

To freshen her lipstick, Ginny pulled the visor down and used the vanity mirror. Her voice was soft, reflective, when she said, "You might not be so fond of this arrangement, but with you on board, I'm really not frightened." She looked at Nicole. "So, whatever happens ... thank you for taking this job." She turned back to the mirror to close it and startled Nicole when she shouted, "KEEP GOING! Don't pull in!"

The words were a command, so Nicole kept going. "What? You just said you're not frightened, and now you're screaming! What is it?"

"The Explorer is behind us. I don't care if they know I'm with you. Seriously! I don't!" She was looking at Nicole, then back to the vanity mirror. "But I doubt you want anyone tipped off to our destination."

Nicole was not an eye-roller, but she made an exception before looking first into the rearview mirror, then the side. The boulevard they were on had two north lanes, two south, and one in the middle for turning. The only vehicle that fit Ginny's description was in the outer lane about four cars back. "Okay, Ginny, let's see." They were driving in the right lane and stayed even with the car next to them, so no one could pass. Coming up on a traffic signal, Nicole slowed, hoping it would turn yellow, but no luck. She tried something else. If she kept to a crawl, all the cars in the left lane would pass and, eventually, so would the Ford Explorer. So, Nicole crept along in the right lane. Somewhere behind them a car was honking, and cars were passing, just as she wanted. All except the Ford Explorer. It stayed back. *Hmmm.* Another light was coming up, and this time luck was on her side; green was turning to yellow. She slowed significantly, ignoring the blaring sounds from the angry driver behind her, who would have made the light if not for Nicole. Ginny looked at Nicole, then looked behind them. She worked at keeping composed, but she had a pinched look on her face.

Nicole inched forward and, as she anticipated, the light turned red. It would take perfect timing for Nicole to flush him out. The cross traffic would start, and within seconds her window would close. She had to be precise. Nicole watched. The cars were in motion. She had to go, quickly. She kicked the accelerator ... and jetted for the small gateway that the intersecting cars were closing. And they honked. Vicious honking. It came from every direction as she made it through. Barely. She pulled to the curb and watched the Ford Explorer to see if there was a reaction.

"Well, what do you know," she said. The Explorer pulled around the outside of the cars in front of it, using the empty turn lane to get to the intersection. Edging forward, he threatened to cross, but he didn't have an opening; traffic was brutal, and Nicole didn't wait around to see how he was going to get through it. She continued and took a right at the next corner, then right again, and floored the accelerator until she saw a sign blinking "15 Minute Oil Change." Wheeling the BMW into the parking lot, she pulled around the back of the changing bay. They were fortunate; the building was a crimson red, and at least it helped to hide their candy-apple sports car long enough for the Explorer to go by.

Nicole waited a few minutes, and when she didn't see him circle back, she pulled out onto the road and took another right to get redirected to Smiling Tribes.

"How long did you say this has been going on?" Nicole asked Ginny.

"About the last five months, but like I said, it's intensified since my accident."

"Hmmm ..." was all Nicole offered. She found a parking space in the lot next to Smiling Tribes, got the business card off the dash, and slipped it into her pocket for quick access. "I won't be long," she said, stepping out of the car, but Ginny followed her.

"I'll go in with you," Ginny said. "No one in there knows who Senator Vinsant's wife is! You're the one they'll notice ... you're the celebrity."

Nicole stopped. "We have one shot and can't afford to mess up. I know you're footing the bill here, but just NO."

"I'm married to Tom. I have a PI following me around. You don't think I can handle this? Leave your shades on, and let me do the talking."

"A catharsis, huh? I'm thinking multiple personalities," Nicole muttered under her breath, but she didn't have to worry about anyone hearing, since Ginny was already inside.

"Actually, I'm thinking of fostering a few children, you know, if there are siblings that don't want to be separated, that would be perfect." Nicole heard her, already in full animated conversation with the employee, and Ginny was good. Everyone was watching her, and Nicole went unnoticed, sliding over to the various racks of brochures, perusing them while getting a feel for the place. Ginny had been asked to take a seat to wait for the next available agent.

There was a glass partition so the conversations in the offices couldn't be overheard, and Nicole saw a middle-aged woman with dark hair leaning over a coworker's desk, saying something to her. When the woman straightened, her eyes made contact with Nicole's, and recognition registered on the woman's face. To hide her own surprise, Nicole turned abruptly, putting her cell phone up to her ear as though she were accepting a call, and meandered toward Ginny, keeping her back to the glass wall. "Is there a woman coming out from the back offices? Dark hair pulled back? Mid-forties?"

Ginny casually glanced up from her magazine, then looked back down and said, "She's not coming through the door, but she's pretending not to look at you from the window."

"She was at the Chastang house yesterday before me ..." Nicole immediately caught herself—not knowing how Ginny would respond could jeopardize their situation.

"Now she's retreated down a hallway," Ginny said, and kept turning pages. "I've lost sight of her."

"There has to be an exit. She could be leaving." Nicole casually took another brochure, then walked out the front entrance.

"Mrs. Brunswick's ready for you now," the receptionist said.

Looking from the receptionist to the door, Ginny said, "I'm going to have to call her back. I've got her card. Thank you." She ran out to catch up with Nicole.

They heard a car crank and within seconds saw the reverse lights from a Honda Civic, but by the time the Civic left the parking lot, they weren't far behind. "As soon as we're close enough, write down the tag number," Nicole said. The Civic was racing in and out of traffic. "If I wasn't already convinced she had something to do with Theresa Chastang's death, this would do it for me. A legit agent for Smiling Tribes would've confronted me back at the office and asked why I was taking her picture, or demand to see some credentials."

Ginny was quiet, and Nicole glanced over to see her writing. She had gotten the tag number. "Where'd she go?" Ginny asked, when she looked up.

"Traffic is on her side today." Nicole handed Ginny the business card from Theresa Chastang's. "Will you dial this number for me?"

Ginny left the phone on speaker, and it went to voice mail after two rings. "You've reached Mrs. Smith's office. Leave a message and I'll call you back."

"Now look at the brochure I took from Smiling Tribes and check the phone number. Is it the same as the one on the business card for Mrs. Smith?"

"You're genius. No! They're NOT the same! The brochure has a 323 area code and the business card has 818. That's a Valley number. Probably her cell phone."

Nicole was nodding, thinking. "Yeah. And it just rang from an unknown caller, so she probably knows we're onto her. Okay. Dial the brochure number."

Ginny bobbed slightly as it rang, urging someone to answer. "Smiling Tribes Foster Care, may I help you?"

"Yes. Mrs. Smith, please," Nicole said over the car mic.

"I'm sorry, we don't have anyone by that name."

Nicole and Ginny shared a glance. "Hmmm, she's the one who's been helping me, and I really need to speak with her. Actually, I was in your office earlier today and saw her in a blue Honda Civic. She has dark hair."

"I think I know who you're referring to, but her name is not Smith." Ginny's face was pinched, watching Nicole, and she had pen in hand, ready to write down whatever came next from the woman, but all they got was, "Hold the phone while I get the supervisor." As soon as she placed the call on hold, Nicole disconnected.

"So, Mrs. Smith is an alias when she's riding in bogus rental-company vans and hustling foster children. I bet the Gramble Street case isn't even in their system." Nicole was talking out loud and didn't expect or wait for Ginny to answer. She added, "What went so wrong, Mrs. Smith, that you had to overdose Theresa Chastang?"

By the time they got back to the Range Rover dealership, the window was fixed on Nicole's car, and she had caught Ginny up on "Mrs. Smith's" cohorts and why they had stolen her camera. "You can't go home!" Ginny said. "They know where you live!" Her face was animated, "I know! I have a beach house where you can stay."

"Wouldn't that go over well?" Nicole said. "Me, staying at Tom Vinsant's beach house." She smiled at Ginny, "Actually, I see my house as the safer of the two."

"Tom hates it there. He only goes when we're entertaining guests from out of state, and on the other hand, he loves it when I'm there, because I'm secluded and out of his way. We could go together and hide your car in the garage." Ginny pleaded, "I'm sure you could stay at a hotel, but I'd really like the company. This is getting weird, quick."

CHAPTER 29

"Gabriel, did you see Nicole Portman?" Rand asked. Gabriel was next to a pushcart that carried a large plastic water drum and, with the nozzle in hand, he was watering plants in the lobby.

"Yes, sir."

Rand stopped abruptly and turned back to the other man. He slowed his pace and slid his hands in his pockets, appearing composed as he waited for Gabriel to elaborate.

"Her car alarm was sounding, and she ran out to stop it. Then she left." Noting the concern on Rand's face he said, "I watched after her to make sure she was safe."

"Thank you, Gabriel," Rand stared at the custodian a beat or two, thinking of what Nicole had said. *She thought he was familiar. How might she know Gabriel?* He left the thought for now and started toward the exit. All that was left in the spot where he had parked Nicole's SUV were fresh shards of glass along the driver's side.

Rand pulled out his cell phone and dialed up Jocko, who answered with the same upbeat energy he always did. "Hey. What's up?"

"That's what I'm calling you to find out," said Rand. "Got an ID from the pictures, yet?"

"One of them. It's running the second now. You want me to send it to you?" Jocko asked.

"*Great*," Rand said sarcastically, in a hushed tone.

"What is it?" asked Jocko.

Detective Graves and his partner Detective Ortega had parked and were walking toward Rand. He moved away from the empty parking space and started toward the door, diverting them away from the glass, and he said to Jocko, "Something just came up. Let's meet at my place. Give me two hours."

"Copy that," said Jocko.

Rand slid the phone in his pocket and reached his right hand out to greet the detective. "Couldn't wait to take me up on my offer, huh?"

"Actually, we've had an incident around this area, and I'm hoping you can help."

"Involving Theresa Chastang?" Rand asked as he walked them into the building. He looked around for Gabriel, who had been there, but now was nowhere in sight. Not even his watering cart. Bethany was at her desk talking to a group of kids. "Bethany, we'll be in the conference room; please tell Gabriel I'd like to see him when I'm done."

As they walked, Graves said, "No, this has nothing to do with Theresa Chastang." He settled his large frame into a chair along the side of the conference table and continued. "A young black male, described as thin, erratic behavior, with thick, medium-length dreadlocks, was last seen running toward your parking lot yesterday morning. We suspect he's still in the vicinity and considered armed and dangerous."

Rand showed no surprise or recognition. He had given his word to let him try rehab, as long as Nicole was on board, so he wasn't going to give the boy up. But he also couldn't lie. He had to let this one play itself out.

"Well, our doors stay locked, so unless he had a key card, or came with a member, he couldn't have gained entry." Rand stood and pulled out his card to show the detectives. "Someone would have had to let him in. Like I did with you two."

"So that's not unusual, then. He could've come in with someone else."

"True. Other than the erratic behavior that you've described. We have excellent security here, and they wouldn't allow that conduct in the building." Rand shook his head, then slid his hands with his card back into his pants pockets.

"What about video? I noticed cameras on the light posts in the parking lot and on the building. Think we can see yesterday morning?"

"I'll have to check." Rand could find a way to stall for time, but Bethany showed up at the door with the arrangement of pastries leftover from Rand's office and a carafe of coffee.

"I thought you'd enjoy these," she said to the officers, then turned to Rand. "I looked for Gabriel, but evidently he left, Pastor."

"Thank you, Bethany. Is Paula still here?" After she left, Rand explained. "Paula is our in-house techie; we'll know soon if we're able to pull that video up for you. Please, try one of Bethany's desserts. It'd mean a lot to her."

Ortega reached over to get a napkin and one of the pink-colored squares. "You don't have to twist my arm. I'm assuming this is strawberry." Biting into it with obvious delight, she tempted Graves to join her.

They didn't have to wait long. Rand's techie, Paula, walked in shortly after.

"Thank you for coming so quickly. Would it be possible to see security camera video from yesterday morning? Do we even save it?"

"Sure, Brother Coleman," was not what he was hoping she'd say. "I can retrieve it from here if you'd like." She pointed toward the computer at the end of the conference table.

Graves told Paula exactly what they were looking for, and she booted up the computer.

"So, what has this kid done other than seem erratic?" Rand casually asked while they waited.

Detective Ortega spoke up. "It's alleged he assaulted the security personnel of a commercial building a couple of miles south of here, after which he was seen waving a gun and screaming, banging on car windows as he moved northward." She wiped her hands on a napkin and reached for one more pastry.

Paula interrupted. "Okay, Brother Coleman, I have the video for you."

Rand's mouth was dry. He picked up his coffee cup and sipped, then all three walked to stand behind Paula and watch over her shoulder as she worked the digital footage. "Is there an approximate time you're looking for?" Paula asked them.

Ortega was busy chewing so Graves answered, "Between eight and eleven yesterday morning."

Paula ran the footage with ease, fast-forwarding, then slowing when relevant, and the black Range Rover entered the frame. Rand stepped back from the two detectives and moved toward the door. "Excuse me, I need to make an important call," he said.

Both nodded, their eyes never leaving the screen. Out in the hallway, Rand leaned against the wall to wait. Graves would be livid that he held out, and rightly so. He called Nicole's cell phone number, and it went straight to voice mail. "It's Rand. Call me." He held the phone, looking at it a moment longer after ending the call. The door handle of the conference room turned. "And ... we're rollin'," Rand muttered to himself.

"Sorry if we kept you from anything, Pastor. We can show ourselves out. Thanks for your cooperation," said Graves, then Ortega added, "Tell Bethany her cakes were fabulous." She gave him a wave as they fell in step with one another toward the lobby.

The confusion on Rand's face was apparent. Paula was talking to him, but he kept staring after the detectives. "Pastor?" The volume on Paula's normally soft voice turned up. "Pastor? Is everything all right?"

"Can you pull up that same segment you just showed the detectives? I'd like to see the last part that I missed."

"Sure." Paula's brows drew together in concern, and when she pulled up the familiar scene, she was sharing Rand's anxiety without knowing the cause.

The Range Rover came into view and parked. Rand clasped the back of Paula's chair, knuckles tight, and waited. The video was in fast motion, and as others were coming and going to their cars, there was still no activity around Nicole's car. No one exited her car, or walked toward it. Rand's puzzled look gradually switched to anger. He had personally watched her drive into the parking lot yesterday from the front door, and waited only two or three minutes before walking outside and witnessing Timbo getting into her car.

"How much time elapsed in the footage we've just watched?"

She read the specs, "Twenty minutes."

"Thank you, Paula."

Urgency fueled Rand. He was in his truck with a newly printed-out personnel report on the seat next to him, and he called Jocko. "I need you to find out what you can on Gabriel Simon. Late forties, five-ten, medium-brown hair, no apparent accent."

CHAPTER 30

Trader's Car Wash didn't simply tend to your automobile. It was a complex. A sophisticated outfit with a small gourmet market and trendy coffee shop, but it didn't stop there. They capitalized on the relationship Southern Californians had with their animals and offered dog grooming. With a full-service detailing of your car, the dog grooming was free. They sold frozen yogurt for the children and had complimentary massage chairs and shoe-shining. They strived to keep the courtyards pleasant, with fans and misters along the market lights strung high above them. At five o'clock sharp Charles "Fuzz" Keel and Harp Grisholm were there, following instructions from their contact at The Network.

There was so much activity no one noticed the casual meeting of the three men at the chess table, although one of the players completely outdressed the other two. He wore slate-grey trousers and a grey silk crewneck. His putty-colored calfskin loafers and the navy, two-button sport coat were both Hermes, not that the two who joined him would know the difference, and his Swiss-made IWC watch alone cost more than their vehicles combined. He had a regal air about him and didn't hide his disdain of the two in their denim pants and running shoes.

Stuart Greystone moved his bishop eight spaces to capture Fuzz's knight and put it with the other pieces. "I got a call from Martha earlier today."

Fuzz ignored Grisholm's twitching. He kept his eyes on the chessboard and asked, "Yeah? Everything okay?" Without thinking it through, Fuzz went in for an obvious move, his rook ahead four spaces, and took one of Greystone's pawns.

"She was leaving work early with a possible identity issue. Someone who could place her at one of your partnering houses came into her office today, so she's going to take a little time off. I've been assured everything was clean before she left.

"You two will be appointed another bird-dog and your schedule deferred to another team. Get a good rest. If a cleaning is in order, see to it before Friday. Friday you'll get your new assignment." He paused to be sure they understood him, then addressed Fuzz intensely as he placed his fingers on the head of his queen, "Recklessness loses the game." He picked up his queen and placed it in line with Fuzz's king. "Checkmate." He rose from the table, leaving them without another word, and disappeared behind a screen panel near the detailing area.

Fuzz stood, and looking back down at the chess pieces, picked up his king. Turning it over in his hand, he contemplated Greystone's words. *Is the game over?* He shook his head, unsure. He tossed the piece in the air, once, twice, then slammed it on the table.

"What do you think he meant about Martha? Should we call her?" Grisholm asked, jarring Fuzz from his thoughts.

"And what if he's tracing her calls? No. We keep our distance for now and follow up on the two women tonight like we planned. Let's go turn the van in and get my car."

Grisholm followed, his bushy mane shaking up and down, agreeing with his partner, then suddenly he reached out and pulled Fuzz back by the shoulder. "What the ..." Fuzz started, but then saw what had come over Grisholm. His eyes were locked on the television screen across the courtyard. The news was on and so was Martha's picture.

They moved closer to hear. "... An employee of Smiling Tribes Foster Care left work early today and fell victim to a stray bullet during a tragic drive-by shooting. We'll have the complete story ..."

They were in the van, idling on the freeway in the evening rush-hour traffic, but neither seemed to care. It was Grisholm who finally broke the silence and he only had one word: "Greystone."

Fuzz nodded. "We better clean up our mess before he finds out."

It was dusk by the time they parked the van at the company warehouse and climbed into Fuzz's Saturn Sky convertible. They kept the top up and headed to Malibu.

CHAPTER 31

"Stay here. I'm going to throw a few things together," Nicole said to Ginny, encouraging her to stay in her car. After the Smiling Tribes visit and picking up Nicole's newly repaired Range Rover, Ginny had followed Nicole to her beach house and parked the red BMW in the driveway beside her.

However, it didn't work. "I'll help!" Ginny cried, scooting past Nicole in the driveway and jiggling the handle of the gate. It was locked.

The idea of Ginny Vinsant in her house was unsettling. "No, you stay with the cars." But when Nicole saw the perplexed expression coming from Ginny, she softened, adding, "Seriously! That will help us most right now. We don't need anyone else tampering with our vehicles. Lock your car and lay on the horn if you need me."

"All right ... but hurry!" Ginny's pace was much slower returning to her car as the gate closed behind Nicole, automatically locking.

To Nicole, the van people were no longer simple stalkers and camera thieves. She was certain they were Theresa Chastang's killers, and somehow the children were involved. And even if Theresa Chastang's kids were not the same as Ginny's, they had fallen into a dire fate and needed help. However, Ginny mentioned the same black Mercedes van that

Theresa did when the children disappeared. It had to be related; she just wasn't sure how, yet. "And now I've exposed Ginny to a killer!" Nicole was shaking her head, angry at herself, but a sliver of reasoning took over, "However ... if Tom *is* involved, then she already *was* in danger!"

Until she had more to give to authorities, Nicole had to stay under the radar, and the killers had her address, so to keep them both safe, Nicole had found a beach rental, a condo, and rented it under Mike's name. It was within walking distance of Ginny's beach house, where Ginny would leave her car. A perfect illusion for the Ford Explorer.

Working quickly, Nicole packed a few things in a duffle and maneuvered through her home grabbing necessities, not losing momentum, until she left her bathroom. She stopped on the same spot she had that very morning, when Rand appeared at the threshold of her bedroom with his muscled arm propped up confidently against the doorjamb. She shivered and was still standing there when she heard the bell chime. And it chimed again. And again. *Ginny!* Nicole snapped out of it, grabbed her laptop and chargers, reset the security alarm, and hurried out.

"What? Did something happen?" Nicole asked, throwing her bags in the Range Rover.

"It was taking too long, I got worried." Ginny was jittery. She pulled on the sleeves of her jacket, then folded her arms.

Nicole shook her head. "This isn't good. I was wrong to take you to Smiling Tribes and expose you to these people." Nicole closed the cargo door, walking past Ginny. With keys in hand, she opened her driver's door, but Ginny hadn't moved. Nicole raised her hands. "Now what are you doing? I thought I was following you."

Ginny took one step toward her car, then stopped and turned to Nicole. "Please don't shut me out. Granted, I got scared and it's got me a little excited. Okay, a LOT excited." She unfolded her arms. "... But, Nicole, the heartbeat in my throat? It's reminding me that I'm alive. Please, I'll do better."

The wind blew, flinging Nicole's hair, and when she pushed it back in place, it uncovered a smile playing at her mouth. "Let's go."

She followed Ginny up the Pacific Coast Highway, or as the locals say the PCH, to the Vinsants' beach house and left Ginny's car in the drive for her shadow to find, then Ginny rode with Nicole to the rented condo. The décor of the small beach rental was geared for tourists. The kitchen walls were lined with pictures of In-N-Out Burger, Bob's Big Boy, Musso & Frank Grill, and even Zeke's. The living room walls featured surfing posters from the early twentieth century through the present, showing the difference in swimwear and surf boards, and there was even a board leaning in the corner. Seashells and rock collections were displayed in bowls and filled the clear base of a lamp. None of it was Nicole's taste. She would have described the furniture as "nondescript meets wicker," but it was immaculately clean and that was the only thing that mattered to each of them upon arrival. Nicole went onto the deck overlooking the beach and chose to work on the counter-height table with high-back stools, so she could see over the railing and watch the world when she needed to.

Music, laughter, shouting, and crashing waves from the beach surrounded her and she was in her element with a couple of hours before sunset. Nicole booted up her laptop to download the van pictures that she had transferred to her cell phone, but getting an identity on the two killers was going to be challenging since her resources had been cut. Ginny stuck her head out. "The kitchen is bare, I need to run to the store, do you mind if I use your Range Rover?"

When Nicole was alone again, she shook her head at her situation. Mike, her best friend, hadn't driven her car once, and now she had loaned her SUV to the second person in two days. *A preacher and Senator Tom Vinsant's wife, of all people!*

The breeze outside was light, a perfect evening, and Nicole moved through her notes, stopping at her notation "SOTIS," remembering Detective Ortega's remark. She downloaded the picture of the witness's statement she got off Graves's desk, then did a search. One article led to another, and after copying a few selections to a working file, she switched gears and typed "Smiling Tribes Foster Care" in the search line.

The first page of options was filled with articles about the organization, but even before their website, there was a trending link getting all the activity. It involved a shooting. The internet was slow at the rental, and when the article finally loaded on her screen, Nicole subconsciously leaned toward the picture centered in the middle of her monitor.

One of her van people had just been identified.

The sun had set by the time Nicole went in. "Something smells wonderful," she said, finding Ginny busy in the kitchen.

"Linguine with shrimp scampi. Also, spinach and garlic bread. I hope you eat shrimp." Ginny placed a cheese platter with grapes in front of Nicole at the counter. She retrieved the two chilled glasses from the freezer, lifted the bottle of wine from the ice bucket, and poured each of them a glass of chardonnay.

"I'm sure I will love everything. You know, you could've just ordered takeout." She took the glass Ginny offered and closed her eyes when she took a sip, allowing her senses to fully appreciate the taste. "Nice."

"I needed this. Something to keep me busy. So, how's it going?"

Ginny asked. She took the bread from the small toaster oven, then turned back to Nicole.

Nicole opted not to mention Martha Vaughn, yet. "Can you go back to the night of your accident one more time? You mentioned Batman. I need to know why. Could it be from a billboard? On a car? How did you mean it?"

Ginny shook her head. "I wish I hadn't told you that. I don't know where it came from. All I can say is, it flashes in my mind when I relive the incident ... and I don't know why."

"Well, the black van is significant because Theresa Chastang mentioned the same van before she died. A Mercedes."

"WHAT!?" Ginny popped up. "Nicole! It's something, isn't it? A clue!?" Excited, she paced. "I really saw a black van! It wasn't my imagination! Wait!" She stopped. "Why didn't you tell me earlier? I've been feeling stupid about it and you let me." Ginny's lips pulled into a tight pout.

"I'm processing everything as it comes. Putting it together. I don't just 'react.' And anyway, the Batman comment took its share of processing!" Nicole took a sip of her wine, grinning at Ginny. "Is dinner ready?"

Ginny's phone rang. Her expression changed three times over when she looked at the caller and she turned her back. "Hey," she answered, her voice low. "No. Just at the beach, like you wanted." When Nicole was working, she gave herself a free pass on the etiquette of eavesdropping. It was part of the job. And since Tom Vinsant was on the other end of that call, she needed to hear every word, however, Ginny was walking into the other room, keeping her voice down. Nicole's trust detector was bottoming out, and the longer Ginny was in there whispering, the worse it became. Instinct took over, and by the time Ginny walked back in, Nicole had everything back in her duffle and was putting her laptop in her tote.

"Wait! What are you doing? Are you leaving?" Ginny asked, her panic echoing.

Nicole lifted a brow. "The woman we saw today? The one we chased in the blue Honda? She was shot and killed shortly after." Nicole zipped up the duffle. "I don't know what's going on, yet, but I WILL find out, and in the meantime, I need to know I'm making good decisions. This one," she held her arm out to the room behind her, "isn't good. I need to be alone."

"Why? What will I do?"

"You can walk to your car, anytime you want. It's only three blocks away. In the meantime, no one should know where you are, unless you just told whoever was on the phone, and if you trust them, you're safe. It's me that's not."

"What did I do wrong? Tell me!" Tears began rolling from Ginny's eyes, and she followed Nicole to the door.

"Listen, I have trust issues with members of your family, which unfortunately extends to you, but I will be straight up with you. I'll stay on this job as promised and will check in when I find out more, but I need to find my own hideaway. The body count is one a day now, and you're whispering to Tom Vinsant in the other room, when he could be involved ... that doesn't work for me." Nicole opened the door like she couldn't get away quickly enough.

"Please don't leave!" Ginny sobbed. Nicole lifted her brows high at the unexpected reaction. "I'm not conspiring with Tom! I—I promise." Ginny's voice broke. "Tom was guarded—like—like he couldn't talk. Then I ... I heard a woman's voice." Her hands covered her face. "I said I'd come home, hoping I was mistaken and that he'd ... that he'd want me to. Instead, he told me ... NO! To stay. Actually ... he demanded it!" She looked up at Nicole, mascara smeared under her eyes. "I just didn't want you to know."

* * *

The linguini with shrimp scampi was delicious, and Nicole and Ginny ate with hardly a word between them, each in their own thoughts. As soon as she was finished, Nicole started clearing the table and loading the dishes in the dishwasher. Anything to avoid a repeat of Ginny's confessions of the Vinsants' dysfunctional private life.

"You're a good person, Nicole." Ginny said, scraping the leftovers into plastic containers she found in the cabinets.

"No. I'm not. I was just hungry." Nicole was wiping the stove.

Ginny's smile was tender, reflecting her gratitude. "Of course, I already knew you were. You'd have to be to deserve such loyalty from Mike. He said you've been his best friend since college."

"Mike's amazing. Anyone could be friends with him," Nicole said flatly. They were finished in the kitchen.

"You didn't leave me. Thank you."

Nicole softened and gave Ginny a smile for the first time that evening. "Let's get some rest. First thing tomorrow we go to the foster kids' school."

CHAPTER 32

"So, anything on Gabriel Simon?" Rand asked Jocko as soon as he came through the door. Jocko and his wife, Special Agent Sylvia Green, had arrived at Rand's condo first and had already set up a workstation in his dining area.

"Not yet. I'm still on the second facial recognition from Nicole's camera," Jocko said, handing a water bottle to his wife.

"Okay, Jocko, what do you need from me?" asked Sylvia.

"You can start the Gabriel Simon ID. As a custodian at The Rock, he doesn't add up. Here's what I have on him from Rand." Jocko handed her a folder. "It's the basic info from the center ... an address, home number, automobile description."

Sylvia opened the folder and read, "Late forties. No distinctive accent, so unless he's hiding it, I'll assume he's from this country and start with West Coast. Medium-brown hair, height approximately five-ten." She called out over her shoulder, "There's no eye color here. Do you guys have an eye color?"

Rand thought back to the smiling eyes. "Brown."

"Begin with the DMV," Jocko said, then went back to work on his laptop. Within minutes he called out, "Bingo! The second one just came through." He now had the pictures and personal information of both on the screen.

Rand looked over Jocko's shoulder, read the basic description of the pictures profiled, and nodded. "Print that out for me." He stepped away with stealthy movement and walked the room as he talked. "I could've picked these clowns up yesterday, but we need them active. Next, I need a GPS tracking on a cell phone." He read off Nicole's cellular phone number.

"I can't do a tracking from here; I'll send a message into the office. They'll do it for us."

Rand left Jocko to his work and walked into his kitchen, dialing the number of The Rock. He skipped the usual pleasantries when Bethany answered. "Is Gabriel Simon there?"

"I haven't seen him, Pastor Coleman. I don't think he came back, but I'll check." Bethany started to place him on hold.

"Wait." Rand stopped her. "Do you have his cell phone number?"

She read it out to him, and Rand stepped into the other room, repeating each number for Jocko to write down and motioned for him to trace that number as well. "All right, Bethany, now if you'll check to see if Gabriel is there." It didn't take her long to return. It was as Rand suspected. He hadn't returned.

"I sent both numbers in for tracking," Jocko said. "What do you want to do when we get a location?" But before Rand could respond, Jocko said, "Hey man, you need to come see this. There's been an update on one of the suspects we profiled."

Rand walked back over to Jocko and looked over his shoulder at the screen: *Martha Vaughn, 47, died in an apparent drive-by shooting today at approximately 3:00 p.m. Mrs. Vaughn worked for the Smiling Tribes*

Foster Care and was delivering papers to a client. The case is under investigation led by Detective Ernest Graves and Detective Roma Ortega, South Station.

Rand didn't believe in coincidence and the other two thugs had Nicole's address. He turned quickly to Jocko. "I have to check on something. You two stay with the tracking and let me know as soon as you get an answer. Also, the Gabriel Simon ID and detail on Martha Vaughn. To get popped, she messed up somewhere and it involved Theresa Chastang. I shouldn't be long," he said, and was out the door.

The beach highway was filled with cars and pedestrians, all enjoying the Southern California lifestyle. It was electric, and Rand was a little more charged than any of them. He parked a few blocks away from Nicole's house and walked the distance to scan the area.

Nothing stood out as overly suspicious, but since Nicole still hadn't returned his call, he climbed the vines along the right of the gate, as he had that morning. When he got his footing on the top ledge, he pushed off to the other side, landing in a squat. Crouched and alert, he waited until he knew he hadn't been seen or heard, then stood, staying to the shadows, and walked around the right side of the house to the back deck, stepping over the wood railing. The house looked empty, but he still scanned the rooms he could see from his position. Satisfied everything was secure, he was about to leave when he overheard whispers, followed by movement below in the sand. The two from the white van.

Rand drew back into the dark.

CHAPTER 33

It was dark by the time Grisholm and Fuzz arrived in Malibu, and the cars on the highway were steady. The air was cool, but milder than recent nights at the beach, so the locals were taking advantage of it. Drivers with convertibles had the tops down, the cyclists were out in record numbers, and even the pedestrian traffic was impressive. A perfect night to go unnoticed along the edges of all this activity. Fuzz parked his car on the opposite side of the highway from Nicole's home, and as a group of loud college students walked past, he zipped his jacket, pulled the hood over his bald head, and slid in with them. There was nothing Grisholm could do to hide his fuzzy mane, so he just sauntered behind the group until he saw Fuzz break away and cross the street, and he followed.

Taking the first accessible alley between houses, they made their way to the beach. "It's the sixth one down," Grisholm said. Counting their way, they stopped behind Nicole's.

"She's not here." Fuzz said, his voice low.

"How do you know?" Grisholm asked, attempting to use the same hushed voice, but like his size and his hair, everything with Grisholm was bigger and unrefined.

Fuzz looked around to make sure no one was nearby. Quietly, he explained, "We know what she's been doing today." He counted off her activity on his fingers. "She's been to the police, we busted her back window and took her camera, then she was at Martha's agency and chased after Martha." He finished by sticking his hands in the pockets of the hoodie. "She'd be hyped up, so there'd be more lights on than this ... or at least she'd be on her computer or TV ... but they produce a distinctive light and we'd see it with all these windows, so there's no way she's here." With the hood still secured on his head, he nodded toward the street. "Let's wait out front, we'll be able to see when she comes home."

They didn't notice the man in the shadows who followed them, watching the two as they split off. Fuzz climbed into the driver's side of his blue Saturn, and Grisholm kept moving toward the small stores and eateries that lined the street.

The buildings along this stretch looked like fifties or early sixties architecture, and were all brightly painted in pinks, blues, greens, and yellows—and with the reggae music that blared through the area, it truly had a Caribbean feel. Laughter and animated conversation surrounded Grisholm as he made his way through the worn café tables to the counter. "Two large coffees. Black." It might be a long night, so they would need the caffeine. Tapping one of his big, brown sneakers to the beat, he waited. Although his order was simple, the bartender had a few drinks ahead of Grisholm's.

Finally, with two coffees in hand, Grisholm worked himself through the social clusters and was close to the street when he heard the familiar sound of a silenced gun. The pop wasn't loud enough to create a disturbance, and on such a busy night it could have easily gone undetected except for the destruction it created. Grisholm's head snapped around toward the bloodcurdling scream. A group of girls stood in the cross-walk near the Saturn clutching each other as one pointed a trembling arm at Fuzz's car. The sheer hysteria caused others to scramble without understanding the cause or origin and people were running into each other to get away, wildly looking about for friends, or ducking behind the closest object for cover.

When Grisholm saw the motorcycle, he understood. It was an all-black Kawasaki with a soldier suited up in full black, wearing a masked helmet. His arm was raised and pointed at Grisholm, who dropped the coffees. Before he could think to dive, he heard the "pop" again. Twice. And his mind was in slow-motion as he looked down at his chest for the bullet to enter. Nothing happened.

Lifting his head again, he looked straight into a set of intense, dark eyes that were behind the wheel of a black Ford Raptor. The passenger door was open. "GET IN!" the driver demanded. The bike made a U-turn and was heading back. Grisholm didn't have a choice. He jumped into the truck, and the driver dove down into the seat, pushing Grisholm down with him when the motorcycle passed, barely missing another bullet. "Fasten your seat belt," the driver told him, then threw the truck in drive and took off after the motorcycle.

Grisholm reached across his shoulder for the belt just as they passed Fuzz's Saturn and saw the damage. "Fuzz loved that car," he mumbled in a hushed tone. "He would hate seeing the window broken out like that."

The driver's window was shattered, and the parts that were still there were splattered in blood. Fuzz's head lolled backwards, wedged between the doorframe and the headrest. Grisholm fixed on the scene, his hands working the metal of the seatbelt, missing the connection once, twice, then finally fastening it as the driver raced after the motor-cycle. Grisholm was unresponsive as the man with the dark eyes drove through the streets, weaving between the cars. The motorcycle did an-other U-turn, changing direction and came at the truck, taking another shot as he did. The driver ducked, pushing Grisholm's head down again, then turned the truck, sliding it around one-hundred-eighty de-grees, and speeding after the bike as it turned off the PCH onto Topanga Canyon Road.

Topanga Canyon winds through the Santa Monica Mountains, and the stretch starting from Malibu is one of the most precarious. While it's exhilarating to take the curves with a great, road-grabbing sports car, it's not recommended for a car chase, and the truck was having difficulty keeping up with the agility of the motorcycle. It stayed in a rhythm, racing on the straights, then slowing enough to make the curves without going off the edge. The driver was relentless. He was af-ter this motorcycle; however, the assassin was an equally skilled driver, so unless they caught a break, the shooter was a free man tonight.

The bike had gotten one bend ahead of them, and although it was dangerous to watch the action at the next bend while maneuvering the present one, the driver had to so he could keep track of the shooter. The bike, about to turn another corner, was leaning into the opposing traffic's lane when the driver saw a restaurant supply truck coming from the opposite direction. Before the shooter could react, the front tire of the bike hit the left-front bumper of the truck and turned the bike in a ninety-degree angle. At the speed they both were going, the bike bounced off with such velocity it sent him backwards, over the side of the road, and down into the canyon.

The Ford Raptor driver waited until he could find a place to safely pull over, and then he got out. He didn't worry about his passenger, since he seemed to be in shock. He looked over the edge, but it was dark, and there was nothing else to do here, so he got back into the truck and proceeded up the mountainside, away from Malibu.

CHAPTER 34

Nicole awakened. Disoriented. Taking in the room around her, she gradually recognized the surroundings. The digital clock on the honey-colored armoire claimed it was three in the morning. The moon was full, and it was eerily beautiful, entwining itself with a mass of fog just beyond the large window in her room. Nicole could draw the shade, darken the room, and try to go back to sleep, but it was no use; the events of the past few days wouldn't stop nagging and poking. They didn't care about the time.

The kitchen had a counter with stools and a small dining table. In her own home Nicole gravitated to the counter, but these stools had no back to lean against, so she opted for the table, and spread out the contents from her tote and opened her laptop. Earlier in the evening, she had downloaded important findings in the foster system. Cases of abused, neglected, or missing children specific to Los Angeles County, as well as information or complaints connected to Smiling Tribes, and now she had time to dissect them.

With as much objectivity as she could muster, Nicole studied the reports, and as she read, she had to intentionally remember to breathe. The accounts summoned images of frightened little children betrayed at the hands of their caretakers. Abuse, pain, hunger, neglect. Nicole read each for as long as she could, then moved to another. The reports were draining. *Maybe I should go back to bed ... I'm sure I could sleep now. But I'm almost finished, and the sun will be up soon. A splash of cold water would help.*

Nicole went to the half-bath near the kitchen and turned on the faucet. With eyes closed and head leaning over the sink, she scooped the cool water in one hand and held her hair back with the other. The cool contact was liberating. She poured a second handful over her face, then a third. *I need this over my whole body,* she thought. She felt for the knob and turned the water off, but nothing happened. Gripping tighter, she turned it harder, but the flow not only kept coming, it intensified.

Peeking through the droplets hanging from her brows and lashes, Nicole tried to examine the handle, but couldn't see through the red. She wiped her hand across her eyes to see, and red was everywhere! The water coming from the tap was red. Her hand was red. "Did the pipes burst?" she asked out loud, reaching for an explanation, and looked up into the mirror. The eyes staring back at her were deep-set and frightened, with red streaks down the face. She absently reached toward the familiar image inside the glass, and the liquid on her hand congealed, helping to ease her fingers through the surface, to the other side, as she touched the young girl's face.

"Nicole?" A voice called her name.

"Debbie?"

The liquid level in the sink was getting higher. It too had thickened and was clogging the drain, and it kept coming. Overflowing, it dripped onto the floor and splashed her feet, jolting her away from the girl in the mirror. She had to stop it. With both hands she frantically worked the knobs, and still nothing happened. Panic slammed her. "No! GINNY?" she shouted.

"Nicole! Nicole ... wake up!" Ginny stood over Nicole, shaking her, and when she didn't respond, she increased the intensity. Nicole's head was laying on her folded arms on the table, next to her laptop. Her breathing was erratic, and Ginny feared something was seriously wrong. She pulled Nicole by the shoulders and leaned her back in her chair. Nicole's eyes fluttered, her chest rapidly rising and falling, and Ginny lightly popped the sides of her face, as she called out, "NICOLE!"

The stimulating smell of fresh coffee was Nicole's first connection back to the present. She saw Ginny standing over her, mouth moving, but Nicole couldn't hear what she was saying. Had she been in an accident? Blood. She remembered blood. She looked down at the hands resting on the table. Everything looked normal.

"Nicole, can you hear me?"

The sound was back on. "Yes, I'm sorry. What were you saying?"

"Are you all right?"

Nicole sat up straighter and pushed her long hair back, "A cup of coffee would be great. It seems I fell asleep."

Not masking her concern, Ginny got two mugs from the cabinet, filling each before coming back around to Nicole. "What would you like in it?"

"Nothing. Black," Nicole said. Steam rose from the mug placed inches in front of her, but Nicole didn't trust her hands to pick it up yet. "Thank you."

Ginny looked squarely at Nicole, almost as a challenge, and said, "Do you want to tell me your dream, or should I say, nightmare?"

"Why nightmare? Did I say anything?"

"You didn't have to. It was evident. But, yes. You called out my name."

Nicole slid both hands around her mug and lifted it to her lips.

"Also, you mentioned Debbie," Ginny added.

Nicole rose with her coffee cup and walked over to the windows to look out. The sun still hadn't come up, but she loved knowing the ocean was just yards away. She blew into her cup, then took a small sip and closed her eyes for a moment to savor it, but they flew back open. She couldn't close them yet or she'd see the bloody image from her sleep. The nightmare had opened a deep wound, and her head was pounding. She turned abruptly and left the room.

Searching desperately in her bag, Nicole found her medicine and took it, not noticing Ginny had followed her.

"I know you're here professionally, that you took my offer only because there was nothing else. I get it. But I'm a person, and I have feelings, and I'm going through hell right now." Her arms were crossed tight against her ribs. Her hands squeezing her flesh.

Nicole watched, but her head hurt too much to do more than give an uninterested stare.

"For a week now, I've been tormented over the idea I might have hit those kids. To make it worse, I find they were running away from an absolute horrid situation. Probably abused. Definitely neglected. And what if we find out I DID hit them. Will I go to jail? Meanwhile, my ambitious husband is steadily controlling me and his campaign, while sleeping with whomever comes along and rubbing it in my face.

"I understand you've had a bad dream, and you want to be alone, but I'm TIRED of being dispensable to everyone!!" She had unfolded her arms and was leaning forward, her hands on her hips.

Nicole pulled clothes and her toiletry bag from her duffle.

"I deserve a response!" Ginny's tears were returning.

"What is this? Emotional blackmail? Is that what you're doing? We don't have time, Ginny. You want a reaction, but everything you just said?... I already know!"

Ginny looked like she'd been slapped. She retreated toward the door, then turned back. "I respected you so much. I had just hoped we could be friends."

Before Ginny turned again, Nicole shot out, "You're all over the place. Angry, sad, despondent. I can't go there, Ginny. My head is killing me, and I'm trying to focus on the job you hired me for. But that's not enough. Now you're mad this morning because I won't be your friend? Ginny, you don't want me as a friend! The only best girlfriend I've ever had died on my watch, so consider yourself lucky!"

Nicole stormed into the bathroom and slammed the door.

An hour later she was on the back deck, looking out to sea, when she heard Ginny step outside. The personal tragedies in Nicole's thirty years had shaped her. Known for her integrity, her associates also described her as tough, driven, and brutally honest. Acquaintances might add exceedingly guarded. But no one would have called her cruel. However, that morning she had been uncharacteristically cruel. It wasn't sitting well.

"My best friend was Debbie Zbinden." Nicole's back was to Ginny, her voice barely audible. "All through elementary school and junior high. We dressed alike, loved the same movies, giggled at the same silly things, and shared our most intimate dreams and fears; everything young girls do. She was there for me when my parents died, and since I had no other family except my great aunt, we told everyone we were sisters." She stopped. Ginny's mouth opened to speak; there was so much to ask, but she caught herself. If she interrupted, Nicole might not continue.

"I was in her mother's wedding with her the summer after eighth grade as a junior bridesmaid. Her mother had been divorced for years, and we were so happy for her, and Debbie was getting a father like she'd always hoped." Nicole paused. A seagull landed on the railing and squawked at her. She tossed him a piece of the toast she was holding. She was stalling.

"Two months into the marriage, the stepfather wandered into Debbie's bedroom in the middle of the night. He told her she would break her mother's heart if she told. Put all the guilt on Debbie. I was the only person she could tell, and she swore me to secrecy. I was helpless, and he kept coming.

"Debbie decided that she was the problem. Said that her mom loved the stepdad and the stepdad would stop cheating on her if Debbie left. Any normal teen would have been thinking, 'Why doesn't my mother see this? Why is this happening to me?' But not Debbie. She worried about her mother. When she came to me, she had bags packed to run away, and I was in her corner. Run. Get out of there! So I helped her."

Other seagulls showed. They'd heard there was a bounty, but Nicole had no more bread. She ignored them and talked through their loud cawing. Ginny stepped closer.

"We went to the local drugstore and bought blonde hair-dye. Debbie's hair was a beautiful chestnut brown. There was a service station diagonally across from the drugstore and we used their ladies' room to color her hair. When we were done and she looked in the mirror, she screamed! It was red." A sad smile found its way, but it was short-lived. "After the initial shock, she actually loved it, and we thought we were so clever. No one would recognize her with her new hair color, and she could start a new life ... without abuse. She had just turned fourteen. I gave her what little cash I had saved, and she was off to look for a job as a live-in nanny. Said she would write me when she got settled in her new location and give me her address.

"Her mother had reported her missing and searched the streets for her daughter night and day. She was in agony. Two weeks later my aunt received a call. My best friend, Debbie, who ran away with my help, was found in a nearby wooded area. Her decomposing body revealed evidence of rape and strangulation." Nicole stood and walked to the rail. "I never told her mother or anyone about the day she left, and how I helped her. Looking back, why didn't I simply offer for her to stay at my house? Why didn't I urge her to tell her mother about the stepfather?" She turned and met Ginny's concerned look head-on. Her neck was flushed, her steel eyes cold, but damp. "So ... it's not that you're dispensable. It's like I said, I'm not a good friend."

Nicole picked up her water glass and walked back inside.

They were on the freeway before anyone spoke again.

"What happened to your friend was horrible," Ginny said gently, and watched Nicole for a response. Nicole was driving and looked straight ahead at the road. The only sign she was listening was a flared nostril. Ginny continued, "I can't imagine. However, that was not your fault. Or hers. You two were only fourteen." Ginny's passion grew and her volume grew with it. "Do you realize WHY you didn't offer other options...? Because, Nicole, at fourteen, NEITHER of you knew there WERE other options!"

Ginny stopped and got control of her emotions before continuing with a softer tone. "I've never had a close friend die, but I can identify with your feelings. I didn't report those abused children at The Rock, and I've been told they no longer come in." Like Nicole, she looked straight ahead at the road before them, anticipating their destination. "What if they were in Debbie's situation at home and now are missing? But Nicole? I did that as an adult!

"Now, I know we can't change yesterday, but what we're doing today might make a difference! A difference in the lives of some overlooked foster children. Children that no one else was looking for, and no one else would help." Nicole glanced at Ginny, who was tugging at the front of her hair again, smoothing it. Sorrow flooded Ginny's eyes, but her message was confident. "These kids need you, Nicole. I need you."

Ginny turned to look out her passenger window and missed the soft smile that brushed across Nicole's face.

CHAPTER 35

"I'm glad you rode with me," Nicole said to Ginny, as she drove to the elementary school that Theresa Chastang's foster kids would have attended.

"Really?" The eagerness in Ginny's voice matched her expression.

It was a little after seven in the morning, and Nicole was jockeying to get across six lanes of traffic to the inside track. "Yeah, now I can take the carpool lane. The congestion is so bad today, I wouldn't have made the school in time."

"Oh. Right." Ginny readjusted her seatbelt. "So, why the elementary? Aren't Angel and Jorge in middle school?"

Nicole nodded her head. "Even though we don't have names for the younger kids, elementary ages are more likely to talk than middle-schoolers." said Nicole.

"Good point."

Their conversation was strained, but without friction. Nicole had gone through the cycle of resenting Ginny for causing her to spill her story about Debbie, then to embarrassment, and finally withdrawal. But actually, Debbie had already surfaced. By discovering the foster children and their plight, the voice that taunted her had been awakened. Then, when she researched case after case after case of abused or missing children, they were all reminders of Debbie and the vulnerability of children - sufficient fuel for the bloody dream. Nicole bit her lip. Her grip tightened on the steering wheel. *Ginny's right—we can make a difference this time.* "I also need to call Kim Argnaut again," she said aloud.

"Who's she?"

"She's the rep from Family Services that gave me Angel's address on Gramble Street. I want to see what she knows about Smiling Tribes Foster Care."

Her telephone suddenly rang over the sound system in the car, jolting Nicole. She saw the source and quickly terminated it, but Ginny read the caller ID and asked, "Pastor Coleman? Why didn't you answer?"

Nicole didn't respond.

"Hmmm," Ginny offered loudly.

"What?"

Ginny's smile did the talking for her, and she nodded her head as if her suspicions were confirmed.

"Ginny, you do have a flair for drama," Nicole said more sharply than she'd meant to, then pulled to the curb on Claiborne Ave. They had arrived. "I'll be right back," Nicole said, as she got out of the car. For the next few minutes, she mingled along the fence line, asking about kids that had been absent for the last week.

A couple of children offered information, but Nicole knew they didn't understand what she was looking for. She was watching for the time and watching for the yard duty monitors, trying to stay clear of their vision. A young boy who looked about six was watching her. "Are you lookin' for Jackie?" he asked her.

"Well, that depends. I have something for a couple of students that left in a hurry last Tuesday. Is that Jackie?"

The little boy simply stared at Nicole with sad eyes too large for his small, round face. His bottom lip hung in a pout.

"Do you know where they were going? Did he say?"

The little boy just looked at her.

Well, that wasn't working. Nicole needed a new strategy. "I'm sorry. I can't talk with you. It's not Jackie." She moved slightly to the left and scanned the playground, looking for another child. "I need to talk to someone else."

"Is too, Jackie!"

"I don't think so." Nicole kept looking past him, dismissing him.

He stomped his foot. "He the only one that's gone. Him an' Kiandra!" Boom.

Nicole shook her head. "That's not enough for me to be sure. I'm only helping the ones who left Tuesday."

"I don't know what day!" Tears filled his eyes. "Me and my sister saw 'em runnin'. He waved bye, said he was flyin' to a new family. He ain't never been in no airplane 'fore an' he was in a hurry." The bell rang.

Nicole's eyes darted all around watching the children run in. She had upset the little boy, and he had to go. "Listen, you're right. It is Jackie, and because of you, I know where to look for him. I have something very special for him! Thank you!" The little boy smiled, exposing a gap where a front tooth had once been, then he took off running.

Nicole took a deep breath.

The yard duty's whistle blew fiercely just before she rounded the building, coming into view, and Nicole quickly hit the sidewalk. As briskly as she could, without drawing attention to herself, she moved in the opposite direction from her car. Opposite the direction of the advancing woman. There was no plan, other than wait until the yard monitor went back inside, so Nicole kept walking. By the time she made the next corner, a black Range Rover pulled up with Ginny behind the wheel.

"Well, aren't you coming in handy!" Nicole said, buckling her seatbelt as Ginny blew past the school.

"Did you get anything?" Ginny asked.

"A name." Nicole flashed a quick smile. She had her phone up to her ear and held up her index finger. "Just a minute."

"This is Mrs. Argnaut's office."

"Is she in, please?" Nicole asked.

"She is, but she's with someone. Can I tell her who's calling?"

"Nicole Portman."

"Oh yes, Ms. Portman, hold just a moment."

Kim came on the line sounding winded, but remarkably friendly. "I wasn't expecting to hear from you until next week. Something must have come up."

"Yes, and I hate to bother you, but there are a couple of things that have stopped me, and you might have advice or answers."

"I'll do what I can."

"First, Angel Davis. I have him associated with Smiling Tribes Foster Care. And second, two other children, siblings, Jackie and Kiandra, were placed along with Angel, and I believe Smiling Tribes handled them as well. Would you have any way to confirm each?"

"Smiling Tribes just keeps coming up today! Can I tell you something off the record?"

"Of course, Kim. I know we just met, but I feel like we've been friends forever." She looked over at Ginny with an impish smile for stretching the truth. "You can trust me not to repeat it if you tell me it's confidential."

"Nicole, I feel the same! Well," her voice got softer, "the FBI is in my office. It seems one of the employees at Smiling Tribes Foster Care was shot and killed yesterday evening." Which explained her eagerness; the feds were in her office, and she was almost exploding to tell someone. "I'm not sure how I can help them, but since we did refer cases to that agency, I guess they're covering every angle."

"I heard about that shooting!" Nicole said, her voice equally conspiring, matching Kim's. "It's just awful. Was she a close friend?"

"No. I've dealt with her on the phone a time or two, but I don't know her well. Her name was Vaughn. Martha Vaughn."

"So sad, Kim, and I know you have people waiting for you. You don't know how much it means that you stopped to take my call."

"I'll look into it as soon as they leave." And they disconnected.

"See," Ginny said.

Nicole looked at her. "See, what?"

"You make friends. People like you."

"That is not friendship. I'm doing my job ... so whatever it takes."

"That's not what Kim thinks. Or Rand Coleman." Ginny was grinning, and before Nicole could respond, said, "I have to make a quick call, you mind?"

They were at the light, so Ginny dialed, then left her phone in her lap, in case the light changed. "Pa-ci-fic Co-ast B ... M ... Double You..." the sultry female voice drew out every ... last ... syllable. Looking toward Nicole, Ginny crossed her eyes, catching Nicole by surprise. The laughter that erupted from Nicole shocked them both, and Ginny could hardly speak to answer.

"Hank Crabtree, please," Ginny said, working to suppress a laugh. She sounded more like she was crying.

The voice, again, caressed each word. "Just one mo … ment, de … ar."

"My new car is being delivered today," Ginny explained while waiting on hold.

Nicole left Ginny with her call and used the map feature on her phone to look up airports in the area. Other than commercial airports and a private airstrip, there was only one small airport nearby. She saved the directions, and as soon as Ginny was off the phone, Nicole said, "Go four blocks, then take a left on Bullard Street. Stay south for three more miles. Our next stop is the Bullard Street Airport."

The Bullard Street Airport was a general aviation field in the middle of gangland, but since 9/11 and the new terrorist laws concerning airplanes, the locals stayed away, and it was relatively safe. The terminal was a small building with one main room as the lobby, furnished modestly, but included two extra-long couches in an alcove to the right for pilots who needed a place to rest. It had a break room toward the back right and a full bath, then to the left was the airport manager's office. Hal Sorensen was career Air Force and when he retired after serving twenty years found the challenges of managing this airport to be a perfect fit for him.

Hal was in his office opening mail when Nicole and Ginny arrived. His desk was strategically placed so when his office door was open, he could see past the front counter at anyone entering the lobby; however, he'd already watched the two ladies from the monitors mounted on his office wall. Hal ran live video from cameras throughout the property, and his backup consisted of a loaded Glock 45 automatic and a combat shotgun. He and his staff had turned this airfield into one of the most efficient general aviation airports in the region despite the rough area, and he was pleased that two beautiful women felt comfortable enough to come there unescorted.

"Good morning, ladies," Hal said, as he walked out into the main area making his way behind the counter. He pulled up a stool to encourage a visit. "Let me guess. You'd like flying lessons."

"Well, not today," Ginny said, smiling her perfect campaign smile for him. "But perhaps very soon. Today I'm needing a little help with some of the inner-city kids we've been assisting."

"Sorry, ladies," he stood. "We don't donate flights or flying time."

"Oh, no," Ginny laughed softly, and placed her hand on his arm, as though his comment was delightful. "I'm just disturbed about something that happened here at your airport." That got his attention. Someone insinuated a flaw in his facility!

"Last Tuesday night a few of the kids we work with at The Rock were coming to meet me. I didn't realize they didn't have a ride, or I would've offered to pick them up. Anyway, they had to cut through neighborhoods to get to me, and when they passed here, some men in a white van harassed them. Scared them, actually. By the time they got to me they were frantic."

His brows pulled together and his eyes narrowed at Ginny, then he looked at Nicole. Nicole had left her shades on and didn't comment, not knowing where Ginny was going with this, but after seeing her in action at Smiling Tribes, she let her run. Surely some of Tom's skills had rubbed off. The man looked back at Ginny. "Lady, the kids that roam these streets, especially at night, don't get frantic over a couple of delivery men. They're usually the ones doing the harassin'."

"I'm sure you would know, being a fixture in this area. I bet you've seen your share of action." She smiled demurely. "By the way, I'm Ginny, and this is my friend Nicole." She intentionally left out their last names, hoping he wouldn't recognize them and clam up. Nicole nodded, but stayed behind Ginny.

"I'm Hal Sorensen, nice to meet you." He relaxed, somewhat. "So, what is it you think I can do for you?"

"Well, I need to know if I can trust these kids," she said, smiling, then leaned toward him. Closer. "So, I was hoping you saw something to back their story."

Hal shook his head. "I'm sorry." But Ginny didn't reply. She just kept watching him, hopeful, and it worked, causing him to use the stereotypical signs of thinking back—looking up at the ceiling and scratching his chin, he shook his head again, then he finally went to the computer at the counter and pulled up the log from last week. "Yep, just as I remembered. Ezra comes in around seven during the week, and I leave shortly thereafter, but Tuesday I stayed later. My friend flew in from Colorado at seven thirty, and by the time we refueled his plane and tied it down in the hanger, it was after eight. We left after that. I didn't see any trouble, and Ezra didn't mention anything."

"Do you still have the security footage from that night?" Ginny asked, her large brown eyes searching his face, pleading silently.

Hal scratched his right ear. Cleared his throat. And the women watched his every move. "I don't know. Probably not." He looked down at his feet, uncomfortable at telling those big eyes "no." When he looked back at Ginny, he was shaking his head. "Unless I specifically save a day in a folder, it's programmed to reset after a week."

Ginny turned to Nicole, sincerely deflated. Her shoulders dropped. It had been a week. Hal caught their exchange. He stood from his stool and left them, going into his office without a word.

"So, what's next?" Ginny asked.

Nicole didn't have a "next" planned out, so she tapped her fingers on the counter. She thought, *I could call Rusty at CMbz, see what he's found, or wait on Kim's call, definitely do a license check on black Mercedes vans. Okay ... I have something.* But to Ginny she said, "I don't get it. Maybe ... if we could see a list of flights in and out on Tuesday." Nicole started behind the counter. "Keep watch."

The loud static eruptions from the radio scanner echoed the lobby, causing Ginny to start at each outburst, and her eyes darted from Nicole to the door where Hal had disappeared. In between the radio sounds she heard the clicking of Hal's keyboard. "Well, I'll be ..."

Ginny's brows deepened. She stood up on her toes, leaning, trying to see who Hal was talking to.

"Looks like your kids' lucky day," he shouted.

"Excuse me?" She waved frantically at Nicole to come from behind the counter and cleared her throat. "Are you talking to us?" She was distracted by Nicole, who nodded her head and then jerked her thumb in the direction of Hal's office, nudging her on. "Hal?" Ginny called.

"Yeah, sorry. Push that swing door from this end of the counter. You need to see this."

They did as instructed, trying not to rush in. Six different frames from six different cameras were on the large screen for them to view. Hal pointed and explained, proud of his setup, and as he restarted the segment for the ladies, Nicole pushed her sunglasses up into her hair. The white van was the initial movement. It came into the first frame, and

Nicole gasped, but Hal didn't notice thanks to Ginny's nervous chatter. He manipulated the segments so they could follow the path of the van. It wedged between a hangar and the fence as though it was hiding. There was no reason for a vehicle to be in that area, and now that he was seeing this a second time, Hal's jaw clenched. This exposed a hole in his tight ship and without these ladies he wouldn't have known.

Next, the bigger man with wooly hair, who Nicole had seen in the passenger seat yesterday, was in a frame, facing the woods and was talking. His hands moved in front of him as he talked, reinforcing his words.

Another frame came alive when someone ran into view. It was the bald driver Nicole had taken a picture of, and it looked like he was chasing after something. At first his movements were consistent with sneaking up on someone, but quickly changed to wild urgency. Hal froze one of the pictures that showed the driver grabbing at something; the man's face was intensive fury. Hal hit play again, and the man ran out-of-frame.

The bigger man ran back in the direction of the hidden vehicle, then suddenly the van bolted into view from another monitor. It stopped, picked up someone, then raced out-of-frame.

Nicole was chewing on her bottom lip. To Hal, she might have looked concerned, but she was concentrating. Processing a story to fit what she saw.

Ginny didn't try to hide her disappointment. "Well, I see the van, and whatever they were doing doesn't look legit, but you couldn't see who they were chasing. It could've been anybody." She batted her eyes sadly at Hal. "I don't understand how this is the kids' lucky day."

Hal stepped right in. "Saving the best for last. I have cameras at either side of the far property lines, and since it's so dark back there, they're night vision lenses." Hal moved his mouse controller around and brought up a grainy but surprisingly clear video. Initially it looked like a still shot. Nothing was happening, then suddenly, from the left of the screen, movement so quick and desperate came into play that he had to slow-motion it to see what it was. The fear on the faces of the four children and their actions told the story.

Two at a time, their small bodies shimmied under the fence. Not enough room for two on a normal day, but these kids were terrified. The last child to come through was caught on the fence and trying to get free. She had a backpack, and with her free hand, threw it to a smaller boy and motioned for him to keep going. But he stood. Frozen. His confusion felt, even through the grainy, greenish hue. The other two kids were out-of-frame now, and he held the backpack tight against his chest, crying, screaming at the man about to grab the girl. Ginny's hand was over her mouth, and Nicole's was across her stomach. Their brows were pulled together, both holding their breath, watching the footage. A mere second before the man caught the girl, the video showed her tearing loose of the jagged link, and the two women exhaled. Ginny reached over and squeezed Nicole's hand. With the girl on the outside of the fence, they watched as she took the backpack from the boy, grabbed his hand, then they turned and ran.

Nicole gasped. Eyes fixed on the screen. "Hal, would you mind going back to when the girl grabs the backpack?"

"I don't mind." He reversed the video to just before she took the backpack from the boy and pressed play. Nicole watched closely. As soon as the girl had the backpack, she said, "Stop. Can you enlarge that picture?"

Ginny's color was draining. She caught what Nicole was after.

There on the screen. On the front of the little boy's shirt.

Batman.

CHAPTER 36

"I'm just the muscle," the big man with the lion's mane kept telling them. When Rand brought him in the night before, they said nothing to him. If he spoke or asked questions, no one answered him. They'd given him water and a couple of bathroom trips, but other than that, he'd been zip-tied to a straight chair, hands behind his back, and ankles tied to the legs of the chair. Rand and Jocko took turns keeping watch over him, so by mid-morning he was ready to talk. "The organization is big and has different divisions. The information they gave me was on a need to know. Like I said, I'm just the muscle."

His head hung forward. They learned his name was Harp Grisholm, and he confirmed the identity they had gotten on his partner, Charles Keel, or Fuzz, as he was known to Grisholm. Jocko had obtained a digital picture from the crime scene of a bloody bullet hole through the side of Fuzz's head. He froze the gruesome picture on a large monitor so Grisholm could see it each time he raised up, which he did frequently to readjust his arms and get relief from the pressure in his shoulders.

"They recruit folks and I transport them. The ones I transport have been through the welfare system, foster kids. That, or undocumented immigrants."

"RECRUIT?" Rand removed his jacket and rolled up his sleeves, then stepped closer, getting in Grisholm's face. "RECRUIT? You didn't RECRUIT anyone! You KIDNAPPED! Say it like it is!" The veins in his neck bulged, supporting his intensity.

"Kidnapped," Grisholm said hoarsely.

"How many others like you?"

"I don't know. I know there are other teams, but I don't know how many."

"Where do you take your victims?"

Grisholm tried lifting his arms again, then took a deep, ragged breath. "We took them to a warehouse. I think they transfer them to the water-front, but I'm not sure. It's done in pieces, so one department doesn't know too much about the other."

Jocko was standing arms akimbo, watching. His trusted tweed flat-cap was on, twisted backward, as usual. "So why the hit on your team?"

"I guess we messed up. A news lady got wind of us, somehow, and," he started rocking his head from side to side, "it all started falling apart."

"Is there a hit on her? The news lady?" Rand asked. He was still flushed. His scar deepened through his brow.

"Not that I know of. Fuzz and I were cleaning up and seeing what she knew. But then, we didn't know we had a hit on us, either."

"Who do you answer to?" Rand asked.

Grisholm once again hung his head. It was easier all around, especially to avoid the intense, dark eyes.

Rand tried another tactic. "The man who ordered the hit on you, what's his place in the organization?"

Nothing.

"You're going to protect him? He's ordered a hit on you! He sells children! And you protect him?" Rand asked him.

He lifted his head and fear darted through his eyes. "I just don't think about any of it. I can't think about it. I have to eat too. Where else would I make this kind of money? Anyway, like Fuzz always said, 'Once these kids become wards of the state, no one really cares about them.' At least we take them out of poverty and give them a life. This way they'll always have better food and shelter."

"Have you actually convinced yourself of that? Did you know your organization uses some of these people for organ harvesting?" Rand asked.

"What are you saying?"

"I'm saying that not only did you deliver little girls and boys, too young to even have pubic hair, to perverted grown men that will violate them physically and emotionally, scarring them for life, but they will also use some of them for their organs! They will be coma-induced. A machine will keep them alive while the body parts are sold for top dollar. Do you know how much a lung or heart goes for on the black market?" Rand's voice had steadily gotten louder, and he was now back in Grisholm's face, who was shaking his head no. "Well, your employers do! And you've been helping them! NOW, WHAT IS HIS NAME?!"

"Greystone. Stuart Greystone. Dominic is our team leader since January, but we're all under Greystone. I don't know his rank, like I said, the organization's big, but that's who we reported to." Grisholm had tears dripping from his nose as his head flopped downward.

Rand got Jocko's confirmation that this last statement was recorded, and they both agreed their guest didn't know anything above Greystone's rank. Exhausted himself, Rand had to get away, but there was one more question. "What did you do with the camera you stole from the black Range Rover?"

Recognition crossed Grisholm's face when he lifted to look at Rand. "That's where I've seen you. You were driving her car!"

Dark eyes turned ever colder and angrier at the big man when he referred to Nicole, and it wasn't lost on Grisholm. He answered quickly, "We ditched the camera, but Fuzz gave me the memory chip. It's in my things." Rand walked over to the counter where they'd laid out his belongings.

"WHERE?"

"It's in my wallet. Hidden in one of the slots."

Rand went through the man's wallet, until he found it and slipped it into his pocket. He grabbed his jacket off the back of the chair, nodded to Jocko, then walked out.

Jocko lifted a black, hard case next to him, laid it flat on the counter, and, using a combination, opened the case. Grisholm strained to see what he was doing behind the lid. He didn't know whose custody he was in, only that he'd had no choice but to get in the truck. It was a professional hit, and when he jumped into the opened truck door, the truck caught the bullets meant for him. He would have been dead. However, if these men were the law, wouldn't they have taken him in last night? Who were they, and what were they planning?

Becoming more alarmed, with his arms behind his back Grisholm struggled to see Jocko's hidden hands and gasped when Jocko walked around the case, exposing the syringe of fluid. Since childhood, Grisholm had been frightened of needles. Instantly, he turned into the big, cowardly lion that Fuzz labeled him, and began thrashing against the restraints; but Grisholm, already weakened emotionally and physically, wouldn't be around to experience the gift in store for him. Before Jocko could inject him, he was out.

A couple of agents were on their way to assist Jocko with the arrest and transfer of Harp Grisholm, so Rand headed back to The Rock. "Good morning, Pastor Coleman!" was Bethany's ever-faithful greeting.

It brought a tired smile to his face. "Did Gabriel Simon come in today?"

"No, sir. I haven't heard from him since he left early yesterday. Oh, and Mr. Blind Dog is here. He wants to see you."

Rand stopped by Mike's office, who was ending a call. "Okay, baby. I'll see you tonight." Mike had been at his desk and stood, waving Rand in. "Hey, Coleman!"

"Was that Nicole?"

"Ummm, no." He walked to the small grouping of chairs and motioned to one, offering a seat to Rand, but Rand didn't bite. He kept his distance, frowning, so Mike didn't sit either. "Somethin' wrong, man?"

"I don't mean to be nosy here, but that sounded like you making a date."

"Yeah."

Rand's head tilted, looking more puzzled than angry. "What about you and Nicole? You told me she was your 'gal.'"

It was Mike's turn to look puzzled, until it hit him. His Blind Dog smile took over, almost breaking into a chuckle. "Your intro, right? No, no, I didn't mean it like that." He gave Rand a hearty pat on the shoulder. "Nicole's my gal, because she's like my family. The only family I have. We've been best friends since college ... but that's it. Sorry, man, if I made you believe otherwise."

"So, Nicole is single? Not—" Rand stopped. "Wait! If she wasn't with you last night, where was she?" Rand casually slid his hands into his trouser pockets. It was his style anyway, whether he used the side pockets of his pants or his jacket, and in certain situations like this, it helped him to stay calm, or at least to hide it.

"She shot me a line, let me know she wasn't staying at her place. Why? You looking for her?" Mike was playful enough, although his vibe had changed.

Rand kept it light. "Yeah, she ditched me yesterday." He slid into one of the chairs offered earlier, and threw in, "If you hear from her, could you tell her to give me a call?" Mike nodded, and Rand asked, "Now, what did you want to see me about?"

Mike went with the flow and lowered himself to a seat across from Rand. "You remember Jeremy Franklin and his crew?"

"Yeah, Sure. Jeremy's the little guy that gets so much air on the court. What's up with them? Ready to start a league?" Rand asked.

"Actually, they're missing."

"Talk to me." Rand straightened. Mike had his full attention.

"It reminded me of Philip's story about his friend missing. Kids there one minute ... the next, they're gone, and no one is looking for them. Circumstances are different, but same thing ..." Mike paused, as though considering something, then added, "Nicole's working on a story like this. She promised not to be writing about our kids, but she needs to hear this!"

"Hold off on that! Give me the details."

"Jeremy was last seen talkin' up someone in a black Mercedes van. The way they described it, it has to be the Sprinter model, and you know that's not a regular vehicle in these woods. If a brother has a Mercedes, it's either going to be a jacked-up Escalade or a sedan, and I guarantee it's gonna have some swag to it," Mike said, his signature radio voice peeking through.

Rand nodded. "Listen, so you'll know, I'm still working on Philip's story. I just don't want to cause alarm around the center. With that said, I WILL follow up on this, too. Thanks for letting me know."

Later, before Rand left the center, he circled by Mike's office again. It was empty. Rand went straight to the computer to pull up Mike's email. Just as he'd hoped, Mike's password was saved on this system and, in one stroke of the mouse, his account was opened.

Looking through the contacts, he found Nicole's email address and opened a new memo from Mike. He wrote only two words, "Stuart Greystone," then hit "send." After confirmation of delivery, he deleted the email from the sent folder, then logged out, leaving Mike's office as he found it.

CHAPTER 37

"Batman WAS there, Ginny! You saw the same kids from that video! Angel and Jorge and Jackie and Kiandra! We have names! And faces for the names!" Nicole was driving back to the rented condo, since they were both too wound up to think about anything but the footage they just saw. Her smile was brilliant.

Ginny was more subdued and kept thanking Nicole, but by the time they got to the condo, she was withdrawn.

"Ginny? Talk to me. What is it?" Nicole asked, sitting on the sofa next to her.

"I'm sorry. I am happy. Actually, it was incredible, the feeling I had when they first came into view. And it proves that I'm not crazy, Nicole, but ..." Ginny's pained look was filled with guilt. Nicole recognized it. It had been her companion for years after Debbie. "... But now, now that I've seen those frightened little faces, not knowing what happened next is even worse."

It was warm in the room. Nicole walked to the sliding door and opened it, allowing a breeze through. She stood in the threshold, welcoming the cool air. So much had happened in the last few days that she hadn't even been on her morning runs, and she missed it. Missed the clarity it gave her. Playful sounds were coming from the sand, and Nicole closed her eyes and listened. It massaged Nicole's spirit, and gradually, everything clicked. Her eyes flew open. "Ginny! You didn't hit them!" Nicole quickly moved toward the couch where Ginny was and sat next to her.

"You don't know that." Ginny looked at Nicole, but only for a beat or two before hanging her head.

"Yes, I do! Look at me, Ginny." Nicole was smiling.

Once again, black from Ginny's makeup was smeared under her eyes, and she swiped at her nose with the back of her hand. "Nicole, you're saying that to make me feel better, but I don't want to feel better! I want to be punished!"

"Ginny! Stop this! Listen to me. Remember the thugs I saw at Theresa Chastang's? At Jackie's foster house? They were the same men chasing him, right? They were at the scene of your accident." Nicole was sitting up straight and pulled Ginny forward to look up at her. "Now, if you hit the children, why would they have gone back to the foster home looking for the kids to show up?"

They sat in a brief silence, then Ginny's eyes finally revealed she had caught on. She grabbed Nicole and hugged her. "Oh, Nicole ... You're right!"

Uncomfortable, Nicole was unresponsive to the hug and separated herself politely, saying, "You did this, Ginny! You got this started. When no one else believed you ... don't stop now."

They were on the patio later, and Ginny was elated, filled with questions. "What about Tom? Do you still think he's involved somehow? If the children aren't hurt, then there's nothing to cover up." She had her sunglasses on and sat under the umbrella, shaded from the magnificent skies.

"I wouldn't be so sure," Nicole said through a crooked half-smile. "If he is, it will unfold. And if he isn't, it doesn't matter anymore. We have another goal here. A purpose bigger than Tom." Nicole sat across the deck from Ginny, soaking up the sun.

Nicole's voice softened. "When you first told me about seeing Batman, I figured you were hallucinating from a really bad concussion!" A light chuckle passed between them, and Nicole shook her head. "Wow. What a story. Batman." Then she ran her hand through her thick hair, pushing it back. "But still, you trusted me with it, and in just days we've gotten a solid tracking on your kids! So, let's find that black Mercedes. It's the only logical explanation to their whereabouts."

"I'm in! But first, let's eat. I'm starved." Ginny was back.

Walking out to the Range Rover, Nicole said, "How about we go to Stanley's? My treat." She winked at Ginny and added, "Since I'm on an unlimited expense account." Stanley's Green Café was completely organic, and Nicole loved their black beans and jasmine rice.

"Rich client, huh?" Ginny grinned at Nicole, then slowly, she turned thoughtful. "The Smiling Tribes woman. Martha. You don't think that was an accident?"

"Not even." Nicole stopped and faced Ginny, with hands in motion. "Think about it. Martha visits Theresa Chastang, and within minutes Theresa is dead. Then, we stumble on Martha at the agency, and the same night she gets *accidently* shot in a drive-by? No. It's all connected. I just have to find out how. And why. It's someone's cover-up ... I'm just not sure it's Tom's."

Ginny's phone started ringing, and when she saw the caller ID said, "Nicole, I need to take this, and I might be a while. Why don't you go ahead? I'll just find something here."

"Sure," was all Nicole said, but instinctively she stayed where she was, watching, listening, as Ginny turned toward the condo. Nicole was curious who changed Ginny's mood and her mind so abruptly. This sudden private conversation. No longer starving.

"How do you do that? You always seem to know when I need to talk." Ginny strolled slowly outside the rental property, where Nicole could still hear. "Actually, I do need your help. We're looking for the driver of a black Mercedes van. The large model, I believe it's called the Sprinter. Have you seen one anywhere near the center?" Then she froze. "What do you mean? What kind of trouble?" She started walking again, but with purpose, and without looking back. The last Nicole heard was, "Do you have my beach address?"

"I don't believe it!" Nicole said aloud, not caring if Ginny heard her. She extended her arm, pointing toward the condo, "We have a clear lead like the van, and she gives it away to the first caller! This is what I get for sharing with someone!" She stormed to her SUV and got in, slamming the door. The resounding thud could be heard from inside, but Ginny was too engrossed to notice.

When Nicole arrived at Stanley's Green Café, she was still steaming, and the lunch crowd was thick. Nicole ordered her rice and beans to go. From somewhere near the entrance, someone shouted, "Hey, it's Nicole Portman!" Turning, she saw two figures with press badges from Drummond Media. "Retirement sure is treating you well!"

"Um, hello," she said half-heartedly, then the comment registered. "Wait, retired? Who said I was retired?"

"That's the word," said the lanky guy with camera bags draped across his chest. Everything about him seemed to be drooping, starting with the beret over his brow and ending with the shoelace of his Converse that dragged the ground. The woman with him was his polar opposite. Perky was best used to describe her, like an enthusiastic wind-up doll, and she was dressed for the camera. They were evidently a roving team.

"So, you're working on a book now, right? Is it a tell-all?" the woman asked in a hushed tone, leaning into Nicole as though only the two of them shared the secret.

"Ummm ... It's on hold temporarily, since I've been commissioned to an exclusive story."

"What's the story?!" The woman almost bounced.

"Sorry," Nicole gave her head a slight shake, "too early to give away details. So, what brings you guys out to Malibu in the middle of the day?" She asked, trying to be civil to these two, who probably knew everything about her job ... or lack of one.

"The shooting."

"Shooting?"

"Dude ..." The woman was going to answer, but the cameraman stepped over her to tell it himself. "Happened right in the middle of Malibu last night. Guy was shot outside of the HangOut. Just sittin' in his car. It was a bloody mess."

"Oh. That shooting. Yes." Nicole crossed her arms, and worked her camera face. The HangOut was across the street from her house.

"Portman. Order up!"

"That's me." Nicole grabbed her order, then turned back to the two. "By the way, was a black or white van involved?"

They both shook their heads and looked puzzled. The woman offered, "No."

"Good to see you guys." Nicole quickly took her food to her SUV and headed to her own home. Two police cars were in front of the Hang-Out, and they'd cordoned the area off with yellow tape. Her garage door lifted and, after tucking the Range Rover inside, she rushed to her kitchen counter to set up her laptop. It was second nature to eat behind her computer, and she took a bite of her food while punching in relevant keywords. They produced the story within seconds and KDLA's report included a video, live from the scene from last night's news. Nicole clicked "play." The newscast started, but was muted. Nicole raised the volume to hear, "... shooting in Malibu."

Panning the scene, the camera offered the viewers a glimpse into the chaos of police cars, flashing lights, yellow crime-scene tape, and crowds of people, then cut to an eyewitness interview. "I was crossing the street with my friends. We were laughing and talking, when someone said they thought they heard a shot. I, like, didn't hear it, but my friend said it was definitely a muffled shot, like a silencer. I wouldn't know, because I've, like, never heard one, and then—" she stopped. Her face crumpled and was turning red as she held her hands over her mouth, holding back sobs. Her friend took over and said, "That's when she saw it and started screaming. She pointed at the car, and we turned and saw it too. The man was shot in the head. Like, blood, everywhere." His hands spread outward in a circular motion, and the original witness was nodding in agreement. The camera found the reporter. It was the perky woman from Stanley's Café, and she finished the account as told by other witnesses.

"It seems the victim was sitting alone in a blue 2009 Saturn. The car, registered in the victim's name, was parked along the shoulder of the Pacific Coast Highway in front of the busy strip known to locals as the HangOut. Several eyewitnesses said a black Kawasaki motorcycle pulled alongside, and they heard small popping sounds, which are consistent with the sound of suppressed gunshot, as he fired into the car, killing the driver. Additional shots were fired, but so far there are no other reported injuries. Eyewitnesses attribute that to a black Ford Raptor truck that slid in, just in time to block the crowd from the spray of bullets, then just as quickly left, chasing after the motorcycle. As of this report, no one has come forward with a tag number on either. Some said the motorcycle didn't have a tag. Police are reaching out to the public. If you have any information on last night's shooting, including our *mystery hero* in the black Ford truck, please contact the Malibu Police Department."

The video switched from the reporter to a still shot of a driver's license photo of the victim. "The victim has been identified as fifty-two-year-old Charles Keel. His injury was an apparent gunshot to the head, and he was pronounced dead at the scene." Nicole dropped her fork. It hit the chair, then landed on the floor, but she didn't react; she was glued to the picture on the screen. The camera went back to the reporter. "Keel was also known as 'Fuzz' by his friends and family, a name he earned from years of service as a police officer with the LAPD. Of course, cause of death will be determined by the county medical examiner, and we will keep you informed of the details as they are released. Reporting from Malibu, I'm Renee Heller."

"The van driver! Across the street from my house? Dead!" The rapid-fire questions were stacking up as high as the facts, and she paced. "LAPD? Where's his partner? ... A black Ford Raptor!" She dialed Ginny. When it went to voice mail, she left a message. "There was a shooting here in Malibu last night. Call me!"

Nicole picked over her lunch while searching the internet for news updates, not only on this latest shooting, but Martha Vaughn's as well. She turned on the television, hoping for something new, then tried Ginny again. It went to voice mail. Rap-tap-tapping. She caught herself tapping her hand, her fingers, her pen. *What if they were looking for me? I owe Ginny, for keeping me away from here last night ... but whatever those thugs got themselves into, the police are involved now and are all over the area. I should be safe to come home!*

Back in her Range Rover, Nicole headed north to the rental to get the few belongings she'd left there and to check on Ginny again.

The rental wasn't large, so it didn't take long to see no one was there. Nicole went to Ginny's room, then checked the bathroom. Ginny's toiletry bag, made of a loud, quilted print, screamed for Nicole's attention, but what was beyond the bag was what captured her. An electric toothbrush. Nicole ran her thumb over the white bristles. They were dry. The crease between her brows deepened and concern fueled her pace, examining the rest of the condo for any sign of activity: glasses, lunch dishes. Nothing. "You said you were going to eat something here," she thought aloud.

The back deck was visible from the living area, and it was empty as well, but Nicole still walked out and scanned the beach. *Ginny sat under the umbrella earlier, I don't see her walking the beach in this heat.* "Unless ... she did ask the mystery caller if they knew her beach address ... she's probably there!"

The Vinsant's beach house was only three blocks away, but Nicole still drove. There was a new, white BMW parked outside of the garage. After knocking on the front door and waiting several seconds, she rang the bell. Twice. Then tried the handle. It was unlocked. Nicole pushed the door open and called, "Ginny?"

The foyer was a landing. Brilliantly placed where the visitor could stand - like on the end of a runway - and gawk at the view through the glass wall of the entire backside of the enormous living area. And Nicole did. It was a small resort; the interior not missing one detail, and could've been on the cover of *Condé Nast Traveler*.

"So, this is what our tax dollars are doing." Nicole stood tall, her hands on her hips, and took it in. "Actually, I bet it's those waterfront kickbacks." She scanned it again. "Or even one of your bogus bills pushed through to line your pockets." She was openly stunned. "And Ginny doesn't question this?" She shook her head slowly, then, stepping down from the foyer, Nicole walked softly. Mainly because she was trespassing, but also from pure reflex, because the tumbled marble was flawless.

"GINNY? TOM?" Nicole called. Still no answer. The house was large, but it was quiet. *If anyone was here, surely they heard me, unless they are in the shower.*

Nicole eased her way around the entire house. "Ginny? Tom?" she repeated before entering each room, but was met only with an eerie silence. The beautiful tumbled marble extended out to the patio decking, and Nicole followed it, and still, there were no signs of anyone being here. *But the front door was unlocked.*

The breeze was blowing steadily on the deck, whipping Nicole's hair around her face, and she fought it to see the display on her phone. She pushed "connect" for Ginny's number. The ring on her end was echoed by the slight sound of a ringtone that started close by. Tilting and turning her head, it was hard to determine the direction it was coming from with the wind in her ears. After a few steps around the deck, it was obvious it was coming from inside, and Nicole released a huge sigh of relief, running toward the door. "Ginny!"

The ringtone had stopped, and on Nicole's end she heard the same stale recording to leave a message, so she disconnected and tried again. Three groupings of furniture were in the open living area where she stood: the main setting, then two smaller settings for more intimate conversation. The ringtone was louder now as it began, and Nicole followed it toward the smaller grouping closest to the far windows. "Ginny?" She walked softly, circling around the sofa, expecting her to be lying there, but it was empty. The phone kept chirping. The low, glass coffee table in front of the sofa held a beautiful, white multi-tier shell as a centerpiece and there, in the bottom of the shell, was Ginny's phone.

Slowly lowering herself onto the cushion, she disconnected the call. "I should have never left her by herself, with everything that's going on." Leaning forward, Nicole put her fingers to her temples and rubbed. Several seconds passed, then her eyes opened wide. "The detective!"

Nicole bolted out of the house. The beach road in front of the Vinsant's was busy, and vehicles of every size were parked along the shoulders, but after quickly scanning her surroundings left and right, there was no tan Ford Explorer. Methodically, she looked at each car parked along the shoulders in case he had switched vehicles. They were all empty. Nicole's frown deepened, and she was back inside the Vinsant's house before it hit her. "Wherever they are, the detective would have reported it to Tom!"

Rolling south down the interstate in her Range Rover, Nicole called Mike. His greeting through her speakers was grounding. "Hey baby! About time we caught each other. You coming my way?"

"Actually, I'm headed to Tom Vinsant's office."

"Excuse me?"

Nicole gave him a broad stroke of what was happening as she drove in and out of traffic. She took a deep breath and finished with, "So far, two people tied to my visit on Gramble Street are dead. Make that three. I shouldn't have left her alone, Mike, but at least Tom has her followed. He should know where she is."

"Baby, it's time to call the police."

"And tell them what? I have nothing but speculations! If I say Ginny's missing ... what's my proof? Also, it's only been a couple of hours, *and* Tom would have to report it." Nicole dug in her tote for her sunglasses case. "So, I have no choice. I have to go to Tom."

"You don't need to be flyin' solo with no one to watch your back. Circle by and pick me up, or I'll meet you there."

"I'll be fine. Think about it. Although the police still think Martha Vaughn was a drive-by accident, this latest shooting has the markings of a hit. They'll be investigating. Widely. So, I actually feel safer now, and when I really have something, I'll turn it over. Promise. In the meantime, I'll keep calling so you'll know where I was last seen." She chuckled, but it didn't hide the disturbing truth of that comment.

"Call me after each move, or I come along." He waited for a commitment, which she finally obliged him under her breath, then he changed the subject. "You remember Ginny saying a couple of kids that she suspected of abuse had stopped coming in?"

"Yeah."

"Well, one of them was a kid named Jeremy Franklin. Him an' his foster brothers had it bad at home from what I understand, so they hung at The Rock. Everyday. No one has seen them around lately, and the kid who saw them last gave me a description of a vehicle that could be involved."

"Wait, don't tell me," Nicole said. "A black Mercedes Travel van."

"Of course, you'd know. So, what are we looking at here?"

"I'm not sure, but the piece fits," she said. "Thanks, Mike."

"We passed this on to those two detectives, Rock protocol ... so *maybe* they're gettin' enough juice to believe your speculation ... so *maybe* it's time to include them now."

"Eventually." Then she asked, "By the way, who's Stuart Greystone?" The sun was bright, and the search for her sunglasses didn't produce anything, so she opened the console where she always kept an extra pair. The Diors.

"Who?"

"Stuart Greystone. You sent me the name. What does it mean?"

"Sorry, baby, not me. You sure you won't call the police?"

"I will! Soon!" Nicole said.

As soon as the call ended, her phone rang again. Nicole slid on the Diors as she answered, "What did you forget?"

"Nicole, this is Kim."

"Oh, Kim! Hi." It was three o'clock in the afternoon. With school traffic adding to the congestion, and now Kim on the phone, Nicole stopped trying to maneuver quickly through and gave in. She moved at a snail's pace with the rest of them, listening closely to her caller. "Did you have time to find out anything on those names I gave you?"

"This is very strange, Nicole, but none of them are in my computer system today. Even Angel from the other day. I had it then, but today? Nothing. By the way, was the address I gave you correct?"

"Yes. It was. Unfortunately, I've lost his trail because his foster mom overdosed." She didn't bother telling Kim it was only two days ago and she was the one who found her.

"Hmmm, maybe that's why I can't find anything. Perhaps they transferred him to another county or state, but even so, I should be able to track him. One thing I did find, however, was a hard copy of a few transfers from the county to private agencies. They were in a 'To Be Filed' folder, even though I can't locate the permanent folders or find them in the system, but two of the documents have the first names you gave me. The last name is Spence. Are you wanting to spotlight these kids? Because I'm not sure you can, Nicole. I'll have to ask our legal department."

Nicole's pulse had quickened. "No! Never! They'll stay anonymous. I'm only using the circumstances. Just to complete my notes, did you place them, or did you turn them over to a private agency?"

"They were placed with Smiling Tribes Foster Care. That name just *keeps* coming up!"

CHAPTER 38

"Tom?" Rita called softly, peeking into the senator's office. She could have used the intercom on the phone system, but at every opportunity she enjoyed distracting him, like now. With folders in her hand and a pen stuck behind her ear, her props looked as though she were working so hard she didn't notice a couple of buttons on her blouse had come undone. "I hate to disturb you, but your new partner is holding on line one. And Tom, you never had a break today, is there anything I can do for you?" she asked coyly. It would have made Marilyn proud.

He picked up the receiver, but before punching the button said, "This will only take a minute, why don't you close that door and lock it, then fix me a scotch on the rocks." With that, he connected the line and turned his back to her. "Tom Vinsant here."

"I'm just making sure we're still on for tomorrow. We've gotten the paperwork back from the attorney. He's finalized the terms, so we're ready to go."

It was Tom's new financial backer. "Great news. Yes, I've set the entire morning aside for our meeting. How about eight thirty at my office?"

"Fine. Fine, Senator. I will see you then." The call ended, but Tom held the receiver longer and kept his back to Rita, reveling in his good fortune in solitude. After Thursday, he would have the funding he needed not only to win this reelection, but to invest with his new international partners. He was finished being the water boy for the superwealthy, slipping in appropriations bills that either funded their bogus programs or tripled their stocks. They were turning their fortunes into billions while he settled for their measly kickbacks. No more. With this new group and their money, he was going to find out what the title "billionaire" tasted like.

For Tom, there was no aphrodisiac like power and money. Hanging up the phone, he leaned back in his chair and turned around to Rita, whose blouse was fully unbuttoned now. "Someone looks hungry," he said. "Crawl to me, Rita. Very slowly. Show me how much you want it."

His sultry, redheaded assistant actually got on her hands and knees and did as she was told, and Tom's breathing grew heavy. His desire to control was incredible. Rita was a mature woman, just shy of forty, and having this kind of power over her was even better than the child in Washington ... Duke's girl. He loosened his tie and was starting on his belt when his private phone rang. Rita jumped when he slammed his fist on the desk. "Stay," he told her. Like ordering a dog. And she did. He kept his eye on her breasts toppling over the top of her bra as she awaited his next command. He picked up the phone. "Yes?"

"Your mess has been cleaned up; however, your poor judgment needs to be addressed. Perhaps your lovely wife could help us." And the voice hung up. Before Tom could process the conversation, his office door swung open, and Nicole Portman was standing there.

Whatever Nicole was expecting when she made the decision to go to Tom about Ginny couldn't have been close to the scene in front of her. Once all parties recovered from their own form of shock, they were all talking at once. "I can't imagine what you've been asked to do, but you owe me! Big!" Nicole said to Rita, who was still on the floor on her hands and knees. "I've saved you from further disgracing yourself."

"I thought you locked the door!" Tom raised his voice at Rita. Then to Nicole, "What the hell are you doing in my office? Leave, or I'll call security!"

Rita jumped to full height, grabbing the folders she came in with and holding them in front of her opened blouse, addressing Tom, "I did lock it! I'm sorry, Tom, ummm ... Senator," and she scurried out of the office door, closing it behind her.

"You're still here? Did you not hear me?" Tom stared at Nicole and picked up his desk phone.

"I only came to ask you one thing, AND I won't share what I've seen here today if you'll answer my simple question."

He paused momentarily. "No one believes you anyway, since Sidney canned you. Do you think I'm worried about who or what you tell?" However, he placed the receiver down. "What one question is so important that you would risk another public humiliation, like being thrown out of my building?"

"Have you heard from your wife today?"

"That's it? Have I heard from my wife?"

Not playing into a banter, she nodded her head yes, her long hair dancing over her shoulder, and the simple movement seemed to amuse Tom. He stood, grinning at the leggy, live, breathing version of his nemesis, with her captivating eyes. "Now why would you want to know about my wife?"

"She and I were supposed to meet today, and she's not responding to my calls. I'm very concerned."

"Well, isn't that sweet." He stepped around the front of his desk, eyes combing the length of her body. "The news shark of LA is taking a break from her ball-busting to have lunch with my wife. And since my darling wife is as inconsiderate with you as she is with me, you're concerned. I. Am. Touched." He patronized her, leaned back against the desk, and tilted his head back, arms crossed. Watching.

"Senator. Please. Have you heard from your wife today?"

"No. No, I haven't. It might not occur to you, but I'm a busy man. I avoid her idle musings when I'm working."

"But you know what she does. You have her followed. So, if something has happened to her, your man would know about it ... unless he's had something to do with it."

He stood straight. The amusement gone. "How dare you walk into my office and accuse me of harming my wife. Get out of here!" His face turned red as he took a couple of steps toward her.

"Let me rephrase." Nicole closed her eyes briefly, then looked squarely at the senator. "She knows you have her followed, Tom. If your man has any idea where she is ... I just want to know she's okay. Can you call him and ask him?"

"Are you recording this? Is this some kind of setup?"

With her hands held high, Nicole showed him her car keys and the dark face of her hibernating cell phone. It was all she carried. The tote would have been searched downstairs, so she hadn't bothered with it.

"How do you two know each other?"

"We're working on a charity project, for children."

Tom rubbed his face, then walked back behind his desk. "I see. She's talked to you about her mysterious 'kid' sighting." Tom spread his hands on the desktop and leaned toward her. "You think I'm stupid enough to buy into the charity thing, huh?" He was smiling. "Her, yes. You? No. Not enough excitement. You're a newshound." He lowered himself into his leather chair slowly, watching her. "So, what is it this time, Ms. Portman? Using my wife to get to me? Using her instability to hurt my re-election?" The smile was replaced with a look meant to disable. "Just try it. I will ruin you!"

Nicole walked toward his desk, slowly. Three chairs faced him in a half-moon, and she stood behind the one in the middle, her right hand braced on the back, keeping eye contact the entire time. "I'm not interested in the war between us. She's genuinely missing."

"Why this newfound interest in my wife?"

"Honestly? I don't know. Maybe it's only because I love a mystery. Would you call your investigator?"

"She's not missing. She's at the beach."

Nicole let go of the breath she was holding. "So, you heard from him?"

No comment.

"I told you, I know about him ... and today it works in her favor. Where, exactly, at the beach?" She caught the struggle in his eye. He wasn't admitting anything to her, so Nicole tried again, "I'm not judging. And I'm not writing about this ... unless ... if you refuse to help me find her. Her public wouldn't like that."

"If I had her watched so closely, don't you think I'd have known you and Ginny were together?"

"No, Tom, I don't. Because I'm a professional. I'm better than him."

The veins down the sides of his neck bulged, and Nicole tried not to show her satisfaction. He seethed, "Ginny doesn't need you. Butt out."

"But she needs this?" Nicole lifted her brows as she swept her hand where she'd seen Rita crawling on the floor.

Tom's fists tightened. Nicole took an easy step back. "Yeah, it comes with the deal." His lip pulled to one side, almost snarling, when he said, "You think I'm corrupt? Ginny wrote the book on it!"

With little movement, Nicole looked like she was shifting foot to foot, restless, but was actually adding slightly more real estate between them. Tom's eyes had glazed over, his knuckles whitening. "... Oh yeah, so if you're going to sniff around our private life, make sure you get both sides. Did she tell you how she tricked us? Me and my family? Yeah, she knew my family were devout Catholics, so when she conveniently became pregnant, she knew what would happen." He leaned forward like he was sharing a secret, but the spiteful smirk kept her on alert. "And guess what? After we eloped, there was an equally convenient miscarriage. Surprise!" His hands flew in the air with the word, then his smirk turned into a full grin at Nicole. "What? Did I shock our star newshound that our little Ginny could be so deceitful? So manipulative?"

Nicole had already heard a slighter version from Ginny, so she didn't bite. "Yes, I've seen what a devout Catholic you are."

But Tom chuckled like he was actually enjoying their confrontation. "I made sure it wouldn't happen again. Lucky for me, one of my fraternity brothers became a urologist." He leaned back in his executive chair. "My campaign is clean. And I plan on keeping it that way, so yeah, I have my wife watched. I can't afford not to. Every day, it's something with her." He picked up his scotch, "Care for one?"

A pig. Bigger than I ever imagined. Nicole reached into her back pocket and produced a business card, holding it up. "If you'll call me as soon as you hear from her or see her, just to let me know she's safe, then, like I said ... this encounter never happened." She laid the card on a table next to the door.

He took a swig of his scotch, eyes steady on Nicole. She was about to walk out, then turned to face Tom again. "However, if I find you had anything to do with her disappearance, I will make it my mission in life to see you rot in prison." And with that final promise, she left.

Tom didn't bother nursing the remainder of his drink; he threw it back, then walked to the wet bar and poured himself a new one. The landline started ringing and kept ringing. Evidently, Rita had left. Tom went back to his desk with his fresh drink and lifted the receiver. "Yes?"

"Senator! Oh, Senator, I'm SO glad I caught you!"

"May I ask to whom I am speaking?"

"Senator, it's Ashley! Remember? Ashley Martin?"

Tom's legs folded and he lowered into his chair.

"Senator? Are you there? Hello?"

"I think you've dialed the wrong number."

"Tom, it's me! From the engagement party with my Uncle Duke! Oh, Tom, it's so good to hear your voice and I've been looking for a reason to call, but ... it's about Uncle Duke. He should have been home by now, and we're starting to get worried. Tom, you're so strong. I just needed to hear your voice."

"Is this some kind of prank? Like I said, you've got the wrong number."

"Oh, Tom, don't say that! I haven't stopped thinking about you—"

Tom disconnected.

CHAPTER 39

Stuart Greystone stood in his foyer that Wednesday afternoon, tossing something in the air and catching it. A thumb drive. It was the way he prepped for his three o'clock call with Dr. Xavier Howard, the "voice" behind The Network. The thumb drive had every incriminating piece of evidence to destroy the Doc, as he called him, and the entire operation. A duplicate copy was kept in his safe-deposit box with specific instructions to his estate attorney if he should meet with an untimely death. Tossing it now, holding Doc's life in his hands, gave him inexpressible pleasure. Enough to withstand the boring conversation he was about to have.

It's like those bloody meetings in the headmaster's office. A not-so-happy childhood memory. Each week at Stuart Greystone's boarding school, his single father would call in from different parts of the world to get a report on his son. Never in person. The headmaster was always involved, keeping the call on speakerphone, ready to share Greystone's shortcomings academically or socially, even trumpeting the boy's poor eating habits to his father. Greystone was expected to stand in front of the headmaster's desk through the entire ordeal, then was dismissed as his father rung off. By time Greystone went off to university, he was accustomed to being alone and embraced it, actually, thankful to be rid of the humiliating calls.

Over the years Greystone dabbled in a few businesses, but with his father's wealth he didn't have to concern himself with success; that is, until his father died suddenly. The inheritance was substantial, but Greystone feared it dwindling, feared living without extravagance, and sought ways to secure his fortune. He considered it pure luck to find a business partner in the wealthy, eccentric Dr. Xavier Howard, and by the time he caught on that it wasn't a partnership, it was too late. The Network owned him. And here he was, like that child summoned to the phone, waiting on a call.

He still had ten minutes, and contacted Dominic, his lieutenant, who answered the same as Greystone always did, on the first ring. "Anything?"

"No. Only what I've heard from the news. Half of the assignment was completed, but we won't know about the other half until he makes contact, and that might not be possible if he's sheltered down in that canyon. There's no cell service," Dominic said, then reassuringly added, "He's one of our best, boss. We'll hear something."

"Keep me informed," was all Greystone needed to say before abruptly hanging up. As usual, with a firm sense of his strengths and limitations, he got right to the point with his men.

Greystone ran the trafficking division for The Network, overseeing the entire West Coast of the United States. He had come to consider transferring stolen military property, illegal weapons, and even humans, acceptable; they were businessmen's commodities. That twisted sense of justification, however, stopped at drugs, but not because of conscience. Greystone had proclaimed, with his self-righteous snobbery. "Drugs are for street thugs," and because he was such an asset, The Network conceded on this one issue and farmed the drugs to another.

The burner phone rang. It was three o'clock and he answered on the first ring. "Greystone here."

"Stu. Punctual as always," was Doc's greeting.

Greystone scowled. To him, the nickname was offensive and he was certain that was Doc's intention.

"Your IT department has shown incredible talent at altering records; however, actual inventory and movement has fallen. What's the problem?" Doc asked with a slight accent. Greystone had researched Dr. Howard and knew his unique delivery was due to the years spent between his parent's home countries, Spain and Ireland.

"We realize this," Greystone said. "Some of our transfers have been sabotaged. We are investigating and whatever is happening, we will find it."

"SOME? Over half! We're behind our projection in the live market by over fifty percent! If you're being sabotaged, then someone's getting your information. How?"

"Like I said, we'll find whoever is doing this." Greystone flipped the thumb drive in the air and watched it fall back into his palm. Expressionless.

"Until the problem is dealt with, the domestic operations from the social systems are on hold. As of this afternoon, switch solely to the structure set for Mexican immigrants. Illegals. It's clean. No paper trail; no one is looking for them. 'Operation Pilgrim,' it's called, will take over. Beef up the teams at the border to pose as *coyotajes*. We already have two other enterprises working in Mexico, so let me know if you need manpower. As soon as they're transported to our safe houses in California, coordinate their destination. We don't want them here for an unnecessary length of time. It allows opportunities for issues. And I don't like issues."

Greystone was silent, watching his own reflection in the mirror across the hall in the foyer. Although he was only in his forties, his hair was a striking silver color and one of his obsessions. He absently groomed it, disengaged from Doc's concern.

"And the four runaways?" Greystone heard Doc ask over clopping sounds. Doc always called from his stables. He was a veterinarian in another life, and still loved his horses, much more than people.

"We're examining theories. They disappeared after the commotion from an auto accident. Senator Vinsant's wife. We can't be sure if she saw them ..."

Doc cut him off. "Don't worry about the wife, we'll tend to her. Tell me about the reporter she's taken up with. Isn't she the one who rattled your contact at the agency? Martha?"

Greystone hid his irritation. "So you know this already? She's being watched, but she has nothing. A foster home and Martha were the only connections, and they are no longer a problem."

"If anything changes, I expect to be notified immediately." The braying and snorting of horses became excessive, distorting the conversation, and Greystone strained to follow the quick change of subject. "I ... customer, The Company Keeper ... escapee ... import from Haiti. Do you ... details?"

Greystone was still watching his reflection, turning right then left, checking all angles of his hair. The British accent was exceptionally heavy when he answered, "Yes. We provided them with a lanky sixteen-year-old who went by the name Timbo. They claimed he was difficult, so they kept him chained." Greystone shook his head, remembering. *Timbo, what a ridiculous name. And the male clientele thought the chain was part of his act. That whole situation is ridiculous, actually.*

Greystone continued, "His aggression worsened, so they drugged him, but he still got away, and the customer wanted a replacement. I assured them we do not warranty, so this is history, and I'm sorry you were bothered by it."

"So, you have the boy?" The connection was better.

Same routine. Doc asked, but usually knew the answer. Greystone started walking the foyer. "We're working on it."

Dr. Xavier Howard's voice tightened. "One neglected detail can take down an entire empire, and I'll not tolerate it." Silence followed. All background sounds stopped. Not a breeze or even a horse's nay. The call had been muted. Greystone waited.

When the call came to life again, Doc said, "Time to reign in the senator." Doc talked a few more minutes before disconnecting.

Greystone had his orders. He tossed the thumb drive in the air again. "Before this game gets any deeper, I have one more thing to add to this drive ... the WHO on the chain above Doc Howard." He tossed it again, thinking. Greystone had his theories, but nothing solid. Yet.

Dominic called. "He's been found at the bottom of Topanga Canyon. Him and his motorcycle."

"What about the big guy?"

"Nothing."

CHAPTER 40

Scraping bottom wasn't something Tom Vinsant was afraid of. He was quick to share his barroom philosophy. "Without the highs and lows in life ... there's no range of motion, you're just stuck in the middle."

Warning Ginny early in their marriage, he said, "Mediocrity would be my death sentence, so don't expect it from me." He told her, "If you're looking for Mr. Safe, you know, the guy who places ten dollars on the roulette wheel and walks away happy whether he wins or loses, then you've got the wrong person. That man won't remember anything about his life." Then he'd pointed his finger into his puffed-out chest with a grin playing across his lips, "I'm the man who will bet it all on one hand of poker. I'll walk away either broke or loaded, but I guarantee my journey will be remarkable."

And all of his highs and lows were just that. Remarkable. However, the current turn of events was heading somewhere deeper than a mere low. In one more day his backer's funding would come through, but not if a scandal blew up around Tom.

"Duke sets me up with a child, then subtly threatens to expose me if I don't let him in on our waterfront action. Next, I get that two-sentence call about my poor judgment and threatening my wife. Then the news leech shows up saying my wife is missing and immediately after, the jail-bait calls my office to confess her love, which Duke was probably recording." Tom was racing through traffic to get home and sounding off in the privacy of his car. When his cell phone rang, he attacked.

"What?"

The now familiar voice that came over the speaker system was distressed. "Oh, Tom, I admit I was looking for a reason to call before, but this ... this ... is so, so horrid!" Ashley, the unwanted jailbait, was crying in the phone. He rolled his eyes, expecting her profession of love again, and his thumb rested on the steering-wheel button that would make her go away, but he needed to say something first to insure she never called again.

"I don't know who is giving out my private number, but as I said before, you have the wrong person! Do NOT call again!"

"Please, Tom, NO! It's Uncle Duke! He was ... was ... he was only minutes from his house when it happened." Jagged breaths overcame her. She was crying again. He kept toying with the button that would disconnect her, but she'd piqued his interest. Tom waited, and eventually she recovered and continued. "His car left the road. At Harold's Bend." She sniffed and her warbly voice pierced his ears: "He's dead!"

His thumb pushed in, and she was gone. Tom tried Ginny's phone. He waited through three rings, then heard Ginny's soft voice asking him to leave a message. He punched another contact in his car system, and this time, the recording was filled with too much testosterone and someone's poor attempt at humor. "Ivan here. I'm not going to insult you ... you know what to do." Tom had never heard the message before, since his private-security man, Ivan, the one who was supposed to keep an eye on Ginny, always answered Tom's calls.

Tom pulled the business card Nicole had left and flipped it over, then absently flipped it again, and again with his right hand as he drove with his left. Thinking. Coming up on an intersection, Tom moved to the left-turn lane. The light was red. He dialed the number.

"Hello?"

"It's Tom Vinsant."

"You've heard from Ginny!" She blurted out.

"No."

"Is that why you're calling? You believe me?"

The light turned green. Tom needed to make a move, and he didn't have a lot of options. "We need to talk. I'm headed to the beach. Can you meet me there?"

Silence.

"Hello?" Tom asked.

"Ginny said you never go to the beach."

Now it was his turn to be silent.

"Okay, meet me at Zeke's," Nicole said. "It's public, but the area in the back, past the dining room, is fairly secluded. What time?"

Tom made a U-turn. "I'm leaving Beverly Hills now. Depending on traffic, I should be there by six forty-five."

* * *

Nicole looked at the phone in her hand, then at the clock. It was six. Zeke's was only ten minutes away. Biting her lip, Nicole tried Ginny's phone again. And again, no answer.

Next, she tried Sidney. He wouldn't still be at the office, so she called his cell.

"My dear, how are you?"

"Sidney, if I have an exclusive that I know will make HUGE head-lines, am I still a leper? Or would you run it for me? I'm not asking for my job back; I just need a platform for my story."

"You never were a 'leper,' my dear, it was damage control, to protect our interests. Just a little distance until the dust settles."

"Again, if I bring you a good story, will you run it for me?"

"Not if it has anything to do with the senator. I heard you were seen with his wife recently. I thought I told you to leave them alone, Nicole."

"And where did you get that information?"

"You need some real journalism. Maybe a trip to the Middle East? Or, I have a lead on something BIG in Central America. You could get in the middle of it. Why don't you come in Friday?"

"Goodbye, Sidney." Nicole threw her phone aside. "It all goes back to you, Senator. No one wants to believe me or Ginny ... not the authori-ties, not my boss ... all because of Tom and his tentacles. Ginny, you re-ally have been living in hell!"

The struggle fueled her. She opened the odd email that Mike denied sending and copied the two words, Stuart Greystone. Public data re-sources gave minor details and no images when she ran the name, but Drummond Media had access to extensive records. If only she could still get in. Watching the time, she pulled up the website and entered her passcode. The searching icon went 'round and 'round and 'round. There were rumors before Nicole left KDLA that a shield was installed to at-tack hackers. If her authorization code was canceled, would she appear as a hacker? Nicole anxiously tapped the desk. *I don't even know if that's possible, but my files are all backed up, so I'll see.* The seconds stretched out. A full minute had gone by, possibly two. It was in a loop. "Something's wrong." Nicole stopped tapping. She laid her finger on the escape button, about to press it, when her monitor came to life with the familiar database.

"I'm in!" She waved her hands, excitedly. She had twenty more minutes. She got to work.

Greystone's name generated several hits, but the information was scattered. Watching the clock, Nicole printed everything she could find, even a couple of related images, then placed everything into a folder to take to Zeke's. She could read it while she waited for Tom. It might be premature, but she also added Greystone's name to her outline and his image to memory.

Zeke's had a beach-casual atmosphere, so Nicole didn't bother changing. She was wearing light-denim jeans with a black blouse, and slipped in her silver loop earrings to add a little polish, with a pair of pewter-colored ballet flats, *In case I have to walk a lot tonight ... or run*, she thought. The pale shade of lipstick she applied was more to moisten her lips, and she grabbed a sweater from the closet.

It was happy hour in the bar area when she arrived, and the guests were thick, milling through fumes of alcohol, coconut suntan oil, and trendy colognes. Nicole followed the hostess to a table in the back, as requested, and with time to spare she read through the printouts of Stuart Greystone.

Greystone was born Stuart Oglethorpe in Vancouver, British Columbia, to a single mother, Jean Oglethorpe. There was no further information on her. Shortly thereafter, he was adopted by Edward Greystone, from an affluent London family, and his name was changed to Greystone. It listed the university he attended, then a couple of investment write-ups, one from five years ago and another from eight that alluded he was still wealthy. The sources listed his residences as California, Vancouver, and London, but no specific address on any of them. No other details, and strangely, there wasn't a clear, posed photograph in his file. The few images available were candid shots, which best showed him resembling a younger version of British actor Michael Caine. Just with thicker, light hair. *Odd. Why wouldn't someone of his financial status have more images on file ... AND why would someone send me his name?* She replaced the file back into her tote and tapped her fingers on the table.

Her tapping fell to the beat of the song playing, and when Nicole realized she was doing it, she smiled and looked around. Everyone else was just as guilty. The deejay's mix was perfect for this Wednesday crowd of beachgoers, until he faded out to a softer tune, an oldie by Billy Ocean. Nicole relaxed, enjoying the diversion, giving the Stuart Greystone mystery a rest, but the crowd didn't follow her lead. The ballad had to fight the laughter, conversations, and clattering dishes for their attention. Nicole simply closed her eyes and listened. *"Suddenly, life had new meaning to me ..."* It was soothing, and she relished in the simple message of the song. Until, *suddenly* the air around her changed. It alerted her to a physical presence entering her space. Nicole's eyes popped open.

"You left without saying goodbye." The minty warmth of his breath embraced her, and Rand slid in next to her in the booth, their thighs lightly touching.

"Can I get you anything?" Came a voice from behind Rand, and the server had to ask a second time.

It was Nicole who finally answered, "No. Thank you. He's not staying." The initial shock of seeing him jolted her heart rate, but she was regaining a drop of composure. She straightened in the seat. "I'd already taken enough time out of your morning. I should have thanked you before I left, but I had an appointment to make."

"Yes. So you'd said. With a broken window?"

Nicole lifted her chin.

His voice was low. Confidential. "Folks talk." He looked away, staring off at nothing. "I left you a couple of messages. I was beginning to wonder if I should be concerned, because someone like you wouldn't simply ignore my call."

"I'm here in a business capacity." Nicole picked up her water glass, but set it down again. "You really should go. If you're here, he won't come in."

Rand nodded. He sat for another minute without conversation, hands folded on the table, then turned, his face within inches of hers. His cologne, his breath, melded together, and the result was as dangerous as his eyes. Nicole stirred, moving a few inches away. "I'm going," Rand said. "But like I said before, we need to talk." He paused. "You still have my number?" Her nod was slight, and he continued, "Good. Eight o'clock? Your place. If you won't be home by then, please call and let me know." Then he was gone.

Nicole picked up her water glass and rolled the contents around, watching it, then set it down once more. Like a tidal wave, Rand had rolled in, creating an all-consuming energy. Now Nicole was left in the aftermath. The void. The vacuum of emptiness that was just as overwhelming. She took her notebook out and found her pen. It was imperative she recover and prep for Tom. He would be there any minute. She jumped when he slid into the seat across from her, and he kept sliding until he was completely against the wall. "I almost left," Tom said.

"I'm listening."

"Why were you talking to the feds?"

"Excuse me?"

"The man that just left this booth. Tell me what he was doing here, and I need to believe you, or I'm gone."

"Mistaken identity. The man who was here is a pastor," Nicole said. "Anyway, I don't have to explain my friends to you." Tom squinted at her in the same manner as he used in his office earlier. It could have been accusation or evaluation. But it wasn't friendly. "What?" she jabbed.

"I'm trying to decide if you think I'm stupid, or if you actually believe this crap."

"That man is not the reason we are here."

Tom's face was getting red, but he kept his voice down in a hushed strain, and leaned forward. "I'll ask again, why a special agent from the Sacramento office was sitting here playing chummy with you in the booth?"

"Special agent?"

"Yes. Special agent." Then he drew out slowly, "Of. The. F. B. I."

"I know what *of*, Senator!" Nicole hissed. "And I'd love to hear how you could possibly recognize every FBI agent from here to the Sacramento office." The vein at Nicole's temple was growing. "But first, let's discuss why you even called this meeting ... what's your game, Tom?"

"Ms. Portman, my game is survival. I actually thought you and I could help each other." Tom stopped, his stare bore through her, and Nicole met it, not backing down. He continued, not taking his eyes from her. "However, you made the mistake of bringing *him* here." He pointed toward the front entrance. "You want to know how I recognize him? I make it a point to remember faces that can help me or harm me. The man who just left qualifies." Tom broke contact and moved against the wall again, his eyes scanning, taking in their surroundings. "He probably feels safe down here in LA, but I remember him *and* his team from when they took down Governor Bartlett. So, don't tell me I'm mistaken." When he caught her stricken look, a sickly grin covered his handsome face. "Well, I'll be. My pain-in-the-ass-ball-buster didn't know."

Get it together, Nicole. Pose for the camera. Don't let Tom Vinsant get the best of you! Nicole took a long, silent breath, keeping her head high, and she released it slowly. It was working. She looked calmer. More poised. In a tone of indifference, she asked, "Is there a point to all of this?"

"Yes. Had you known, I would've left and been on the phone to the state's attorney working up some kind of charge against the two of you for entrapment. Is that why you cooked up that story about my wife? You knew I'd bite?"

Nicole leaned back and crossed her arms, trying to enjoy Tom's discomfort. "Entrapment? That's rich, Senator!" Getting her footing back, she continued, "I find truth, unlike you. I don't 'cook up stories.'"

Tom rubbed his hand across the back of his neck. "A very low point ... to call you," he said aloud, but it was to himself. The hostess was leading a party of four by their booth, and Tom waited until they passed. His mood took another turn. "So ... Ms. Portman ... from what I understand, you are the last person to see Ginny." Placing his forearms on the table, he leaned in, ready to pounce. "So it's *you* who has some explaining about my wife's whereabouts."

He might have rattled her earlier, but this side of Tom she was prepared for. Nicole's cool stare met him squarely. "I have a great slogan for your campaign, Senator. *Prey, or be prey.*" Nicole's notepad was on the table. She gathered her things and stuffed them into her tote as a crooked smile broke across Tom's face.

"Love it!" He was a little too loud and gave her a conspiratorial wink. "How about you come work for me?"

Nicole's forced laugh was his answer and, from across the room, the two smiling at each other in the back booth would look like friends. With a leftover grin, Nicole said, "I'm a newshound, remember?" She pulled her bag over her shoulder. "We're done here, Senator. It's evident I'm not going to find out 'how we can help each other'," she did the quotation marks with her fingers over his words. "I have work to do." She stood. Her mask gone. "Because, unlike you, Tom, I actually care where Ginny is tonight, and if I don't hear from her by morning, twenty-four hours or not, I'm going to the police."

Tom, all about appearance, wrestled with his smirk, holding it in place as he watched Nicole disappear.

CHAPTER 41

The tragic shooting from the day before was having a reverse effect on Malibu. Instead of repelling the public from the beach's nightlife, a crowd of lookie-loos had converged on the streets in the short time Nicole was in Zeke's, and after leaving her encounter with Tom Vinsant, the chaos from the streets matched the commotion in her head. *What was I expecting? ... Whatever weak moment caused Tom Vinsant to call me, sure didn't last. Or was it a ruse? And I ... I bought it! ... but ... no ... on the phone he had a purpose ... I'm certain of it!* She pulled onto the highway and joined the crowd.

The stark quiet that greeted her when she finally arrived at home magnified her loud mental ramblings. *He was unsure when he called me ... almost frightened ... I wasn't wrong on that. But then he saw Rand ...* "Rand!" The one spoken word stunned the other thoughts bouncing around, and her breathing kicked up a notch. It was outrageous that Nicole would believe anything Tom Vinsant said, but it fit. Mike told her Rand was from the Sacramento area, and she'd known something was different about him, something more than the apparent. She shook her head. *I let him con me! So taken by him personally that I ignored every sign. But the worst of it ... Tom Vinsant got to deliver the blow!*

Nicole poured a glass of wine, but she let it sit. What she really wanted, needed actually, was to go on a run. It had been a couple of days and her skin was tingling. She rubbed her arms, and when the bell sounded for the gate, she whirled around, knocking over the wineglass, and the ting of crystal echoed from the stone floor until the second round of buzzing began. Nicole looked at the clock. Eight. It was him.

The heavy, wood door creaked when Nicole pulled it open. It was a soothing sound to her, expected. It was the beach, where everything was a little salty or damp. She held onto the solid door, drawing from its support, ready to confront the deceptive agent on the other side. But he wasn't there. Instead, Nicole stood facing the familiar dark eyes from outside the music room. The same rugged face that rescued her from the carjacker, and the reliable shoulder that convinced her Theresa Chastang's death wasn't her fault.

The night breeze swept in from behind him, tousling the dark waves around his head. She looked away. "It's late, and I'm tired. We can talk tomorrow."

The last time Rand was at her door, his expressions dove into a mélange of emotion, and it was happening again, but in a reversed sequence. From pleasure in seeing her, to confusion, to concern. "It's only eight." His eyes narrowed, and he took a step toward her. "Nicole? I heard something breaking. What's wrong?"

"Tomorrow." She was curt and stepped back to close the door, but Rand's foot stopped it.

The lines in his forehead deepened, and his cool disposition was replaced with urgency. In one quick move he pushed past Nicole, through the door, keeping his right hand at the small of his back where the Glock hid under his jacket. He methodically scanned the room. It took only seconds, and after dropping his hand along with the puzzled expression, he closed the door behind them, smiling. "Sorry, I couldn't hear you with the wind and the cars at my back."

Nicole lifted one brow. In her head was Tom Vinsant's mocking voice, *"Special agent."* Keeping distance between them, she circled the island into the kitchen side, careful to avoid the broken glass, as well as the broad shoulders that were following. They caused an undercurrent that she felt even from her side of the counter. "So ... *Pastor* ... What is it that cannot wait until tomorrow?"

"Nicole?" His head tilted, waiting for her to look at him. "What is it? You don't seem yourself."

A wide smile replaced her stoic features, releasing an edgy laugh. "Well, that's quite ironic, isn't it?"

Walking around the counter, Rand stepped on a shard of the crystal, crunching it under his boot. The scar in his brow deepened. "Are you alone?" His right hand hung free, close to his back, ready, waiting for her answer while he skillfully combed the room.

There was no music, no television, and since Nicole hadn't been home long, she hadn't had a chance to open her French doors and allow the beach in. There were no soothing sounds. Only harsh noises from the traffic. *Whoosh. Whoosh.* The cars passed.

Nicole didn't answer him, but holding onto her smile folded her arms across her chest. "So ... Pastor, I'm curious ... Where was it you went to seminary?" She caught the flicker in his eye. The faint twitch in his cheek. "And you're here from Sacramento, right? So ... how long are you planning on staying in L.A.?"

The deep lines in Rand's forehead slowly receded. He glanced at the broken glass again, noticing the liquid mixed within it. He breathed in, deeply; his exhale measured. As he raised his head, a car horn blared, then faded down the highway, but somehow it lingered in the room, leaving a message that enhanced his blatant stare.

He started toward her.

With one hand, Nicole motioned for him to stop. "You can lie to me from over there."

There was no flicker in his eye this time. "I haven't lied to you, Nicole."

"Really?" Nicole walked to the French doors to open them. She needed air. Facing him again, she re-crossed her arms. "You are nothing that you led me to believe." With a catty grin she added, "I nailed it when I joked about your mission work, as if you were 'on a mission' … like 'under cover.' It was the truth, but you let me feel foolish for even teasing about it. You had the opportunity to come clean then, Special Agent Coleman. Or is it even Coleman?"

His large frame stepped toward her again, but she lifted her brow in warning, and he spoke from where he stood. "I'm everything I've said. I'm working at The Rock. I'm those kid's director for now."

"For now?" Her laser-eye coolness watched his every reaction. "Which means your time here is limited."

Rand looked down at the floor beside him. "Do you have a broom? I'll help you clean this."

"Leave it." Nicole only waited a breath or two. "You said you wanted to talk."

When he raised his eyes to her, the intensity behind them contradicted his voice, which was even. Calm. He took a step. "First, we clear this." He brushed his hand between them. "The location of The Rock fits a need, Nicole. And I fit The Rock's needs, as a director. It has nothing to do with you."

In the next moments, the faint whooshing of waves from the shore joined the voices and treads of the street. The lone bark of a dog added to the chilling stillness inside, until Nicole finally regained her voice. "That's all you have to say? Okay, I get it. It has nothing to do with me. So, personally, you owe me no explanation." She matched his stare, her eyes narrowed. She'd lost the smirk. "However, professionally, I can't keep quiet on this. Lying to little children. Pretending to be a pastor. No matter what the feds think, there's a line you don't cross."

With no change to his features, Rand nodded. Not in agreement, but more like he was simply listening.

"Who else knows? Mike? Ginny?" She asked, and Rand's head changed direction, moving once from side to side, indicating no. She continued, "They will. I'm not lying for you."

"I don't mind you knowing, Nicole," he said, moving closer, and her eyebrow shot up again, warning him, but he ignored it. He kept coming. Nicole's arm flew toward him in an attempt to push him away, and he stopped it in mid-air. With his fingers clamped around her wrist, he rotated her arm back behind her, leveraging the position to jam her body against his. Whispering into her hair, he said, "Actually, I wouldn't mind you knowing *everything* about me." Starting at her neck, a shiver traveled down her spine, and she twisted to break free. He held her tight. "But those kids are off-limits. I meant it when I said that before." Rand wrapped a small lock of her hair around his free hand, his voice flat, unemotional. "If you expose me, you could put the kids in grave danger, Nicole. Anyway, I am, or at least was, a pastor once, so like I said, I'm not lying."

She pulled at the arm he held. It was met with slight resistance, then he let her go. "Fine. I'm sure you're just doing your job, Special Agent," she said. "And since it has nothing to do with me ..." Nicole started toward her front door to send him out, but spun back, a gasp escaping her open mouth. "Wait! I want to see your truck!"

Rand slid his hands into his pockets. "My truck is being repaired."

"So—that WAS you chasing the motorcycle shooter last night!" Watching for his reaction, she got nothing. "Why were they outside my house, Rand? Why were you?" The vein above her left temple was rising from her growing tension, and Rand looked at the ground. "Answer me!"

When he looked up, his dark eyes were filled with accusations of their own. He was slow to answer. "Did you think I didn't notice those two following us from your house yesterday? I wasn't the only one watching you take pictures of them, Nicole ... they saw you, too. But you already know this, so, I'm not the only one holding back."

Embarrassment only served to fuel Nicole's anger. Her elbows stiffened at her side, with fists so tight, she didn't care that her nails dug into the flesh of her palms. "Why would I have involved a pastor? That's who I thought you were ... or have you forgotten, since you play so many roles? Even pretending not to notice me take their picture. To what purpose, Agent Coleman? What is it you're after?"

Nicole's chest rose and fell heavily, waiting for his answer. Their eyes locked. Since first meeting, their deepest conversations had been non-verbal and this one was filled with a range of emotions that left Nicole unblinking, intensity building between them. When Rand's phone rang, neither acknowledged it. Neither were backing down. Until it rang again. Rand was still on the job and duty trumped. He broke away to look at the display, then back at Nicole, and brought the phone to his ear. "Yeah," he answered in a voice huskier than normal.

Nicole turned from his penetrating stare and started toward the broken crystal. She knelt and picked up each piece like they were still a treasure, and she held the stem and turned it slightly. It had been Great Aunt Naomi's.

"Send me the address," Rand answered, then slid his phone in his pocket. "We'll have to talk later. I'm sending a team to watch your place."

Nicole was hidden by the counter as she soaked up the spilled wine with a towel. She didn't stand. She kept cleaning. "I don't need anyone."

"For me to do my job tonight, I have to know you're safe." He waited. "Trust me, Nicole."

She didn't answer. She didn't have an answer. Nicole used her energy to scrub the stone tile, until she heard the forlorn sound from the door hinges, then a solid clump. Slowly, she stood, the soiled towel in her hands, and she was alone.

CHAPTER 42

Jocko's voice had been urgent on the phone to Rand. "We've finally gotten a signal from your missing custodian's phone. It must have been turned off, so he's likely to shut it down again at any time. If you want to check it out, we should move. Quickly." The address he gave Rand was in Venice Beach, which was a straight shot down the Pacific Coast Highway from Nicole's home in Malibu. Although it was only twelve miles south, it took Rand twenty-five minutes with traffic. By the time he arrived, Gabriel Simon's cell phone had moved from Pacific Avenue to Speedway. Like veins branching off, there were clusters of small alleys in that area all the way to Ocean Front Walk, so Rand and Gabriel were on foot, following the signal that had become oddly inconsistent. "Are you reading this correctly?" Jocko asked. He was on the phone with their office, who had a read on the location and were guiding them.

Jocko nodded toward a homeless woman to their right, who was walking in figure eight circles in a public parking lot. "It's coming from her," he said to Rand.

Known only as "Cher" and dressed like the popular icon, the woman was flipping her long, black wig from side to side and babbling into the phone pressed against her ear. Rand shot Jocko a side glance with his brows high, then looked back at Cher. "You know her?" Jocko was a local and had a strong street network.

"Just know *of* her."

They slowed, but before they could agree on their next move, she had spotted them. She spun her body erratically, looking all around, then broke her earlier pattern and started walking across the parking lot, heading south on Speedway. Jocko called out to her. "Hey Cher! It's me, Jocko. Can I ask you something?"

And she took off. With an unexpected agility, she sprung like a gazelle, racing to the maze of alleys ahead of her and darted down the first one. Rand wasn't far behind her, but when she shot left again, between two houses, she lost him. He froze to listen for her footfalls, but all he heard was Jocko running up behind him. Together they combed the small lanes ahead, and just beyond an air conditioner unit, Rand saw a slight movement. Fabric. With stealth silence, Rand pulled out his ID and moved closer, with Jocko on his heels. They parted to go around the unit from both sides, and Cher was there, leaning against the hard metal and breathing heavy. Her eyes were closed, like a child playing hide and seek. Rand held the ID before her and asked, "Had enough running?"

Cher's eyes flew open wide, and a shriek broke free from the depths of her throat, echoing in the night between the cluster of homes. Jocko placed his hand on her shoulder. "Cher, you know me. You know I'm not going to hurt you." He let a moment pass for his own heart rate to slow. Cher watched him like a trapped animal. Her breathing was still rapid, but not in distress, and Rand gave a slight nod, so he continued, "We only have one question."

From a window somewhere above they heard a voice, "We're callin' the cops!"

Jocko shouted back, "FBI. Don't bother!" Jocko reached to help her up, but she wouldn't stand. "All right then, we'll talk here." He leaned in. "The reason we came to see you ... it's about the phone you were using."

Cher started rocking. Her arms crossed tight around her waist. "You can't take my phone! He said it was mine! You can't take it. NO. Unh-unh."

"*Who* told you that, Cher? Do you know the man who gave it to you?"

The rocking increased, and she turned her head away from Jocko, but her eyes strained to keep him in her sights.

"Cher." A new voice, deeper, softly delivered her name, and Cher slightly relaxed the grip on her waistline. Rand knelt next to her. He continued in the same tone, "I'm sorry we chased you, Cher. I hope your shoes weren't damaged, they're great shoes. Are they new?" Cher tilted her chin down a fraction and smiled a little shyly, nodding yes. "Well then, we did the right thing to stop all this running. Let's find somewhere else to sit so your dress doesn't get soiled." With the caution of a frightened animal, she watched Rand, and after he stood, she was still wary, but allowed the strong hands to help her up. Dirty, broken nails lined the fingers that Rand supported. From a distance, she had looked to be in her early fifties, but at a closer perspective, it was possible she wasn't more than thirty years old, which explained her sprinting abilities.

They found a sidewalk café, and Rand ordered her something to eat. "Cher, you know we'll ask about the phone again, but if that's your only source of communication, we can get you another one. See, the person we think gave it to you is missing, and the phone could help us locate him."

"You'll get me another one?"

"Absolutely."

"Tonight. Right now."

"Jocko, do you think you can find Cher another phone?"

Rand and Cher stayed at the café to wait on her food, and Jocko took off in search of a burner cell phone. The acoustic guitar playing inside the café drifted out to them, a classical Latin piece dripping with passion. Rand sat quietly, appreciating the music.

"You're thinking of a girl," Cher said to him and swung her hair behind her shoulder.

He smiled. "Guilty."

"I knew it!" She laughed, rocking forward and back, clapping her hands. The server brought her food, and before the platter could touch the table, she grabbed the sandwich on it. "What'd you order me?"

"A grilled chicken-breast panini."

"I thought I was gettin' chicken and waffles." But her mouth was already full, talking between chews. "I usually get shooed away from places like this." She looked around, then took another large bite. "You gonna start talkin' 'bout God, mister?"

"Rand. My name is Rand. I'll talk about whatever you'd like."

"Humph ..." A piece of spinach was finding its way out as she chewed, and with childlike movements she pushed it back in, but still watched Rand with the hardness of the streets. "Usually, to get food like this, we have to listen to a preacher talk 'bout how much God loves us and sent Jesus to save us. Thing is, nobody's saved me yet! I'm still here."

Rand looked over her head for Jocko. "So, how's your sandwich?"

"Ain't no chicken and waffles, but it'll do." Cher gave a brief smile. Bread was stuck between two of her teeth. "You want a fry?" She held one toward him.

"No, thank you, Cher."

She turned the fry toward her mouth and shoved it in. Her brows drew together. "So, you believe in God?"

Rand nodded.

"You believe He loves you?"

Again, Rand nodded.

"You know why? 'Cause you have a fancy house. You and those preachers! But what about me? And they keep saying that He loves me!"

The guitarist from indoors was taking a break, and it was turning cool. Rand and Cher were the only two left outside, and she was getting jumpy waiting on his answer. Rand put his hands together on the table. "I understand why you'd question that. Life is tough."

Hard eyes squinted at him. "You as bad as them."

Rand's voice was low, calming. "Cher, listen, I believe He loves us all the same. But ... I also believe this world is imperfect, filled with sadness and evil, along with the good ... and sometimes, even when we're doing good, we get hit by the sin in the world."

"What chu you mean, get hit by it?" She cocked her head back, and her mouth hung open, displaying the mashed remnants of her last, un-swallowed bite.

"Well, let me see ... I'm a visual kind of guy, so ... picture sin flying around us." Rand moved his hands around, creating the effect. "It's all over the world, being slung about by people. Most of it's just your basic stuff, but sometimes serious evil gets mixed in." He gave her a slight smile. "Now, with everything that's flying around I feel I'll eventually be hit by it unless I specifically ask for God's intervention."

"So, you don't think He jumps out and blocks it unless we ask? Why not?"

"Because He gives you free choice to live. He's not a puppet master." Rand brought his hands together, his fingers entwined. "So, if He isn't forcing His will, that unfortunately includes His protection. So we ask. Daily. And even if God doesn't make it go away, He helps me through it."

Cher picked up the remainder of her sandwich. She was nodding, but watched him guardedly, and Rand shrugged, "You know, I have a list of questions myself to ask God when I see Him one day. Until then," he gave her a sincere smile, "I try to see Him in the small things ... like a free meal, or a new cell phone, and even good conversation. His way of sending something special in our direction."

A crooked smile broke across Cher's face, and with an impishness, she asked, "And what if you die and find out that being good and telling me about God was a waste of time? What if there ain't no heaven or hell?" A twinkle danced in her eyes, and for a flash, the spirit of a young, untroubled Cher was exposed. She popped the last bite of the panini into her mouth and chuckled.

"Well, then at least I did something positive in the world. Spoke an encouraging word, lent a helping hand. I don't see a downside ... AND ... I won't be disappointed, since I wouldn't be conscious for it to matter anyway, huh?" He grinned back at her, then leaned in toward her confidentially. "However ... the big question is ... what if I am right? Then what? There are no 'do overs' after that last breath, and eternity's a long time to be wrong."

She dipped her french fry into her soda. "I'll digest that right along with my fries," she said, then she stuffed one into her mouth, grinning. "You have a funny way of explaining things, Mr. Rand, but nice. Real nice. You the one that should be a preacher."

Straightening, he winked at her. "So I've been told." She was calm and on her last fry, so Rand didn't chance waiting on Jocko. "Listen, Cher, about the phone. How did that happen? You said he told you that you could have it. Did Simon just walk past and hand it to you?"

"Simon? You know him?" Her eyes popped.

"Yes. We've worked together, but I think he might be getting himself in a little trouble. I need to help him."

The food did her well, because suddenly she was more lucid, her eyes still wide. "Wait a minute! If you traced this phone to me ... can 'his trouble' trace it too? Like you did?" Without waiting for him to answer, she pushed the phone away with her napkin. "Here. I don't want it anymore."

"I'll get it away, just tell me what you can."

She played with her hair, then flipped it to the opposite side and drew her brows together. "I was somewhere near Marina Del Rey. You know where the Cheesecake Factory is?"

Rand nodded.

"Near there. A couple came down the sidewalk in a crazy hurry and out of nowhere, he turns and hands me that phone." She pointed to the cell phone across the table, then leaned further away from it. "Said it was mine if I wanted it."

"Can you describe them? Or recall anything special about them?"

Like switching channels in her head, she was her old self, agitated, and started humming, then she nodded toward the sidewalk. Jocko was coming toward them.

"Cher?" Rand asked, but she just hummed.

"Hey, look what I found." Jocko held a new cell phone out toward her, and she moved quickly to snatch if from him, but Jocko was quicker. "Yours first."

"I gave it to him," She pointed to Rand, and he held it up in the napkin for Jocko to see. She grabbed the new phone from Jocko's hand and took off running. After about twenty feet, she turned back and said, "Thank you for dinner, Pastor!" Then she was gone.

CHAPTER 43

Hidden in the hills of Malibu was an elusive mansion that housed a private gentleman's fraternity. The Stapleton.

The Stapleton had been around since the turn of the twentieth century, and due to the deep pockets of its members, it thrived no matter the economy, although most Malibu residents didn't even know it existed. It was nestled in the mountainside across the highway from the ocean, down a dusty turnoff that twisted through the hills. The road had no markings except for a no trespassing sign, and its one-laned trail ended at the Stapleton's driveway which was heavily monitored with cameras. The only entry was through an electronic keycard gate.

It was a sanctuary for the ultra-rich to be off the grid for a while. Whether they wanted to disappear or to simply over-indulge without witnesses. Every need was considered.

Tom Vinsant was one of those members, and he was tucked away in a side room off the dining area, enjoying his Chivas Regal, stewing, after leaving Zeke's and the meeting with Nicole. "So that's where the ball buster likes to hang out. That, or she was planning something with her friend," he said, staring into his glass. "What was I thinking, calling her? She heard a weakness in me, and like the rest of them, was ready to set me up ... not going to happen." He took a swig, then slammed his glass down.

"Who are you talking to, Tom?" Sidney Drummond demanded as he casually walked up to Tom's table and pulled out a chair.

"Sidney! Surprised to see you tonight." Tom stood so abruptly, he knocked his own chair backward, and grabbed it before it hit the floor, then extended his hand to Sidney.

"Sit. Sit. That's unnecessary." Sidney came with drink in hand, and lowered himself across from Tom. "So, what are you doing in Malibu on a weeknight?"

"Staying here for a few days." Tom took his time settling into his seat. Facing the intruder, he tapped on the table. "And how's the news business, Sidney?"

"Doing good, doing good. One thing about the news, Senator, there's always plenty of it. Sometimes more than others, like this week. Real shame about your buddy, Duke. You know, Congressman Duke Stanton. I assume you've heard."

"Yeah, I heard. Like you said, real shame."

Sidney nodded. "I talked with him recently, too. He seemed real proud of your accomplishments. So much that he wanted to share them with me ... hell, he wanted to share them with the world and was planning on it, too." He swirled his drink around in his glass. It was dark, with no ice, and Tom was mindlessly watching, waiting to see if Sidney was going to take a sip. Tom had never seen Sidney drink. He always played with his glass, but never drank. "He was especially interested in your ability to attract young girls..." Sidney's grin looked almost painful. He swirled his drink again, then held it up in Tom's direction as a toast.

"To Duke." He kept his hand raised for a moment, then set his glass back on the table. Being of keen mind was Sidney's elixir.

Tom emptied his glass and looked around for Dixie, his server. He loosened the button at his collar, and when she came into view carrying a tray and a couple of empty glasses, Tom squeezed his eyes shut to refocus. Dixie was an alpine of a woman. A tall figure even before the four-inch heels and the thick, brown hair piled high atop her head. But now, ironically, the instrumental version of "Rocky Mountain High" was playing softly, and Tom was dazed, watching her tower over the tables in her brown spandex with a plunging neckline. Normally, he'd find that deep valley intriguing, but tonight, as his world was clouding and she twinkled her fingers at Tom, it was comical, and he burst into laughter, forgetting about his drink. Dixie saw his empty glass, however, then winked and bouldered away toward the bar.

"What in the hell's so funny?" Tom heard coming from across his table. His private table that Sidney Drummond had invaded.

He was brought back to the moment. Shaking his head clear, the humor was replaced with irritation. He took a deep breath. A snake of smoke from Sidney's Cuban cigar slithered artfully toward Tom's face and went right up his nostril, catching him off-guard, and Tom began coughing uncontrollably. He stood to catch his breath. Had his vision not been flooded by the involuntary production of tears, he would've seen the slight smirk Sidney wore. "Put that thing out! I need fresh air." And Tom started off.

"Don't leave so soon, we haven't had a chance to discuss your meeting with Nicole Portman. Since when did you two become so ... friendly?" Sidney asked.

Tom spun about. "So, that's what this 'coincidental' visit is about." He swept his palm over his red, watery eyes. "Business must be slower than you let on."

"No, no, it's busier than ever, which is why I don't have time for the veiled threats from every new enemy you make ... or for Doc Howard's rantings how you're about to screw your partners. You've been making some bad decisions, so you're going to sit down and listen."

"Nobody owns me." Tom said, then stormed away, stopping only at the front desk to sign his ticket and under his breath said, "Not anymore."

* * *

After a couple of quick pulls on his cigar, Sidney muttered, "I own everything." He leaned back in his seat, looked through the contacts in his phone, and took one more pull before the other party answered. "He just left," Sidney said. "Going to his beach house, and other than making him a little uncomfortable, the Duke Stanton news didn't move him, so if you plan on getting his attention, it has to be effective, and it has to be tonight. If his deal with his new financial backers closes tomorrow, you lose your puppet on Capitol Hill." Sidney's expression was always the same when talking with Doc Howard. Sour. He detested the man. The working relationship had begun before Sidney realized all of Howard's twisted ventures, so Sidney kept his distance and vigil over Howard and his top men, anonymously studying them to make sure he was never the one taken by surprise.

"I'm flying out of the country tonight, so Stuart Greystone will handle it. I'll direct him to the senator's location," was the icy response. "I also understand the senator was in the company of that newswoman tonight. I thought you took care of her."

"I have. She's not an issue," Sidney quickly countered.

"Reporters are always an issue."

"I don't like repeating myself," Sidney said.

"She could jeopardize everything, but you don't think clearly where she's involved, Sidney. She has something on you, and since you won't take care of it, Greystone will."

"I've spoken on this matter for the last time. She IS NOT an issue, and no one goes near her!" He paused for a response. "Do you hear me, Howard?! Howard?" Nothing. Looking at his phone, the connection was cut. "YOU DO NOT hang up on Sidney Drummond!" Sidney's face turned red. He called back, but it wouldn't ring. Three attempts, and the connection kept going directly to voice mail.

"Mr. Drummond? Are you okay?" Dixie had appeared beside Sidney, concern dripping through her voice. "Can I get you something?"

"I believe I've had too much to drink for the night. I'm going to lie down in the blue room. Sign my ticket out, will you? And this is for you." He laid a one hundred-dollar bill on her tray. A clammy film of sweat began to creep over him.

"You know, I could come check on you during my break," she said, pressing her breast against his arm as he rose.

"Dixie, you are truly exquisite, but if I disappointed you in my inebriated state, my ego couldn't bear it. I must take a raincheck. Goodnight, my dear."

Dismissing himself, Sidney walked down a hallway toward the rear of the building. Certain he was out of sight, he went out the back door and was on the highway in minutes, dodging traffic and pedestrians, racing to

Nicole. The route to Nicole Portman's beach house was simple for Sidney Drummond, since it was one of the guest cottages near his compound, but the drive had never felt as far as it did tonight.

CHAPTER 44

With Rand gone, Nicole actually considered going on a run, although she never did at night. "Bad for your ankles," she'd say jokingly, but she meant it. Beachgoers often dug holes in the daytime, and at night they weren't easily seen, a lesson she had learned firsthand. "I need to consider a treadmill!" She said aloud. Her insides were grating at her to move, so she started stretching, creating good energy that stimulated her thoughts, which circled around Ginny, the kids, Tom Vinsant, and now Rand—in a totally new role.

Slowly, she moved across her living room. *SO ... How did Rand know I was at Zeke's tonight? And what job would the FBI be doing from The Rock? Maybe it involves the local gangs and drugs. OR ... Detective Graves's partner mentioned the gang SOTIS. One of the charges on their sheet listed trafficking. That would definitely bring in the feds.* She stopped, her arms came up, fists tight with excitement. "And that could be how Rand found me at Theresa Chastang's! They're tied together." She picked up her pace, walking to the glass door, back to the kitchen, then around the counter, in big circles. "Rand warned me again tonight not to mess with the children, but actually, he's trying to warn me! If we're following the same thread ... he needs my information!"

Nicole hurried into her bedroom to get her laptop, "I let my pride get ahead ..." She slammed to a stop. Her bedroom curtains were partially opened. Nicole knew she'd closed them earlier, before leaving for Zeke's, and no matter, she never left them halfway. Her drapes were always completely opened or completely shut. Other things were moved. Small things, like the shade on her bedside lamp, was turned. Walking toward her closet, she slowly opened the door. Two drawers weren't completely closed, and Nicole's eyes were wide. She darted out of the room, back to get her purse, and scavenged for her mace. Holding the can high, Nicole moved quickly, collecting her work, jamming it into her tote, and ran out of the house into the garage.

The garage door had never been slower, humming and popping as it lifted, and Nicole threw her belongings across the seat of her Range Rover. She heard a voice calling from the dark driveway, "What's the hurry?" and didn't wait to see who it was. She jumped into her SUV and locked it in one quick swoop, then started the engine. An image appeared in the side mirror, coming from the shadows, and she threw her car in reverse, gassing it, almost hitting Sidney Drummond. "Whoa!" he shouted, scanning her garage. His hand was jammed in his coat pocket.

"Wait! Nicole! I'm staying here at the compound tonight. Come with me to the big house. You had something you wanted to share with me, right?"

Nicole simply looked at him, incredibly, hearing every other word. "Move, Sidney," she said, then sped out of the drive. She looked around to see if Rand's agents were there yet, and figured the only way she'd know is if they followed her, so she took off toward LA.

She watched the road behind her for a tail, but it was night and Malibu was alive with cars and lights. It would have been difficult to discern one headlight from another, so she kept plowing forward. Activating her command system, she said, "Call Ginny Vinsant." It was a hopeful attempt, but soon the interior of her car was filled with Ginny's soft, recorded voice asking her to leave a message again, so she did. "Ginny, we've got to talk! Someone's been in my home. I'm going to the police ... with or without you!" She didn't want to disconnect. "Ginny, where are you? I don't believe you'd intentionally frustrate me ... why didn't you take your ph—" With an instant realization, Nicole abruptly ended the call. Her eyes wide. "YOUR PHONE! That's it!" Without hesitating, Nicole made a U-turn in the middle of PCH and headed back toward Ginny's beach house. "I've got to find out who that last call was from!"

* * *

Nicole was spooked. Had Sidney approached her any quicker, he'd have been hit by the pepper spray in her hand or by the SUV when she reversed past him. He kept his hand tight around the trigger of the Glock in his pocket, waiting for someone else to come bounding out of the house. But the garage door started down, and before it was completely closed, she was gone.

Sidney ran back to his car and raced to catch her, but the car in front of him was stopped by one of the few traffic lights in Malibu. He loosened his collar and turned up the air. He found a roll of antacid tablets in the console, popped two in his mouth, and drummed heavily on the steering wheel. When the light finally turned green, he gunned the accelerator, going around the lead car from the shoulder, then edging back onto the highway, he kept his foot down until he spotted Nicole's SUV pass by in the oncoming traffic, heading back into Malibu. "What in the ..." He hit the brakes and turned the wheel, making a quick U-turn. The loud squeal of brakes and rubber skidding from behind didn't faze him, nor did barely missing the rear panel of a Toyota minivan in the opposite lane. The only thing he knew once he got control of his car was he had lost sight of Nicole.

With streetlights and businesses lining the street to the right, it was easy enough to make out the cars, but there wasn't a black Range Rover ahead. Sidney started scanning the parking lots. When he got as far as the market, he turned in and got out his cell phone. His hands were trembling as he found her number and pressed "call." Every second that ticked by, Nicole was getting further away and perhaps closer to danger.

After two rings it went to voice mail. He ended the call and tried again, receiving the same message, so he tried reaching Dr. Howard again. That call also went straight to voice mail. Sidney was used to getting what he wanted, when he wanted it, and was now swimming in unknown waters. It had been years since he felt this form of helplessness and anxiety. Grabbing his chest, he pulled back on to the highway. He might not have known where she was headed, but he knew where Howard's men were, so he traveled north.

* * *

Tom stopped at Sandy's Liquor and Mini-Mart for his essentials, and by the time he loaded his purchases in the car and started for the beach house, his fuming over the meeting with Sidney had settled into unease. Even his backers weren't a secret from Drummond. *How long have I been under surveillance? They could be watching Ginny, too.* Instead of turning into his driveway, Tom drove past his beach house for about a hundred yards to a small alley between two homes and parked. Pulling off his shoes, he walked down the familiar stretch of sand, staying in the shadows until he was outside his own house, looking in.

* * *

Rand and Jocko were eager to check Gabriel Simon's call log after recovering his phone from Cher. They had a long walk back to their vehicles and were almost there when the phone rang. Rand looked at the display. "Only the letter G is showing on caller ID," he said.

"Cher wouldn't have had time to plug in her contacts."

Rand nodded in agreement. He motioned for Jocko to be quiet, then answered, "Yeah?"

CHAPTER 45

Everything seemed quiet at the Vinsant's beach house when Nicole arrived. The white BMW still in the drive. If Tom were here, he would most likely park in the garage, so Nicole knocked. Then knocked again before trying the knob. It was unlocked as it was earlier. She called out, "Ginny? ... Tom?" No answer. Stepping beyond the foyer, she tried again. Nothing.

Everything looked the same as before, but an unexplained tremor shook her. "Keep moving, don't think," Nicole whispered softly. She rushed directly to where she'd last seen Ginny's phone. It was still there. Her pulse accelerated as she picked it up, and within seconds she had access to Ginny's call log. The missed calls, including the ones from Nicole, were all highlighted in red, so the one she was looking for was easy to spot. It was the last number in black, the last conversation Ginny had before disappearing that afternoon, and the call had lasted twelve minutes. It was THE call that swept Ginny away. Nicole had seen the way she confided in the caller, so it had to be someone she had a special relationship with. It began with area code 310.

With anticipation, Nicole engaged the number immediately. The loud pounding, coming from her increased heart rate, distorted her hearing, so when a familiar male voice answered, "Yeah?" Nicole held the phone away from her head and looked at it in bewilderment. She listened again, waiting, until the same voice came through, only louder. Clearer. "Hello?" And there was no mistaking it.

"Rand?"

Silence. Breathing. Finally, the voice asked, "Nicole?"

"Is this some sort of game you two are playing? Where's Ginny?"

"Slow down. Whose number are you calling from? Ginny's?"

"You asked me to trust you ..."

A door closed and jerked Nicole's attention from the bizarre call. Holding the phone away from her mouth, she called out, "Ginny? Tom?" and started toward the sound, straining to see who was inside with her.

"Nicole? NICOLE!" Rand called out from the cell phone, and Nicole moved it behind her back, clasping her hand tightly over it as she called out again, "Hello?"

Still no answer, but someone was inside. Instinct told her to get out. Nicole turned and wasted no time heading to the front door. Rand was still connected on Ginny's phone, and just as she held it to her ear, a voice behind her said, "I can't believe our good fortune. Is it really Nicole Portman?"

"AAAHH!" Nicole screamed, jumping backward, and brought her clutched hand to her hammering chest. "Where did you come from?"

The silver-haired man smiled, "I'm so sorry if I gave you a fright."

"Nicole, who is that? Where are you? NICOLE!" Rand called from her closed fist, but his muffled words were barely audible.

"Did I interrupt your phone call?" The impeccably dressed stranger was looking at the hand still locked against her.

"Ummm ... no," she said, staring into the face of the man she'd recently been made aware of. Stuart Greystone. "I ... uh, missed my opportunity to leave a message. Ummm ... I didn't realize anyone was here." Without disconnecting, Nicole placed the phone in her shirt pocket.

"I'm simply waiting on Tom. He'll be here soon. Come, you must stay and keep me company while I wait." The British accent offered, "Would you care for a glass of wine?"

"I'm not really thirsty." Nicole stepped back. She didn't attempt to leave yet; it was an opportunity to ask questions, but she still kept her distance from him.

"Wine's not about thirst, my dear, it's an experience; an art, actually. We're so close to the vineyard country, you must feel the same. What will it be? Red or white?"

"I guess white. Chardonnay." She watched him comfortably working his way around the kitchen. "So, Mr. Greystone, how do you know Tom and Ginny?"

"You know my name. I'm impressed. But of course, you *are* the great reporter." Greystone poured a taster amount in a glass for Nicole.

"I'm sure it's fine," she said, so he finished filling her glass to halfway, then poured the same in his.

"Let me see, where does Ginny keep her beverage napkins?" Greystone took the glasses with him to the pantry, and when he came out he had a couple of small, white cocktail napkins with the letter V in script, and with a polite nod, walked to Nicole with her wine. "I'm pleased we are finally meeting," he said, as he raised his glass to her.

Nicole held hers, not responding to his suggested toast, and asked, "You never answered. How is it you know the Vinsants?" Nicole tilted her head and waited.

"Tom and I have been business associates for years."

"Oh? Associates in what business, exactly?"

"Come, come. You're not going to just leave me here, are you?" He motioned with his raised glass, sending it toward her again, for her to toast him.

"I'm sorry. I'm not feeling well. Please tell Tom and Ginny I stopped by." Nicole sat her glass down and headed for the front door.

"Ms. Portman! I cannot let you rush off like this."

The statement was off. It sent a shiver of warning up her spine, and Nicole already knew what she'd find when she turned around. The wineglass in his hand had been replaced, and although she didn't recognize the exact make of the gun he held, anyone who had reported the news as long as she had knew this one was an automatic with a high caliber—and that the silencing attachment on the end wasn't good.

* * *

Listening to Rand's one-sided conversation on Gabriel's phone, Jocko watched his friend's face change from confusion to alarm as Rand asked, "Nicole, who is that? Where are you? NICOLE!"

They were still on foot making their way back to their trucks, and Rand put the call on speakerphone, then muted their end and told Jocko, "From her comment, it's got to be Ginny Vinsant's phone. I think she's covered the receiver, but we still have a connection." Before they'd made another block, they heard Nicole's voice again, clearly. She was talking to someone else. Then a man's voice.

"That was Greystone!" said Jocko, but Rand was already running to the Jeep.

CHAPTER 46

Parked on the shoulder of the road across from the Vinsant's beach house, Sidney Drummond spotted Nicole's black Range Rover and pulled in behind it. Within seconds he was at the front door and rushed inside. "Tom? Nicole!" There was a clambering sound coming from the left, and he followed the noise, making his way to the grand living area just as Stuart Greystone was coming in from a door off the kitchen.

"Terribly sorry I didn't hear you knock. I'm Stuart Greystone," he said, and moved toward Sidney, offering his hand. "I believe you're Mr. Drummond. So good to meet you!" Greystone's casual manner didn't camouflage the significance behind his ruffled hair and wide, shifting eyes. Drummond knew all about Stuart Greystone. Doc Howard referred to him often, and he knew his idiosyncrasies. One being his obsession with his perfect hair. Sidney's heart was hammering in his chest.

"Where's Nicole?" Sidney asked, walking right past the offered hand, scanning the room.

"She's resting and doesn't want to be disturbed. Is there a message?"

"She'll want to see me." Sidney started toward the hallway, shouting, "Nicole!"

"She really doesn't want to be disturbed, Mr. Drummond, and I'm just waiting on Tom. Here, let me walk you out."

Sidney squinted at Greystone. "Tom had plenty of time to get home. He left the restaurant before me." Sidney's large frame pounded toward Greystone. "I'll ask you one more time, WHERE IS SHE?"

* * *

Between the intense flashing of the emergency dash light suctioned to the Jeep's windshield and the occasional blaring of his horn, Rand maneuvered through intersections and around congestion, making remarkable time toward Malibu, slinging Jocko against the window without apology.

"Well, she just confirmed it's Greystone," said Jocko.

"We didn't need confirmation, there's no mistaking that cold, smug voice." Rand kept his eyes glued to the road, barreling along. "They both mentioned Tom and Ginny. I left Nicole at her home, and she couldn't have made it to Beverly Hills this fast, so it has to be their Malibu house. Get an address. And get us backup. There should be a team in front of Nicole's now. Give them the Vinsant's address and get 'em moving FAST!"

Jocko didn't seem to notice the quick braking, jerking, and fitful accelerating as he contacted the office with Rand's instructions. He worked with the agent on the phone to get the Vinsant's address and a GPS location on Nicole's personal phone. They were still connected to the cell phone she had called from, and with Gabriel's cell paired to the Jeep, they could clearly hear Stuart Greystone offering Nicole a "toast" over the speaker system.

"DON'T drink it!" Rand shouted. "NICOLE! DON'T DRINK IT!"

"If Greystone hears you, too, he'll take the phone. We'll be cut off."

Rand cast a piercing look to his friend, then looked back to the road.

Jocko calmly said, "Rand, this is what we've been working toward. Don't blow it. We need to tie Greystone in with Doc Howard and Drummond."

"NOT at Nicole's expense! This guy isn't just a boss! He's their top eliminator ..." Rand stopped talking. Bits of muffled dialogue had started again, and they strained to make it out.

Rand didn't back off the accelerator and was making good time, but they still had a few miles to go. Suddenly sounds of scuffling and a loud bang echoed in the cab of the Jeep.

"That doesn't mean anything," Jocko said, but Rand ignored him, and tightening his grip, he swerved onto the shoulder of PCH.

* * *

"Well, well. Isn't this interesting," was heard from the back of the house. Stuart Greystone and Sidney Drummond both jerked their heads around at the sound of Senator Tom Vinsant's voice. He was walking in from the deck with his HK45 leading the way and was wearing a ghoul-ish smile that was nothing like his campaign version. "What a nice little setup. I bet you're discussing my reelection. I know you've been working hard on it ... just not in the way I'd prefer." Tom motioned with the barrel of his sleek handgun toward Greystone and said, "You sent your top dog here, Sidney. I'm impressed. You and Doc must already have my replacement picked out for your little racket on Capitol Hill."

Sidney's eyes narrowed at Tom, then darted around the room and behind him, looking for Nicole.

"What is it, Sidney? It's all between friends, right? Let's get everything out in the open." Tom egged him on. "You think I don't recognize your hit man? Doc's underboss?" Then Tom spoke directly to him. "It's Greystone, right?"

"I came only for Nicole, and she'll be leaving with me. Now." Sidney turned to Greystone. "Tell me where she is!"

"Nicole? The news leech is here, too?" Tom asked, then chuckled. "Well, this just keeps getting better."

Greystone eased his steps backward, into the kitchen.

"Stay where you are," Tom ordered, pointing his barrel directly at Greystone's chest.

"So, you seem to be the one with the answers; where is Nicole? Is Ginny with her?"

"You needn't be concerned about your wife," said Greystone, "Doc Howard said I wasn't to worry about her. She should be fine."

"Then you aren't as smart as I gave you credit for." Tom turned his aim on Sidney. "Tell him why Doc would say that, Sidney. Who ordered a hit on my wife?"

Sidney stared coldly. "Don't be absurd, and I'm not discussing anything in front of your guest."

"First of all, Sidney, as you are aware, he is not my guest, and second, he's here doing your bidding, not mine. So, before I put a bullet through you for threatening the safety of my family, call him off!"

"I knew it!" Greystone watched Tom and Sidney's interaction and was grinning even though he was being held at gunpoint. Tom's confession confirmed everything he suspected, and he was almost jubilant.

Sidney winced, putting his hand to his chest. "I need to sit."

"Yeah, right. Like I'm an idiot," Tom said.

"It's not a trick," he said through labored breathing as he lowered himself onto one of the stools at the counter. "Greystone, I want Nicole here! Now!"

"I had my orders," Greystone responded.

"WHAT HAVE YOU DONE TO HER?" Sidney yelled, and was visibly trembling when they all heard a moan—then something fell. It was coming from behind Stuart, in the laundry room.

"Greystone, open that door," Tom ordered. Greystone didn't move. Tom pulled the slide back on his gun to release a bullet into the chamber. "Perhaps this will help your hearing."

Moving cautiously, Greystone went to the laundry door, and when he pushed the door inward, he went in with it.

"Get back where I can see you!" Tom ordered, and Greystone came back out with the SIG Sauer he'd left hidden in the small room. The silencer tip was pressed against Nicole's temple as he prodded her to walk in front of him, and she struggled to keep her balance.

With gun in hand, Greystone's smile was cold, emotionless, "My good fortune just keeps getting better! I believe the dynamics have changed here, Senator, so my turn to give the orders. Put the weapon down."

"The hell I will. You think I'd fold that easy for her? You'd be doing me a favor, buddy."

Sidney looked at Tom. "I'm begging you, don't. Whatever you want, Tom, it's yours, just don't provoke him." Then, addressing Greystone, he said, "That will be all, Greystone. Your services are no longer needed. You're dismissed. I'll tell Doc."

"She's on to us, Drummond. She knew me by name when she saw me here tonight."

"She's mine and you *will* do as I say. Let her go," Sidney's words were threatening, but his delivery wasn't. It was getting weaker, and as he shot up from the stool, he grabbed his chest and fell back on the seat. He watched helplessly while Greystone tightened his grip on Nicole, keeping the barrel against her temple. Her eyes rolled back, closing, then strained to open again.

"What did you do to her?" Sidney asked, a damp film forming over his top lip and forehead.

"She'll be all right. Just a tiny dose of Rohypnol or, as the kids say, 'roofie,' to help her relax."

"Relax? She can't hold her head up! I need to get her to a doctor."

"It did come from the doctor!" Greystone threw his head back in laughter, and when he did, Tom charged, but Greystone quickly caught the movement and fired. Tom dove to the floor. Greystone was enjoying it. "Mr. Drummond, you may leave. I'll clean this up."

Greystone didn't notice Sidney's ill coloring, and with a manic look in his eyes, kept talking to him. "You can print the story for the world tomorrow, Mr. Drummond. I see the headlines—'The news reporter who caused Senator Vinsant so much grief was found overdosed in the senator's home.' Actually," he said, rubbing his chin against the side of Nicole's head, "we're only a condom away from adding rape to his list of sins."

Greystone's hair was standing up, and his wild eyes were searching for Tom. He feigned a laugh. "Did you hear me, Senator? This will be your legacy. It's your parting gift for breaking your bond with Doc Howard."

Tom stayed low, peering from around the counter with his gun in hand. He didn't have a clean shot, since only Greystone's head and gun arm were exposed, but he had no choice. He'd have to be precise to miss Nicole. "Sounds good in theory, Greystone, but you forgot about this."

The bullet from the HK45 whisked past Greystone's cheek, taking a small chunk of flesh with it, and on impact Greystone dropped Nicole and pulled the trigger of his silenced SIG before Tom could back into cover. The discharged bullet nicked the edge of the bottom cabinet before ripping through Tom's jacket, knocking him backwards.

"Stuart! Put the gun DOWN! Nicole WILL NOT be harmed." Although Sidney's command was still powerful, it was barely audible, and Greystone didn't react until he saw the gun Sidney was pointing at him. "She's my daughter, and if you hurt her, you die."

Greystone froze. Bright red dribbled down his shocked face onto his collar, and he simply stared.

Sidney ordered him, again, "Put the gun down!"

"You're lying, Drummond." Greystone's tone had sobered.

Sidney took a deep breath. The pain lessened enough for him to raise up from the stool and look Stuart square in the eye. "I'm her father and I WILL protect her at any cost." He kept the gun as steady as he could on Greystone. "It's why I suspended her job. Her story about the waterfront would've gotten her killed, so, you see, I control her. Now ... leave her alone and get out of here!" He slowly, methodically, breathed, willing himself to stay calm. He couldn't get medical help until he got Nicole away safely.

"Stop talking about my father." Nicole tried to get her feet under her to stand. Her words were slurred, and she fought to speak clearly. "You didn't know him."

"Is she your sole heir?" Greystone's eyes were growing wide, his smile returning, and blood dribbled over his lip onto his teeth.

Sidney nodded. He had to rest again. He worked to steady his breathing, then coughed deeply a few times, stimulating his heart.

"This changes everything. You're right, I can't hurt her." Greystone helped Nicole to her feet, and his voice pitched higher. "This is perfect. Sidney! You, me, and Nicole, together. We don't need Doc Howard."

"Nicole is not a part of this. She WALKS!" Sidney cried. His arms constricted across his chest. The gun dropped and he collapsed, face down on the counter, gradually sliding until he landed on the floor.

With Greystone distracted, Tom had been inching himself closer to his gun, leaving a small streak of blood on the marble floor. By the time Tom noticed the new movement coming from the hall, it was too late to calculate his options. He could reach his gun in seconds, but his right arm was numb, and he was no match for the man approaching from behind. However, instead of drawing on Tom, the man put his finger to his lips for Tom to stay quiet. Then he motioned for him to stay down, and called out, "Greystone?"

"Dominic? What are you doing here?" Greystone asked, as Dominic emerged from the shadows.

"Doc said you might need help, but it looks like you've got everything under control," Dominic said. He was watching Greystone carefully, stepping closer. Greystone had always been cold, but predictable, unlike his present condition. "How'd you get Nicole Portman here?" He passed Tom, slowly making his way to Sidney.

"It's providence! I've been preparing to take over the organization for years, and it seems today is the day. Nicole is my ticket! Clean this up for me. A good house fire should do it. I'll contact you from Vegas."

"Vegas?"

"Yes. We'll hold out there until I figure how to use this to our advantage." Greystone turned back in Sidney's direction. "As my father would say, pip, pip, old sport," and he ushered Nicole out of the house.

Leaning over Sidney, Dominic felt his pulse. "I've already phoned 911, they'll be here soon," Dominic told Tom, as he began CPR on Sidney. "How's your shoulder?"

"Numb."

"You'll have to use your good arm and take over until the EMTs get here. I'll be back."

Tom worked his way to Sidney as quickly as he could. "Who are you?" But Dominic was already outside chasing after Stuart Greystone.

The white Audi came flying out of the neighbor's driveway, and with Dominic in its path, it veered a hard right and bounced over a flower bed. The detour slowed the car, and Dominic dove for the back door, beating on the window. "Open up, Greystone!! Let me go with you! I can help drive!" He worked the handle, but it was locked. Nicole was in the back seat, and her eyes met his as she sat up and reached for the lock, but Greystone gunned the car. Dominic's hand was caught in the hardware, and his finger snapped backwards. Darkness washed over him, and he struggled to see through the cloud of pain. Deep, even breaths helped to break the veil away in time to see the headlights of a Jeep headed directly at him. He jumped out of its path as the Jeep skidded.

"Gabriel! Stop!" Rand yelled with urgency, coming out of the car. His gun was drawn and pointed at Dominic, who looked identical to his twin brother, Gabriel.

Dominic shook his head. "I'm not Gabriel, and there's no time to explain." With his good hand, he pointed toward the road. "Stuart Greystone is in that white Audi. He has Nicole Portman in the back seat and said he's heading for Las Vegas."

Rand didn't hang around for questions. He and Jocko bolted back down the highway in pursuit. Dominic pulled out his phone. "Greystone has Nicole Portman and is speeding toward Las Vegas. He's in his white Audi A8. We still have a tracker on it, so head him off." He started to disconnect, then added, "Oh, and Rand Coleman is chasing in a black Jeep Wrangler."

CHAPTER 47

"Where are we going?" Nicole asked, attempting to sit up. Her tongue was thick, and her words were slow, but she was more alert.

"To meet Ginny Vinsant. I'm glad to see you're feeling better. Just rest, we'll be there soon."

"Ginny? You heard from Ginny?"

Greystone made a sharp left turn onto Malibu Canyon Road to get up to the 101 freeway, and Nicole slid on the leather seat in the back, hitting her head on the side panel. "Ouch! Can we slow down?"

"I'm sorry, but we must hurry. There's a party in your honor."

Nicole rubbed her head and tried to get her seat belt fastened. "Did I win something? I don't remember. And where's my usual driver? They always send me Roy. Did he quit?"

"We're getting into the canyon now. I'll go slower ... Just relax."

Nicole looked at Greystone's rearview mirror and caught a partial reflection, then looked around the seat for her purse and cell phone. Nothing was there. Studying his reflection again, she recognized who he was, then looked around the car again and out the window, getting her bearings. Suddenly, her eyes flared with alarm, and she felt the front pocket of her shirt. It was empty.

* * *

Rand sat tall in the Jeep Wrangler, his fists tight around the steering wheel, and said, "Greystone will turn onto one of the canyon roads to get to the 101 freeway. We need to get a visual before then, or we could lose him." He was driving down the PCH, passing on shoulders and doing whatever he needed to bridge the distance between him and the white Audi.

"What about his aversion to heights?" The feds had a file on Stuart Greystone, and Jocko had studied his every strength *and* his every weakness.

"He'll see it as a necessary risk. It's his quickest way out of here," Rand said, just as two unmarked cars and an emergency vehicle passed them coming from the opposite direction, en route to the senator's beach house. He nodded toward them and said to Jocko, "Send all extra units our way."

"Copy," Jocko said, and was on his phone.

Their first option, Kanan Dume, was coming up at the next intersection, and Rand lifted his foot from the accelerator. He thoughtfully looked in its direction, coasting, then shook his head and pushed the pedal to the floor, barreling past.

Jocko muted his call and said to Rand, "We have backup."

"They'll need the description of Greystone's vehicle. Have someone take the road we just passed as a precaution. It's longer and winds the whole way, but the roads are wider. In some places it's four-lane, so it's possible it'd be more appealing to Greystone. I'm still betting on Malibu Canyon. It's narrow, but it's shorter and it straightens somewhat after the tunnel. If neither of us catch him on the canyon roads, tell them we'll meet up on the 101."

"Got it," said Jocko, steadily working his phone and his laptop, one step behind Rand's orders.

"Anything on Nicole's phone?" Rand glanced briefly at Jocko.

"No. It's stationary. Left at the beach house."

He didn't ask about the other phone. The one they'd assumed was Ginny's. It had been disconnected or simply abandoned after muffled conversations and a distant gunshot. As unthinkable as it was for Nicole to be in the car ahead with Stuart Greystone at the wheel, it was better than the images Rand had conjured up from the disturbing audio. He shut off the emergency lights so he could close the distance to Greystone without alerting him, then turned at the next main intersection, onto Malibu Canyon Road by Pepperdine University.

"I went to college here," Rand said, slamming the accelerator to the floor. "The first time I was able to really appreciate this road, I was driving my friend's Corvette." His jaw stopped clenching for a brief moment, remembering. "There was a girl I wanted to impress, and he encouraged me to take her out in his car." He backed off the gas before rounding the first bend. "It took these corners as smooth as butter." His eyes narrowed, coming out of the curve and he gassed it again. "I made that car sing."

"What happened to the girl?" Jocko asked.

"Never wanted to see me again. Thought I was too dangerous." There was a flicker of a smile, then Rand's face intensified, and his jaw started clenching again. The next four miles would be two narrow lanes of the familiar twisting, and this Jeep wasn't conducive to the same smooth ride as the Corvette, but he had no choice. He pushed it, because once he got to the tunnel through the mountain rock, the roads become somewhat straighter. At that point, Greystone would regain his confidence. They had to catch him before then.

"There." Jocko pointed ahead on the next turn. Headlights from another car illuminated the white Audi, and Rand was already fixed on him. He counted four cars between them, and within a few hundred feet, Rand passed the first.

* * *

Inside the Vinsant's beach house, Dominic and Tom heard the wail of sirens coming closer. Dominic had left the front door propped open and took over Sidney's CPR until they arrived. Just as they descended on the house, Dominic went out the back, and with his one good hand, flipped over the railing, onto the beach, and into the night.

* * *

The driver of the Audi A8 was uneasy on the mountainous drive and was fixated on the road ahead, slowing the car to a crawl on each bend. Nicole rode with her head back, peeking through heavy lashes. If she could get her door unlocked without notice, then she had a chance of getting out of the car the next time he slowed for a sharp turn. But suddenly, he was squirming in his seat and flexing his tight hold on the steering wheel. It had to do with whatever he was watching in the rearview mirror. Nicole eased upward with minimal movements and slowly turned. A Jeep was recklessly working its way around a car on the stretch behind them. When she gently turned back around, her eyes made contact with Greystone's reflection, and although she closed them quickly, their clarity didn't get lost on him. He swerved to the shoulder, threw the car into park, and was at her door in seconds.

"Get out! You drive!" He grabbed her arm, yanking her out of the back and into the driver's seat. With his SIG trained on her, he ran around the car to the passenger side. "DRIVE!" Greystone yelled before his door was closed.

"I'm not able. I can't see clearly."

"You're faking! DRIVE!" His hand was shaking, and he looked over his shoulder at the traffic behind them, "NOW!!" Greystone shouted.

Nicole put the car in drive and gunned the accelerator as instructed, forcing the Audi into a vintage VW Beetle that was struggling up the hill. The nasally little horn blasted a weak attempt at expressing anger, but it only served to agitate Greystone more. He turned the gun toward them. "Greystone!!" Nicole screamed. His shock at her cry brought his attention, along with his barrel, around to her, but she responded with unusual calm. "Please don't hurt them. It was my fault."

There was another sharp curve coming up and immediately afterward went into another, and another, like writing a big S over and over in the road, and the cars behind them disappeared into the bends. Stuart Greystone became eerily quiet. He'd placed the gun into his lap and was gripping the armrests. It was a couple of miles before the route relaxed enough to see the Jeep again, and it had gained ground, successfully passing two more cars. There was only one car left between them. A straighter stretch was ahead; however, it led into a tunnel that went through the rock of the mountainside.

Greystone shifted in his seat, and Nicole juggled her attention between him, the road, and the Jeep that was now directly behind them. The entrance loomed ahead. Just as the Audi entered the dark mouth of the tunnel, the Jeep caught up to them, riding alongside in the oncoming lane. The thick, black wheels dominated Nicole's peripheral view and cut into the Audi's path, pushing Nicole over toward the right side of her lane. "Don't pull over." Greystone had the gun in her side. "Floor it!"

Nicole closed her eyes for a second, then did as he said and punched it. Exhaust spewing, she fishtailed, trying to reclaim her lane, and broke free of the entanglement with the Jeep, just as Greystone swung his gun around toward their pursuers and took aim. "NO!" Nicole screamed, pulling the wheel hard left. It threw Greystone sideways, and his gun hand slung skyward, firing through the roof.

The loud discharge rung in Nicole's ears, disorienting her. There was a muffled shout, "Do that again and you die!" She didn't quite make out the words, but understood the message when Greystone delivered the smoldering tip of the gun against her head. The Jeep backed away a car length. "Now get us out of here!"

Nicole corrected the Audi and tried to regain her speed up the climbing grade. Greystone kept an eye on her and the Jeep following, until he saw the change in her features. Nicole's brows drew together, rapidly changing from questionable to incredible, then finally shock. Greystone followed her gaze and rubbed his eyes. At the exit, a black Mercedes Sprinter van was sideways, blocking both lanes of the tunnel, its headlights shining into the rock of the mountainside.

"Don't stop!" Greystone ordered.

Her ears were still ringing but the order was clear. Shaking her head, she said, "I have nowhere to go unless I turn around."

"Get up enough speed and you can wedge behind them, perhaps clip them into a turn."

"I can't go behind them! There's only a small guardrail near the road. If we don't hit them just right, we could end up in the canyon."

"Then go in front. Plow between them and the mountain wall! It'll swing them out of the way, at least enough to get through." Nicole didn't move for a few beats. "GO!" he demanded, watching the van, but instead Nicole threw open the car door and threw her legs in motion with everything she had. She ran toward the Jeep. A pop from Greystone's silencer echoed on the tunnel walls, and from pure reflex she ducked, freezing, until she realized she hadn't been shot, then started running again.

Greystone climbed into the driver's seat. And with the door still open, he leveled his SIG at Nicole's back and pulled the trigger once more. Rand was out of the Jeep. He dove for Nicole, knocking her to the ground, and blocking the bullet, which cut through his thigh. He rolled, coming off her in a defensive stance with Glock in hand, and locked Stuart Greystone in his sight. His bullet ripped through the tunnel with an urgency. Twirling. Arrowing. Searching out its target, until it connected with the Brit. This time it didn't graze his cheek like Tom's. It entered his unscathed left side with an angry velocity, slinging his head backwards across the front seat of the white Audi.

Jocko was out of the Jeep, his gun aimed high, making his way to the Audi, and Rand left it for him, turning to Nicole.

"Rand!" Nicole pushed herself up from the pavement and ran into his outstretched arms.

Time stood still for only a moment. Sirens were no longer faint and the red strobe from the emergency vehicles confirmed this was not simply a nightmare. The sound of tires quickly braking over gravel and the shuffling of the first responder's feet joined the symphony of shouted commands, and Nicole's head didn't want to leave the comfort of Rand's chest, but his embrace was weakening. "Oh, Rand! Your leg ..." Nicole lost all color when she saw the large, red stain growing on the side of his pants. Just as the EMTs wheeled a stretcher over, he collapsed on it.

"I'm riding with him!" Nicole said, running after the medical team. Before climbing into their emergency unit, she looked at the tunnel exit. "The van. It's gone!"

CHAPTER 48

"You saved my life," Nicole said, and lightly brushed her fingertips over the bandaged leg. The evidence that yesterday really happened. The bullet had torn through the flesh of Rand's thigh, but other than blood loss there was no major damage. The paramedics had insisted Nicole be checked out, but she had only ingested a small amount of the wine Greystone spiked, so other than being bruised, physically she was fine. Her damage ran much deeper. She was still processing the bizarre events and, most importantly, Sidney's paternity confession.

"My pleasure." He watched her eyes roam further, her hand touch his flesh. She was reflective, not meaning to arouse him, and she didn't notice his expression deepening. Rand covered her hand in his, pulled it to his lips and laid a kiss in her palm, bringing a soft smile to her face.

"Mike called." She paused, and slowly, reclaiming her hand, she looked at her watch. "Said he'd be dropping by this morning. How do you feel?"

"Great. Now." Rand's eyes delivered a message he made no apology for. "How about you?" he asked. Nicole was wearing black long sleeves that were pushed up, and white denim jeans. Her long hair was loosely pulled back, and she had on no jewelry except the watch and Great Aunt

Naomi's ring. She was lovely, but the solemn smile and the dark circles under those grey eyes cautioned him to take it slowly.

Nicole turned toward the large picture window and looked out over the busy street below, and shrugged.

"Nicole?"

She shook her head, and Rand unclipped the monitor from his finger, then turned the machine off. He lifted the IV bag from its stand, and with it tucked under his arm, he carefully worked his way to her, and when she finally spoke, her voice was delicate, and he lowered his head to catch each word.

"Before ever seeing your face ... you stepped up from behind me as you are now. I was in the hallway of The Rock and beguiled by the bassist's beautiful melody. So, beguiled that I didn't know the exact moment it changed from me to us. It was an emotional intimacy that I'm unfamiliar with. Your voice. Your breath in my hair. They became a part of it. It was as though I'd always known you ... and ..." she stopped. She licked her bottom lip. The words were stuck.

Rand wrapped his free arm around her, and the same warm breath brushed against her neck when he spoke. "And?" he asked with an added rasp.

"I hadn't noticed until that afternoon."

He waited. But nothing came. He nudged. "What, Nicole? What didn't you notice?"

She placed her hand on the arm he had around her and said, "How very lonely I've been."

Rand closed his eyes and said a prayer of thanks as she continued, "But —just as you awakened this in me, you were almost taken away. I don't know if I can do this, Rand." She turned to him, and it was there. The single tear sitting on her long, dark lash that he'd seen the first time he stood this close to her outside the music room. This time, however, he did what he'd wanted to then. Placing his fingers under her chin, he gently lifted her face and pressed his lips against her lash to kiss away her tear.

Her breath caught, and he pulled away just far enough to see her lips parting. Rand lowered his mouth slowly, barely brushing over hers until they were soul to soul, with the lone, salty tear pressed between them.

The wave that rushed Nicole was not met with resistance this time. Like a carnival ride that took her stomach in a daring sweep, not knowing where you were headed next, she let herself go. Nicole brought her hands up to touch Rand's face as she kissed him back and gave her mouth fully over to his, then slid her hands around his neck and pressed her body against his. The muffled sound of his moan was primal, and her knees weakened, causing her to briefly slip, but Rand caught her, pulling her even closer as his kiss went deeper. His tongue savored the woman who'd visited his dreams, only to be gone when he woke. But she was here, in his arms. The woman herself, and not a dream.

The hospital room door swung open.

"Knock, knock!" Mike's voice arrived before he did, blaring out jovially with his trademark smile, then he came up short, looking from Rand to Nicole, still held in an embrace. "Hey, you could've at least warned a guy. Hung a sock or something."

Nudged from their intimate world, Nicole took a beat or two before rejoining reality. "Can I help you back into bed?" Her flesh burned at the look that Rand answered with.

"Listen, I'll come back later," Mike said, waving from the door.

"No, no, come in, Mike." When Nicole turned to greet him, her color was still high, and she was smiling. She pulled a chair close for Mike while Rand hung his IV back up, just as the nurse charged in, fussing and fuming under her breath. She gave Rand the eye and reconnected the monitor.

"'There is no greater love than to lay down one's life for one's friends'." Mike shook Rand's hand. "And you were willin' to do just that. Solid, man. You're what my gal has been missin'." While still holding right hands, the two men closed in an embrace, their left hands patting shoulders.

"Wait, Mike ... wasn't that Scripture?" Nicole asked, looking from Mike to Rand. Her brow lifted, and Rand winked at her.

"Yeah, baby." Mike lowered himself in the chair, "Gotta believe in somethin'. So, any news on Ginny?" He asked.

"Not yet. We know Ginny and Gabriel Simon were in touch with each other." Rand glanced at Nicole.

"And he's missing too, right?" asked Mike.

"Wait!" Nicole's face became animated, and she looked up toward the ceiling, recalling a memory, then back at Rand. "It's cloudy, but I may have seen Gabriel at the Vinsant's beach house when I was leaving with Greystone."

"I saw the same guy ... but it wasn't Gabriel," Rand said, adjusting the bed to a sitting position. "Are you up to talking about it?"

Nicole nodded.

"And you heard about Sidney? That he didn't make it?"

Again, she nodded.

"First, the man you saw was Gabriel's twin brother, Dominic. Simon is not their last name. Let me start from the beginning." Rand took a sip of water, a tactic he used in meetings to think his sentences through before delivery. This delivery was important to him.

"Your waterfront investigation? You were on the right track, and because of that, your legs were cut out from under you," Rand said, affectionately. "The Network owned Senator Vinsant, and his name surfaced because they had him muscle the port authorities to position inspectors and customs agents. Placed throughout the dock area, they could wave vessels through, unchecked. With the right people in place, The Network was free to traffic guns, drugs, and even humans.

"Sidney got a percentage of the racket, simply because he arranged contact with the senator and manipulated the media. When he sabotaged your story, he brilliantly used your alleged 'vendetta' against the senator to keep it buried. Tom simply milked it, as is his nature. But it was the beginning of Sidney's fall."

"Why's that?" Mike asked.

"Sidney kept layers of insulation around him. He would have never risked exposure, but Nicole became involved." Rand looked at Nicole, his words softening. "Sidney fired you to protect you. The Network would have eliminated you if he hadn't."

"But instead of backing off, I started the investigation for Ginny, which had loose threads that led back to them." Nicole was nodding.

"Exactly. Their ring was tight. Clean. If Sidney hadn't gotten personally involved, it could have taken thousands more man-hours to flush him out." Rand took her hand and rubbed his thumb over it, caressing. "But he had to protect you."

"So, he risked everything for her." Mike glanced toward Nicole, then back at Rand and added, "Then he did have one redeeming quality. So, what about this Doc Howard? Where's he in all this?"

"He's the mastermind behind the smuggling, using Sidney and Tom like pawns. We assume he left the country, but thanks to Stuart Greystone's 'insurance policy,' there's enough evidence on his thumb drive for an indictment, and Tom Vinsant will be testifying. He cut a deal with the FBI."

"Heavy." Mike shook his head, and looked over at Nicole.

Nicole was staring at a pattern on the hospital room floor. "Do you think Ginny's dead?" She looked to Rand, her eyes hopeful, begging for him to tell her otherwise.

"There's nothing to indicate that. She and Gabriel are both missing and are being investigated. We all know they were in communication with each other."

The room was becoming stuffy to Nicole, and she rose and walked to the window again. Rand called, "Nicole?"

She didn't turn around.

"I would've never suspected Sidney!" Mike said.

Nicole shook her head, echoing his sentiment. She was wearing Great Aunt Naomi's ring, and she twirled it with her thumb, reflecting, then suddenly she became rigid, and her eyes narrowed. When she turned to meet Rand's, her sorrow had shifted. She was angry. "But you did, didn't you?"

Rand didn't answer. The hum of the air conditioner grew louder.

"You already suspected Sidney was involved when you met me!" Nicole said, staring at him in disbelief. Her chest started rising and falling rapidly. "Did you know about his possible relationship to me?"

"Drummond's been on a watch list for several reasons, but like I said, he'd built a fortress around himself: he *and* Doc Howard. We got lucky ... thanks to you."

"That's not an answer." Her head slowly shook. "All of this ... and you said nothing!"

"Nicole, I couldn't. I wasn't at liberty to," Rand said, as the light in those beautiful, pale eyes dimmed, and the wall around her heart began to rebuild. It could be heard over the air conditioner and he watched, helplessly.

"There will always be something you can't tell me, won't there? Sidney was the reason you got close to me. It was a case to you. It was a job!" Angry tears were developing, and before Rand could see them, she snatched up her bag and slung it over her shoulder.

"Nicole," Rand called after her, "you don't believe that!" But she had already marched out of the room.

* * *

Before she left the hospital, Nicole had a stop to make. Taking several deep breaths and slowly releasing them, she had calmed enough to finish what she needed. "Excuse me," she said lightly, knocking, and eased open the door to Room 1214. "May I come in?"

Tom Vinsant waved her in. He was hooked up to a monitor, and his right arm and shoulder were heavily bandaged and in a sling.

"I just wanted to say thank you. I understand you played a part in my rescue," Nicole said awkwardly, standing near the door.

"Who'd a-thunk, huh?" came out through a crooked grin.

She worked at returning a smile. "You and I probably won't ever see eye to eye, Tom, but I understand you're testifying for the FBI. I know it'll be tough. I'll be pulling for you."

"It's nothing noble, Nicole," Tom shrugged. "I'm only covering my own ass, so don't go giving me a medal."

She nodded, her smile sad. "Anything on Ginny?"

Tom didn't say anything else, simply closed his eyes and shook his head.

* * *

The following morning was another effervescent day in Southern California, but it was lost on Rand. Released from the hospital, he waited at the curb for Jocko to bring around the rented Jeep and heard someone calling, "Hey, Pastor! I hear you've been a real busy guy."

Rand kept looking straight ahead at nothing particular. "Yeah. What's up, Graves?"

"Coming to get a statement from the senator, next I'll be taking a ride to see your friend, Ms. Portman. Sounds like she's been real busy, herself!" Detective Graves said. "Hey, everything all right? You almost make me look happy."

The Jeep stopped, and still without looking at Graves, Rand worked his leg into the passenger seat. "Treat her gently, Detective." He closed the door.

CHAPTER 49

"Baby, you're rich!" Blind Dog said to Nicole. "Ha, not only that, but you're my boss! Can I have some much-needed vacay time?"

Nicole and Mike were having lunch at Samm's Beachside after her appointment with Sidney's attorney. The meeting lasted two hours and could have gone longer, but she left while he was finishing the details of Sidney's will. Nicole was still in shock. "He left everything to me, Mike! Everything! It's like having blood money. I can't accept it."

"Not all of it was made illegally. Drummond Media is huge. The money you think is bad? Donate it to charity! The Rock's a great place to start!" He held his glass high for Nicole to toast, but it was lost on her. She was staring out toward the water.

Sidney's attorney had explained the details of her birth and subsequent adoption by Casper and Margaret Portman. Everything was in Sidney's legal files: *Your birth mother was actress Vivian Malone, and Vivian had been nineteen years old when she was impregnated by a sixteen-year-old Sidney. Vivian was the love of his life, but she dropped him cold, fearful of a scandal that would ruin her career before it ever started. She was on her way to terminating the baby when Sidney caught her and threatened to expose the relationship if she had an abortion. Re-*

luctantly giving in, Vivian would have the child privately and give it up for adoption IF he would never try to claim it or tell anyone of their relationship. The birth parents kept to the agreement, until years later after Vivian Malone died in a plane crash. By then, Sidney was powerful and had the clout to find the child.

Nicole watched a yacht leaving its slip, the slow, graceful movements that would remove it from the safety of the harbor. Each time, it fascinated her. She turned to Mike. "Every day as a journalist, I've chased after the truth." She feigned a laugh. "I had no clue my own life was a lie."

Since that interview when they met ten years ago, Mike had seen the student who seemed too worried to relax, worried it would all fall apart if she did. He knew a part of that young woman was still in there. "It's not a lie, baby. Maybe your beginnings weren't as you thought, but that's because your loving parents never had the chance to tell you about it. Not their fault." He dropped his sunglasses down just long enough to make sure he had her attention. "Your story is still the same, and all the details of life that were possible to control, you did. Now eat. You haven't touched your salad."

Nicole watched him a long minute, then looked at her food, and after pushing it around the plate with her fork, she gave up and tried her tea instead. Mike pretended not to notice and kept talking, "Now, you and I both know the *only* thing that's changed," he glanced at her, grinning, "other than your financial status ... is your perspective, and you just need a little time to adjust to this new Nicole."

She smiled softly, knowing where he was going with the comment. Her emotional involvement with the kids, the story she had chased, and her full circle with Ginny. It had thinned the armor she'd worn most of her life. It was still around, of course, but by lessening the layers, things *did* look a little different.

"Then you have this whole Rand story, which needs a good rewrite, and you're in luck. I know a good writer that could fix it." Mike leaned back, smiling, proud of his play on words. He crossed one ankle over the other.

But she didn't bite.

"Over a hundred and sixty years ago, Tennyson dropped his famous line about love and loss being better than no love at all ... it still holds water, baby."

"Normally I can follow you, Mike, but are you just trying to be poetic, like using Scripture in the hospital?"

"Hey. That wasn't *trying* anything. That was real Scripture. And you know what I'm getting at. Tennyson knew his stuff, and you need to think about what he said!" Mike uncrossed his legs and reached for the french fries left on his plate. Nicole watched him as he dropped a few fries into his mouth. Watched his freedom to be comfortable in himself, even with an upbringing so much worse than Nicole could imagine. And he shared his wisdom, because he loved. He loved her. And he loved others. She also watched him rinse the fries down with the remainder of his tea, and when it was empty he pointed a finger at Nicole, "Baby, you're a professional. If ANY woman could understand Rand's circumstances it would be you. You're always on an assignment you can't tell me about. He needs a woman like you, so like I said, this needs a good rewrite."

Nicole chewed on the inside of her cheek before turning back to the water, searching for her sailboat. It was past the harbor and about to be free. "I wouldn't ever be sure if he played me or if it was real."

"Uh-uh ... no. This isn't you, baby. You don't play victim." Mike paused and waited for Nicole to look at him. It was with reluctance, and it was challenging. He tipped his head forward to meet her challenge over the top of his sunglasses, "You just got lucky when you found a good reason to shut him out, 'cause you got scared." Then he broke eye contact, picked a baby tomato off Nicole's salad, and popped it in his mouth, grinning. "None of us are gettin' out of this alive, you might as well live while you can."

Nicole's eyebrows lifted, watching him eat her tomato on top of the french fries, and she shook her head, almost smiling. "Time to change the subject."

"He took a bullet for you."

"He was doing his job." Nicole was dismissive, but much lighter. Almost playful.

Both sat behind their shades, but even so, Mike could read her. Satisfied he'd gotten through, he changed the subject. "So, let's talk about the headlines." Mike clapped his hands. "You've been vindicated, baby!"

"Yes. Personally, I got my vindication ... but my relationship to Sidney is what made headlines. My waterfront and trafficking article only got a sliver of recognition."

"Don't try to sell me that," Mike grinned. "It got you an offer, and I've been waiting to hear. Did they agree to do the documentary you wanted, or will they fluff it into a movie based on a true story?"

"Fluff." Nicole pushed her plate aside. "But I'm good with it." She shifted in her seat, sitting a little taller, then told Mike about selling the movie rights to her story, as long as she could work with the screenwriters. "If I'm going to make a difference in human trafficking, I have to allow it the exposure that a feature film can give, *and* they've agreed to the name *Gramble Street*." Mike nodded. He understood. To her, that's where life had taken a new turn. "The movie will have it all: the waterfront corruption, weapons and human trafficking, murder, conspiracy to murder. All the juicy elements for a great action drama ... it *could* be big."

"I hear ya." The server appeared, gathering their dishes, and Mike put in an order for a bottle of champagne. "Don't want to force the issue, but I think we have some celebrating to do." Mike saw the grin in her eye. "What?" Nicole's smile that threatened to surface earlier finally sprouted, and Mike tried again. "You're holdin' out, baby. What's goin' on?"

A trace of her animation returned. "Well ... about halfway through the meeting with the attorney today, a lightbulb went on." She knocked her palm to her forehead. "If I'm Drummond Media ... I don't need offers for my documentary." A light chuckle escaped. "I can do it myself!"

The champagne arrived, and after the server poured, they toasted. "You have a title for it?" Mike asked her.

"Yes!" Nicole took a hurried sip, like she couldn't wait to tell him. "It will be titled *Without a File, Do I Exist? A Child's Life in The Foster System*, and will be about all of them. The abused, the missing, the unnoticed, and even the ones that are unscathed or actually become adopted. It will also spotlight the system that let them down. I'll get Kim Argnaut from the Family Services Department involved as a technical advisor.

"Because of our findings, the entire county system will be reconstructed, Mike, and Kim is helping Child Services through the transition. She had campaigned to change it for years, and now she can. She plans to assign full teams to small groups of children—an actual support system for each one, where no child slips through. It's a start!" She lifted her glass to him.

"Baby ... so cool!" Mike met her toast. "You always were meant to change the world. And these little lives *are* the world!"

The conversation lingered in the air around them, then Nicole added, "I'll dedicate the documentary to Debbie." It was a positive affirmation, and Mike squeezed the hand he was still holding. Then Nicole locked eyes with him. "However, with all this, Mike, no one has information on our four foster kids. They simply disappeared."

Mike shared her concern and reminded her, "Before you and Ginny, they didn't have a voice, and now the authorities are looking for them. They'll find them, Nicole. You did good." He waited for an appropriate pause, then asked, "So ... other than the documentary, what else you gonna do with all that money?"

It didn't take her long to reply. "Look for Ginny."

"You know the FBI is on it, right?" Mike reached in the backpack at his feet, pulled out a plain white envelope, and handed to Nicole.

"What's this? Your Christmas list?"

"Good one!" he said, and laughed. "You think my Christmas list could fit in here?" Then in a more serious tone he said, "No. Rand said I was to give you this, since you won't accept his calls or open his email."

"Do you know what's in it?" She was suddenly reluctant to take it.

"It's about Ginny."

She tore the seal and unfolded the letter. It was very informal, not even on federal letterhead. It was a brief on Ginny's disappearance and her affiliation with Gabriel. They were both still under investigation and it ended with a personal promise to keep Nicole updated.

"The FBI is still investigating Ginny! That means they officially have reason to believe she's alive!" Nicole looked up, and every inch of her face illuminated the message of hope.

"I'm beginning to think you actually care about the senators' wife."

"Ginny is *nobody's* wife. She's her own person." Nicole folded the letter and placed it in her handbag. "And I need her to be okay, Mike."

CHAPTER 50

A couple of weeks had passed since Nicole took on the role as president and CEO of Drummond Media, and between the demands of the position and the hours spent on her documentary, she and Mike hadn't had time to talk, but that morning she had received an email that she couldn't wait to share with him. "Hey, Mike!"

"Baby, you sound great—*and* sounds like you're rollin'. You heading my way? I'll meet you at Samm's."

"Can't. I got an email from a friend, and I'm going to see her!"

"No! Nicole! It could be a setup! You heard Rand. Doc Howard? The one that wanted you terminated? He's still swarming!"

She let out a light laugh. "Howard is in hiding, Mike. I'm not worried about him."

"How do you know it's her?"

"It's her, Mike." She was exuberant and it was clear through their connection. "Anyway, I just wanted to let you know. I'll call you later with details." She started to disconnect, then paused, "And Mike?"

"Yeah, baby?"

"I love you."

He exhaled, then in his deep, soothing radio voice, said, "I love you, too."

Nicole pulled her Range Rover into the prestigious motor court, and a black sport-coat opened her door. "Welcome to the Bacara."

Walking through the large archway of the foyer, she continued through the building to the waiting golf cart, just as she had over a month ago. *More beautiful than I remembered.* The bougainvillea latched onto the sides of the ivory stucco, and the palms were waving at her again, beckoning for her attention, but she couldn't slow. She had someone to meet.

This time, however, the black coat drove her to the upper pool and stopped at a white, canvas cabana. Tea was set up, along with a silver-covered tray and a delicate bouquet of pink peonies. An envelope leaned against it with one word: "Nicole." The smile she'd been wearing all morning left. The tea was set for only one person.

She picked up the note and looked around. A few guests were milling about, but she didn't recognize anyone. She opened the letter.

Nicole ~

I'm sorry I left before saying goodbye, but under the circumstances it wasn't possible. Evidently, someone had ordered a hit on my life, thanks to Tom, and I left my phone behind so they couldn't trace it to me. Not only was I in danger, but Gabriel Simon had to disappear for a while, too, so he came to get me. And guess what he was driving!!

You'll understand everything when you see the enclosed photo. Gabriel said until the authorities have a better system to protect these children, he and his brother Dominic decided to take action. They experienced childhood suffering firsthand ... however, they were fortunate enough to be adopted. His real name is Gabriel Mancuso-Sullivan and when he noticed a flicker of recognition in your eyes when you met at The Rock, he figured his cover was blown. Evidently, one of your first stories at KDLA was on their elusive father's passing—he was Sullivan Oil.

I'm sending a message to Tom to let him know I'm okay, but filing for divorce so Gabriel and I can move on and perhaps build a life together.

I love you, Nicole. Your friendship is a gift I'll forever cherish. Without you I might've stayed in that cocoon I'd been existing in. PLEASE, allow yourself this same freedom. You deserve happiness more than anyone I know. Yesterday's sorrows have a special place in our hearts, but they should never stop it from beating.

Always,
Ginny

Nicole searched the envelope for the picture. Ginny and Gabriel were in the center of the photograph, their faces lit up, and arms around each other. The man on Gabriel's left with a cast on his hand looked almost identical to him. "That must be Dominic! The man at the beach house," she whispered. There were hundreds of children around them all laughing and playing ... and there it was! In the far-right background, a black Mercedes Sprinter van. "Well, I'll be!"

Every figure told a different story, and Nicole's fingers brushed over each one. She moved to the dark, lanky teen standing on the other side of

Dominic. Ginny was right, this picture said it all. It was Timbo. He was still gaunt, but he looked happy, clean, and well-dressed. No sign of drugs *or* the animal desperation. Gabriel and Dominic had done that. They had rescued him and all these other kids at risk. Her heart was filled with a satisfaction like no other news story had done and was on the verge of bursting at the childlike joy that filled Timbo's face. However, as brilliant as *his* smile was, it was not the brightest. No, that label belonged to the little boy leaning into Ginny with his arms wrapped around her legs.

He was wearing a Batman T-shirt.

Nicole pressed the picture to her chest and all the emotion from the last few weeks overcame her. With her eyes closed, she didn't notice the shadow coming up behind her. The hand touched her shoulder, and Nicole whipped around. Standing there was her friend. Ginny. With her arms open wide.

"We did it, Nicole," Ginny said through tears of joy, and they embraced in a hug that covered every unspoken word between them.

Before separating, Nicole whispered softly, "Thank you, Ginny, for everything."

Ginny placed a kiss on Nicole's cheek, then dabbed her own eyes. "I can't stay. The FBI will be here any minute – I'm a fugitive, you know," she said, laughing at her own words.

Nicole lightened at Ginny's playfulness, but assured her, "I wasn't followed."

"Oh, we know, but Gabriel figures they've tapped into our email ... probably yours too, in case I contact you."

"What?!" Nicole's brows pulled together, bewildered. "Then why did you do this?" She motioned toward the grounds of the resort. "There were other ways to contact me!"

Ginny couldn't contain her smile. Her expression was the total opposite of Nicole's, and she nodded to her right, toward the lower pool. "To lure him here."

There was no mystery in Ginny's words. It was written all over her, and Nicole knew before turning around to see him. Rand was coming around the cart path at the far end of the Bistro Restaurant. The sharp intake of breath was her only reaction, and Ginny caught it. "He's a good man, Nicole, and he's crazy about you."

"So you arranged this?" Nicole twisted back to Ginny again. The cool, grey eyes were accusing, but her words were more teasing than angry. "A fugitive for less than a month, and you think you have all the answers!"

"Nicole, you were reluctant to let me in, too ... and look at us. Was that a mistake?"

"He could have this place surrounded! I can't believe you'd risk that ... just ... just to start butting into my private life."

"First, we don't feel it's a gamble. We bet he's alone. And second ..." Ginny stood a little taller. The ocean breeze lightly lifted her blonde hair around her face, cheering her on. "... it's what I do now. I don't cower in the shadows. I take risks, like you." Ginny didn't notice Nicole's subtle flinch. "This is my gift to you. Please, read my last line once more. It's not as eloquent as something you would write, but it holds truth."

The letter was lying on the table, the edges fluttering as the air whispered through the cabana. Nicole glanced at the walkway Rand was advancing on, then back at the letter. Lifting it, the sincerity of Ginny's words came alive again, and she read the last line: *Yesterday's sorrows have a special place in our hearts, but they should never stop it from beating.*

Nicole turned to Ginny, but she was gone. Quietly, in the direction Ginny had come, she breathed, "You always have taken risks."

Folding the letter, she slipped it, along with the picture, deep into her purse, as Rand steadily made his way up to the cabana. His limp was slight, but paired with the denim jeans, it added a rugged edge to the navy sport-jacket and crisp, white shirt. The Ray Bans completed his look, which could have been an advertisement for the resort, or for the cologne that was blowing in her direction. It was his same solid fragrance, and it triggered an overpowering connection to the man approaching. Nicole chewed her bottom lip. *Snap out of it, Nicole! It's textbook psychology. Through life-threatening events, strangers develop special bonds that are mistaken for other things. That's all it is!*

Striking his standard pose, Rand slid his hands into his pockets, his jacket open. "You won't answer my calls."

It was the low, intimate voice from outside the music room at The Rock, before their history. And even if she could explain away the rest, his voice alone ignited a familiarity that transcended nostalgia. Nicole was having trouble holding onto her anger. She took a step back. "So, what brings you to the Bacara, Special Agent Coleman? I figured you'd be back in Sacramento by now."

The words were meant to be challenging, and she crossed her arms in a defensive move, although none of it reach her eyes. The steel had softened. Stray strands of hair danced around in the sea breeze that ruffled her blouse, and she watched him, waiting for his response.

Seconds stretched into a long, awkward impasse, and Rand shifted restlessly, then pushed his shades up on his head, and stared, unfiltered, at Nicole.

Pure reflex had her clutching her throat. The bold eyes were just as she remembered, demanding, but the dark circles beneath were new, making them more dangerous than ever.

Nicole relied on her professional training to keep her composure, and summoning her camera smile, she plastered it on to move the situation forward. "Actually, I know why you're here, Agent Coleman. And ..." She stopped. An unusual disturbance challenged the peaceful setting around the resort. It was an engine, followed by a heavy *whooshing* sound and Nicole looked up as a helicopter rose above the rooftops. The movement inside was visible from where they stood, and when she recognized the occupants, a genuine enthusiasm had her finishing a little too loudly over the noise of the aircraft. "... And she's getting away!!"

For a fleeting moment, Nicole's face reflected her joy over Ginny's escape, until she turned back to Rand and realized he hadn't looked up. His eyes never left her.

Although the voice was low, even the loud whirling of the blades couldn't distort his honest message, for she watched the lips that translated his words. "I'd be a fool to let her."

Contrary to Ginny's earlier comment about Nicole's heart, it was having no problem. It pounded her chest as though it was trying to break free... and when Rand took three steps to close the space between them, it finally did.

'In the United States, traffickers prey upon children in the foster care system. Recent reports have consistently indicated that a large number of victims of child sex trafficking were at one time in the foster care system.'

*U. S. Department of State **2019 Trafficking in Persons Report:***
https://www.state.gov/reports/2019-trafficking-in-persons-report/
Excerpt - page 4

ACKNOWLEDGEMENTS

Many people have helped me in the writing of this book, but none more than my muse, literary agent Paul Fedorko. Thank you Paul, for your encouragement, professional guidance, and most importantly, your friendship.

When snippets of a plot and a growing cast of characters refused to leave my head and I decided to give them life, I never dreamed of the support that I would receive – From family and friends, from my local community, and even from the community of other writers, all to whom I'm truly grateful. However, one author in particular came alongside me when I faced the proverbial fork in the road with publishing decisions and I have no doubt it was Divine intervention. Thank you, Cap Daniels! You took time from your own writing to share a wealth of experiences, resources, and solid advice. I cannot thank you enough–and also, to your lovely wife, author Melissa Mason, for being a champion of *Gramble Street*.

To my husband, Richard Blackwell, and my children, Chandler and Amelia Blackwell – You were proud of me before my first draft was ever finished, and when it was, helped me to realize the depth of my accomplishment. But then the editing began – the grueling rewrites. And after my fourth one, you never shouted, "Aren't you finished yet?!" Instead, you admired my persistence to see it through and patiently cheered me on. I love you guys. You are my home.

To my developmental editor, the multi-faceted, Maya Sloan – I cannot thank you enough. Maya, you knew how to get the best out of me. You helped me become a better writer and Gramble Street would not be the novel it is without you.

Of course after all the work is done, a good novel cannot go out without a final coat of polish, so to my grammar police - my fabulous proofreaders - Cathy Dee and Lynn Mostyn, Thank you!

There are many others to acknowledge because of their continued support – Barbara Blackwell, Gene Blackwell, and Sam Bogosian, my bonus parents. My brother, David Sweatt, who offered assistance and even his beach house–whatever I needed to complete Gramble Street; I love you forever. To my sisters, Alice Brown, Bren Browning, Pam Roberson and Jojuan Jones – to extended family – and to numerous friends – a few whom I must mention… Ginny Smith, Diane Corrales, Toni Davison, Dona Moore, Terri Maier - your encouragement mattered more than you will ever know, thank you.

My largest source of inspiration comes from my role model and mother, Joyce Sweatt. Joyce has accomplished more than anyone I know and does it with a grace that blesses everyone around her. In additional to her own achievements, she's helped two children write books, one build a successful business and another become a corporate head. She finally retired this year from a lifelong career, only to start a new venture with her fiancé. By example, she's taught me to persevere, love unconditionally, and when aggressively challenged by those holding bigger sticks, I hear her voice, "Just keep going and don't make eye contact." I love you, mom.

It all began with a seed inside, and I'm thankful to God for giving me that seed, for helping me follow through, for the thirst to keep being a better version of myself, and the desire to make a difference.

Two relatives who are no longer with us influenced my love for stories, although I never saw either reading a novel. Their gift was orating tales and as a young girl, I listened and absorbed them all. One was my maternal grandfather, whose tales were mostly fabricated and told with a twinkle in his eye, but the ones I loved the best were from W.C. Sweatt. My dad. Although he left this world many years ago, his stories still live on in me because they were his real life adventures. Sometimes it would be just he and I as he shared them – my older siblings would be off with friends, and my mother had heard all of the stories – so like a sponge, I soaked it in. When his aunts and uncles came to visit, there would be a revival of repeated tales as we gathered around the kitchen filled with the aroma of freshly brewed coffee and the choruses of laughter as tears rolled down the weathered cheeks of his elders. I'm left with treasured, vivid memories and I actually used one in the first draft of Gramble Street, but it was one of my 'little darlings' that ended up on the edit room floor. It needs to be told, so I'm going to slip it into my next novel and you can tell me which one you think it is.

I cannot leave out my furry family who helped me write the book in its entirety and expected nothing in return. As long as I wrote at home, they followed me to whatever writing space I chose that day and stayed right by my side. WE did it, Rhynn and Enzo! Now, let's finish book two!

Lastly, to all my readers, thank you for sharing your time with Nicole, Ginny, Blind Dog, and me. I hope you thoroughly enjoy **Gramble Street**.

ABOUT THE AUTHOR

L. S. Blackwell began her writing career creating content in the marketing world, however, with her training and love for literature, she was always creating more than content and over the years, produced a growing collection of her own short stories.

Married to a stuntman and living in Los Angeles, her writing took on a new twist when she saw a need in the stunt community and approached a monthly magazine for her own column. She was awarded the column and titled it, *In Stunt Company,* to give spotlight to the unsung heroes of Hollywood, featuring interviews, stories, and action shots of this glamorous but dangerous work.

On a visit to the culture-rich environment of the South, she stood on a veranda overlooking the grand magnolias and knew it was time to write her debut novel. With this southern backdrop, her west coast lifestyle, and a love for thrillers, L. S. Blackwell presents her compelling debut novel, ***Gramble Street***.

www.lsblackwell.com

Made in the USA
Columbia, SC
04 December 2020